BOUND IN MAGIC

A FANTASY ROMANCE ANTHOLOGY

Copyright © 2023 Priscilla Rose, Elayna R. Gallea, Ruthie Bowles, Daniela A. Mera, Danielle M. Hill, Mimi B. Rose, E. Milee, and Alisyn Fae.

All rights reserved. This book or any portion thereof may not be reproduced or used in any manner whatsoever without express written permission by the organizer and authors except for the use of brief quotations in a book review. Thank you for purchasing an authorized copy.

This is a work of fiction. Names, characters, places, and events either are the product of the author's imagination or are used fictitiously. Any resemblance to actual persons, living or dead, events, or places is entirely coincidental.

Organizer: Priscilla Rose

Cover design: JV Arts

Formatting: Jess Wisecup

Map Artwork: Eternal Geekery & @alecmck

Bound In Magic

A FANTASY ROMANCE ANTHOLOGY

ELAYNA R. GALLEA   RUTHIE BOWLES   PRISCILLA ROSE

DANIELA A. MERA   DANIELLE M. HILL   MIMI B. ROSE

E. MILEE   ALISYN FAE

FOREWORD BY
PRISCILLA ROSE

Heat Levels

STEAMING:
Kissing only or fade to black.

SMOLDERING:
Lots of sexual tension; on-page, but not especially graphic steamy scenes; not much explicit language.

HOT:
Detailed steamy scenes; increasing use of explicit language.

SCORCHING:
Extensive steamy scenes with heavy description and explicit language.

Foreword

In 2022, there was an article written highlighting ten authors with fantasy romance debuts. A discord group chat was formed, and some of us discussed starting an anthology. As the anthology was coming together and more authors joined, it became clear that we needed a leader of sorts.

Hi! It's me, Priscilla Rose. I'm a pretty cool person, but these other seven authors? They're truly amazing!

Whether we're from the USA, Canada, Mexico, or Kuwait, everyone here brings something unique to the table. Our stories have varying levels of heat, cozy energy (or darkness), and even varying levels of fantastical elements. I'm not being hyperbolic when I say there's something for everyone.

I hope you'll give each story a try, and if you see one (or many) that you particularly like, check out the other books we've published or are in the works.

Elayna R. Gallea and Daniela A. Mera both publish fantasy and dystopian romance. They've even written books together!

FOREWORD

Danielle M. Hill writes swoon worthy fantasy and contemporary romance novels.

Ruthie Bowles is not only an amazing author, but also an audiobook narrator and sensitivity reader.

Mimi B. Rose, who is quite lovely, writes both fantasy romance, and books of the paranormal variety.

Alisyn Fae is our reigning queen of fae fantasy romance.

E. Milee has a delightful sapphic YA fantasy romance in the works.

And lastly, I publish fantasy romance, with some monster romance on the horizon as well.

I'm endlessly proud of these amazing women and the things they've accomplished. Happy reading!

Contents

HEIR OF STORMS AND SORROWS Elayna R. Gallea	1
WORDS, WOUNDS, AND WARRIORS Ruthie Bowles	61
SPELLS FOR ETERNAL BLISS Priscilla Rose	133
THE HIDDEN GOVERNESS Daniela A. Mera	177
FROM STEEL AND STONE Danielle M. Hill	239
A FATE OF FEATHERS AND FAE Mimi B. Rose	303
BE CAREFUL WHERE YOU BLEED E. Milee	367
LORD OF WEBS AND WHISPERS Alisyn Fae	415
Coming Soon From Our Authors	517

Heir of Storms and Sorrows

Heir of Storms and Shadows

ELAYNA R. GALLEA

Heat Level:
Steaming

Content Warnings:
Mild language and violence

Once Upon a Time

MAREENA

Once upon a time, in a faraway land in the depths of the deep blue sea, there lived a young princess who was forced to marry a much older male. After a time, the male became king. The princess bore his many children, never to be seen by the world again. She lived a sad and lonely life within the walls of the castle until the day Nontia, the goddess of the sea, came to claim her soul.

That was the story of my mother, her mother, her mother's mother, and so on, and so forth, as far back as the dawn of time.

Everyone knew how the story went. Females were born. They got married and bore children. Then they died. The end.

That probably would be my story too, if my father had his way. He was constantly trying to find someone who would, in his words, take me off his hands. Unfortunately for him, I had no intention of marrying any time soon. Seeing as how I was his only child, I had some sway over him.

I had hoped.

Adjusting the pearl-lined bands covering my breasts, I whispered my mantra under my breath, "I am Mareena, Crown Princess, and Heir to the

Coral Throne. I am fully capable of ruling the Indigo Ocean on my own. I am a Mature mermaid and I don't need anyone by my side."

I ran a comb through my black hair, the tight coils bouncing back almost instantly. The water moved gently around me, caressing me as it lapped against my skin, and I glanced down. Nibbling on my bottom lip, I ran a smoothing hand over my scales. My dark brown, almost black skin was rich and made the violet of my tail seem even brighter in the watery sunlight. Each individual scale shimmered in the light.

A knock came on the door. "Princess Mareena, your father is waiting."

I nodded, though the servant couldn't see me. "One moment, Lyril."

Reaching over, I grabbed the gilded coral diadem resting on the side table. Placing it on my brow, I took a deep breath as I ran my finger over the family heirloom. Given to me by my mother before she passed away, the diadem was purple like my tail. Shaped like a wave, the ends came together to form a shell in the middle. I ran my finger along the edge of the headpiece, smirking.

Coral was everywhere in this place. Coral City, the Coral Throne, the Coral Crown. My ancestors lacked creativity. Of that, I was certain. If it was up to me, I would have chosen far more imaginative names. Even my father's guards were known as the Coral Soldiers. I mean, who did that?

Lyril's voice came through the door again, tinged with more urgency. "Princess, please hurry. Your father is in a mood today."

I swallowed, swimming to the door. As I did, I grabbed a pearl necklace and matching earrings. Something told me that today, I would definitely want to look my best. When my father was in a mood, no one was safe. Not even his heir. One would think that position would keep me safe, but alas, it usually put me in the direct line of fire for his anger.

The High King of the Seven Seas was nothing if not an angry bastard. Perhaps it had to do with his age, or maybe he was just a jerk. Knowing my father, it was probably the latter. He didn't have a kind bone in his body. Some people compared him to the vampire queen of Eleyta. Apparently, Queen Marguerite could give Father a run for his money in the cruelty department, though I had never been to the Surface to meet her.

Taking a deep breath, I swung open the door. "Good morning, Lyril."

My maidservant dipped her head before pinching her lips together. Her pink hair swirled around her, a few shades lighter than the band around her breasts.

"You must hurry, Princess Mareena." Her voice dropped to a whisper. "Rarely have I seen your father in such a foul state. He has already destroyed three priceless antique vases from the Surface, and it isn't even mid-day."

My stomach plummeted, and I adjusted my diadem. Straightening my back, I kept my hands loose at my sides. It would not do for the heir to the throne to appear nervous in front of her king. Even if said king was known for his outbursts.

"I'm ready," I said, ignoring the guppies fluttering around in my stomach.

The water stirred beside me as my personal guard came to my side.

"Good morning, Calix," I said, nodding in his direction.

As he had every day for the past ten years, my personal guard grunted. This morning Calix's chest was bare, allowing his sculpted muscles to be on full display. He gripped a trident in his left hand, his expression impassive as his eyes swept the room. He was always on guard, always looking for any danger.

Someone else might have noted the way the golden rings around Calix's upper arms accentuated the muscles on his tanned skin. They might have also noted the way his dark brown, almost black hair had glimmers of gold in it when the sun landed on it. That same person would have probably also noticed the dark green of his tail and the way it flicked back and forth as he stood guard. They would have probably seen that his brown eyes weren't one solid color, but filled with promises of strength and surety in the midst of a storm, like a steadfast friend.

I, of course, did not notice these things.

Calix was my guard. He was here to protect me and keep me safe against any potential dangers. Not that there were many. Father rarely allowed me out of the castle, and if that happened, I was heavily guarded.

Besides, in all the years Calix had been a part of my personal guard, the male barely spoke more than three words at a time. I wasn't even sure he was capable of such a thing. On top of all that, I was fairly certain Calix hated me. All he did was swim stoically in the corner of rooms, looking scary. Even when I tried to get to know him, he shot down my questions. My other guard, Oliver, was an open book. He worked when Calix was off, and he was more than happy to tell me about everything he and his boyfriend did around the city.

But Calix?

He just stared straight ahead.

"Let's go," I said, adjusting the band around my breasts. My tail swished, moving water around me as I began to swim down the coral corridors of my home. I didn't have to look back to know that Calix was right behind me.

The palace was surprisingly empty despite the morning hour. The coral walls shimmered in the watery sunlight as we passed one priceless artifact after the other.

I narrowed my eyes. Usually, the West Wing was bustling with servants at this time. Especially since the Summer Solstice was only a few days away. They were supposed to be getting all the rooms ready for the dozens of dignitaries and visiting royals from the lesser seas coming to take part in the Solstice Celebrations.

Where is everyone?

Forcing all of these thoughts aside, I waited for Calix to swim ahead of me. His muscles bunched gloriously as he pulled open the giant golden doors separating the West Wing from the main part of the palace.

"Thank you," I said.

As expected, a grunt was my only reply.

We turned a corner, and I glanced down another corridor. It was empty too.

Strange.

"You're looking well-rested, Calix," I said conversationally, as though we were simply out for a swim and not on the way to see my volatile father.

He made a male sound that was a cross between a grunt and a word that I took to mean *yes*.

Glancing to the side, I studied my guard. I didn't know when he found the time to exercise, but one simply did not have a body like that without spending a significant amount of time training. I knew this was true because I enjoyed spending my spare time indulging in delicious treats from the Surface like chocolate and wine. Life was short enough without having to add the pain of daily physical exercise to it. Or at least, that was what I told myself.

Obviously, Calix did not share my opinion. The male was a head taller than I, and he carried himself with the air of someone who was confident in his abilities to do his job. He was my protector, and I always felt safe around him. That feeling had existed since the moment we met. Although he was large, there wasn't a single moment in our acquaintance where he had made me feel uncomfortable. Even though the massive trident in his hand should have frightened me, or at least reminded me he was incredibly strong, I knew I was safe around Calix.

I couldn't say the same about many other males in my life. The number of times I had to endure a horrible male's company and deal with their groping hands and rude jokes simply because they held a title was obscene.

Soon—too soon, in my opinion—we found ourselves in front of the gilded doors of my father's throne room. Many centuries ago, one of my ancestors hired the acclaimed artist Julius to make these doors. They depicted a rather gruesome scene. Kano, the first High King of the Seven Seas, loomed over his subjects with an expression of violence etched onto his face. He brandished his trident in the water as the other six monarchs of the seas bowed before him.

It was a reminder to everyone who passed through these doors that the one who sat on the Coral Throne was the ruler of all. No matter what else happened in the Four Kingdoms, no matter what tomfoolery was taking place on the Surface, the ruler of the Seven Seas would do whatever it took to maintain the balance in their domain.

If I ever became High Queen, I would have this door, and all the others like it in the palace, replaced in a heartbeat. I hated them.

Brushing a hand over my hair, I adjusted the band around my breasts before nodding at Calix. "I'm ready."

Swimming over to the door, he held it closed for a moment as he studied me. "Good luck."

Before I could reply, he yanked the doors open.

The throne room was eerily quiet as I swam in the doorway. The pounding of my heart thundered in my ears, far louder than normal. A hundred pairs of eyes turned towards me as one and the courtiers of my father's court stared at me. They were as unmoving as the statues that lined the walls of the palace.

To call my father temperamental would be an understatement. He liked to play games—deadly ones. The last time he summoned me to him when he was in one of his moods, he made me wait for thirty minutes at the doors before allowing me to enter.

Perhaps if Nontia was smiling down on me, today would be better.

A minute ticked by. The nearby clock on the wall was a gift from a fae lord who lived across the ocean. Enchanted to survive beneath the water, it was a reminder that life existed on the Surface.

Father still didn't call me.

Two minutes went by. Five. Ten. I kept my gaze trained on the ground, knowing that if I looked up before he called for me, I would be inviting his wrath. Studying the smooth coral floor, I noted the golden strands interwoven with the blues and greens that made up the palace.

That clock kept ticking. With every passing minute, anticipation grew in the water. Soon, it was hard to breathe.

When twenty minutes had gone by, a bang resounded through the throne room.

"Come forward, Princess Mareena," my father commanded.

Instantly, I obeyed. I kept my gaze trained on the floor as I swam with confidence, approaching the royal dais. When I could see the edge of the gilded throne in my vision, I bowed. My tail bent nearly in half as I stretched out my arms before me.

"Your Illustrious Majesty," I murmured, enunciating clearly so as to not give him any reasons to be angry with me. "How can I be of assistance?"

"You're a disappointment, daughter of mine," he spat.

I tensed, biting my lip. So this was how this was going to go. Not for the first time, I wished that Nontia had seen fit to bless me with a parent who wasn't the epitome of cruelty. Unfortunately, my mother had died before I even Matured, so here I was.

"Yes, Father," I replied after a moment. "I'm sorry."

"I'm glad to hear that," he said in a thundering voice, "because I have a task for you."

My heart thudded against my ribs, and my lungs tightened.

"A task, Your Majesty?" My gaze remained trained on the floor.

The king cleared his throat. "A way for you to redeem yourself."

For a brief moment, everything stopped. Redeem myself. To my knowledge, I hadn't done anything wrong. Every single year of my life had been spent living in the palace, learning everything a crown princess needed to know. I had no friends, no one to talk to. I didn't have fun—I wasn't even sure I knew what "fun" was.

But if my father thought I had done something wrong, then I must have. Right?

"Princess Mareena," my father said sharply. "Look at me."

Instantly, I complied.

The king's gray eyes were sharp, his mouth twisted into a grimace. His waist-long blue and gray hair was in a low knot at the back of his neck, his crown of jagged coral reaching high above his head. He reclined on his throne, his sea-green scales shimmering as the light hit them. The king ran his eyes over me, sighing. "Well, I suppose this will have to do."

I furrowed my brows. "Your Majesty?" The question was clear in my voice. "If I may—"

"You may not," he snapped, coral ribbons escaping his palms and swirling around him, awaiting his bidding. My own magic thrummed in response to his, but I knew I couldn't beat him. He had the power of the throne behind him.

I kept my mouth shut, and Father said, "It's high time you did your duty to me and the kingdom."

Duty.

My stomach sank and heavy knots formed in my stomach. It wasn't that I didn't understand what he meant. Of course not. Even before Mother died, I knew what my duty would be.

Marriage.

Countless times, my father had lamented the fact that his only merling wasn't born a male. While it wasn't unheard of for females to ascend to power in the Seven Seas, there had never been a female High Queen of the Seven Seas. Never had a female sat on the Coral Throne in her own right. Since I wasn't born with the right parts, my father wanted me to give up my birthright to someone who was "better" simply because he was a "he."

Never in my life had I wanted to scream more than I did at that moment. I was perfectly capable of holding the Coral Scepter on my own. I didn't need a male by my side, nor did I want one.

Ever since I Matured, my father had paraded dozens of suitors in front of me. Foreign princes and dukes from the Seven Seas, lords, and knights. He even proposed finding an elf, vampire, or shifter for me to wed from the

Surface. Any sea witch worth their salt could enchant them to be able to remain underwater, he reasoned.

I refused every single one of them.

Not that I hadn't given them a chance. On the contrary, I gave them far too many chances. They had groped, touched, and kissed me against my will far too many times to count. When my suitors weren't making physical advances, they were proving that being male did not, in fact, guarantee any modicum of intelligence.

I wasn't opposed to the entire institution of marriage.

I was just opposed to marrying anyone who wasn't kind, loyal, smart, and capable of upholding a conversation. It wasn't like I was expecting a bonded mate to appear out of the clear blue water, or something like that. The gods only knew how rare those were.

All I wanted was a male who wasn't an absolute idiot.

Was that too much to ask?

Apparently, it was.

"Who do you have in mind, Father?" I asked. My voice was steady, unwavering, as I forced myself to hold the king's gaze.

He cleared his throat. "Bring them in."

The Epitome of Cruelty

MAREENA

T*hem?*
 The king's words were barely out of his mouth before the doors on the right side of the throne room opened with a bang. I jumped, holding my hands in front of me as my eyes widened.

A dozen young mermales entered the throne room. Swimming in a single file, they held their heads high as they formed a line beside the throne.

I swallowed as minnows erupted in my gut.

This was... not good. In fact, I would go so far as to say that this was very bad. If my father had gone to all the trouble of bringing this many suitors here, it could mean only one thing.

My freedom slipped away like a piece of kelp between my fingers.

"Princess Mareena." The High King's voice echoed through the throne room, and I stiffened. "You are hereby commanded to marry."

Commanded.

To.

Marry.

The words echoed around in my skull painfully. I clenched my fists at my side, my breath coming heavier. Blood left my face and my lungs tightened as my entire body urged me to do something. Instead, I forced myself to remain still. "But, Fath—"

He held up a hand, the gold bands around his wrist shimmering. "Enough!" he yelled. "I have given you time, Princess Mareena, to find your own husband. Time to decide for yourself who you shall marry. I am a patient male, am I not?"

There was no way in hell I was answering truthfully.

"Of course, my king," I lied smoothly.

"Which is why I am willing to give you one more chance."

"Father?"

His gaze pinned me. "You have seven days, Mareena. If you do not take a husband within that time, you will forfeit your claim to the Coral Throne and be cast out of my presence. It is your duty to wed and continue the royal line."

Cast out.

The words echoed around in my head. Would he really do it? Not even a second went by before I knew the answer. Of course, he would do it. My father was the epitome of cruelty. He would likely find some twisted pleasure in throwing his only daughter to the wild sharks that called the Indigo Ocean their home.

The king continued. "In order to assist you in your search, I have invited these kind gentlemen to come and remain at the palace with us. They will spend every single day with you until you get to know them. You *will* marry, daughter of mine. But I will be gracious enough to allow you the privilege of choosing your own husband."

Behind me, hushed whispers came from the gathered courtiers. I couldn't spare a thought to try to understand what they were saying, though. My every focus was stuck on the males before me. Their expressions ranged from bored to lecherous, but each of them had a commonality.

They were clearly my father's males. There was no way he would choose anyone who would defy him as a potential suitor for me. I already knew what kind of males these were. They were the same ones who always flocked around my father at the balls he threw, the same ones he had thrown at me countless times since I had Matured.

Rude. Mean. Only interested in pursuing physical affections. Dangerous.

There wasn't really a choice here. I wouldn't marry any of them. So I could string them along or...

A plan began to take shape to form in my mind. It was insane, and more than likely would result in the loss of my birthright. But if it would save me from this horrible fate, then it was worth a try.

I cleared my throat. "You say I must find a husband in a week's time, Father?"

The king nodded curtly. "Yes."

"Or I will lose my birthright as your heir."

"Correct," he growled. "The entire court has heard me, daughter. Do not think you will make me go back on my words. I swear on all that is good in Nontia's blue ocean, you will marry within seven days."

I smiled. "Oh, that is not what I am trying to do at all."

He narrowed his eyes. "Then you will marry?"

This was it.

"Yes." Gathering all my courage, I continued. "I would ask for your leave to go into the city and search for a husband."

A collective gasp came from the courtiers behind me. The water in the throne room felt as thick as soup as my father stared at me. He pushed himself off the throne, his muscles bunching with absolute power as he swam towards me. His eyes flashed as coral power rippled off him.

"You dare defy me?" he roared.

I shook my head. "Of course not. I will marry," I said quickly. "But I would like to choose my own husband."

He seethed. "What would you have me do with them?" He gestured to the suitors lining the wall. "They came here for you, daughter. You would have them leave without so much as a taste of their prize?"

Anger bubbled up within me. I was not a prize to be won, just because I'd had the misfortune of being born female.

"Send them home?" My voice was quieter than I hoped.

He glared at me. "What?"

"If you please, Father, send them away. If I am to do my duty,"—I gulped as a shiver ran down my spine—"at least allow me to search for someone with whom I am compatible. Someone who cares for me. Maybe someone who could, one day, love me."

The king stared at me. His gray eyes pinned me, and he stared and stared and stared. The weight of his gaze was heavy, the coral ribbons swirling in the water around him both a threat and a reminder of his power. My own magic, that same coral power, cowed in my veins. That usual constant hum was dimmed until I could barely feel it. Until I took my throne—something which seemed unlikely, at this point in time—I would never be as powerful as him.

My heart pounded, the coverings around my breasts suddenly feeling like they were nothing at all as I swam before him. I was laid bare before the court, waiting for my father's response.

He stared, and I waited.

Then, the strangest thing happened. My father, the High King of the Seven Seas, laughed. He roared, and mirth roiled off him like a wave at high tide. Everyone froze for a moment before nervous giggles and chortles rose all around us.

I couldn't do anything except stare at my father. I had *never* seen him laugh. Ever. In all my years, even in my youth before I Matured, he had never so much as snorted in front of me.

And here he was, laughing.

"My daughter is a *romantic*," my father choked out. Tears streamed down his face as he slapped his hand against his tail. The sound echoed through the watery throne room, and no one even dared to breathe. "May the gods have mercy on me. A romantic!"

He laughed until he was blue in the face. Then he swam to the throne and sat as he gasped for air.

Still, I did not move. I did not breathe. I just waited to find out my fate.

After what felt like an eternity, Father canted his head. "Alright."

"Alright?" I repeated, unwilling to let hope enter my voice.

He nodded, a glimmer of violence in his eyes. "You have a week, daughter. I'll send these suitors home." One of them groaned, but Father ignored them, continuing. "Find yourself a male who is 'worthy' of your love, or get out of my ocean." He sat back, clearly proud of himself. "It's your choice."

One week.

Seven days.

How could one find a husband in that short of a time?

But I looked at the males lined up against the wall, their tails moving slowly in the warm water of the throne room, and I knew that I would take it. I had to. I wouldn't marry them.

Swallowing, I dipped my head. "Thank you, Father."

"Oh," he said, holding up his hand as a predatory smile crept across his face. "One more thing."

A frisson of fear ran down my spine. "Yes?"

He snarled. "You will leave now. Be gone, Princess Mareena. Remove yourself from my sight. You are not permitted to return to your rooms, nor may you take anything with you from the palace."

I gasped. "But how will I survive?"

It was becoming exceedingly clear that I did not think this through.

Father raised a brow. "That's no longer my problem, daughter." His voice was colder than I had ever heard it before. "You'll figure it out or die trying. Either way, you will get out of my sight."

Nontia help me.

Knowing that my father was not one to be trifled with, I turned and swam as fast as I could toward the back of the throne room. My eyes stung with unshed tears as I rushed past the couriers. They stared at me, venom in their expressions as they watched me pass. Some of them hurled insults my way.

"... Ungrateful..."

"... daughter of a sea witch..."

"Should be sent to the beaches of Ithenmyr..."

"... Teach her a lesson..."

"Ugly bit—"

I forced myself to ignore them, keeping my eyes trained on the exit. From the throne room, it wasn't a long swim before I found myself at the main entrance of the palace. This place had been my home for my entire life. I had never been allowed to leave through these doors on my own. Every time I left the palace, I was under heavy guard.

But now, things were different. I was leaving with nothing but the band around my breasts. I wished I could say that at that moment I was fearless. That courage had run through my veins. I wished I could have said that I was ready for the challenges coming my way.

But that wouldn't have been true.

Fear ran through my veins, like frigid waters on a bitter winter day. I was afraid of the world that I was going to enter. I was afraid of what I would find. That I wouldn't find someone who could love me or even tolerate me. But more than that, I was afraid of being used as nothing more than a womb and locked in the palace, never to escape. I was afraid that if I remained, I would become nothing more than a figurehead. A female whose sole purpose was to exist.

And so I took a deep breath, ignored the stinging in my eyes, and pushed open the doors.

Coral City was nothing as I had imagined. My father's palace was filled with muted colors. Grays and blues and greens. Colors were few and far between. It was as though darkness itself ebbed off the king in waves, leeching color from his surroundings.

That was not the case in the city. During the first few minutes of my freedom, I did nothing but swim down the steps of the palace onto the main street. My jaw fell open as I stared at the vibrant colors. The brightest blues and deepest greens were intermingled with brilliant pinks, deep purples, and bright yellows.

It was more than incredible—it was magnificent.

Schools of multicolored fish swam around me, filling the great seas with their colors as they went about their days. Kelp rose from the sandy sea floor, moving gently in the currents. Everywhere I looked, there was more beauty.

Suddenly, understanding flooded me. *This* was beauty that inspired art. Colors like this were the reason that artists painted, composers wrote music, and thespians acted in plays. These colors spoke to a part of me I hadn't even known existed. They called upon an appreciation of beauty that I had never known.

Looking at the beauty of the city, my heart swelled. Even when I had gone into Coral City in the past, I had never seen it like this.

It was as though I had been seeing things in gray-scale until this point and now I could see what life really looked like.

It was stunning.

And the people!

There were hundreds—no, thousands—of merfolk out in the streets of Coral City. I had never been out of the palace unescorted. The merfolk did not know I was here. They were just living their lives.

It was so incredibly loud. Every possible sound filled my ears. Tails slapping against each other were the backdrop to conversations that abounded. Raucous laughter from merlings intermingled with shouts coming from the streets.

It was so much, and yet, it wasn't enough. There was so much to see, and I had just bought myself a few days of freedom. Surely that was enough time to explore. Just a little. Just enough to see the world that I had been denied.

"Do it, Mareena," I mumbled to myself as I swam down the busy road. "Live a little before you find yourself a husband."

A laugh came from beside me. "I'll be your husband, baby! We could *dance* together all night long."

I turned to see a mermale swimming along, raising his white brows as he gazed at me lecherously.

I shuddered, shaking my head. "No, thank you."

"Suit yourself," he replied before lifting his hand in a rude gesture and laughing at me.

I snarled at him, showing him my sharp teeth, before turning around. I didn't have a map, and I'd never learned much about the inner workings of Coral City, but I figured that if I headed down the street, I was sure to encounter something interesting.

And so I swam.

An hour turned into two as I played the tourist in my own city. The city I would—hopefully—one day rule.

I didn't have any coin to spend, but that didn't stop me from observing the small families out with their merlings or the busy merfolk as they swam to and from their places of work. Everyone was so busy that they didn't seem to notice the princess in their midst. That was good.

The further I got from the palace, the more chaotic the city became. Near my home, the streets were long and orderly. But as I continued into the city and past shops where vendors were selling food, things began to change. The city evolved. Long, tall structures rose up from the sandy floor, the coral buildings filled with windows that provided glimpses into their inhabitants' lives. From them came sounds of life. Children screaming, newly birthed merlings crying, and adults yelling at each other.

None of these things happened when my father was around.

I swam down the sandy streets lined with rows upon rows of tall green plants, watching as people around me *lived*.

I was observing two adolescent mermaids flirt nearby when the hairs on the back of my neck prickled. I stiffened, but nothing seemed amiss before me. The same two girls were now holding hands, whispering as they swam off together. I was just about to turn around when a hand landed on my shoulder.

A deep voice growled in my ear, "I've been looking everywhere for you."

A scream rose in my throat as my eyes widened. Before I could yell, a large and calloused hand landed on my mouth. I tried to bite the hand at the same moment that my assailant jerked us both backward.

No, no, no.

This could not be happening.

My heart hammered in my chest and I whipped my tail as hard as I could. Gathering my strength, I rammed my elbow into a very hard chest. Pain radiated through me, but I didn't stop fighting.

"Stop it, Princess," my attacker hissed, grunting as my elbow connected with their stomach. "It's me."

Me?

In my panicked fog, I didn't recognize the voice. I reached up, clawing at the arm holding me still as I shook my head back and forth. Whoever this person was, I would not go with them willingly. I swung my tail around, knocking into them. The moment my attacker's grip loosened around my mouth, I snapped my teeth. I tasted salt and flesh and copper as his blood seeped into my mouth. My assailant cursed, wrenching their hand away from me.

I spat, blood tinging the water red.

"What the hell?" I yelled as I turned. "Don't come any clos—"

My words dried up in my mouth as I stared at the large mermale currently shaking his injured hand in the water.

"Dammit, Princess," he said. "That actually hurt."

"Calix?" I asked.

He crossed his arms, his trident catching the light as he glowered, grabbing my arm. I inhaled sharply at the contact. My entire body felt alive as he touched me. I was so entranced by the feeling; I didn't fight as he dragged me into a secluded courtyard, where our only witnesses were the orange and yellow fish swimming all around us.

When we were alone, he released my arm and snarled, "Do you know any other mermales?"

I shook my head. I truly did not. Other than my guards, the only other men I had ever met were the potential suitors thrown at me by my father.

Apparently, he believed males could be bad influences on the female mind. It made me wonder why he was so eager to have me married.

"That's what I thought," Calix said. He crossed his arms, and I couldn't help but notice the generous bulge of his muscles.

"What... What are you doing here?" And why was he talking so much? Calix had said more words in the past minute than during our entire acquaintance.

He tilted his head. "I thought you might need some protection." Lifting his hand, he winced at the bite mark. His blue eyes flashed, and his mouth twitched. "Apparently, I discounted your abilities."

My heart slowed in my chest as I pondered his words. His *many* words. Nibbling my lip, I studied him. "You left the palace? And followed me? But my father sai—"

"Someone has to look out for you," he said. "If the High King isn't smart enough to see that and assign you a guard, then I will have to do it myself."

"What about your job?" There was no way that he would be allowed to just waltz back into the palace. Not now that he left without warning.

He shook his head. "I can get another one."

"But—"

"Look, Princess, as much as I *love* answering all of your questions, can we not do this right now?"

I stared at him. "Do what?"

"This." He gestured around him, and the water rippled. "Night is coming," he said gruffly.

"And?"

He huffed as if speaking this much was physically paining him. Which, to be fair, it might have been. "And unless you plan to spend the night sleeping in the streets with the common fish, we need to find somewhere to be."

I blinked at him.

Somewhere to sleep.

I hadn't even thought about that, to be honest. I had been so focused on *not* marrying those twelve idiots that I hadn't really planned much at all.

Calix stared at me. "Did you even have a plan?"

I bit my lip, my gaze wandering. "Not so much of a plan as an… idea."

He narrowed his eyes. "Of course, you didn't have a plan." Sighing, he grabbed my arm. "Come on then. Let's go."

"Where?"

"Somewhere safe."

Without waiting for a response, Calix swam away. I stared at him for a minute before sighing and hurrying after him.

Night was falling, and whether it was prudent or not, I trusted Calix.

I only hoped I was right to do so.

What Was Wrong With Me?

CALIX

What a day. This morning, when I rolled out of my bed at half past four and made my way to the courtyard to swim laps before coming on duty, I would never have guessed that this was where I was going to end up.

Swimming through Coral City with Princess Mareena, of all people.

"Come on," I grunted, leading Mareena out of the courtyard.

A quick glance behind my shoulder told me she was following. Her eyes were wide, and she looked around with awe as I led her through the city. She was silent, which was fine with me.

I had a lot of thoughts to parse through.

For the past ten years, I had grown used to my job. Comfortable. Relaxed, even. I came to expect the routine that came with guarding the princess. When I was first assigned as her personal guard, I had been less than pleased. I knew the circumstances of my birth meant that I would never be allowed to work on the king's guard, but I had hoped for something more stimulating than guarding the princess.

All that changed when I got to know Mareena, though.

Nothing about her fit the mold of what I thought the princess would be. She was strong, kind, courageous, and utterly unlike the horrid male who had contributed to her conception. Given the chance to reign, she would bring about real change in the Indigo Ocean. Change that was desperately needed.

I already knew that Princess Mareena would be an incredible queen.

Not only that, but she was beautiful. No, wait. Beautiful wasn't the right word to describe her. It was too pedestrian, and there was *nothing* pedestrian about the princess. She was magnificent. Impressive. Exceedingly skilled in every facet of her life.

She was amazing, and her father didn't know her at all.

But I did. I knew her better than I knew my own mind. I had spent the last ten years watching her. Protecting her. She had invaded every second of my life. The problem—and it was a problem—was that somewhere along the line, I lost sight of who I was. Who she was.

And now, I broke the cardinal rule of my job. The one rule everyone knew to follow.

Like a stupid mermale, I forgot my place. I forgot all the horrible things my father had said to me growing up. I forget where I had come from, and I had made the biggest mistake of all.

I had fallen deeply, madly, irrevocably in love with the one female I could never have. The Crown Princess of the Seven Seas.

What was wrong with me?

Obviously, I knew I couldn't have her. To be perfectly frank, I was fairly certain the princess barely knew I existed. She was polite when she spoke to me, but then again, she was polite to everyone. Unlike her horrible father, she actually treated those around her with kindness.

What a revolutionary idea.

So this morning, when I was ordered to take her to the throne room, my stomach twisted. I just knew something was wrong. Call it a gut feeling or intuition, but I knew that today would be the day everything changed.

When her bastard of a father told her she had to marry one of those blustering idiots who were undressing her with their eyes, I barely restrained myself from swimming over and stabbing him with my trident over and over again. The only thing that stopped me was the knowledge that if I did it, I would have proven every single horrible thing my father said about me right.

So instead, I kept my white-knuckled grip on my trident, swimming near the door as the insufferable courtiers muttered under their breath about Mareena.

She was so brave. She looked her father in the eye and defied him. It was incredible. I had seen mermales three times her age quiver before their king. But not her. She stood before him, unwavering in her bravery.

As soon as she left, I knew I had a choice to make. I could stay and keep my job, or I could go after her.

It was barely a question. What good was employment if the female I loved was no longer swimming in the same waters as me? If her laugh never again filled my ears? If I never again saw her eyes glimmer as she got an idea? She'd never been out in the city alone. She didn't know the dangers of the city.

If someone hurt her...

A shudder ran through me at the thought.

I couldn't let that happen. Mareena was the hope for the people of the Indigo Ocean. More than that, though, she was the female I loved. The tiny fact remained that she wasn't aware of that last part, but I wasn't going to be the one to tell her.

The moment the palace doors swung shut behind her, I handed in my notice. Packing my bag with as much as I could carry, I told Kvrim that I was done and swam out the front doors of the palace.

By the time I left, Mareena had disappeared. It took me three hours to find her. Three hours too many, if you asked me. By the time I locked my eyes on the princess's black hair and shimmering purple tail, my heart felt like it was about to explode out of my chest.

"Where are we going?" Mareena's voice broke through the fog of my thoughts, and I blinked. It took me a moment to process her question.

"I know a place." I shifted my trident from one hand to the other.

She stopped swimming, her tail flicking angrily as she crossed her arms and glared at me. "Do you care to elaborate, Calix?"

I ran my fingers over the bite mark on my palm. It was healing—I was Mature, it would be gone by nightfall—but I still couldn't believe it. She *bit* me. I hadn't meant to frighten her. I just wanted to take her off the street so we could speak in private. I wasn't angry that she bit me. On the contrary, I was very... not-angry about the entire situation. To know that this female was not only strong in character but willing to fight made me feel things that I really shouldn't have been feeling for my crown princess.

Especially since she was in the market for a husband. I always knew she would marry. She had to. It was her duty to produce heirs. And of course, she couldn't marry me. Notwithstanding the secrecy of my affection for her, I was a guard, and she was a princess. There was a world of divide between us.

But that didn't mean I was going to be happy about it. To see another male smile at her. Kiss her. Take her to their bed. The thought made me want to destroy everything around me. But I didn't. Using every ounce of self-control I possessed, I didn't do a single thing. I pushed down those thoughts, shoving them deep inside myself until I could barely feel them.

"Somewhere safe," I said gruffly.

She could sleep, and I could finally think in peace. And the gods only knew how much I needed to think. I had already decided I would do everything I could to make sure she found a male who would be, at the very least, tolerable.

Of course, she didn't just deserve "tolerable". No, Mareena deserved far more than I, or anyone else, could give her. She deserved to be unconditionally and wholeheartedly loved. She deserved a male who was going to treat her as the absolutely incredible female she was.

That was why I was taking Mareena to Shipwreck Cove.

She whispered, "Thank you, Calix."

I grunted a reply. The more words I said, the more I chanced telling her how I felt accidentally. That would not be good. She could never know that I loved her. It was my secret and mine alone.

"Come on," I said. "The city isn't safe at night."

That was an understatement. The sharks that called the Indigo Ocean their home were the least dangerous predators that swam through the dark, moonlit waters.

Mareena's eyes narrowed, sweeping over me. "Why are you helping me, Calix?"

My name on her lips had never sounded so good.

I grunted, "It's the right thing to do."

And it was. Of that, I was certain. Before she could pry any further, I tilted my head. "Let's go."

We swam in silence through the Anemone District. Mareena naturally attracted attention. We passed schools of fish, merlings, and entire families going about their days. Everyone's eyes were drawn to Mareena, but she was completely unaware of their attention.

That was part of what made me love her. Mareena had no idea how incredible she was.

Soon the seas opened up around us. In the distance, vast wooden structures rose in the distance. They had been claimed by the ocean floor. Reefs and kelp grew around the wood. Shafts of dying sunlight illuminated the shattered bellies of massive ships that had once carried humans, vampires, werewolves, witches, and elves alike across the surface of the ocean until Nontia decided to claim their souls for her own.

Mareena slowed, her tail moving behind her as she turned in a semicircle. "Where are we?"

I pointed my trident at the land in front of me. "Shipwreck Cove."

"Shipwrecks?" She glared at me as a flash of coral sparks appeared in her hand. "As in, a graveyard. You brought me to a graveyard."

I swallowed, swimming backward just a touch as her eyes hardened. I had never seen Mareena use her magic before, but based on what I'd seen her father do... perhaps angering her was not in my best interest. But I'd be damned if seeing that flash of violence in her eyes didn't make me feel all sorts of improper things about my princess.

"Well... not technically." I tilted my head. "As you know, mer don't need graveyards."

When merfolk Faded, our bodies returned to the sea. There was a balance in the Indigo Ocean. Everything had a give and take. Magic, that incredible power that few mer had, demanded it. There would be no life down here without it.

"Calix," the princess asked, her voice hard, "are there bodies down here?"

"Ah..." I nibbled my lip. Then, deciding that it was better to just tell her quickly, I blurted, "Yes, there are."

She swam up to me, staring me in the eyes. Suddenly, I was aware that we were alone and there was only a foot between us. My chest squeezed, and I tightened my grip on my trident.

Mareena glared up at me. "You brought me, a princess of the Seven Seas, to a graveyard?"

Now I was beginning to question my sanity. Perhaps this hadn't been the best course of action after all. Maybe she would have preferred if I'd stayed behind in the palace.

"I'm sorry, I just thought that you should have somewhere safe to stay. I know this isn't much, but I can keep watch over you here, and we won't be dis—"

"Oh my gods," she chuckled, shaking her head back and forth. The movement caused her hair to billow up in the water, and I stared at it, captivated. "Calix, I think you have said more words in the past minute than you have in your entire life."

I stared at her, blood rushing to my cheeks. "Your Highness?"

What else was there to say? I didn't think *I'm staying silent so I won't say I love you* would go over well.

She snorted. "It's fine. Did you say there's somewhere to sleep?"

I nodded. "Yes, I come here sometimes to..."

Escape. Get away. Forget about my family. Steal a few minutes to myself. I didn't say that, though. I just stared at her like an idiot.

"To get away?" she suggested.

I nodded.

"Perfect." She groaned. "This day has been absolutely exhausting."

Without a backward glance, Mareena swam into the nearest shipwreck. I shook my head, watching her go.

How could I ever watch her marry someone else?

Shipwrecks and Sporting Matches

MAREENA

I'd never been inside a shipwreck before. It was not exactly what I could have called a pleasant experience. The interior of the ship was decaying before my eyes. Kelp and seagrass reclaimed the wood like a starving beast. Fish swam through broken boards and around mangled furniture that, at one point, was probably useful. Although Calix had admitted that this was a graveyard, I couldn't see any evidence of bodies—physically, at least.

The waters told a different story. They swirled around me, carrying echoes of screams of the men and women who had died. My heart ached for them.

What a terrible death, dying in a place you never belonged.

We entered what appeared to have once been the main eatery, and I turned to Calix.

"The people who were on the ship when it wrecked," I said slowly, "do you know where they came from?"

Calix tightened his grip on his trident, his tail flicking and stirring the sand as he avoided my gaze.

"Ithenmyr, probably." He spoke over his shoulder, swimming through the nearest door and disappearing around the corner. "I was just a merling when this ship came down fifty years ago. This place was... I came here to get away."

I tucked that piece of information away for later. Like me, Calix was Mature. Maturing made us stronger. Not immortal, per se, but very long-lived. Long enough that my father had been High King of the Seven Seas for eight hundred and twenty-nine years. Unless we were killed by unnatural causes, merfolk didn't die. We Faded.

Remnants of the Surface people who had once occupied the ship were all around me as I swam after Calix. Old tables lay in pieces, the wood sanded smooth from years in the water. Bits of fabric floated around, their colors muted to an indistinguishable shade of gray. Broken plates littered the room, and assorted silverware stuck up from the sand. Empty frames lay on their sides, and there was a heaviness to the water that made it difficult to breathe.

Not wanting to remain in this place on my own, I shivered, hurriedly swimming away from the haunted room. By the time I caught up with him, we were swimming down what had, at one point, been a corridor. Now, it was little more than a few planks of wood holding together a roof. Eventually, Calix came to a stop in front of a door that was somehow still standing, despite the destruction all around us.

He pulled it open, revealing the remnants of what had once been a bedroom. Now, the coral had claimed the wooden frame of the bed, and sand was strewn across the floor. But the space had a roof and four walls, which was a feat considering the state of the rest of the shipwreck.

Holding open the door as I swam inside, Calix slipped in after me and swam over to the small trunk at the base of the bed. He pulled it open, rifling through it before pulling out a packet of something green the size of his palm.

Turning around, he shot me a look of chagrin as he handed me the packet. "Here."

I eyed the interesting green leaves as I ran them between my fingers. I'd seen some of the guards eating something similar in the past, but I had never tried it before.

"What is this?" I asked.

"Roasted kelp." He shrugged. "I thought you might be hungry."

Bringing it to my nose, I sniffed. It smelled salty, which wasn't a surprise, and it was rough beneath my fingers. Breaking off a small piece, I popped it into my mouth. It was crunchy, and though the salt was powerful, it was somehow balanced by a bitter aftertaste.

"It's delicious," I said, proceeding to eat the rest of the packet as Calix pulled out for himself.

When all the food was gone, we stared at each other awkwardly before Calix cleared his throat. Gesturing to the bed, he said, "You can sleep here, Princess. I'll keep watch."

And he did.

Calix was a silent presence as I slid into the bed, pulling a blanket made of woven seaweed over myself before finally closing on this long day. As I drifted off to sleep, I couldn't help but consider the mermale standing at the entrance of the room. I was grateful he had come after me. What would I have done without him?

I wasn't sure. But I had survived the day, and now I needed to sleep. After all, tomorrow, I had a husband to find.

I woke to a soft grunt coming from the other side of the door. Pulling myself out of the last vestiges of sleep, I shook my head as I stretched out on the coral. Though it wasn't as luxurious as my bed back at the castle, I had slept well.

Another grunt hit my ears, and curiosity got the better of me. Taking care of my needs in the small pot in the corner, I washed my hands before swimming over to the door and pulling it open slowly.

My eyes widened.

Calix's bare back was to me as his arms reached high above his head. Holding onto one of the remaining wooden support beams from when the ship was still in one piece, he pulled himself up with his arms. His muscles bulged, and he lifted his entire body with ease. Switching from using both arms to just one, he curled his tail up beneath him as he stretched his muscles.

I would be lying if I said it wasn't *very* attractive. My mouth dried and warmth flooded through me as Calix exercised. No wonder he looked so good. He pulled himself up a dozen more times before letting go of the beam.

Deciding it probably wasn't very princessly to get caught ogling my guard, I cleared my throat. "Good morning, Calix."

He straightened so fast, his tail slapped against the wall as he turned around. "Good morning, Princess," he said sheepishly. "How did you sleep?"

I smiled. "Well, thank you." Sunlight shone through the cracks in the ship's walls, and I glanced out of a hole that probably hadn't been part of the original structure. Chewing on my lip, I tried to decide how best to tackle the issues at hand. "So, Calix... I need a husband."

He stared at me, and I could have sworn his face paled slightly before he swallowed. "Yes. A husband."

"Before the week is up." Therein lay the problem. While I didn't want to marry any of the pricks Father had invited to the castle, I wasn't exactly sure how one went about meeting available males. Especially ones that are not... horrible.

Calix was still staring at me, and I shifted beneath his gaze. "I'm not looking for a mate, you see, but someone who is... kind. Would you know... I just... I'm not exactly sure where to start."

My plan hadn't gotten me that far.

Calix ran a hand over his face, his muscles rippling with the movement. "Someone kind," he muttered.

I nodded. "And preferably not ancient." I shrugged. "I just... I want to be married to someone who isn't complete garbage."

The male nodded slowly. "Alright, Princess."

He stared at me for a long moment, seeming to resign himself to something. Then he turned, picking up his trident where it rested against the wall. His powerful tail moved back and forth, disturbing the water around him as he swam through the ship.

I hurried after him, not wanting to be left alone. By the time I had caught up with Calix, we had left the shipwreck behind us. Seaweed swayed in the current and large schools of fish swam through the clear blue water.

"Wait!" I called out. "Where are you going?"

The guard turned around, raising a brow. "You need a husband, right?"

I nodded. "Yes."

"And I'm assuming that you don't want to marry someone like those... young lords at the palace?"

"Never," I seethed. "They are horrible. I want someone real."

He raised a brow. "On that, we are in agreement, Princess." He waved the trident in the water, pointing in the distance past the crowded streets of

Coral City. "If it's someone real you're looking for, I know the perfect person."

I stared at him.

He was going to... set me up? This was not exactly how I thought this was going to go. However, since I didn't have any other ideas, I swam after him.

Maybe this wouldn't be so bad.

The roaring of a crowd was the first thing I heard. The swirling water carried the voices to our ears, and an undercurrent of excitement filled the water. I followed Calix as he led me through the same streets I had traveled yesterday, but this time, we weren't going toward the palace.

Instead, he swam in the direction of the large coral amphitheater that bordered the western edge of Coral City. Made of rare black coral, the Onyx Arena was visible from the palace. Father had never allowed me to go there—all my trips out of the palace had been closely guarded and curated. I only took part in activities that were deemed "appropriate" for princesses.

In other words, I had taken part in more tea parties than I could count, and I was adept at reading out loud. Theater and sports, though? Those were inappropriate for a female like me.

A bubble of excitement grew in my stomach. Perhaps here, in this place that Father would never dare frequent, I might find my husband. Curious about who Calix was bringing me to meet, I peppered him with questions. Unfortunately for me, he barely spoke other than to ask me to be patient.

Eventually, I gave up trying to figure out who we were going to see and just took in the city. The water was warm and full of bubbles as fish and other animals intermingled with merfolk, waiting to gain entrance to the amphitheater. Calix and I joined the rather disorderly line, waiting for the gates to open.

By the time a loud gong sounded, the noise rippling through the water, the energy was nearly frantic. Merfolk trickled through the gates, their chatter joining the sound of bubbling water as tails slapped against the sand.

"This is taking too long," Calix grumbled.

"I'm fine waiting," I assured him.

"You're a princess. You shouldn't have to wait." He shook his head. "Come with me."

Calix's powerful tail swished forward. I wasn't sure if it was the trident in his grip or the thick ridges of his muscles, but either way, people took one look at him and swam out of the way. I kept my head down, swimming closely behind him.

The mermale came to a stop in front of the gate. "Greetings, Bartholomew," he said, addressing the blue-haired guard stationed at the entrance.

The guard nodded. "Calix. Coming as a spectator, for once?"

I raised a brow. Calix competed here? That was interesting. I didn't even know where he found the time to do that.

My guard nodded. "We're here to watch."

A grin crept over the blue-haired male's face. "Ah. Who is the lucky lady?"

I swam forward, sticking out my hand. "I'm Mar—"

"Marie," Calix interrupted, speaking over me. "This is my friend, Marie."

Glancing at him, my brows furrowed. Before I could ask why he changed my name, he reached back and threaded his hand through mine. I was so shocked by the touch—and the sparks that ran from the point of contact all the way up my arm—that my words dried up in my throat.

Bartholomew waggled a brow. "I see how it is. Will you be wanting your usual seats, Calix?"

"Yes," the guard holding my hand grunted. "And let Silva know we'd like some refreshments sent to us."

"Of course." Bartholomew extended a hand, and Calix led me into the amphitheater.

That was... odd.

Things only got odder from there. Calix swam through the amphitheater with the ease of someone who had been here many times before. We went up a set of seats, past a viewing area already filled with an eager crowd, and to another door. This one was black and guarded by a mermale wearing a seaweed tunic. As soon as the male saw us, he pushed open a door.

Nodding at the guard, Calix led me into an enclosed box. He let go of my hand as soon as the door slipped shut, enclosing us in the box. Three of the four walls were made of light pink coral, and the last was made of clear glass, allowing us to see into the arena. A settee sat in the middle of the space, and a counter ran along the back wall.

Calix rested his trident near the door, and I took a moment to look at the arena. It was enormous and could probably hold thousands of merfolk. A raised platform was in the middle of the stadium, surrounded by a net made of braided seaweed.

Here, the deafening noise of the crowd was quieter, muted by the walls, and the water moved calmly around us.

I raised a brow. "You brought me to a... sporting match?"

The guard looked nervous, and he paused, running a hand through his hair. "Yes," he said eventually. "My—"

A knock came at the door, interrupting him. I wondered what he was going to say. Who was I here to meet?

Calix swam over to the door, slipping it open. He murmured, and a few moments later, he came back with a tray of food.

As soon as a warm, spiced aroma hit my nose, my stomach grumbled. Calix chuckled, handing me a bowl full of something fried. The witches involved in the cooking of this food must have been very skilled, because when I picked up the food, the water simply moved around it. I may have moaned when the food hit my tongue. The breading was still crunchy, and hiding beneath it was a smooth cheese that must have come from the Surface. It was delicious.

I quickly devoured the entire bowl. By the time I was done, a bell was ringing in the middle of the area. I set the empty bowl on the settee, swimming over to the windowed wall. Looking out, my breath caught in my throat.

The huge amphitheater was packed to the brim, with merfolk crammed into the seats. The water seemed to buzz with eager anticipation as a door opened in the middle of the ring. A pair of sharks swam into the arena, pulling a male in a shell behind them. They brought the male to the center of the stadium, in front of the elevated dais, and he lifted a conch shell to his mouth.

"People of Coral City," he proclaimed in a loud voice, his voice booming throughout the entire stadium. "Welcome to the Onyx Arena. As I'm sure you are all aware, today is no ordinary sporting match."

The mermale lifted his arms, and two bare-chested males entered the stadium. Each wore a ribbon around their upper forearm. One was dark green, and the other was as black as the night sky.

Deafening applause and the sound of slapping tails filled the water as the two males made their way to the stage.

When the applause died down, the announcer continued. Gesturing to the male with hair as white as the sand dusting the floor of the arena, he said, "The Champion of the Green Tides, Siveril of the House of Aqua has challenged none other than Coral City's own Champion, Byron of the House of Syreni."

The other male—Byron, I assumed—had bright red hair. He raised his arm, waving as he turned in a slow circle. The crowd cheered, but my attention was caught on his face. He looked *incredibly* familiar.

"Is that your brother?" I asked Calix, swimming closer and pressing my nose to the cold glass separating us from the crowd. The fighter and my guard looked almost identical, except for the color of their hair.

Calix grunted. "Half."

I turned, a dozen questions landing on the tip of my tongue, but before I could ask them, a gong sounded in the middle of the arena. The sharks pulled the announcer out of the ring, and then it began. People waved flags in the water, some green but most black, as the two warriors swam around each other in circles, their fists raised. Tension rose. The crowd quieted. I held my breath, waiting to see what would happen.

It seemed like an eternity passed before Siveril darted forward. He was a flash of white hair and muscles as he raised his fists, aiming for Byron. Just when I thought the match would be over before it even began, Byron darted out from beneath the punch. He slammed his tail into the Siveril.

The two of them went tumbling away, and the crowd roared.

Family Ties, Bastards, and Loneliness

CALIX

Byron was winning the match. His fists were raised and Siveril was swimming away from him now, forced into a defensive position by my half-brother. It wasn't a surprise. Byron *always* won the match. Older than me by five months, he was the apple of our father's eye.

I was the scourge of the family.

Father never let me forget that I wasn't wanted. My very first memory was being reminded by Father that my mother appeared on his doorstep when I was only a few days old, thrusting a seaweed-wrapped bundle at him. I was his son, she said, but she couldn't care for me.

Did she know she was condemning me to life as a bastard? Or did she simply not care? I supposed her intentions were inconsequential because I never met her. Father allowed me to be raised in his home and educated alongside Byron, but that was where his kindness ended. As soon as I Matured, I was thrust out of his home and forced to find my own way.

I always found it ironic that Byron had found favor in our father's eyes through participation in these types of events, but no matter how I excelled in my position in the king's guard, nothing was ever good enough for him. I was a bastard, nothing more. That was my lot in life. Nothing I did would ever be good enough for the male who had sired me.

Byron swung out with his tail. The roar of the crowd was deafening, drowning out the slap of my brother's tail as it slashed across his opponent's chest. A trail of red blood floated into the water, and they chanted my brother's name.

"Byron. Byron. Byron."

Mareena pressed her hand against the glass, and her tail swished excitedly as she watched my brother. My heart twisted at the sight, and it felt like part of me was breaking in half, but I pushed down the hurt. I couldn't show my pain—this was the reason I had brought Mareena here. She needed a husband. A good, kind male that would look after her no matter what. Someone with virtue who, while not a lord, would be enough for her father.

Byron was that male.

An overwhelming ache consumed my entire body at the thought of playing matchmaker between the female I loved and my only brother. It was deep within my bones, starting at the tip of my tail and moving through my entire body. I consoled myself with the knowledge that at least this way, I would get to see my princess every once in a while. I could keep her in my life. If she married Byron, she would be happy.

Last night, I spent long hours thinking about this. Not only was my half-brother everything Mareena was looking for in a husband, but he was single. This was the only way to keep Mareena safe. If she married a stranger, who knew what kind of dangers she might be walking into? They could be cruel or hurtful or ignorant.

No, it was better this way. At least this way, I knew Byron would give Mareena everything she deserved.

The crowd cheered, and I glanced outside. Byron had Siveril pinned, and the announcer was counting down from ten. By the time he reached the last few seconds, the crowd was in a frenzy. They stood, waving their hands in the air and roaring as Siveril tried and failed to get up.

"We have a winner!" the announcer declared. Swimming into the arena, he held up Byron's hand.

The crowd went wild. Screaming. Cheering. They partied, waving their flags in the air as they celebrated their champion's victory. Mareena swam at the glass, watching as the celebrations continued.

Eventually, the members of the crowd began filtering out of the stadium. Mareena pressed her hand against the glass. Every time she moved, I knew it. I always knew where Mareena was in a room, even without looking at her. It was as though there was something tying us together—but there wasn't. It was just wishful thinking.

When the stadium was nearly empty, Mareena turned to me. "So you brought me here... to watch a wrestling match? Not that it wasn't enjoyable, or anything, but I thought—"

"I have a plan," I said gruffly.

"A plan?" She raised a brow. "Do you care to elaborate, oh Silent One?"

Her tone was teasing, but there was a curious edge to her voice. It prodded that part of me that loved her. If only she weren't a princess. If only I weren't a bastard guard. I would love to do nothing more than show her exactly how *loud* I could be.

But I was a bastard, and she was a princess looking for a kind, decent male to marry.

Shoving my desires deep within me, I growled, "Yes."

The weight of Mareena's gaze was heavy as she eyed me.

Luckily, a knock came on the door. Thankful for the interruption, I swam over and pulled it open. The water moved around the door, and on the other side, a mermaid with long black hair in a tight braid held a basket.

"Your brother sends you and your... friend his greetings." She handed me the basket. "He asks that you wait for him. He will be up as soon as possible."

I wasn't surprised Byron knew we were here. As soon as we swam into the arena, I knew the guards would alert him to my presence. Byron was the member of my family who cared about me—he was too good to care that I was a bastard. Without him, my childhood would have been unimaginably terrible.

Thanking the mermaid, I shut the door behind her. When I turned around, Mareena swam a few feet away from me.

"What's that?" she asked, eyeing the woven basket.

"A gift," I replied.

Placing the basket on a nearby table, I pulled open the lid and reached inside. My fingers met the soft fabric, and I withdrew two garments. Mareena gasped, reaching out and taking the smaller one from me. Our fingers met, and a jolt of electricity ran up my arm.

For a moment, the water seemed to still. Our eyes met, and her mouth opened as she stared at me. Did she feel it too? For a single moment, neither of us moved.

Then Mareena inhaled sharply. Her gaze dropped, and she swam back, putting space between us. My heart fractured as she ran her fingers over the black silk, making the sound of appreciation that only females who enjoyed fashion ever seemed to make.

"It's from your brother?" she asked, holding the black silk around her breasts as though she were trying it on.

I forced myself to drag my eyes away from her chest. "Yes," I said, my throat suddenly dry.

Leave it to Byron to send us something in his colors.

"It's lovely." She ran her fingers over the material. "Can you... will you turn around? I'd love to try it on."

My mind emptied, and suddenly, thinking became difficult. She wanted to get changed. Now. While I was here.

She needs to find a husband; I reminded myself. *One who isn't you.*

Forcing my tail to move, I did as she asked and turned around. Facing the door, I clenched the black tunic Byron had sent me, doing my best to ignore what was happening behind me. The walls felt like they were closing in on me as I tried—and failed—to forget about what was happening behind me.

I couldn't do it. Picturing her curves was as easy as drawing breath. I could see the swell of her breasts in my mind's eye. Imagine the softness of her skin beneath my fingertips. Every part of her was carved into my memory.

It felt like an eternity passed before Mareena tapped me on the shoulder.

"It's safe to turn around," she said.

Slowly, I did so.

The black band was wrapped tightly around Mareena's breasts, accentuating her female form, and the excess fabric swayed gently in the water. She looked into my eyes, and everything seemed too tight. Breathing was too difficult. This room was too small. Too tight. She was too beautiful.

These were forbidden feelings. I wasn't supposed to feel this way towards my princess. I shouldn't have felt drawn to her.

So why did the way my heart beat faster when she was around feel so good? Why was my body straining to move towards her and draw her into my arms? Why did every part of me yearn to kiss her senseless?

Mareena eyed the fabric clenched in my fist. "Are you going to put that on?"

I dropped my gaze to the material between my fingers. I had forgotten all about it. Pulling the woken material on in one swift movement, it had barely settled over my torso when a single knock came from the door, followed by a, "I hope you're decent, brother!"

I grinned, swimming over to the door and pulling it open. Taking Byron's fist in mine, I slapped him on the back.

"Good match, brother," I said by way of greeting.

Byron grinned. "I wiped the sand with him."

"You did."

My brother turned, and I knew the moment he noticed Mareena. His lips curved into a smile and his eyes glinted as he swept into an overly dramatic bow.

"My lady," he said, taking her hand and pressing his lips against her hand. "How is it possible that I have lived in Coral City for my entire life and I have never met you before?"

"I'm... visiting," Mareena replied, her eyes flicking up to mine.

I nodded, and she relaxed.

Byron continued. "Imagine my surprise when the guards informed me my brother was seen arriving with none other than a beautiful mermaid. I could scarcely believe my ears, and yet, here you are."

His flowery words might have sounded insincere to others, but this was just how Byron was. Kind to a fault, well-spoken and generous. If he wasn't my brother and the only member of my family who tolerated me, I probably would have been disgusted by it. As it was, my heart cracked in half when Mareena smiled.

"My name is Marie," she said softly, using the fake name I had given the guard earlier. "It's a pleasure to make your acquaintance."

Byron smiled, tucking the princess's hand into the crook of his arm. "The pleasure is all mine, my lady. Do you plan on remaining in the city for a while? I cannot believe I've never met you before. I certainly would have remembered someone as stunning as you."

Mareena smiled. "This is my first time here. Calix is... showing me around."

"You're not working, brother?" Byron asked over his shoulder.

I shook my head. Picking up my trident, I gripped it tightly before saying. "I'm off."

Permanently, but that wasn't important. I would explain the logistics of the recent change in my employment after they were married.

My half-brother grinned. "Then you must stay with me. Both of you."

Mareena glanced at me. "Oh, we—"

"I insist," Byron said. "Allow me to show you some hospitality. Please."

Mareena paused, glancing at me over her shoulder. I dipped my head, tightening my grip around the trident.

"Alright," she agreed. "We'll stay with you."

"Marvelous." Shooting me a look over his shoulder that said, *can you believe this?*, Byron led Mareena out of the room.

I followed them out of the arena and into the busy streets, the sound of their murmured conversation filling the water. My stomach sank further and further with every passing moment.

I was right. The female I loved and my brother got along splendidly. That left me as it always did.

Alone.

Maybe Nice Was Good Enough

MAREENA

Half of my allotted time was gone. As soon as I woke up this morning, I realized that Father's deadline was looming closer and closer. Soon, my week would be up.

The past three days had gone by in a blur. Byron was a fantastic host, and he had taken me under his proverbial wing. Being Marie was fun, and I found myself looking forward to spending time with the fighter. Byron was an excellent tour guide, and over the past few days, he showed me all around Coral City. We went to museums and swam in the park, watching the merlings play when they weren't in school. It was nice, being in the city.

No one recognized me—I had barely been allowed out of the palace, and no one expected their Crown Princess to be meandering around the city without a massive escort. Being outside of my father's watchful eye was freeing in a way that I had never expected. Even so, I couldn't shake the knowledge that this freedom was temporary. I had to find a husband or I could never claim my crown.

How was this fair?

If I ever became queen, I would get rid of this nonsense. In *my* Indigo Ocean, females were going to be equal to males. It didn't matter what one looked like or how one was born. Being male wasn't a great equalizer. I was in this predicament because there were far too few good males in existence. Byron seemed to be a good one, just like his brother.

Since we left the amphitheater, Calix had barely spoken to me. Reverting back to that silent statue of himself, he was always nearby, just… watching. If I hadn't known better, I would have said he looked sad.

Last night, Byron's chef had cooked a five-course dinner. After dessert had been served, Calix informed me he had an appointment and had to leave immediately. As far as I knew, he had yet to return. Byron had assured me this was normal behavior for his half-brother. Just Calix being Calix.

It felt… strange being here without him. The guard had become such a welcome presence in my life that now his absence was like a hole in my heart.

Taking care of my personal needs, I threw my hair into a quick bun on top of my head before slipping out of the guest room. The water in Byron's townhouse was warmer than I was used to, and though the furnishings made it clear he had money, there was a distinctly homey quality to this male's abode that I had never known in the palace.

Byron greeted me as I entered the dining room. He sat at the table, his tail moving the water slowly around him as he dined on a simple breakfast of toast and fried kelp.

"How did you sleep, Marie?"

I blushed, still not entirely used to this name. "Fine," I said. Swimming over to the side table, I helped myself to some breakfast before taking a seat across from Byron. "How about you?"

He raised a brow. "I always sleep better when there is a beautiful female beneath my roof."

His words were always like this, I had learned. As beautiful as the flowery coral that adorned the garden outside his townhouse, and yet, he was sincere.

"You're too kind," I murmured.

Byron placed his hand on mine. Inhaling sharply, I met his gaze. His touch, while gentle, was… just nice. Everything about Byron was nice. The way he looked. The way he treated me. He was smart and strong, as evidenced by his performance in the arena. He was kind to his servants and to his half-brother.

He was nice. Nice was good. Nice was what I was looking for, wasn't it?

If nice was what I wanted—what I needed—why did I feel nothing when he touched me?

"Marie, I was hoping... since Calix is gone for the day..." Byron stumbled over his words, his skin turning red as his eyes searched mine. "There is a troop of performing artists from the Crystal Sea in the city, and I was hoping you would come with me. As my date."

I stared at him. Byron wanted to take me on a date. That was a good thing, right? He was a good male, and I needed one of those. That was why Calix introduced us. I knew this was the way things had to go. So why was I wishing that his brother was here instead? Why was I picturing Calix's strong, silent form next to me instead of his brother?

I was delusional. That was the only explanation for these feelings. Calix wasn't even here. He was my guard. That was all.

My silence must have stretched on because Byron's eyes shuddered. "Unless, if you don't want to, in which case please forget—"

"I'll do it," I said, forcing a smile onto my face. Calix was gone, doing Nontia only knew what, and I was running out of time. I needed a husband because the gods only knew I did not want to give up my throne. And Byron was nice, and obviously interested in me. I would be a fool to turn him down. "I'd love to join you."

Byron grinned, and he looked so happy that my stomach twisted. Maybe I was wrong. Maybe nice was good enough.

The theater was crowded and smelled like salt, the dark blue walls a beautiful contrast to the paler coral of the seats and stage. The last performer, a stunning mermaid with long silver hair, sang on the stage. Like a siren, her voice was entrancing.

Every breath felt too loud as the mermaid sang a tale of lost love. She told a tale of a dragon shifter from Ithenmyr who fell in love with a mermaid long ago. The two of them petitioned a sea witch to enchant the dragon shifter so he could live underwater, but the witch tricked them. Stealing their magic, she lured them to the middle of the Indigo Ocean before killing them both. They died in each other's arms, sealing their love with one final, fatal kiss.

For a long moment after the mermaid sang the last note, no one spoke. Then, as if she knew the tragedy had been too much, she started into another song. This one was beautiful, telling a story of childhood friends turned lovers.

Every note that came out of her mouth was more beautiful than the last. The performance was incredible, and I was blessed to have been able to experience it. But I wished Calix was here.

His absence had been like an itch I couldn't quite scratch all day. After breakfast, Byron had taken me shopping in the Coral Market before taking me to lunch at a quaint café next to the theater. He had been the perfect gentleman, seeing to all my needs and being exceedingly nice. The theater was amazing. Each of the performers was more incredible than the last. By all rights, it should have been a lovely day, but I couldn't help but feel as though I was missing something. Someone.

Calix.

He was missing.

The singer's last note reverberated through the theater, and for a moment, no one moved. Then the sound of roaring applause filled the water. Tails slapped against the coral, the sound a resounding backdrop to the roar of approval. The entire cast of performers made their way onto the stage, and they joined hands, bowing.

Once the applause died down, Byron turned to me. A brilliant smile was on his face, but as soon as he looked into my eyes, it died. I must not have been keeping my feelings as hidden as I thought.

"I see," he murmured softly. "It's Calix you want, isn't it?"

My mouth opened and closed as I tried to find words. Calix was my guard. My silent friend. Nothing more. Right?

Even as I thought it, I couldn't find the words to refute Byron's claim. Not now. Not when my heart was aching because I was missing the mermale who had been my protector for the past decade.

Instead, I closed my mouth and nodded. "I'm sorry, Byron."

He sighed. "It's alright. To be honest, I saw the way the two of you have been looking at each other all week. I should have known Calix had already stolen your heart as soon as I figured out who you were."

My heart pounded in my chest, and a roaring filled my ears. How did Byron know who I was? Wide-eyed, I reached out and grabbed his hand.

My tail flicked through the water as I swam close to him. "Please don't tell anyone. I just—"

"It's alright, Mareena," Byron said softly, his eyes downcast. "I confronted Calix about it last night before he left. He told me everything."

My eyes widened. "I don't want anyone to know who I am. I was just trying to—"

"I won't tell a soul," Byron said fiercely. "Even if you weren't the princess," —he lowered his voice so his words weren't carried through the water—"my brother cares very deeply for you. I would never hurt him like that."

"Thank you," I breathed.

He nodded, extending his arm towards me. I threaded my hand through his elbow, and together, we swam back to his townhouse.

Calix was on my mind the entire time.

Plans and Confessions

CALIX

The past three days were a special kind of torture. Every morning when I woke was a new lesson in heartbreak. A large part of me wished I had never left the palace. At least then, I wouldn't have had to watch Mareena spending every second of every day with my brother. I wouldn't have to watch as she smiled at something he said, nor would I have to witness her laughing at his jokes. She seemed happy here—happier than she had ever been before.

I only wished I was the one making her smile. Maybe if the circumstances of my birth had been better, I might have been the male for Mareena. Perhaps if my father had chosen to claim me, I might have had a chance. If I hadn't been a lowly guard in love with the Crown Princess, my story might have been different.

But it wasn't. I was a bastard, and she was a princess. That was why I left last night. I couldn't take it. Not after Byron figured out who Mareena was. A male worse than Byron would have probably celebrated because of their stroke of luck. How many princesses looking for husbands fell into people's laps?

Even after he knew who she was, Byron was just concerned for Mareena. He was a good male. Far too good, considering the horrible male who fathered us both.

I couldn't deal with it any longer. Instead of staying around and watching Byron woo the female I loved, I left. Going back to Shipwreck Cove, I spent the night wallowing in my pain. When I woke up this morning, I knew I had to go back. I couldn't just abandon Mareena.

It was my stupid sense of morals that had me packing up my things and returning to my brother's townhouse. Three days. That was how long Mareena had left. I would stay long enough to see her engaged to Byron, and then I was going to leave. The Rapid Currents were far from here. Maybe after I stayed there for a while, I would go to the Obsidian Coast. I was always curious about the way the fae lived. If I could find a sea witch to spell my tail away, I could go on land.

Thoughts of my future far away from here occupied me as I swam back to Byron's home. I refused to think of it as running away. Instead, I was simply protecting myself. It was nearing dinnertime and the streets of Coral City were busy. Dozens of merfolk were out. Many were swimming, but some were riding in shells pulled by sharks and eels. The sounds of life filtered through the water, their noise a good distraction from the sorrow taking root in my heart.

Too soon, Byron's red door came into view. Hopefully, they would still be out, and I could sneak in and hide until dinner. Steeling myself for another three days of misery, I raised my fist and knocked.

Barely a second passed before the door swung open. Halpert, my brother's butler, swam in the entryway. His woven tunic moved with the water as he dipped and moved aside. "They're in the parlor, sir."

Just like that, my hopes of hiding out were squashed. Pausing in the doorway, I considered turning around and swimming back to Shipwreck Cove. I was just about to close the door when a door closed in the house.

"Calix."

My name was little more than a whisper on her lips, but it reverberated through my core. I sucked in a breath. Everything stopped. My heart. My lungs. Even the gentle movement of the water seemed to cease for one long, eternal moment.

There was something about the way she said my name that was unlike anything I'd ever heard.

Mareena's eyes met mine, the hallway between us seeming like nothing, and my tail moved of its own volition. Before I even realized what was happening, I was inside the townhouse. The Crown Princess moved towards me, the space between us shortening with every moment. Something sparked to life within me as the door slammed shut behind me.

She was all I could see. All I could hear. All I could think about.

Mareena's lips parted, and she reached for me. Her hand slid into mine, and a shock ran through me. She was so much smaller than me, my hand dwarfed hers. I stared at the place where our flesh connected. Had she ever willingly touched me?

There had been soft brushes between our hands in the past, of course. Accidental touches that haunted me for hours after they took place. But this... It was different. Her hand tightened around mine, and she pulled me towards her.

"Come here," she said. Authority and strength filled her tone, and I was reminded once more that she was the heir to the Seven Seas. She was so far out of my league, I had no business even being in the same room with her, let alone touching her.

But I couldn't have pulled my hand out of hers even if I tried.

I swam after Mareena, my tail moving me swiftly through the gentle waters of Byron's townhouse as the princess led me into the small study on the main floor. Once we were inside, she let go of my hand, shutting the door.

We were alone.

Canting her head to one side, Mareena studied me. Her gaze was analytical, and if it had been anyone else, I would have felt strange. But with her, I was comfortable. She could look at me for as long as she wanted.

"Byron said he knows who I am," Mareena said softly, breaking the silence between us.

I wasn't sure how, but he knew. I made him promise he wouldn't tell a soul. If people knew their crown princess was swimming through the city without much of an escort, they could hurt her—or worse. I couldn't let that happen.

"Yes," I grunted.

She swam closer to me, her eyes never leaving mine. "Byron is nice," she whispered.

All I could do was nod.

This was the moment I had been dreading. I knew this would happen. As soon as I introduced the two of them, I knew she would fall for him. How could she not? Byron was rich, thanks to our father. Not only that, but he was successful, fit, and kind.

He was a catch, and surprisingly, still single.

Until now.

Drawing in a deep breath, I steeled myself for what was coming next. Mareena was going to marry Byron. That was the only way she could maintain her claim to the throne. I was certain they would be happy—after all, how could they not be? She would be queen and I would leave, only coming back when I could handle seeing my brother married to the female I loved.

Clenching my fists at my side, I drew in a deep breath.

"He's very nice," I said.

Mareena swallowed. "And he's... a good male."

My heart twisted, and agony ran through me. "He is," I agreed.

"If I married him, I might be happy." Her eyes widened, and she looked at me imploringly. "He would be a good husband. Father would probably approve of him."

I couldn't respond. I nodded, swimming backward. Everything felt too tight. My skin. My lungs. The water was too hot. I needed to get out of here. Forget waiting until the week was up. I was going to pack a bag and leave tonight.

"I don't want to marry him," she whispered. Her words were barely audible, but they reverberated in my very core.

"You don't?"

She shook her head. "No."

My brows furrowed. "Then... it's going to be one of those... pompous asses your father brought to the palace?"

Why would she pick one of them over Byron?

"What?" She furrowed her brows. "No."

"I don't understand." My fists clenched and unclenched at my side as my heart raced. "Who do you want?"

She had to pick someone. Her father was very clear on that point. She couldn't give up her throne. The Indigo Ocean needed a queen like her.

Mareena swam towards me, her dark purple tail moving her swiftly across the room. When she was a foot away from me, she stopped. Her hair swirled in the water around her and those eyes looked up, meeting mine.

She reached out, running her hand down my arm and lacing our fingers together. Twice now, she touched me. I could barely breathe, let alone understand what was happening. Mareena pulled me towards her until there was little more than a hairsbreadth of space between us. The water moved softly around us both as she squeezed my hand.

"You," she murmured, her eyes searching mine. "I want you."

Then, before I could say anything, she closed the distance between us. Her lips landed on mine, and my mind exploded as we kissed.

A Blessing from Nontia Herself

MAREENA

Calix seemed stunned. For the first few moments after my lips landed on his, he did not move. I wasn't even sure he breathed. He was like a marble statue beneath me as my mouth brushed over his.

I pulled back. "Calix?"

My guard's eyes widened, and he drew in a sharp breath. He whispered my name, and it was as though life itself went back into him. His hand left mine, landing on my hip as he pulled me tight against him. His mouth crashed against mine, tasting of salt as he kissed me.

Every single doubt I'd ever had about his feelings toward me vanished into thin air. This kiss was passionate in a way that I hadn't known this silent male was capable of being. Groaning, I pressed my breasts against Calix, trying to ease the fire coming to life within me. My entire body, from my tingling lips to the very tip of my tail, felt alive from this kiss.

His hand splayed on my bare back, and I moaned, writhing against him. His hands moved over me with the skill of a male who knew what he wanted, and I melted in his hands. Our mouths moved in time with each other, our kisses deep and filled with desire, speaking the words we had yet to say.

An untold amount of time went by until Calix pulled away from me.

"What does this mean?" he asked, his voice raspy.

I blinked. Did he need me to spell it out for him? I wasn't going to marry anyone else. I didn't want anyone else.

He continued to stare at me, his brows furrowed.

Placing my hand on his chest above his heart, I waited until his eyes met mine. "It means I want you, Calix. My father be damned, I want you to be mine. Today. Tomorrow. Every day."

My words seemed to unlock something within Calix. He growled, taking my hand in his and pulling me towards him. His hands cupped the top of my tail as he moved swiftly, drawing me with him.

"Where are we going?" I asked.

"Somewhere private," he said. Then, as if those two words had taken everything out of him, his lips met mine in a storm of want.

Before I knew it, we were outside his bedroom.

This was moving fast...

But I wasn't upset about that at all. We had known each other for years, and even if I hadn't had my father's timeline weighing on me, I knew Calix was the male I wanted.

Why didn't I do this before?

My questions disappeared as Calix reached around me, pulling the door open. A rush of cold water flooded towards me, the change in temperature serving to accentuate the heat coursing through my body.

Calix kissed me again, his mouth moving with an urgency that echoed within me. My heart pounded as we kissed, and when his hand slipped beneath the band keeping my breasts together, I moaned. His fingers moved with deft precision, and I pressed myself against him. His tongue swept into my mouth, and he tasted me as we moved towards the bed.

When the coral mattress was beneath me, he lifted his lips from mine long enough to ask, "Is this..."

"Yes," I said, pulling his mouth back to mine. "I want you. All of you."

He groaned against me. "Nontia have mercy on me, Mareena. I want you too."

Our mouths met mine with the force of desires long since tamped down. Something within me turned, and there was an unlocking in my soul as we kissed. Our hands explored each other, touching in ways that we never had before.

Our passion tasted of salt and light and the future. It was romantic and intense and filled with everything we had yet to say. Something within me sparked and grew, a connection that I had long since believed was never possible for a female like me. The heat of Calix's body against the cool water all around us only intensified the warmth already running through me.

My heart raced as we kissed, and I knew I would never be the same again. Our hands ran over each other, touching in new, intimate ways that left me breathless.

With every passing moment, with every touch of his fingers against my skin, I was more secure in my decision. Calix was the one for me. I didn't care that he was my guard and I was a princess. I didn't care that he wasn't the lord my father probably wanted me to marry.

After returning from the theater earlier, I had come to a conclusion: I loved Calix.

I wasn't sure when it happened or how, but I loved him with every fiber of my being. When I saw him swim up the steps to the townhouse, I couldn't wait for him to come inside. I had to tell him. I wasn't going to marry anyone else. He was the only one I wanted, and if he didn't want me, I would leave. I wouldn't marry someone just because they would allow me to get my throne.

No.

I would have him, or I wouldn't have anyone at all.

Calix pulled his lips away from me, resting his forehead against me. "Mareena..."

Hearing my name on his lips was incredible. It was one word, but it carried so much weight. I looked up at this male who held my heart and moved away from him. Not much—just enough so that I could speak without wanting to dive back into those kisses that were stealing my heart. My tail hung over the side of the bed, my fins dancing with his as I reached over and took his hand in mine.

He watched me, his eyes wide.

"Calix, I want you," I whispered. I knew I would have to be the one to say this. He wouldn't. Despite everything he thought of himself, he was far too much of a gentleman for that. "All of you. I want you to be mine in every way. I want to take you back to the palace with me." Biting my lip, I studied him. "I love you, Calix. I want to show you off to the world."

A long moment passed, and his eyes swept over me. Today they were filled with wonder and darkness and... love. They softened, and a small smile graced his lips.

"Mareena, I have been in love with you for so long I can't even remember what life was like without you in it. There is nothing I want more than to be yours." His voice deepened, and he drew me towards him. Accentuating each of his words with a kiss, he rumbled, "I will be your willing servant. Your husband. Your everything if you allow me the honor of loving you for all eternity."

My heart skipped a beat at his words, and I grinned. "I don't think I've ever heard you say so much at once."

He pulled back a touch, laughing. "You make me want to talk, Mareena. You make me want to do everything."

He put his hand on my chest and then something entirely unexpected happened. The magic within me hummed, bursting forth unbidden from within me. A flash of purple and coral light filled the space between us. I gasped as a feeling I had never felt before ran through me. It was one of rightness. Of love. Of being cared for. One of complete and utter knowing.

I looked down at my arm, watching in wonder as coral, and violent ribbons escaped our palms. They wound themselves around our arms, diving into our skin. The briefest flash of pain was followed by a bead of blood that appeared on my forearm. Staring at Calix, the two of us moved in unison, pressing our arms together.

The moment they touched, a flash of white light filled the space. When it disappeared, matching coral and violet swirls marked our arms.

Raising my wide eyes, I met Calix's gaze.

"You're mine," he breathed, his voice deep and filled with awe. He paused. "If you'll have me, of course."

What kind of question was that? Of course, I would have him.

The corners of my mouth twisted up, and right then and there, I knew that nothing my father could do would ever break us apart. This was more than love. This was a mating. A bond gifted by the gods themselves. Not even my father could go against Nontia's wishes.

Calix was mine, and I was his.

"I'm yours," I whispered. Reaching over, I pressed my lips against his. Together, we spoke the words that would bind us for eternity. From now until the end of our days, everyone would know we belonged to each other.

There was just one thing left to do.

With all the gentleness in the world—something that I hadn't known a mermale of his size could possess, Calix lay me down on the bed. His hands ran over me, his every touch igniting a fire within me.

Our tails entwined, and for a long time, nothing else mattered.

He was mine, and I was his.

Forever.

The End

Thank you for reading Mareena and Calix's story!

Not tired of this world? You can explore the Surface in Of Earth and Flame, as well as Tethered.

About the Author

Elayna R. Gallea lives in beautiful New Brunswick, Canada with her husband and two children. They live in the land of snow and forests in the Saint John River Valley.

When Elayna isn't living in her head, she can be found toiling around her house watching Food Network, listening to broadway, and planning her next meal.

Elayna enjoys copious amounts of chocolate, cheese, and wine.

Not in that order.

You can find her making a fool of herself on Tiktok and Instagram on a daily basis.

Learn more and explore her other titles here:
https://linktr.ee/authorelaynagallea

Words Wounds & Warriors

Words, Wounds, and Warriors

RUTHIE BOWLES

Heat Level:
Hot

Content Warnings:
Strong language, gore, decapitation, murder, colorism, consensual sexual activity, kidnapping (not by a love interest), stalking (by a love interest), profanity, and violence.

CHAPTER 1
Adelola

"Oh no, nothing's wrong. Everything is fine, dear," I heard the woman's voice say. I pushed out a sharp gust of air as I watched the cut appear on her right cheek. She lied to protect his ego, taking on the wounds of his words. I could see them as plain as day all over the visible parts of her body. Talk about death by a thousand cuts.

Sipping the pinot noir I had chosen for the night, I thought for the millionth time how grateful the rest of humanity would be to not have my gift. They would call it a curse here in the United States. But those of us who were connected to the old ways, who were the orishas' hands on this continent, knew better.

I was chosen by Oya, the orisha of storms, change, death, and rebirth. Her gifts were just as potent and powerful for her chosen jagunjagun, her warrior.

"I can always count on you to be here at this time at this table. Ready to hear the specials?" The reason I came to this restaurant for the last three Wednesdays said.

His brown eyes immediately soothed my frayed nerves, caused by sitting in the middle of the restaurant dining room. I avoided large groups of people, because while I was used to it, it could be difficult to carry on a conversation and pretend I didn't see the wounds, some tiny, some gaping, and the horrific scars they carried on their energetic bodies. To my eyes, they appeared as real wounds would on their physical bodies.

"You know me by now," I began, leaning forward, using my eyes, smile, and body to communicate that the specials wasn't the only thing I was interested in. "Lay them on me."

His laughter reached his eyes, and I could see in his energy that our weekly banter lifted his spirit. "Well, I could tell you all of them, but since I know you now, I can tell you that you'll want the lamb, and you won't be disappointed."

He didn't have many fresh wounds, and the ones he did have were small. It was his scars that marked him as a survivor. They were deep and some of them were knotted. I usually only saw these types of scars on victims of abuse. But he seemed past that time in his life and his determination to live in joy attracted more than one magickal being here. At least it had until I discovered him.

"Then the lamb it'll be, Michael. You know, I'll still tip well. You don't have to be so nice to me," I teased.

A blush crept up his tan neck, past the scar that looked like someone attempted to garrotte him. His Adam's apple bobbed and then he said, "I'm not nice to you because you tip well Adelola."

The right side of his mouth crept up in a half smile I've seen him give some of his coworkers. Friends he visited sometimes on their off nights. People he liked.

I smiled up at him and bit my lip and murmured, "I tell you every time. Lola is fine."

He picked up the menu, but his eyes stayed on my lips. "Honestly, I like the way it sounds. And it fits you."

"Well, I look forward to finding out what makes you say that," I responded, resting my jaw on my hand, my smile unwavering. "Perhaps after your shift tonight..." I let the rest of my sentence trail off. I have his patterns memorized, and he never has plans on Wednesdays, so if he says no, maybe he's not ready to go beyond our weekly teasing.

"Ahhh... you know what, why not? No, that sounded wrong. What I meant to say was... yes. Yes, absolutely," he said, finishing strong. I let my grin overtake my face because I was just as excited as he was.

I knew my smile popped against my medium brown skin. I have some of my long braids up in a bun on top of my head, and the others trailing down my back and over my right shoulder. My grey eyes were another sign that Oya was my orisha, as grey as storm clouds.

I leaned back, keeping my smile big, and brushed my hands down the skirt of my yellow ochre and white daisy dress. "Alright then. As much as I'm looking forward to the lamb, I'm looking forward to the end of your shift more," I told him as he backed away.

Thankfully, the restaurant was high-end enough that the servers were expected to be friendly with the diners. So there were no scolding managers to contend with. It was strange because even if there were... he didn't seem to take wounds from other people's words easily. So I couldn't help but wonder what caused the scars on him.

I also had to wonder where my attraction was coming from. Usually I was a lot more focused on my purpose, moving through the world, exacting Oya's vengeance. But there was something about him I obsessed over. Even stalking him like prey. He had no idea how often I watched him, cloaking myself in shadows for the past couple of months.

Taking another sip of my wine, I watched the restaurant's patronage as some had wounds actively heal, but more often than not, more cuts, scrapes, and bruises formed. How did they live with these untended wounds? No wonder so many of them were so angry and sad.

Just then, two women entered the restaurant. Words are my domain, so the leggy blue-eyed blonde asking the host, *"Can you get Michael for me? It's a private matter,"* was not lost to me. What was a surprise was the server rushing to the back while the over tanned blonde giggled at something her equally tanned brunette friend said.

Michael looked through the small window in the door quickly, and I saw him pale before he ducked out of sight. Who was this woman, and why was I starting to feel like she deserved a dagger in between her perky breasts?

Her face brightened with overly enthusiastic joy when he finally stepped into the dining room and started walking toward them. The brunette smirked like she knew something no one else did.

"What are you doing here, Arabell?" he asked, his words clipped.

"Oh Michael, don't be like that? Can't I just want to see you, babe? You're never happy to see me anymore," she responded teasingly. Then she kissed him on the cheek, which he accepted woodenly.

That didn't bother me, though. What horrified me was that I saw some of his healed scars open up and bleed. Which they wouldn't do unless..... She was the one who caused them in the first place.

That bitch.

My power thrummed beneath my skin. Just as storms cleared weak branches and sometimes felled entire trees, and how a single lightning strike could set an entire plain ablaze, so too did Oya's justice clear the way for new growth. Sadly for the perpetrators, that "new growth" often used their bodies as fertilizer.

"No, I was clear before. What we had... it's over. You can't come to my work or my apartment, or anywhere else," he told her firmly, not even sparing her friend a glance.

"Mike... you're just going to throw away two whole years?" she asked, sounding wounded.

I had never heard anyone else he interacted with in the last few months call him Mike.

"Look, I can't do this right now. I'll.... I'll talk to you later, okay? After I get off, or...," he paused, perhaps remembering we had plans, *"or later. Just... not right now, okay?"*

"Alright, we're hungry anyway, we'll just stay for dinner then," and she clapped her hands, beaming at him. Michael walked away as the host finally seated them. On his way back to the kitchen, my gaze caught his, and his face looked pressed. I cluelessly smiled, and he strode back into the kitchen.

I turned my predator's gaze on my new prey, surprised to see them heading outside already. They left their coats in their booth, so maybe they were stepping outside to smoke? I followed them to see what more I could learn.

Another server was just approaching my table with my meal, another sign of how shaken up Michael truly was. I gave them a little wave, indicating I'd be right back.

I stepped outside and discretely stepped into some shadows, listening in on the women's conversation.

"Arabell, do you think he's really going to take you back this time? You fucked his coworker," the brunette chuckled.

"Oh, he only has his word for that, Kara. And before he found out, he was wrapped around my little finger. Between the sex and me giving and taking away the approval he so desperately needs, I'll reel him back in," Arabell said, too smugly.

"Well, you better. You're getting evicted, and his place is nicer than yours, anyway. A change of address will keep some of those bill collectors away for a while," Kara reasoned.

"Worse comes to worst... I'll just cry," she laughed. Then her phone rang, and she started digging through her bag. "I need to take this, and I'll meet you back inside," she said, a new urgency in her voice.

Kara walked right past me, and Arabell picked up the phone with, "Babyyyy, I told you, I'm busy tonight, but I'm reeling him in, I promise."

"To give you what you want, Arabell, I require his blood, and I require it soon," a voice rough with urgency said through the phone.

I had heard enough. Arabell wasn't just going to continue her abuse of Michael, she was sacrificing him to some supernatural. There were a number who dealt in blood, but I didn't care who or what it was. This was over.

"Go into the alley calmly, or you'll bleed out here on the sidewalk," I said behind her, letting her feel the poke of my dagger's tip into the soft area around her right kidney as she hung up her phone.

"Who—" she stammered.

"Say nothing, and walk," I hissed.

We quickly made our way into the shadows of the alley, and I let my glamour drop, revealing the silver glowing tattoos all over my body that marked me as one of Oya's jagunjagun. My braids now contained streaks of white and were tipped in hardened lightning blue crystal tips. They rose of their own volition as if I was under water, small bolts of lightning arcing between them playfully.

"Who are you? What do you want from me?" she asked, her eyes trained on the dagger I held in my right hand, a hand that was now decorated in deadly crystal claws. It made sense that was what she focused on. The dagger was black and silver, and the length of my forearm. Unfortunately for her, that wasn't the most dangerous part of this situation.

"Arabell Bothington," I intoned, "you have been judged and found wanting for crimes you have committed and intend to commit against your fellow human beings. What do you have to say for yourself?"

She scoffed, "Am I being punk'd right now?"

I punched her in the mouth, causing her head to snap back. The lightning in the punch probably made her heart skip a beat. She clutched her face, eyes wide in disbelief. It was then that she seemed to really take in the inhuman parts of my appearance.

"Oh God... what do you mean *against* my fellow humans?" she asked fearfully.

"Michael," I said with bared teeth. "You planned on sacrificing Michael to whatever you were talking to."

"A vampire! He said he would turn me! I need it... Please, I can't be human anymore. My life is horrible, I have no money—"

"Your excuses mean nothing. Your white woman tears will not save you. Especially as I can see your life results from your choices. Would the vampire have killed him?"

Her eyes darted to the side, and I could see that her teeth were coated in her blood now that she had dropped her hands. "I don't know," she admitted shamefully.

"You don't know because you didn't ask. You didn't ask because, ultimately, you don't care."

"You know what? Fuck you! You don't know anything about me..." she trailed off as I laughed.

"I can see back to the day you were born. You may play fuck fuck games with vampires, little girl, but you've never seen the likes of me. I'll make you regret the day you crawled out of the trailer park you were born in," I said with a vicious smile. A smile that widened as I saw a deep cut appear where her neck met her shoulder.

"Your mother was right, you know? You'll never amount to anything, always chasing dreams or chasing a high."

This time, she hunched over, clutching her stomach in pain.

"Why would you think you could come here and actually make something of yourself? You're worthless. And you proved that by being willing to sacrifice someone whose only bad choice was loving someone who couldn't even love herself."

By now she was sobbing, and I could see her ankle was now misshapen. Huh, guess it's not just sticks and stones breaking bones, is it?

In truth, I did not judge her for any of these things. But she judged herself, and that was all my power needed.

The worst part about my power for my victims is that when I speak, it is to the very core of them. There is no delusion they can cling to, no mental gymnastics. Their identity is laid bare before the tortures of my words, and they're helpless to stop the pain.

Finally, I made my move, barring her across the throat with my arm as I pressed the dagger to her chest. I didn't always kill them. Oya is destruction, but also change. Sometimes my words spoken were enough to change the course of a life. But even the terrified look on her face could not quell my rage. She tried to take what was *mine*.

Finally, Michael stepped out from behind the dumpster. I'd been aware of him there for some time. Here in the darkness, I could see a faint shimmer on his skin, suggesting he was more than human. Not a lot more, but more. Maybe he had a distant ancestor who was fae. I'd have to dip further into my power to find out, but I wanted the experience of him telling me.

"You don't have to do this, you know. You're so much better than her. Than them," he said slowly, a touch of pleading in his voice.

"Oh sweet summer child," I said as I slowly drove the dagger into her chest until it hit the brick wall of the building behind her. "I'm so much worse."

CHAPTER 2
Michael

My mouth dropped open as she slowly pushed the dagger into Arabell's chest, not stopping until she hit the brick wall of the building they were leaning against. Adelola never broke eye contact with me, seeming interested in my response.

"Holy fuck," I whispered as she slowly withdrew her weapon, and Arabell's body starting to turn to ash. I could see the tongues of flame licking her insides, preternaturally burning her from the inside out. Adelola still hadn't stopped watching my face, not sparing the rapidly developing pile of cinders a glance.

"Yes, the fire might be considered holy, to some. To me, it's convenient clean up," she said with a smirk as she prowled toward me. There was no other word for it. Adelola was a predator. A predator I had said yes to meeting after my shift. The type of predator I had spent years hiding from. Shit.

I started backing up. "Now, w-wait," The glowing markings began to fade from her skin, and her dagger disappeared from view, perhaps she stored it in the ether, the liminal space where magick waited.

"Oh now," she teased, her smile reminiscent of when I thought she was a human woman intentionally popping into the restaurant when I was working. "Don't tell me a little vengeance has made you change your mind about spending time with me?"

"Ah, well...." I fumbled my words, as my brain tried to wrap around the fact that she might not know who I am. "Adelola, um, you can probably understand why I'd be... hesitant, surely," I said, plastering a nervous smile on my face.

Just as I realized she had backed me up against a wall, she was there, pressing against me. She wound her hands in my blonde curls, and pulled my face down to hers. The moan of satisfaction I heard in her throat sounded better than anything I had conjured up in my head over the last few weeks.

Her tongue played at the seam of my lips, and I couldn't resist. I wove a hand into her braids, and gripped the other on her hip as her hands slid down my chest and coasted over my nipples. Lust washed over me and it felt like all of my blood was competing to take up residence in my cock. Especially when she pressed her hips against me.

"Mmmm," I sounded, coming to my senses. "Just hold the fuck on," I protested, pulling my face away. I put both of my hands on her hips and pushed her back just a few inches. She smirked up at me, waiting.

"We can't just make out after you stabbed my ex in the chest." Who was I trying to convince?

"Huh."

"What?"

She shrugged her shoulders, and pulled her body out of my grip. My cock was moaning the loss while she said over her shoulder, "That was just a really human thing to say." She crouched down by Arabell's ash pile and picked up her purse.

"You can't just go riffling through a dead person's things!" I whispered in a shout, walking in her direction a few steps before halting.

She stood and narrowed her eyes at me. Fuck, this was it. She *was* here to kill me. I tapped the ability I thought I'd never have to use again before she could make her move. Should've known better than to think a smart pretty woman would want me.

The golden glow in my skin brightened, and I knew she would see my brown irises shift to gold. The fact she hadn't taken her chance when she had me distracted with that kiss was her mistake.

She gaped at me, and the magick of the world pressed down upon us, manifesting my will. Her magick was bound, and she was no more powerful than a human woman. One hell of a reverse card, if I do say so myself. I crossed my arms and gave her a smirk of my own. I watched her gaze flick down to my arms before meeting mine in a blaze of fury.

"You idiot! This woman was going to....." she pinched the bridge of her nose and closed her eyes, as if trying to find patience.

"Ummm..." I began, but then stopped. My smirk fell from my face, and I uncrossed my arms, shifting from foot to foot. "Aren't you angry? Furious? You don't want to attack me now?"

"May the orishas take you! I never wanted to attack you. Just fuck you. Repeatedly. For an undetermined amount of time," she muttered, eyes still closed and her fingers still on her nose. "Sad day for you, your troubles are just beginning. You have no idea what this chick was up to, do you? She was going to sacrifice you to vampires, Michael. They want your blood, and while I'm sure you're delicious, I doubt it's strictly for nourishment." Her eyes narrowed again, but in curiosity this time. "What are you? You're not a blessed one."

I just stared at her for a second. Was she just saying that? Or was this a trick to try and get me to unbind her?

"Well, now that you're bound there are no immediate threats. So I guess we'll just go back to my place while I figure out what to do about you, you murderous siren," I told her, trying to get the *rest* of my body onboard with being upset; after all, she spent weeks trying to lure me into her trap. I should just leave her here, but her reaction planted enough doubt in me to feel bad about leaving her defenseless.

"Look, tone down the glow, and stop all that. We need to get out of this alley. Your place isn't safe, so we should go to mine. The vampires won't know about me. I have no doubt this bitch gave them every last bit of info they could get on you."

"Yeah, yeah, the vampires. Nah, we're going back to my place."

She sighed and balled up her fists. "Then allow me some of my power then, in case we're attacked on the way there."

"Nice try, but no. Let's go," I said more gruffly than I meant to, but it was the right move. My emotions kept wanting to respond to her the way I have these last several weeks. I tried harder to ignore my hurt feelings.

"Fine, lead the way," she huffed out, and turned to walk out of the alley.

I gulped as I strode past Arabell's ashes. I had been ready to move on from her. That's why I said yes to Adelola's invitation. What had I gotten myself into?

CHAPTER 3
Adelola

We made it to his apartment several blocks away without being accosted. He somehow managed to create a story in his head that *I* was the one trying to attack him. Men. My last few relationships had been with women. I should've known the first man I'm attracted to in a while would come with baggage.

I side eyed him as I leaned against his apartment's door frame, waiting for him to find his key. *A lot* of baggage.

In all the months I had been watching him, Michael had never revealed this particular binding magick trick.

"Let me go in first," I ordered.

He had unlocked the door, but didn't open it. "Why?" he asked with crinkled eyebrows.

"I'm assuming that you have minimal knowledge of hand to hand combat. You may have bound my power, but I've still got some of my basic advantages over humans. It will be the best we've got over the vampires," I explained, knowing he still wouldn't believe me.

Predictably, he rolled his eyes, "Right, the vampires again. Well, sure," he condescended, "Be my guest." He dramatically waved his hand toward the door, so I opened it quietly and entered the dark space.

Then he pushed in behind me and turned the light on.

"For fuck's sake," I said in a low voice, "Was it not obvious that I was going to clear your apartment? If there's anyone here, now they know we are."

"Mmhmm," he sounded, probably just to irritate me.

I decided to check out his bedroom and bathroom, both of which were clear. After monitoring him for weeks, I knew how he kept his living space, and things looked normal.

I returned to the living room, to find him tending the plants he had growing near his window.

"That's a clever way to use your power," I noted. He glanced up at me and gave me a small smile.

"Thanks, but it's nothing. Just a bit more magic than a hedge witch could do," he demurred.

"Are you serious? You enhance the plants as they grow, and then create medicinal blends that are further enhanced. The way you weave the layers of magick is truly an impressive use of your abilities. You have some Earth affinity, yes?" I asked him, not letting him brush aside his skill. The plants and medicines are the reason he can afford this apartment. It's a nice side income from the local supernatural community. Of course, I had considered hedge witch as one of the options for what he was.

"How... how do you know that?" Michael asked me, turning his eyes back to the oregano leaves he was gathering. He didn't struggle this much to accept compliments from me before. I guess believing someone is trying to kill you makes you suspicious. Aiii, Oya help me.

There was a life to these plants, they practically reached out to him, begging for attention. They didn't move quickly, but I could tell they were following him. He was their sun.

"I just... I just do. Look, Michael," I began, taking a few steps toward him, "I wasn't trying to kill you. You have to believe me, please." Despite what had happened tonight, I still felt an attraction to him. I'm mad, but I still trusted him. I don't believe he would've bound me if he hadn't thought he was in danger.

He sighed, stood up straight, and tilted his head back, his eyes closed. I took this unobserved moment to do some observing of my own, as if I hadn't watched him plenty. But I wasn't usually this close. I took a few more quiet steps toward him.

He must have let out another of the buttons on his work shirt, because I was seeing more of his chest than I did earlier. His skin was just as tan there as anywhere else. The muscles in his forearms tensed and relaxed as he balled his hands into fists and then let them go repeatedly.

"Adelola," he finally said, meeting my gaze, "I- I believe that you weren't trying to kill me. I can't even say why I believe you. But my aunt taught me to go with my intuition, but I just can't believe any vampires would want me for more than food. With Arabell... dead, I'm sure they'll just move on."

I let his wishful thinking pass, as I put the back of my hand against my forehead and pretended to swoon.

"What?" he asked, rubbing an oregano leaf between his fingers.

"Lawd, a man who talks about intuition. You can't cook can you? My clothes might fall off."

He let out a real laugh at that, which was what I had hoped for. There was something between us; he could feel it too.

"I'm decent," he said with a twinkle in his eye. "Oh shit." His eyes got big. "You never ate dinner."

I waved a hand at his words dismissively. "I'm old. I don't get hungry very often."

"What are *you*?" he asked curiously, moving to sit on the couch, indicating I should join him. So I did, although I probably sat closer to him than he expected. Mmmmm, he always smelled like a forest after a rainfall. I felt desire coil low in my belly.

"I'm a blessed one," I said simply, tracing small circles on his thigh. His eyes watched my busy fingertips, fascinated. His features took on a sharpness that made me certain he was some type of fae, I just didn't know which kind. Hell, it wasn't like I had met all the different types of fae in the world anyway.

"Blessed one of what?" he asked slowly as I traced my fingers slightly higher. Ah, perhaps the fierce attraction wasn't one sided either.

"You shouldn't ask 'of what' but 'of who?'" I replied, moving my mouth a bit closer to his ear. I watched goosebumps travel down his neck, and he swallowed hard. My fingers traveled a shade higher.

"Who then?"

"I'm a blessed one of Oya, the orisha of storms, lightning, sudden change, and vengeance, among other things," I whispered, but Oya's thunder crept into my voice anyway.

Michael turned his head, and our mouths were just inches apart. The energy between us was so fraught a spark of static could've set us aflame. "How did you do that? You can't access your magic?"

"I don't know," I confessed with a chuckle, "but I'm pretty sure it's Oya's way of not letting you get too comfortable. You did bind her chosen. A bold move." I darted my tongue out, licking the side of his neck. He shuddered.

I sensed when his demeanor changed. I ran my hand back down his thigh and started to pull my body away. His eyes locked on mine, the brown looking a touch more gold and flashing with green Earth energy.

"No," he grumbled, and brought his far hand up from clenching his thigh to gripping the back of my neck. "It feels like I've waited forever for this, like I've always wanted you." He brought his lips crashing down on mine.

If my lips weren't otherwise occupied, I would've smirked.

As he swept his tongue into my mouth, taking what he wanted, I swung myself up to straddle him. He released a moan of satisfaction. His hand on my neck joined its fellow in grabbing my ass, pulling me against his hard-on. So I took over, grinding my body against his. I hesitated to say I had ulterior motives. Perhaps additional motives? I've been watching him, wanting him longer than he even knew I existed. And this felt so *good*, so *right*.

He felt like... everything.

I traced a line of hot sloppy kisses down the side of his neck and ran my hands frantically underneath his now untucked shirt, loving the feel of his abdomen reacting to my touch. I slid my body down until I was kneeling in between his legs and unbuttoning his black work pants.

He gave me a lopsided smile, and his lust-filled eyes set me aflame even more.

"I thought we were just making out."

I raised an eyebrow, "Is that all you want to do?" I unbuttoned his pants, slid down the zipper, and took his cock in my hand, slowly stroking it. He released his breath slowly as his eyes tracked my hand. Up to the head, then back down his shaft until I reached the base.

"Michael," I sing-songed lowly, and swirled the head of his cock with my tongue. "I asked if that was all you wanted to do."

He threw his head back with a hiss. "Well, fuck. It's not all I want to do *anymore*." He raised his head to meet my gaze. "Now I want to bury my dick in your throat. Then I plan to bend you over the arm of my couch, and fuck you until the neighbors bang on the wall because of your screaming."

I felt myself gush at his words, but instead of letting on, I looked up at him from beneath my lashes. "Well, I can't let a wonderfully detailed answer like that go unrewarded, can I?" I don't think he noticed, but his skin was taking on that golden glow again.

I enclosed the head of his cock in my mouth and circled it and the underside with my tongue in a rapid, repetitive motion. I kept at it until he thrust up into my mouth in desperation.

"Come on Adelola," he groaned, my full name sending shivers down my spine, "All the way."

I laughed around his dick and allowed him further into my mouth, although by no means did I go "all the way." I wouldn't be rushed.

"*Fuuuck*, ahhh. Touch yourself for me. Show me how wet you are," he said roughly. I slipped my hand into my underwear and moaned at the feel of myself. I bobbed more vigorously on his cock, enjoying him sliding in and out of my mouth as I slid my fingers in my arousal. I circled my fingers around my clit and moaned in satisfaction.

"Show me," he demanded again, his golden energy flaring. I stuck two fingers inside my pussy, scissoring them, and moaned louder. Michael wove his fingers in between my braids and made a fist, pulling me off is cock with a 'pop'. I returned his glare with a smile.

"Show me," he said in a firm low voice, giving me a small shake. I raised my hand, knowing what my fingers looked like.

"Sorry, I'm... a bit of a mess right now," I said with saccharine sweetness. One hand still in my braids, he grabbed my other hand in his. After staring intently at my slow flexing fingers, his gaze returned to mine as he sucked each of my fingers into his mouth.

"Oh. Mmm.... Of course, now I want your tongue in other places," I said smoothly, as if my pussy wasn't regretfully clenching around nothing.

"Later," he responded, having just finished licking in between my fingers. "I need to be inside you."

His hand had loosened in my hair, so I took the opportunity to move away from him. "Mmmmm, I don't fuck men who've bound my powers. I'm funny that way."

He narrowed his eyes. "So you'd fuck a woman who had?"

"What a weak 'gotcha'. Have you seen women?"

Michael rolled his eyes. "No sex because I bound your magick?"

"No," I corrected. "No sex, because you've maintained the binding."

He pretended to be at ease, but the grip he had on his knees was anything but. We locked into our quiet staring contest for a few moments, but eventually he said, "Fine. I'm going to take a shower."

I let him get up, tuck his cock back in his pants, and make it halfway across the room before I taunted, "You know an orgasm in the shower isn't going to even come close to satisfying you."

He stilled mid-step, and his fists clenched and unclenched before he continued without remark to his bedroom.

CHAPTER 4
Michael

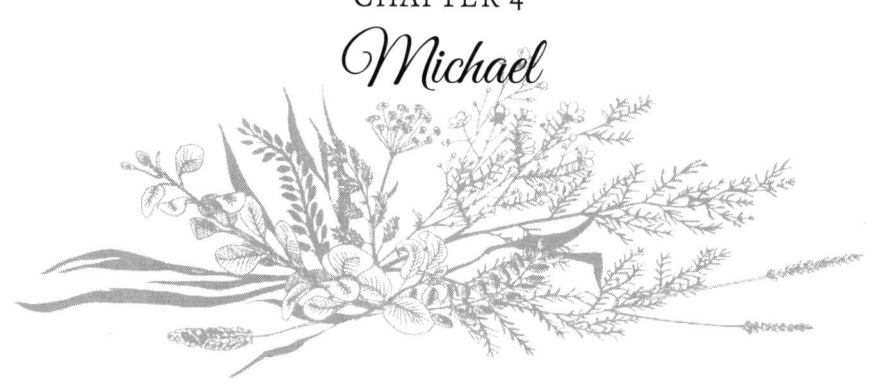

I woke up because something tickled at my awareness. Was it my sexual frustration? I can't figure out how she maintained even a drop of her magick, but she had control of my orgasms. She had said it wouldn't be as satisfying, and it was horrifyingly true. Pumping into my fist had about as much appeal as astronaut food paste did alongside a five-course meal. And now Adelola was lying next to me, untouchable. The fact she successfully cursed me *should* be upsetting, but I still couldn't get over her being here, happily laying in my bed.

But why? Because of this vampire threat she keeps going on about? Or is this another opportunity for her to drive me out of my mind with need so I'd release her powers?

I felt that pressure on my mind again and realized it was my plants. They were distressed. My body tensed, ready to get out of bed, but Adelola gripped my thigh.

I opened my mouth to say something, but the silent shake of her head stopped me. Something in her grey eyes told me she wasn't playing around. What was going on? I closed my eyes to figure it out from my plants.

Plants weren't like people. They had a decentralized sense of awareness, and that made it hard to communicate. But they had awareness, which meant it wasn't impossible.

What is it?
Not him. Not her. Not him. Not her. NOT HIM. NOT HER.

That's all I could get. They weren't even using words, according to how my Aunt Mab explained it to us when she taught my sister and me as kids. Our brains just automatically attempted to process their symbols into something resembling intelligible language on our end.

I furrowed my brow in confusion. I was tired. I just wanted to sleep. If she wasn't going to say anything or let me get up to check, why the fuck were we just laying here?

"Mmmmm, ooooh yes, just like that," Adelola moaned theatrically as she threw her leg across my hips and straddled me. Shit, I was still hard. Her raised eyebrow meant she noticed.

"Wha—" I started, but she slapped her hand over my mouth.

"Yes, ohhhhh fuck me like that, yes, yes, yes," she continued, her eyebrows practically in her hairline, as if to ask, "Why are you being so stupid?" While her face didn't match the sounds she was making, her hips sure did, making my bed frame squeak. And making all the blood not trying to stay—

My mouth transformed into an 'o' as I realized that someone must be here. Thank the gods for plants and women, I suppose. But who would be here?

Just as the thought crossed my mind, my closed bedroom door flew off its hinges. Adelola ducked down over me and rolled us both off of the bed.

"Give me my magick," she whispered at me furiously, somehow still on top of me.

With my heart jack hammering, I nodded, and released some of her magick back to her.

"Give me all of i—" but she never got to finish as someone pulled her off of me and threw her through my closet door.

"Michael, we've been looking everywhere for you," the pale-skinned bald man said, fanged-grin filled with malice. Not a man, a vampire. Oh look, a vampire. Whoops.

I showed him my empty palms. "Uh, hey, so normally you could just knock on my door during the day, er, I guess you couldn't do... HEYYY!" I yelped as he hauled me up by my shirt.

"Hey fellas," I chuckled nervously, including the two other vampires in my greeting, one of whom was wearing sunglasses. Weird. They were all wearing black suits. "Is there something I can help you with?" Silently, I urged the thyme growing in the two hanging pots behind the two vampires who had stayed on the other side of the bed near my window to mature as quickly as my magick would allow.

"You can help us by coming with us quietly. If you do, we'll leave your little girlfriend here," the one holding me snarled.

"Awww, after all of this, you're going to leave me out?" Adelola taunted, right before a black and silver dagger flew through the air and embedded itself in Glasses' eye. Flames consumed his skull from the inside out. I took that moment to encourage the now woody thyme behind the other to stab him in the back.

Baldy tried to turn around, realizing that Adelola was a serious threat. But he realized it too late, and before he could fully turn, his body jolted as her second dagger slid through his sternum like he was made of butter. He gaped at me before his grip finally loosened, and he crumpled to the floor, body already turning to ash.

Adelola grinned at me, eyes white with magick and something like... pride? "What the hell did you do Michael?"

"Sharp pieces of vampire-toxic wood are a bitch. Even if they're still attached to the plant," I replied shakily.

She put a hand on her hip. A hip my adrenaline filled brain now realized was clad in just panties. She took out two vampires, and probably had a plan for the third one, in her bra and panties. Fuck.

"That was... unexpected. What was also unexpected was you giving me only a scrap of my power." Her victorious grin turned into narrowed eyes.

I swallowed. "What is going on?"

"What's going on is 'I told you so,'" she said before grabbing her folded up dress off of my dresser, proceeding to get dressed.

CHAPTER 5
Adelola

"Why did you get dressed?" Michael asked, following me out into the living room. I looked him over as I gulped down a glass of water in his kitchen. The magickal exertion made me thirsty. Goddess, it felt amazing to have even this small bit of power pulsing around in my veins. It had only been a few hours since he bound me.

"Ahh. 'Cause we obviously can't stay here. That bitch obviously gave them your personal information. I chased a few vampires away from the restaurant weeks ago, but thought they were just lingering because of your aura," I shared.

"Weeks ago? How many weeks ago? You've only been coming in for the last three weeks," he countered.

I winced, and explained, "Well, I may have been watching you... a month... or two.... before that."

"Let me get this straight. You stalked me for months before you actually came into the restaurant?" He asked incredulously while sitting on the counter next to the sink. He stared at me intently.

"Well, I was trying to make sure *you* weren't luring *me* in. I thought you might be fae, and you know how some fae survive by luring in the foolish. Ironically enough, you still snared me." I rolled my eyes.

"Hey, that wasn't my fault. How was I supposed to know you were telling the truth, and not just trying to capture me to use for your own devices?" He countered.

"*And*, now that you know I'm not, can you please release my magick?" I asked sweetly, leaning against his fridge.

"No, you'll just leave me. If I keep you bound, then you have no choice but to help me."

"That's faulty reasoning, since I unburdened you of your girlfriend—" I pointed out, but he interrupted me.

"If we're not staying here, where are we going?" he pushed on.

"I have somewhere we can go. My powers might be bound, but it's magickally shielded, in addition to mundane security measures. A friend of mine runs a safe house for new blessed ones, but she helps out all types of beings. I live there permanently, but most people are just passing through."

Michael took a second to think about it. "I guess until we know why the vampires want me, I shouldn't go to any of the places I'd normally be. There's more than one blessed one?"

I sighed. "Can we have this discussion once we relocate? We have no idea how often they're supposed to report in or if anyone knew exactly when they planned on breaching your apartment."

"Breaching my apartment? Who the fuck talks like that?" he laughed.

"My body was a soldier before I took up residence," I deadpanned. "Blessed ones were all someone else. A body has to be prepared to release its current soul before a blessed soul can inhabit it. The blessed ones are favored by a deity with abilities that reflect their own bailiwicks, their own realms of power. Can we go now?"

He had gotten up to go check on his plants by the windows. "So are you Adelola, or was she?" Dim golden power emitted from his hands as he ran them over the herbs.

"That's a really existential question. One I'd be happy to discuss after we *relocate*," I said, stressing the last word. "Michael, I do not have time for this white people shit. We need to leave."

"Wha—Why would you—Are you ser-—" He couldn't seem to settle on how he wanted to respond.

I showed him the car keys in my hand. "My car is back at the restaurant. Let's get there, and then we can talk more on the way to my place."

"Nice car," Michael mumbled as he buckled his seat belt. Once he got dressed and packed a few essentials, it didn't take us long to make our way to my car. I knew he was feeling distressed, the events of the night catching up to him, but I'm glad I could finally pry him out of his apartment.

"I know this isn't top of your list to do, but I really think they would've sent a second team, probably a bigger team, once the first three didn't come back," I said gently as I pulled out of the parking lot.

"Where do you live? Where are we headed?" he asked as we quickly pulled out of the geographical bubble between his apartment and workplace.

"I don't live in the city. I live in what could've been a suburb if we had a homeowner's association and no one minded their own damn business." That got a subdued chuckle out of him. It was a start. "It's surrounded by forest, so that should be nice for you."

"Mmmm, yeah, it's been a while since I could just walk into the woods. I miss it."

"So, what are you, then? I assume they want you for your binding ability, but I also assumed you posed no threat to me... and yet, here we are."

He really laughed this time. "I *don't* pose a threat to you, Adelola. The most I can do, I've already done."

"And that was quite a bit," I muttered.

"I'm an ellyll, one of the ellyllon, a Cymreig forest fae. Or I am in part. You'd say Wel—," he started to explain, but I interrupted him.

"Yeah, yeah, it means Welsh. Go on," I urged as I navigated out of the city. Familiarity with different languages comes with the territory of being hundreds of years old.

"Right, okay. My ellyll grandmother traveled to Costa Rica and mated to my human grandfather, something that surprised her entire family. They had my mother after they came back to the States. My mother, with her bloodline obsession, married as near to full-blood ellyll as she could, hoping it would increase our powers and make our appearance fae. It worked for my twin, or maybe Catrin absorbed all the magick and fae good looks while we were in utero. My mother named me after my grandfather. Well, kind of," he paused, then continued. "His name was Miguel, and she named me Mihangel, the Cymraeg version," he divulged with bitterness.

I let what he said float around and settle. I didn't need my powers to know there were some deep old hurts in what he just shared. That probably explained some of the scarring I saw.

"So, does your sister have this ability, too?" I finally asked.

He snorted. "It's about the only thing she didn't get, but as children, she rubbed it in my face. They never thought I'd live this long, since I didn't have the power to protect myself."

"How old are you?"

"Fifty-two. You?"

"Ehhhh..." I replied.

"Oh, come on now. We both know it's not the same for us as it is for humans."

"Fine, I'm two hundred and thirty-three."

"Holy shit. I was stalked by an—" he began, but I interrupted.

"Yeah, yeah, jokes about my age are not tolerated. And you better get used to it. Blessed ones live a long time."

We sat in silence for a little while, which gave me a chance to think as I navigated the back roads to get to my house. Or rather, the house I shared with Monife.

I had wondered why Michael was with Arabell. She obviously didn't appreciate him, and based on the little I overheard, she used him often. But it sounds like he has unresolved issues with his mother, and thanks to her projecting her insecurities on him, he ended up with women like Arabell.

"So Arabell didn't know about your family and who you really are, right?" I asked, wanting to confirm. Some supernaturals shared this information with their partners to help keep them safe, and in some cases, just to be honest.

"No, definitely not," he responded, sounding disgusted. "Why?"

"Well, if you didn't tell her, then how did she have the information to negotiate with the vampires? They were supposed to turn her in exchange for her giving you to them," I said.

"Wow," he said sarcastically, "if only she hadn't had an unfortunate run in with a magickal dagger. Then we could ask her."

"Hey, we're here!" I said loudly, ignoring his point. Sometimes I get a bit stabby, so what? She threatened what was... mine. I won't feel bad about ending her, despite him having a point. *We'll find answers, regardless,* I thought to myself as I pulled into our driveway that led to the attached two-car garage.

"Whoa, how many rooms does this have?" Michael said in appreciation as we exited my car.

"Ahh, I think four officially, but Monife, my friend, created a few smaller rooms down in the basement as well. So when we have a full house, we have a *full* house. But there's no one here but us for right now."

"Wow, you weren't kidding about her running a whole operation."

"Yeah," I agreed, pulling out my keys to unlock the mahogany wood front door, letting us both into the foyer. Michael put all the things he wanted to bring into a small black duffel bag. He also had his arms around four potted herbs, and there was a small part of me that thought he looked so cute toting around these pots. But we were about to have bigger problems.

"Bitch, where have you been?"

CHAPTER 6
Michael

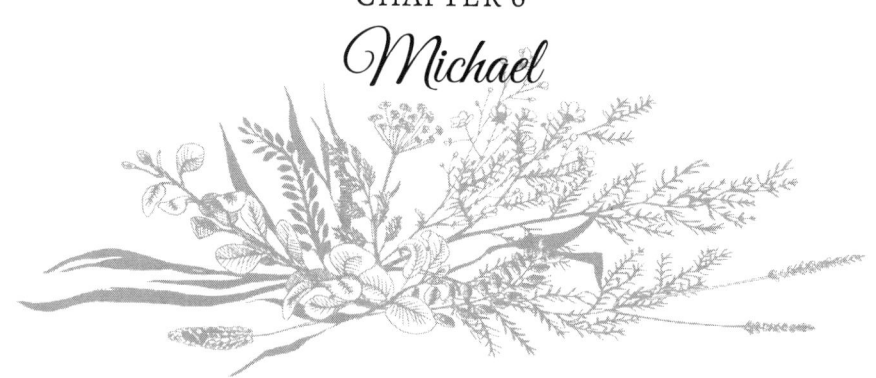

Damn. The lights snapped on to reveal a pissed off looking woman with a fade. She must be Adelola's friend, Monife. I struggled a bit balancing the pots in my arms.

"Moni..." Adelola started, but Monife cut her off.

"Eh, eh, eh, eh, don't you 'Moni' me. What you been up to? Sending me these vague texts and shit. Nu uh. And why you bringing home your toys?" She stood directly opposed to us in the foyer, hand on her hips. With her short hairstyle and silver piercings contrasting against her dark brown skin everywhere someone could think to pierce, Monife cut an imposing figure. She was taller than Adelola, and nearly as tall as me. Despite the early hour, she was wearing a crop top tank top and skin tight leather pants.

"What? Oh no, I'm not—, we're not—" I tried to explain, but Adelola cut *me* off with a "Tssss" of disapproval. How did people have conversations here if they're always cutting each other off?

"I'm happy to explain everything to you, but can we get Michael into a room first? He *does* need help, and he's not my toy," Adelola said firmly. Monife cast a reassessing look my way, taking me in from head to toe, as if she could extrapolate my whole story in that perusal.

"Humph," she sniffed. "Alright, follow me then *Michael*. I'll show you where you'll be staying." Why did she put that emphasis on my name like that?

"Michael is my real name, you know?" I said as I shuffled behind her. Adelola seemed to think I was fine alone with her. She followed us for a second and then broke off to head into what appeared to be a well-equipped kitchen. The lights were dim, which made sense, considering we showed up in the middle of the night. But the minimal light reflected off of the stainless steel appliances and shiny quartz countertops easily.

Monife led the way silently, glancing back at me several times with suspicion written on her face. I sighed heavily. While her suspicion was concerning, I was simply exhausted.

After leading me past two other rooms in this hallway, she turned right and opened the door.

"You can stay here. The bathroom is the first door on the left if you're walking out of this hallway," she explained brusquely.

I stepped through the doorway, taking in the simple furnishings. The full-sized bed was made, a dark blue comforter over medium blue sheets. The carpet was black, which made sense if they had a rotating roster of guests. I couldn't see any stains. There was a small chest of drawers and a nightstand next to the bed.

I turned back to face her. "You seem very suspicious of me, but thank you all the same."

"Yeah, alright." The twist of her mouth showed that her suspicion hadn't waned in the slightest. "You look tired, so go to bed if you want, but there are some cold cut sandwiches ready to eat if you need." Then she left.

I placed each of my plants on the dresser. These are some of the more temperamental plants, and they would've been offended if I had left them behind. Unsurprisingly, all of these are plants from Cymru and aren't known to humans. But they impart their magick in spells and healing tinctures and salves better than most plants. My Aunt Mab would be pretty upset if I requested new seedlings from her because these ones died. Even if I am fleeing what appears to be certain enslavement or death.

I let out a sigh, glancing about the simple room one more time. The bed was inviting, but all of this activity in the early morning hours made my stomach rebel at the thought of sleeping before eating. So I retraced our steps, but stopped just short of the kitchen entryway when I heard Adelola and Monife talking.

"What is going on? I can count on one hand the number of times you've brought someone here without talking to me about it first," Monife demanded.

Silence rang through the shiny room.

"Dammit Lola, don't tell me what you think I want to hear. Just spit it out."

"If I'm being honest... I'm not fully sure myself. There's something about him that has just... fascinated me? But I don't think it's any actual magick. He makes me feel something, something I'm not sure I've ever felt... But Moni, he *does* need help."

"You're not telling me something... Michael, why don't you join us instead of lingering like an eavesdropper?" Monife summoned me. How did she know I was there? The floor didn't creak at all when I approached.

"Um, er, hi," I stammered, giving them an awkward wave as I entered the kitchen. "I was, ah, just coming down for one of those sandwiches you mentioned. Then I'll be out of your hair."

"No, please, sit," she commanded, despite having said please. Why did it feel like I was in danger? She narrowed her eyes at me when I hesitated. That's right, I *was* in danger. I perched on top of one of the barstools positioned beneath the kitchen bar countertop.

"Would you grab a sandwich for our guest Lola?" she asked, giving Adelola a half smile that felt almost.... private. Adelola rolled her eyes, but moved to do as asked. Their interactions thus far make me question the nature of their relationship. Are they just really good friends?

"So Michael... what isn't Lola telling me?" she asked, her gaze intense.

I puffed my cheeks before slowly letting the air out of my mouth. If Adelola was reluctant to tell her, then shouldn't I be afraid to do so?

"I bound her magick."

The entire room changed in an instant, and the stool I was on suddenly fell apart. I landed on my tailbone and then just laid down on my back, stunned for a second.

"Monife, wait—"

"Shut up Adelola, shut up," was the quiet response.

Then she was on top of me, straddling my hips with her hand around my throat cutting off my air.

"Alright, you have a tiny sliver of time in which I will want answers more than I want your death. It's a brief window. When you say that you 'bound her magick,' do you mean to say that she can't access her orisha-given abilities?" she questioned sharply.

"Not fully," I gasped out. "I gave some of it back." Why couldn't I move my arms? Jesus, was that the barstool's legs securing my arms to my sides?

"Gave? You gave back what you didn't have the right to take? Colonizers never change, do they?" She tossed the rhetorical question over her shoulder to Adelola. Her attention returned to me. "Why?" she hissed through bared teeth.

"I thought she was going to kill me. I watched her kill my ex-girlfriend," I rasped out once she alleviated some of the pressure on my throat.

"Right, it was a misunderstanding. One we can discuss, *not* on the floor." Adelola chimed in.

Monife stared daggers at me for a moment. Then she placed the hand on my throat onto my chest, pushing into me to jump from her knees to her feet, and walked back around the counter. In her wake the pieces of the barstool reassembled themselves before my very eyes.

"So you didn't kill his girlfriend?" Monife asked, putting a chip from what was presumably my plate into her mouth. I righted the stool and sat down.

"Ex-girlfriend," I mumbled.

"Oh, no, I did do that. The misunderstanding was that I was also going to kill him," Adelola clarified.

Monife nodded sagely, as if killing random people was a common occurrence. Who knows, maybe for these women, it was. Yes, I was definitely in danger.

"And you haven't killed him and released the binding because...?" Monife left the rest of her question dangling.

Adelola's eyes darted to me and then back to her friend. "I already explained that. Besides, I'm sure once we eliminate the threat, he'll release the binding. He's just trying to ensure I keep helping him."

"By hamstringing you? Stupid, paranoid fae. And if you killed this dangerous ex, then what threat are you talking about, eh?" Monife's eyes were squinted at her now, trying to make sense of the pieces of the story she held.

"Perhaps you should start from the beginning," I suggested to Adelola.

So she proceeded to tell Monife about what Adelola heard Arabell say, her death, my binding, and the vampire attack.

Monife sat there with the tips of her index fingers pressing into her cupid's bow and the rest of her fingers interlaced, ruminating on what we told her.

"Alright," she said after a minute. "We'll sort out our plan of action in the morning. You two need sleep if you're going to be useful."

I didn't need to be told twice. While Adelola recounted our evening, I had polished off my sandwich. I was ready for this day to be over. I'd confront the fact that I couldn't outrun my heritage and my magick after all, tomorrow.

CHAPTER 7
Michael

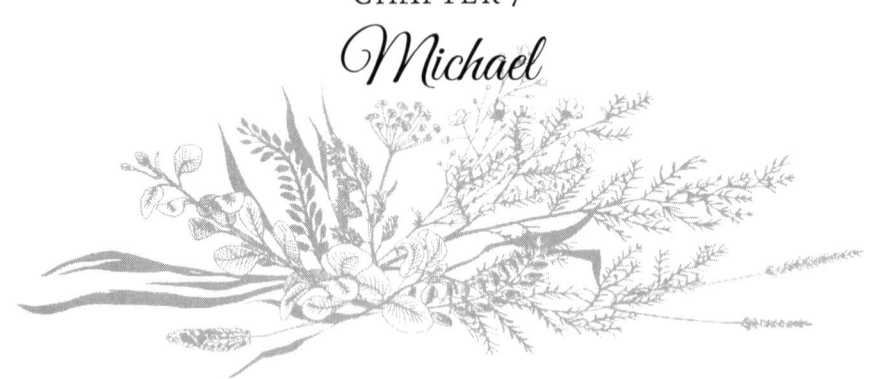

As tired as I was, I couldn't resist seeing the sun paint the forest trees with its light. My people, the ellyllon, took the Cymraeg phrase, Dod yn ôl at fy nghoed, coming back to my trees, to a whole 'nother level. As denizens of the forest and nature being the source of our spirits and magick, it soothed me on a level that nothing else could. Except maybe Adelola's visits over the last few weeks.

I lived in the city, and my human blood helped blunt a lot of the effects of iron, but not much competed with magick rejuvenation like greeting the sun. It was a threshold in time. And to be here, inhaling the air of this forest...I took a deep breath, taking in the smell of morning dew. There were a few clouds in the sky, so the light that preceded our fiery ball was reflecting off of them in bright oranges and pinks.

I exhaled, releasing not just my breath, but some of my stress. The decision had been made and acted upon. I was here. There was nothing to do but move forward. I took a step off the back patio deck and a shudder ran through my body at the feel of the cold blades of grass against my bare feet.

"Making a break for it?" came Monife's voice behind me.

I rolled my eyes. A moment of peace, was that really too much?

"Looking for another reason to attack me?" I asked snidely, looking at her over my shoulder.

"No, I'm looking for a reason to kill you that she'll accept," she replied, looking down on me from the porch in more ways than one. She was dressed much like last night, in black leathers and a sporty tank top, ready for the day. It looked like she changed out the ear spikes she was wearing yesterday for thin silver chains that dangled down to her collar bone.

I might be a magickal creature, but just like almost everything else on this planet, I wanted to survive. Monife would not make me regret choices that helped me stay alive.

I snorted and turned back to face the forest.

"I was just enjoying the sunrise and the forest. A moment of peace and solitude. Or it *was.*"

She was silent for a while, and the sun was fully visible above the horizon when she said quietly, "You can't keep her with you this way."

"What are you talking about?" I asked, turning my whole body around. It was tempting to ask "keep who" but we both knew who she was talking about.

"Binding her to you like this... This isn't the way. She believes you'll release her before it's too late to help you, but if you go beyond her kind nature, and she does have one... you'll regret it," she said reluctantly.

"Because you'll kill me, right?"

"No, because you'll wish I had. Lola is a force. I'm older than the both of you, seen more than most, and I've only seen one Lola. You don't contain a force. You stand in the midst of it, thrilled it hasn't ripped you to shreds," she paused, but I could tell she wasn't done. "Trust her to stay with you, to help you," she finished finally.

I snorted again, "That's absolutely... ridiculous. I may not be fully fae, but I know that no one gets anywhere that way. When she came across me, she thought I was just a human with an unusually attractive aura. Now she knows I'm mostly fae with weak magick and an ability that makes me a useful tool to those more powerful than I. No one wants to align with that." I faced the trees again, determined to ignore her until she finally went inside.

After a minute or two of silence, I thought she had, and I relaxed. Which was the exact moment she forcibly turned me around by my shoulders.

"Fuck, you scared the shit out of me!" I nearly yelled.

"Listen carefully little ellyll. If you bind me, I will kill you. If you try to flee after we've helped you without releasing Lola, I'll kill you twice," she whispered sinisterly, her near black eyes almost absorbing the sunlight shining on her face. And then she mashed her lips against mine, and they *burned*. Dammit, she must have put in iron hoops; they looked silver yesterday. I pushed against her and she released me, allowing me to back up a step. Monife spit on the grass in front of me, her eyes set determinedly.

"A vow sealed in a kiss and iron. It's hard to get more serious than that for you little ellyll." She smirked.

I didn't say anything, just breathed heavily as I felt my body work on healing the four welts on my lips. Shit, it was going to take a while. The iron must be enchanted, judging by the lingering burning sensation I felt.

She raised an eyebrow at me, and when I didn't offer a response, she turned around and walked back into the kitchen, closing the sliding glass door behind her noiselessly.

CHAPTER 8
Adelola

"So if you aren't doing the horizontal tango with the colonizer, why are you carting him around like a pet? Why not kill him and be done with it?" Monife asked as she extended her hand to help me up from the mat. Sparring was part of our normal morning routine whenever I was here, which was more often than not until I started keeping an eye on Michael.

As I accepted I said, "You know he's also Latino, right? He's white presenting."

She sniffed and squared up again, but I maintained my lax body posture. I've known Moni long enough to decipher that sniff.

"Don't. Don't do that. Not all of us can be you, like single sourced tea. I'm not even completely African, and you know it. His mother shits on him for presenting as more human than fae. He doesn't need you playing the colorist on top of that," I warned.

She relaxed about half way through my tirade and held up her palms toward me. "Wow, you are protective," she paused to gather her thoughts. "But I see your point. I've watched this country, the world shit on us, for the color of these meat suits, or where the meat suits were born. I won't make him feel bad. For that at least," she said the last under her breath. As she fell into her fighting stance, she offered, "Say the word, and he'll die. You fighting hamstrung is utterly stupid."

Being a blessed one is to be both human and not. We have human memories, but inhuman levels of power. Most magickal people were like Michael, earning a human living while having a magickal existence. Moni and I didn't have that problem. The consensus in the magickal community is that we had to stay secret since humans couldn't even refrain from killing *each other* over things like religion, skin color, or who they were fucking. We already knew how they'd respond to us.

I resumed my fighting stance, and we went a few rounds, trading jabs, hooks, kicks, knees, and anything else we could think of from the multitude of fighting styles we both had learned. I usually lost, but over the last hundred or so years, I had gotten better at prolonging the amount of time I was on my feet.

I try not to feel bad about it because fighting with Monife made me a better fighter. She's old, like *really* old. To hear her tell it, she woke up in her body aboard a slave ship on its way to Puerto Rico. Being a blessed one of Ogun, the orisha of metalworking and war, she tore that ship apart and made landfall in the Americas herself with a few other Africans.

Interesting thing though, whenever I've asked what happened to the other Africans on the ship, the only thing she would say is not to worry about them because they made their bargain with the sea. I never asked what happened to the slavers. I knew what I would've done in that situation.

Monife was helping me to my feet again when I heard Michael say, "Hot damn, no wonder you were able to take out those vampires."

My emotions immediately lifted and I began to say, "Well, you took out one—," but stopped abruptly when I turned around and saw his face. The smile I had planned to greet him with fell from my face.

"What, no compliments for me little ellyll?" Monife taunted, and Michael rolled his eyes.

What had she done to him? My breaths were coming faster, and I could feel every muscle in my body infusing with rage. Had she... had she... *kissed* him? My brain couldn't hold onto the point that she meant to hurt him with it. Just that she had hurt him and kissed him. And I had assured him I would protect him.

My vision filled with red, and I snapped, tackling Monife to the ground. Once on top of her, I punched her in the face twice before she managed to fling me off of her, using her supernatural strength. Usually, she held back in that department, since not all Blessed Ones had the same base strengths like speed and strength, but I surprised her with my attack.

"What the actual fuck Lola? What are you doing?" she yelled at me. Michael stood shocked near the gym door entrance.

"You hurt him. You *kissed* him." The words ripped out of my throat, sounding growly.

"As a *warning*, fuck," she tried to explain.

"No, you over-fucking-stepped." I walked away from her, and grabbed Michael by the hand, tugging him toward the door. "Never again Monife. Never again."

"I think your body shimmered gold, you know," Michael said quietly as I dabbed an enchanted salve on his lips in my room. I had opted to straddle his lap under the guise of making it easier. Really, the closeness helped me calm down. He barely winced when I made contact with his skin. I knew it had to hurt, though. Many of my friends over the years had been fae with some type of aversion to iron.

"I'm sure if my rage had a color, it would've been black, like death," I tried to joke, but my response surprised even me a little bit. "She shouldn't have done this. I'm trying to keep you safe. The last thing I need is for her to poke holes in you."

"She loves you very much," he said, as I finished. "She's trying to protect you. I was mad at first, but then I realized what an amazing gift that is."

"Did no one protect you?" I asked gently, craving more knowledge of him. I struggled to be concerned about my obsession, but it felt too good.

Michael sighed and dropped his eyes. "Tragic life stories aren't supposed to be attractive to women. Not unless they're like a superhero origin story, right?"

I placed my hand on his cheek, lifting his face back to mine. "That is patriarchal bullshit. We don't get to pick what happens to us, just how we deal with it," I told him, and kissed his nose.

The left side of his mouth perked up in a small half-smile. He slid his hands up my thighs and rested them on my hips. "My Abuelo Miguel and my

Aunt Mab protected me when they could," he confessed, eyes sad. "My mother has a habit of going against tradition. She thought that suffering might bring out latent abilities and strength in me. It took me a long time to realize that other ellyllon didn't raise their younglings like mine did. But my Aunt Mab has immense responsibilities. Honestly, she's not even my aunt, but she took a fancy to me when I wandered into her dreamscape wood one night as a child." I wiped the salve from his lips; it had sat long enough. I examined the healed but still slightly red skin, satisfied the magickal remedy had done as much as it could as Michael continued speaking.

"And my Abuelo Miguel... well, he was human and already an old man when I was born. He had taught me about his country and his people, taught me their language. But after he passed, my mother had a gwehydd cof, a memory weaver, rip the knowledge from my mind because I wouldn't stop speaking it in my child grief. They even prevented me from relearning it, leaving me with that one word, abuelo. She said it hurt her too much, but it made me feel like he was still with me. I also think it reminded her of how human I was. So...."

We stared into each other's eyes. He seemed to be waiting for something. Perhaps my rejection. So I honored his vulnerability with a kiss. I meant for it to linger just a moment or two, but once my lips met his, I couldn't pull away. I shouldn't be comforting the being who bound my magick, my orisha-given magick. On some level, I knew that. But there was something deep inside me that told me he was mine and he just needed time. Hearing how his own mother re-traumatized him on the heels of losing the only family member who he felt like cared for him only affirmed that feeling.

So when his hands gripped my hips tighter and his tongue found the seam of my lips, I opened to him. His moan of relief hurt my heart. I pressed closer to him, twining my fingers in his hair and plundered his mouth. My thighs opened a bit more, allowing me to rock against his erection through his jeans. Everything about me felt primed for pleasure. His hands on my body, our tongues dancing. Even pressing my breasts against his chest brought pleasure, but also served to increase my desire.

Michael skated a hand up my back and tugged on my braids, encouraging me to tilt my head back. He placed wet kisses along the column of my neck.

"I'm salty," I said on an exhale.

"Good, maybe it will help me remember to season my food properly," he said, and we froze. He looked up at me, and we both laughed so hard, I had to slide off his lap to sit next to him on my bed.

"Michael," I wheezed, "I can't believe you said that! Talk about intrusive thoughts."

"I had just thought your skin tasted good before you said that," he tried to explain between laughs.

"That's just a stereotype. I'm pretty sure you season your food just fine. Besides, you're mixed," I jokingly reassured him.

"Yeah, I'm mixed," he said with a touch of bitterness and rubbed his hands over his face.

We simmered down after that. He was looking at his hands when he asked, " Adelola, I know you're attracted to me, but why are you doing this? It made the most sense to kill me. It still makes the most sense."

I sighed. I understood why he thought that, especially with Monife's cold welcome. "Michael, I'm a blessed one of Oya, her warrior. She's the orisha of sudden change and vengeance. I know seeing me kill Arabell might have painted me as a monster in your eyes, but you didn't hear what I heard. I kill when I deem it necessary, and she had it coming."

"That doesn't explain why you're doing all of this. I'm no one to you," he responded, running his fingers through his curls.

"You don't feel like no one. I am a jagunjagun, a warrior, and you are a oniwosan, a healer. You are the moon to my sun, the ice to my fire. If I am the raging storm, you are the new growth that comes in the aftermath. Why would I want you? No. A better question is: how could I imagine myself without you?"

He stood up suddenly. "I should leave you to take a shower or whatever you planned next. I know we need to discuss our next steps." Then he walked out without a backward glance.

He was asking important questions, the same questions Monife asked. But how could I give either of them satisfactory answers when I just *knew* this was my path? That *he* was my path?

CHAPTER 9
Michael

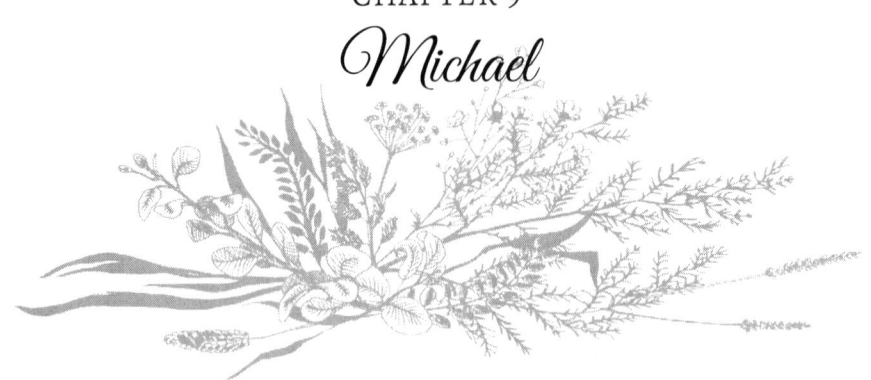

If we hadn't stopped kissing in her room, I might have been convinced to release her. That's why I made the joke, hoping she'd laugh and pop the bubble of sexual tension building between us. Of course, I still had plenty to spare, so I had gone back to my room to jack off and try to get my shit together.

How could I imagine myself without you? she had said.

Normally, I was a pretty easy going guy. The same guy Adelola asked out a few nights ago. But I left home a couple decades ago because I felt like my mother crossed a line when she loaned me out to satisfy a debt. Since I left, I had managed to make friends who didn't realize I kept them at arm's length. They were kind, creating space for me to be as well.

But that didn't mean I shed 30 years of life lessons just because some humans and low-powered beings were nice to me when there were no stakes.

It was nearly 11 AM, a bit early for lunch, but cooking was something I was good at and enjoyed doing. So perhaps I could ameliorate tensions between Monife and Lola by giving them something delicious to eat while we figured out our plan of action. I changed course to the kitchen.

I was just wrapping up some fish cakes when Adelola walked in expressing her appreciation for the aroma of lunch. Monife followed close behind her, an eyebrow raised in curiosity.

"I figured we had a stressful evening and morning, so a solid lunch would help settle us," I said, plastering a smile on my face. My lips only tugged slightly, which made me want to get the recipe for that salve. Those wounds should've taken a day to heal completely, but now I doubted I would feel them by the evening.

"What did you make?" Monife asked slowly.

"Teisennau eog dyfrdwy, salmon fish cakes. It's a Cymreig recipe, with a twist. I make them with sweet potatoes. Kind of a Latine Cymraeg fusion."

"Ha, like you. Well, I'm ready to try it. Gimme," Adelola said playfully, making grabby hands at the platter as I placed the last of the fish cakes on them.

We got lunch on the table, and I waited for them each to have a bite. "So?" I asked. My fish cakes had been complimented many times, but I figured they were used to different cuisines. I had adapted the recipe with the seasonings available in the pantry and used magick to enhance the vitality of the herbs and spices, which makes them more flavorful.

"I have to say, this is—" Monife began.

"Delicious!" Adelola gushed. "I saw you making this for yourself at home, but I couldn't have imagined it was this good!"

Monife turned to her questioningly. "What do you mean you 'saw him' make this?"

Adelola's eyes dropped to her plate, then she said, "Don't worry about it. So what are we going to do?"

Monife narrowed her eyes at Adelola as she took another bite, then said, "Well, we can talk about what to do, but we still don't know which nest of vampires to target."

Adelola nodded in agreement. "So we need to figure out which nest, but I think we sort of already have a solution for eliminating them, right?" she asked.

"What?" I interrupted.

They looked at each other and then said together, "Solar bomb."

"A solar *bomb*?" I asked. "You can make something like that?"

"Vampires aren't inherently bad, but this isn't our first run in with them," Monife smirked.

"Okay," I said slowly, my food forgotten. "How do we do that?"

"*We*," Monife stressed the word, meaning her and Adelola, "will do it.

Adelola has the contacts to gather the necessary parts, and I'll bespell the metal components."

She didn't say it, but the "you're not needed" was loud and clear. Of course. I sighed and turned my attention back to my food.

"Well actually, Moni," Adelola interjected, "Michael can come with me to make contact with my people. His aura puts people at ease, which would be helpful. And don't you make an oil with herbs toxic to vampires that you coat the metal in? Michael would be better at that than you, with his magick. With him working on that, we could get the bomb assembled faster."

I almost spit my bite across the table. Monife's eyes darted around like she was trying to find fault with the proposal. She pursed her lips and let out a reluctant, "Fine," and focused back on her food.

"What about figuring out the vampire nest location?" I asked. "A bomb with no destination just sounds like a hazard."

"Our first stop will be a rootworker I know in the city's magickal underground," Adelola explained. "In fact, we can head over there after lunch. No point in delaying when the risk of them finding you only increases every day. They won't be happy we killed their nest mates either."

CHAPTER 10
Adelola

I could tell stepping through the city's portal to the magickal underground was an experience for him. It throws beings for a loop the first few times as the magick acts on their physical bodies. But I knew that walking through our world would shock him even more. Here, no one is glamoured.

I buried a twinge of irritation mixed with sadness that my own natural form would be suppressed due to Michael's binding. When I come through the portal, my braids are tipped in their lightning crystals, my grey eyes shifted to silver, and the patterns on my skin become visible and glow. It's only if my emotional state goes south that my braids float around my head and become charged with Oya's lightning. With my claws, I was clearly marked as dangerous. As it was, Michael appeared the most magickal of the two of us. I shrugged it off. It shouldn't be a problem.

"Whoa, shit, um, pshh," Michael blew out a breath, trying to center himself.

"Yeah, it takes some getting used to, but you will. It's hard to believe you've never been here. It would be the perfect place to sell your remedies."

He followed me as I led the way down the street, facing us. There were vendors lining both sides. In between vendors, there were doors to various shops. We could buy anything here, from enchanted jewelry and clothes to potions and bespelled weapons.

"Not really," he responded, slipping his hands in his jean pockets. "I was trying *not* to be found. If I had spent time in a place like this, the odds wouldn't have been in my favor."

He looked so good in his dark blue jeans, light blue shirt, and black leather jacket. Without his glamour in place, his ears were pointed, his cheekbones more pronounced, and his eyes shaded from their usual light brown to more of a yellowish gold. Not touching him was a trial, so I stopped resisting, looping my arm through his.

He looked down at me sharply, but smiled a little. Good, he didn't shake me off. If he wanted the physical contact even half as much as I did, then this would feel great for him, too.

I quieted, letting him take in the different beings and sights. He followed my tugs on his arm willingly. Blessed ones weren't overly common, but there were fae of all types here, as well as beings from all over the world. The portals weren't limited to the cities where our undergrounds were located. We could portal to the underground in Tokyo or Cairo if we wanted to. Of course, to do that, I'd need to cash in a favor with one of the portal masters I knew.

Finally, I said, "Alright, this is it. We're here."

We found ourselves in front of a cozy looking vintage bookshop and apothecary.

"This is where we're going to find out where the vampires are and what they want?" Michael asked doubtfully.

I gave him a playful shove. "Hey, don't knock it til you've tried it. If this doesn't work, there are other avenues for us to explore."

Suddenly, the front door opened, and Delilah stepped out. "C'mon in now, I've been waiting for y'all since yesterday," she called out, her Southern accent tingeing her words. Delilah was a beautiful woman, one I had made a move on a few times in the last decade or so. She always wore vibrant colors, today's maxi dress being sunflower yellow. Her shoulder length locs whipped as she turned and headed back inside. Each loc was threaded with a small silver or gold bell, making music wherever she went.

Delilah was one of a few humans in the underground. She went so deep into her craft, her magickal abilities were nearly indiscernible from a being with moderate levels of power. She's particularly good at uncovering secrets, and that was what she was known for here. The cost was that she couldn't live in the human world and lost a human fiancé in her pursuit of power. Personally, I thought that Delilah's dive into hoodoo triggered latent magick abilities she has from one of her ancestors having kids with a magickal being.

"You heard her, let's go," I said as I lightly jobbed up the walk and up the few steps to the wraparound porch. This Southern-style home was so out of place, but I couldn't imagine Delilah living and working anywhere else. I glanced back at Michael while I grabbed the door, suppressing a smirk as I caught him looking around, examining everything suspiciously. I guess he had a right to be wary. There were people out here looking for him. Did he think I was leading him into a trap? I hoped we had graduated from that by now. He had to know I genuinely wanted to help him.

Upon entering, I could see she had rearranged things since I had visited last. She always kept the storefront well-lit, the light catching prettily on the various crystals she had placed around her shop. People came here to buy remedies and spirit-blessed tools. Some came to converse with their ancestral spirits. That's what we were here to do. Deliah was skilled at getting answers from the other side, either from her ancestors or *her* customers.

"Hey girl, how you been?" I asked, taking in the changes with a sweep of my eyes. At this power level, I couldn't see any of the scars that marked Delilah's energetic body. The one welcome change in all of this.

"Lola, I've been feeling neglected. It's been some time since you came to see me," she said reservedly, taking in Michael coming in behind me. "You've also never brought anyone with you, besides Monife. What's going on?"

"That's so unusual that something has to be going on?" I joked, trying to bring a smile to her face.

"Oh the bones and my cards told me something was going on yesterday. The spirits might have told me a bit more, which is why I've been waiting on you," she said knowingly, her hands clasped in front of her.

"I suppose I shouldn't be surprised by that. Things have been rather dramatic over the last day or two," I admitted.

Michael snorted then looked surprised when Delilah threw her head back and laughed.

"Oh yes, dramatic, that's a good word for it. Don't look so shocked. Just because your people don't tend to have these gifts doesn't mean they aren't more common for others. So, what do you want from me?" Delilah asked.

I reached into my tan leather cross body bag for the bit of a shirt I had ripped off the vampire Michael had taken out. When I kill with my dagger, the spirit flames consume everything, but Michael's herbal stake left the vamp's clothes.

Holding out the torn fabric, I explained, "We had a run-in with some vampires. I need to know where their nest is."

I felt Michael tense to explain, but all Delilah said was, "Okay, let's go into the back."

She led the way, and as we followed her, he asked, "Don't you want to know what happened?"

"Well, y'all killed 'em, didn't you? If that's not the case, then do tell. Y'all not killing 'em would be more surprising," Delilah said over her shoulder. We came to a door at the end of the short hallway at the back of her shop. The door was painted black with an antique looking brass doorknob. As she twisted the handle, she warned, "Watch your step here."

There was black salt laid in a line at the threshold of the room. I noticed Michael pausing on his way in to look at the sigils inscribed on the door frame. As Delilah shut the door, I took in the empty room. The walls were a medium grey, at least this time. I never knew what I was going to get when we came in here. I guess we weren't getting much today.

"Alright, have a seat," she said, rubbing her hands together. I watched Michael look at Delilah quizzically.

"What do you...?" he said as turned around. While it was empty before, the room now contained a low black table with three cozy dark red chairs, one seat on one side of the table, and two on the opposite side.

"How did you do that?" Michael asked as Delilah made her way to her chair. I mimicked her, taking my own seat, which encouraged Michael to do the same.

"I didn't," she said simply. "The room knows what we need."

Michael narrowed his eyes and started darting them around the room, like he was thinking deeply.

"No, the room isn't possessed. I became bound to it and the store shortly after relocating to the underground. But then, you know all about bindings, hmmm?" Delilah asked lightly, directing our focus back on our current issues.

The way he narrowed his eyes this time had nothing to do with thinking and everything to do with distrust. "So, do you need the cloth from Lola or what?"

Delilah just chuckled knowingly and held her hand out to me. I placed the scrap of cloth in her palm and glanced at Michael, catching him looking at me.

"Did you know we were going to come here?" he asked.

"What do you mean?"

"Well, how else did you know to grab it? The cloth I mean."

"Ah, I didn't know we'd be coming to see Delilah, but she's not the only one in the underground who could help. I figured it was better to not need it and have it." I explained. Delilah cleared her throat to get our attention.

Both of us looked at her, only to see we missed a bit more of the room's magick. A dull yellow-gold oracle cloth draped the polished black table now. In her hands, Delilah cradled a bloodred cloth drawstring bag, probably filled with divination bones.

"If y'all are ready, I'm going to need your attention and focus. It's your question; I'm just the vehicle. I'll give you a couple of minutes to quiet your thoughts. Then we'll begin."

I sank into my chair and held my head in a neutral position. Slow, deep breaths helped me quiet my mind. Without the chatter, I could sense and see the small kernel of my power I had at my disposal and it threatened to throw me out of my calm state. Inhaling, I reminded myself that Michael would come around. Before it was too late, he would come around.

"Alright now, as you take your next inhale, draw in your intent and shape your question, the home nest of the vampire who wore this on their person, in your mind," Delilah intoned. Following her directions, I even visualized the vampire and infused that vision with my need to know.

"Now, exhale your gratitude for the ancestors' help," she instructed. I blew the air out, letting my gratitude infuse my aura and receiving a warm feeling in response. I was on good terms with my ancestors, although it hadn't always been that way.

Then Delilah tossed the bones onto the cloth. Michael and I opened our eyes and leaned in closer, like we knew what to look for.

"Oh dear," Delilah muttered, her eyes darting around the cloth, "Someone didn't clear their mind, did they?" she asked, looking pointedly at Michael, who had the decency to look sheepish.

"I've had a lot on my mind the last couple of days," he said, running a hand through his curls.

"Is it usable?" I asked intently. If not, we'd have to come back. Spirits don't tend to appreciate the living wasting their time. I'd always figured it shouldn't be a problem because they now had all the time in the world, but maybe I had that wrong.

"Oh no, you were very clear. The answer you need will be found if you follow the crow," she told me. Now you need to leave. I have something to share with just Mihangel."

His body jerked in response to that name.

I opened my mouth but closed it again. If she was saying that she had something for him, it meant the ancestors had something for him. I didn't need to anger ornery spirits on top of everything else.

"Fine."

I took one more moment to convey feelings of gratitude for good measure, and then I left the room to wait in the store area.

CHAPTER 11
Michael

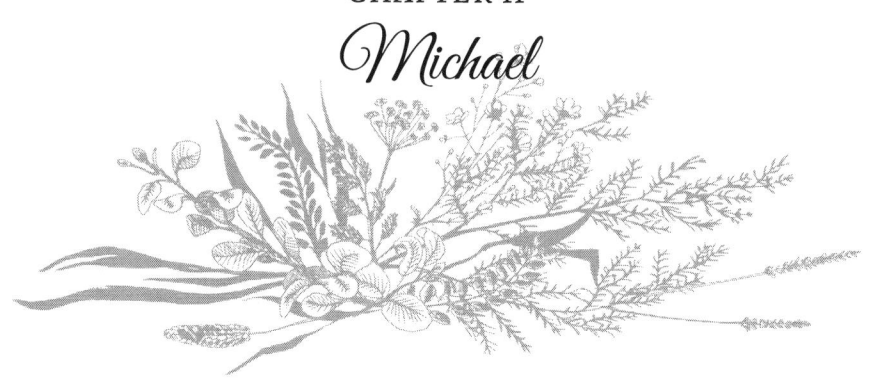

As soon as Adelola left, Delilah turned her knowing eyes back to me. "It's a good thing Lola is focused or else your questions would've obscured the answer you came here for completely."

"Where is that? The answer," I asked, gesturing to the bones.

"That? Right here." She indicated the spot by making small circles with her index finger. There were a few bones just left of center that seemed almost out of place compared to the mess around them.

"So... what do you have to tell me?" I urged. I hadn't meant to interfere with our purpose, but if my ancestors, any of them, had guidance for me, I'd take it.

"Your mind is consumed with the woman who just left us," she said lowly.

"What? No, I want to know why the vampires are coming after me. I've been in the city for years. No one knows who I am. Or at least no one did."

"Well then, chile, you shoulda thought about that, bless your heart."

I may not have lived in the South, but even I knew what that meant.

"Okay, so what? She's on my mind."

"Mmmmm, there is more to her than even she knows, and you may find yourself bound. Although not like the way you've bound her."

I threw my hands in the air and let out a frustrated breath. "Gods and goddesses, how does everyone know my deepest secret now?"

"That's not your deepest secret, Mihangel," she said with a small frown, and a chill went down my spine. Whatever *that* was, I didn't want to hear her say it.

"Is there anything else my ancestors want me to know?" I asked impatiently. I've never liked seers.

"The key to her binding is your complete trust."

I snorted. "No problema then. I don't completely trust anyone." Problema? Why did I say that? I can't speak Spanish anymore. I shouldn't even be able to slip up like that.

"Yes. If you don't trust Adelola," she paused, peering closely at the bones. "You won't have *any* more problems."

Great. Why did she have to say it like *that*?

After we left Delilah's shop, we began walking back to the portal in silence. She seemed to sense that I wasn't in the mood to talk.

"I won't ask," she said quietly.

That surprised me. I figured she would've tried to strangle Delilah's words out of me. I glanced down at her warily. "Oh yeah? Why not?"

"Well, if they wanted me to know, I wouldn't have had to leave the room, would I? Besides... we all need someone who holds space for mental peace."

"And you're going to be that someone for me?" I asked gruffly, trying to keep my emotions out of my voice.

She sighed, "I'm going to be that someone for you right now, Michael. Beyond right now.... I guess that's up to you."

We both fell silent again, my thoughts overwhelming me. Of course, I couldn't trust her. I couldn't trust anyone. But even now, our silence soothed something in me. This feeling made me want to put my head in her lap and rest. Or feast on her until she trembled. Maybe feast on her until she's shaken from the pleasure, and *then* I'd rest.

But if I trusted her... she'd bind me somehow, and I couldn't allow that.

"Don't look, but we're being followed. God dammit, I said *don't* look," she said as she grabbed my arm and dragged me into a clothing store to mask my head turning.

We walked into an explosion of color.

There were clothes of all kinds. The shop floor looked like someone took human cultures and magickal cultures and fused them together in ways I couldn't have imagined.

One mannequin looked like a winged creature, but was wearing an orange and yellow sari that accommodated its wings perfectly. I saw a mannequin that could've represented any number of beings with tails sporting pants that allowed the tail to remain on the outside. While the mannequin's pants were black, the rack behind it contained the full spectrum of colors.

Signs indicated that any garment could be spelled to survive nearly any type of shift, all I had to do was ask.

A dark-skinned man with cornrows in a pattern around the small horns coming out of his head approached us, arms wide in welcome. His vertically-slitted green eyes contrasted with his skin in a stunning way.

"Adelola, how are you?" he said familiarly. I felt my lip draw up slightly. Maybe he was too familiar.

"Gajoon, clear the floor using the back door discretely. Now," Adelola said urgently. While I expected him to protest, he immediately obeyed her.

"What is he to you that he would do that, without question?" I whispered furiously as she pulled me further into the store. Like Delilah's shop, it seemed much bigger on the inside than it did from the outside.

Adelola looked at me quizzically. "I saved him and his family when they were being pressured to pay protection money. Their house was shielded and set on fire to keep them inside it. I brought Oya's vengeance, and no one has bothered them sense."

"Oh, I guess that makes sense," I muttered, feeling somehow justified and embarrassed all at the same time.

"Yeah... Listen, this might get ugly, so I need you to be prepared for that. I'm going to leave you standing here, but I'm not far away. I just need whoever this is to think that you're alone, even for a moment."

Panic shook my bones, but I tried to hide it through anger. "Leaving me out as bait is how you're helping me!?" I said, teeth clenched.

She rolled her eyes. "Don't be dramatic, we don't have time for this. Stay here," was all she said. Then we heard the door open and shut and Adelola whirled out of sight. Great.

I figured my role was to pretend I was interested in these clothes, so I pretended to peruse while keeping my senses alert. Just as my hand touched a forest green shirt made from a material I didn't recognize but was curious about, someone grabbed me from behind and moved with super speed towards the door. I slowed them down as best I could by grabbing onto racks and digging into my heels. They growled, and just as I felt them dig their fingers into me as a warning, we came to an abrupt halt and crashed to the floor.

I pulled myself to my feet as quickly as I could, but not quicker than Adelola had a dagger trained to the vampire's throat. The underground must be enchanted to allow the illusion of sunlight without its impact. She pushed him against a wall, and this scenario felt too familiar.

She snarled at him, baring her teeth. Her braids ended in crystal points, but weren't floating like when she killed Arabell. Adelola's crystal nails had returned too.

"I'm sorry, I'm sorry! I was just supposed to observe, but I thought you left him alone!" He held his hands up by his head, palms open. "I'm not a threat!"

"You were never a threat!" she hissed. "Tell me, what do they want with him?"

"I don't know," he practically wailed. Right then, I realized he was a new vampire, but was a human probably in his twenties when he was turned. Born vampires have silver eyes, and this one's gold eyes made his pale skin look even more grey and ashen with fear.

A blank look settled over her features. "Then what good are you, hmm?"

"Wait, wait. I'll tell you something, you just have to agree to let me go."

"That might depend on what you have to say," she responded, looking down her nose at him despite him being taller than her. She slowly lowered her dagger, and backed away from him.

"They don't want him for his blood, I can tell you that much. And you," he said, flapping a hand towards Adelola, "were an unexpected complication. They don't know who you are yet, so they aren't sure about acting against you."

"Great," and then she hemmed him up against the wall again, dagger poised to strike.

"Adelola, wait! He's just a kid," I shouted.

"I thought you'd let me go!" he cried.

"He has to die. He'll go back to the nest and tell them what I look like, smell like, sound like. And then the caution my mystery has granted us will be gone, Michael," she explained through gritted teeth.

"You don't have to kill every being because they *might* do something," I urged.

"You're not seeing this clearly," she argued back.

But the vampire took the opportunity to push her, giving him enough space to bite into her trapezoid. He only did it to surprise her so he could make a dash for the door. Somehow, she was prepared for that, and he didn't get far as she gripped the back of his leather jacket to haul him to the ground and against her.

I could see her slitting his throat in my mind's eye. I knew it was coming. So I did the only thing I could do. I drew on my binding, blocking her access to even the small amount of power I had released before.

Her dagger disappeared and her appearance returned to human. The glare she leveled at me almost melted the flesh off my bones. She roared as the vampire bit her arm and scrambled his legs, still trying to get away. Without her enhanced strength, he almost managed it, but then she glowed that golden yellow, same as when she saw what Monife had done to my mouth.

Her eyes locked with mine, and if Oya had manifested in this realm, it was in this woman. Her desire for vengeance was as clear as the vampire's death was inevitable. Never looking away, she gripped under his chin and yanked.

I watched the skin of his throat tore, and his wail hurt my ear drums.

"No, no, no, fucking don't! Don't you—!" I started, but she just yanked his chin upward again, and his scream abruptly cut off. She must have broken something in his throat. Blood sprayed out of a torn and exposed artery.

"No one," she said viciously, "will stop me from protecting you." She yanked again, and this time ripped his head clean off and threw it on the floor behind her, spraying blood on the side of her face and neck. Adelola stood, chest heaving from the exertion. "Not even you," she finished. The gold aura faded, leaving her as she normally looked.

Her eyes searched my face, and whatever she found there made her expression shutter. I couldn't hide my horror. "Wait here," she said flatly. "I have to go get Gajoon. I'll need some clothes, and to pay him for the damage." She turned away from me and walked towards the back of the store.

I was rooted to the spot. Why she believed I wouldn't flee was beyond me. Maybe she knew I had nowhere else to go. After I was used to pay off a deal with a demon, I couldn't go back to my family for safety.

I had attracted the attention of a monster... but what if the monster turned on me?

CHAPTER 12
Adelola

Over the last two weeks, we had been pulling together the pieces and parts we needed for our solar bomb. Michael and I didn't leave the house together again. He claimed that he could create a better oil for us to use to bespell every piece of the bomb, but I got the sense he was avoiding me. So Monife accompanied me a few times instead, locking Michael in the house.

We hadn't heard another peep out of the vampires. Perhaps there was something about Michael that they were tracking. Our property was shielded, so they'd find no trace of him here. Even my car was impenetrable, so if they had been magickally tracking him before, they lost him as soon as he sat in my car.

Now though, all three of us were at the kitchen table, assembling all of the pieces. I had finally managed to convince a sun phoenix to part with one of her eggs. I now owed her a price of her asking, which was a very valuable favor indeed. Sun phoenixes believed themselves to be helpful beings, so I hoped she wouldn't call on me to do something terrible. I'd hate to have to kill her.

Michael's hands were glowing as he carefully anointed each piece before placing it on a cloth for me and Monife to place into or on the bomb.

"Alright, put on your goggles," I instructed. "This is going to get bright."

They wordlessly did as I asked.

Monife had been quiet, watching the two of us more carefully since

Michael and I came back from the underground. Now, though, she was in the throes of her magick, holding every piece of metal just so, and she would, until the ritual was complete. The runes on her seemed bright against her dark skin, but they wouldn't compete against the egg.

"Removing the egg," I warned as I untied the drawstring on the black magick bag the phoenix had placed the egg in for safekeeping. I squinted as I took it out, the light blinding even through the goggles.

I placed it quickly inside the cradle we'd constructed for it, and Monife gestured quickly, moving the final metal pieces into place. Michael's head turned this way and that to watch the remaining pieces fly through the air. Once it was all in place and sealed up, she nodded to the both of us, and we removed our goggles.

"So, when do you want to do this?" she asked me.

I looked out the window at the afternoon sun.

"Can we do it tonight?" Michael unexpectedly asked. "I'm ready for this to be over with."

Was he just referring to the vampires, or did that statement include me?

I shrugged one shoulder. "Sure," was my only response.

CHAPTER 13
Michael

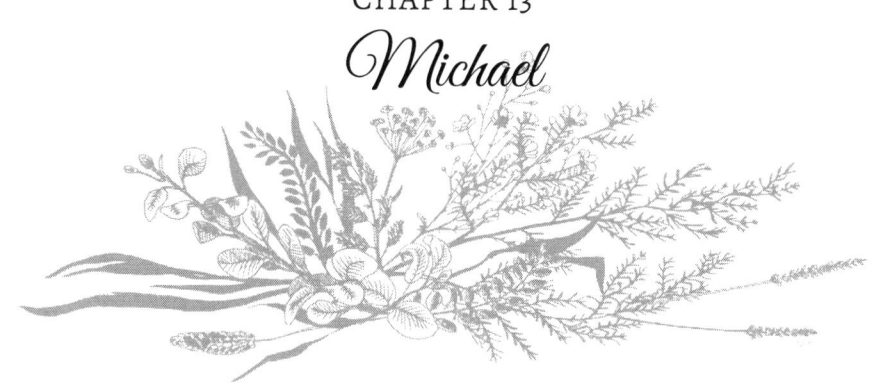

Some research revealed that there was a vampire's nest on Crow Street in the north part of the city. That seemed so obvious, but I guess it wasn't unless you visited a know-it-all hoodoo woman. Monife had confirmed with one of her contacts that this particular nest was known to play with the North American Vampire Convocation Council's laws and even break them on occasion.

We had parked Adelola's car a few blocks away and carefully made our way to the address. Much like Monife and Adelola's house, the vampire nest was a ways into a forest, so we navigated the woods to avoid announcing our presence by walking up the long driveway.

After a few moments of struggle, Monife grunted out, "Want to make yourself useful col—Michael?" She had avoided calling me "colonizer" since she and Adelola had that fight in the sparring room a few weeks ago.

"Oh, right. Sorry, I shoulda thought of that," I mumbled. I was a jumbled mess of nerves, but my golden glow mutedly lit the way for us while also encouraging roots to flatten and branches to fold out of the way of our path until we were just inside the tree line, facing the house.

It wasn't dark yet, so we had time to neutralize the human guards before placing the bomb. I had prepared a few darts dipped in an extreme sedative potion. When I offered them to Adelola and Monife, they politely turned me down. Well, Adelola politely turned me down. Monife just laughed and strolled off.

"Ready?" Adelola asked me. I looked into her eyes. I had waited these last few weeks for her to ask me to return at least some of her power to her. But she hadn't. I waited a beat for her to ask me now, but she just looked at me expectantly, waiting for my answer. The tree I was leaning against brushed its leaves against me comfortably.

Why was she doing this? Why wouldn't she ask? Was she trying to prove something to me? I kept trying to hold that image of her ripping that young vampire's head off his shoulders. But what kept surfacing was the feelings of surprise and gratitude that there was someone out there willing to do the most for me in return for nothing. No one did nothing for something, and until I knew her motive, I tried to avoid thinking about that spark, that moment where I felt... cherished.

Did it say something about me that seeing someone decapitated before my very eyes made me feel treasured? I shook my head, trying to shake out the thoughts.

"You're not ready?"

"No, I'm good," I told her. "I'm good."

The nest didn't have any external patrols, so we ran up against the side of the house, near the basement door. Monife placed her hand over the lock, manipulated its mechanism, then opened the door. We slipped inside.

Back at their house, we had agreed to split up. Monife would scope out the top floor, Adelola would secure the main floor, and I would guard our exit. Just before they left me there, I let out some of Adelola's magick, a bit more than I gave her before. She gave me a smile that needed no words. But if she wasn't going to ask, I couldn't let her do this with just the tangible weapons strapped to her body. I swore that I could almost *feel* her gratitude.

They stalked off, nearly melting into the shadows. The minutes agonizingly ticked by as I waited for them to return or for me to have a run in with a guard. The blessed ones came back first.

Adelola gave me a thumbs up, and we filed out of the door. Monife locked it behind us, and we ran back into the treeline.

"Easy. I told you. Vampires tend towards arrogance. It's shocking they even still exist," Monife said, pulling the detonator out of her pocket.

This detonator wasn't like a human one. It was bound magickly to the bomb, but was also keyed to the three of us. No random being would be able to detonate it. Adelola insisted that any of us be able to detonate the bomb as a precaution, which Monife conceded to, surprising me.

"Now we just need to wait until nightfall, and then we'll be good to go," Adelola said, not that we needed the reminder. We had gone over the plan countless times, and complete nightfall wasn't too far off. Monife thrust an enchanted silver stake into the ground that she said would mask our scent. The sky was already taking on those beautiful dusk hues.

Once the sun had completely released its hold on the sky, I felt us all tense. Sure enough, we saw blurs as older, more isolated vampires entered the house. The vampires they sent after us were younger, so they hadn't been as strong or as fast. These vampires were clearly older, so they usually slept outside of the nest, having the resources to do so.

We heard the first cry of alarm when they must've come across one of the bodies. More and more cries came, and some of the vampires left the house to search the property. I watched Monife looking intently at Adelola until she nodded, indicating the time was right. Monife lifted the small shield and pushed the button.

At first nothing happened, but then Adelola yelled, "Get down!" and she tackled me to the floor. "Shut your eyes!"

I closed them as tightly as I could, and I couldn't deny that feeling Adelola pressed against me again after a few weeks of staying out of her way calmed me and riled me up all at the same time. What a time to get a boner, fuck.

I felt a wave of energy wash over us, and then the whole ground shook as the house collapsed in on itself. The way I understood it, it was the solar energy that took out the vampires. The explosion was just energetic backlash from the force of directing the sun's power. Even in a phoenix egg.

We laid there like that until the forest was silent again.

"Come on," Adelola said, pulling me to my feet. "Create the path. We gotta get out of here. The humans are bound to investigate that. Monife, you got the evidence?" Monife had her hand outstretched towards the house. Pieces of metal flew into her outstretched palm. The remnants of the bomb.

"Yup, let's move," she said, beginning a jog down the path I had opened through the forest.

CHAPTER 14
Michael

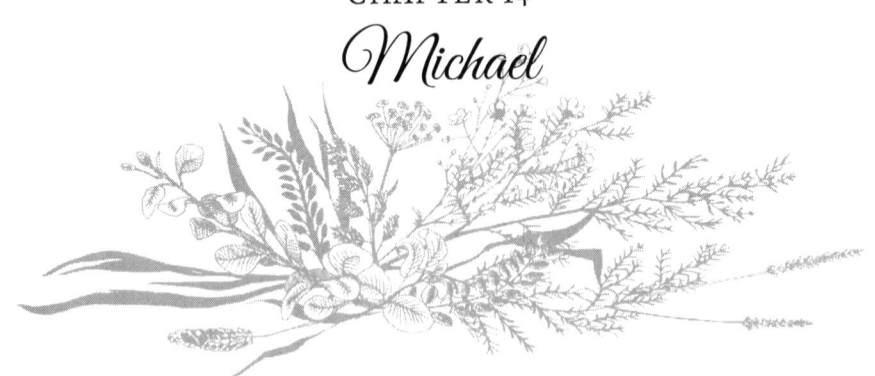

Almost as soon as we made our way back to the car, my mind filled with a pressurized buzzing that could only mean one thing. My mother wanted to talk to me. She hadn't summoned me this way since I left home two decades before, after I fulfilled that demon deal on behalf of her debt. I suppressed a shudder at the memory of how that demon tortured that poor shifter, and in front of her husband....

By the time we returned to the house, I felt like I had the worst sinus headache that somehow involved bees. What could she possibly want now, after two decades of not speaking to me?

"Michael, you have a minute? I had hoped we could talk?" Adelola asked gently. My hand rubbed my forehead and her brow furrowed in concern.

"I'm sorry, I can't. I need to go to my room. I can't right now." I said on my way out of the living room. If I didn't get to a mirror soon, I might pass out.

I locked my door behind me and rushed to the mirror over the chest of drawers.

"Mother, what do you want?" I spat at it. And she appeared.

"We haven't spoken in such a long time, and that's how you greet me?" she simpered, already playing the wounded party. She was never going to change.

I took a breath and moderated my tone. "Mother, it felt like you were trying to buzz my head off my shoulders. My apologies," I replied through gritted teeth. I bowed my head slightly for good measure. I learned long ago that playing along was the quickest way to end a conversation with my mother.

I looked at her now, and Seren, my mother, hadn't changed a bit. Where my hair was dark blonde with golden highlights, hers was a mix between platinum blonde and gold. Her skin tone was darker than mine, courtesy of my Abuelo Miguel. While I had his eyes, warm brown, she had her mother's eyes, vibrant green. Her face reflected the ellyllon's characteristic features, high cheekbones highlighted with gold, tapered ears, and a pointed chin. She was strikingly beautiful, like a poisonous tropical flower.

"Well," she said finally, "I wouldn't have pressed so urgently except that I've heard some concerning news about something you might be involved in." She put on the perfect concerned mother face, but I didn't trust it.

"You've been keeping tabs on me, Mother?" I asked, surprised. When I last saw her, after I returned from my required task to absolve her debt to the demon, she sounded like she was relieved to be free of me. Free of the family embarrassment... the family weakling.

"Oh dear, of course I have! I know we exchanged harsh words when you left Mihangel, but I've missed you. What is going on there? What have you gotten yourself into?" she pressed.

I only just avoided furrowing my brow in confusion. "A vampire nest decided they wanted me, although we never found out why. It's not a problem though. We just returned from eliminating the nest," I sighed. She probably already knew something, if she was asking. *How* did she know, though?

"*We* eliminated a whole vampire nest? Did you make friends with an army?" she asked, not even trying to suppress her laugh.

"No, it only took the three of us," I said defensively. I had been helpful out there. They wouldn't have made it through the forest nearly as quickly without me there to communicate with the trees and bushes.

"Who have you gotten yourself involved with Mihangel? They sound like valuable allies..." she trailed off thoughtfully. Thankfully, I knew Adelola and Monife wouldn't fall prey to my mother's machinations. They were too smart and too powerful.

"It's primarily one of them. She came into the place I was working—,"

"Working like a human," my mother interrupted. The disgust was clear on her face.

Ellyllon worked and lived on the land. We could obtain everything we needed through our magickal bond with nature. It wasn't until I was older that I found out most ellyllon families didn't look down on humans the way my family did.

"Yes, Mother, I had bills to pay," was my only response before I continued. "She came into the place I was working and actually saved me from the first vampires that were sent after me." No need to tell her about Arabell.

"She killed vampires, as in more than one?" she probed.

"I took out one too," I pointed out.

"Who is this woman?"

"She's a blessed one. Do you know about them?"

"Of course I do, son. They're not common, but can be quite valuable allies, as you've learned," she said.

"Why did you never tell us about them?" I asked.

"As I said, they are not common. I've never met one myself actually. How was I to know that one day you'd get yourself tangled up with one?" she quipped back.

"It's more like she's tangled up with me," I muttered, but she heard anyway.

"Are you saying she wants to help you? When you have so little to offer? Why?" she asked flippantly, but I couldn't believe she hadn't aimed that barb intentionally.

Unfortunately, two decades hadn't lessened the sting of her words.

"It might be hard to believe Mother, but she likes me. She *wanted* to help me."

"Ah," she smirked, "But in exchange for what Mihangel? In exchange for what?" She punctuated each word by smacking the back of her hand into the palm of the other when she repeated herself.

"For nothing, as far as I know. What I do know is that she's continued to help me, even after I bound her magick, for whatever the binding is worth," I responded, with a small eye roll.

"Wait," she held up her hand. "You bound a blessed one's magick, and she continued helping you anyway? And what do you mean, 'whatever the binding is worth' my son? Is there something wrong with your power?" The way she asked it made it sound like if there was, she was sure it was my fault. I could feel myself spiraling into the self-hate I used to wallow in before I left. I could feel it, but couldn't stop it.

"I don't think so! It feels normal. But I completely restricted her power, and she still ripped a vampire's head off with some type of golden magick I don't think she wielded before," I rushed to explain. "Maybe there's a type of magick our family ability doesn't work on."

"Impossible...," she paused and stared off to the side, finger tapping her chin. "Mihangel, my son, would you say you're attracted to her?"

"Well, yes," I replied awkwardly, surprised at her sudden change of subject.

"And she to you? Ah, nevermind, the answer to that is all over your face."

I felt the tips of my ears warm as I remembered just how *attracted* we were to each other.

"Have you considered.... that she could be your mate?" I could practically see her calculating ways to use this to the family's benefit. To *her* benefit.

But my mind stopped processing my mother's words after she said "mate." My mate? Could Adelola be my mate? I never considered it because...

"Wait," I interrupted her, "Adelola isn't ellyll. Before she was blessed, I'm pretty sure she was just human."

"She may just have a touch of cymreig in her. But my... father wasn't ellyll either Mihangel, it's not a requirement. Just a preference," she said. Her preference. I never understood how she could love Abuelo Miguel the way she did, but still abhor our human blood so much.

"Shouldn't the mate bond have just snapped into place?" I nearly yelled.

My mother placed her hand on her chest and drew back, shocked at my emotion. "Well, your magic has always been... low. Perhaps that has prevented it from being instantaneous. But Mihangel, if she is your mate, then the golden magick she drew on was *yours*."

"No. She was too strong." I shook my head in denial.

"Well, if she isn't your mate, then I don't know how to explain it. But my son, you're still in danger. The vampire nest you destroyed was working on behalf of one of the sitting members of the North American Vampire Convocation Council."

My blood stilled. The vampires' method of governance was somewhat of a democratic government... until you got to the very top. The Convocation Councils are made of powerful vampires whose job is to govern over their respective continents.

"Do you know which one?" My heart was hammering in my chest.

"No. But it doesn't matter. They could send hundreds, if not thousands, of vampires after you, Mihangel. You can't let your power fall into their hands. You need to come home. The family will protect you. We can keep you safe, like we always have."

I was safe, but unloved. But if I'm so weak I could bind my mate without knowing who she was... maybe I didn't deserve love. I didn't deserve the sense of peace her presence grants me nor the desire she ignited in me.

But I was done not trusting Adelola. Maybe trusting her would be the end of me, but maybe Delilah's words just referred to the mate bond I couldn't sense.

"Mother, I have to talk to her first. I will let you know what I decide to do," I finally said firmly.

"My son, she can't keep you safe by herself! Please, just listen......" her words trailed off as I rushed from my room. Above all else, I had to release Adelola's magick. To do that, I needed to look into her eyes.

I checked her room, and then the living room. I found Monife in the kitchen, eating a strawberry.

"What are you rushing around in my house for little ellyll?" she asked boredly.

"Where is Adelola?" I responded quickly. "I need to talk to her right now."

"She left."

"Left? Where did she go after blowing up a vampire nest?" I asked, dumbfounded.

Monife let out a dark laugh. "She wanted to talk to you, thinking you'd feel safe enough to remove the binding on her magick after she risked her life for you, sneaking into a vampire nest with one arm tied behind her back. But what did you do? Rushed to your room like she had the plague. She just needs some air. She'll be back from the city soon. Don't fuck up again." Then she chuckled and shook her head.

"You have to get her back here, now! The danger isn't over. I just spoke to my mother, and a member of the Convocation Council is the one who wants me. Not just a low level vampire nest," I told her urgently.

"You've got to be fucking kidding me! I *knew* I should have killed you. I *knew* it! But noooo, I let Adelola's puppy dog eyes make me go against orisha-damned common sense. Fuck me. But fuck you if you think this is going to get you out of releasing her magick fairy boy." She started advancing on me threateningly.

I put my hands up pleadingly. "No, I was going to release it right now. I... think she's my mate," I blurted out, which stopped her in her tracks.

"Mate? Like your fated mate? Love of your life?" she asked slowly. "Blessed ones don't have fated mates."

"But ellyllon do. Only one side needs to be ellyll, but both sides will feel it. It's likely why she's so protective of me. But that's secondary. Call her. We need to get her back here."

But Monife shook her head, her eyes wide with fear, something I had yet to see on her face.

"She left it here, which isn't uncommon. She's usually the baddest thing on the streets, except..."

Horror wracked my body. "Except she can't fully access her magick."

I had felt a lot of self-hate, but never more than at the moment I realized I left my fate-granted mate vulnerable to *my* enemies.

CHAPTER 15
Adelola

I had left my car parked in the parking lot near this small park's entrance. A walk in the forest surrounding our house might have worked, but I needed physical distance... as well as air. I liked visiting this park, watching the parents with their kids and the people walking their dogs. There was no one here now though. It was well into the evening by the time we got back from our mission.

Michael rushing away from me hurt more than I'd like to admit. He rushed away knowing what I wanted to ask him. Does he still not trust me after all we've been through? After all I've done? I wanted him before all of this, and I wanted him even more now. How can he not see it?

I looked up at the sky, peering at the few stars I could see through the trees and with the city's light pollution, and let out a sigh.

"Why so sad, pretty lady?" a masculine voice said as something blurred past me on my right. I immediately dropped into a defensive stance.

"Who's there?" I barked.

"Why so serious?" another masculine voice hissed from behind me on my left. I summoned my dagger, its weight comfortably settling in my hand. I didn't have enough of my power to sense the beings around me or they wouldn't have been able to sneak up on me.

Suddenly, there was a woman in front of me, smirking. "Forgive him. He's an irritating movie buff."

"Yeah? And who are you?" I asked snidely.

"You might say..." she trailed off. Then she smiled, revealing her fangs. Vampires.

"That we're acquaintances of someone who's dying to meet you," finished the first masculine voice from behind me. I whirled around and backed up, trying to keep both of them in view. I held the dagger in front of me and summoned a second one into my other hand, ready to go in either direction.

The woman looked picture perfect, like she just finished taking her social media pictures for the week. Her straight brown hair had streaks of red in it, paling her light skin even further in this light. Her partner had long wavy black hair that hung past his pectorals, and light brown skin. They both had silver eyes, born vampires.

Fuck, that would be a problem. Born vampires were stronger than turned. And these two had the confidence that comes with age. Knowing you had strength.

"So, if he's so irritating, why do you keep him around?" I asked, trying to buy myself time to locate him. My eyes roved the trees' dark shadows.

"Oh, he has his uses," the femme vampire said just as I felt arms circle my middle and yank me backwards. Shit, I thought there'd be more talking. I stabbed into his body multiple times and even jabbed at his face. But nothing stopped us from being swallowed up by the portal he opened. Even my howl of rage couldn't make it out.

How did they know to target me?

About the Author

Ruthie is an Army Veteran and former translator from Southern California who now calls Central Maryland her home. If she's not in her soundbooth or writing, you can find her hiking in the trails near her house, playing with her kids, or (of course), reading a book.

While book reading is her top hobby, she also gardens, homesteads, and loves virtual reality. Ruthie's heritage has made her very devoted to bringing books written by authors from marginalized communities to life through audio. It's also the onus behind her desire to write inclusive stories that reflect not just the world she lives in, but also the ancestors who had to come together to create space for "Ruthie" to exist at all.

Stay up to date with all of Ruthie's projects here:
https://linktr.ee/ruthe.narrates.books

SPELLS FOR ETERNAL BLISS

Spells for Eternal Bliss

PRISCILLA ROSE

Heat level:
Hot

Content Warnings:
Consensual sex, profanity, attempted groping (not by the love interest), reference to named character's previous SA (vague; off page), slight mentions of misogyny and homophobia, and violence.

TERRA

North Terra — Winterhurst

East Terra

Mid Terra — Medio, Clearwater Cove, Vero Village, Gretchester Woods, Reditus Castle

South Terra

West Terra

Desert Isles

Chapter One

Sera had spent the last three months preparing for her aunt and uncle's departure, and yet now that the time had come, she found herself uneasy. The Duke and Duchess of Vero were the only family she had left. Primrose, her cousin and other half, abandoned this realm for another. Queen Lilith of Mid-Terra requested the Reditus Family join her court at the capital to strengthen her appearance as she goes into arbitration with the northern queen, leaving Sera the new Duchess of Vero. Sera didn't know how to rule, and she especially didn't know how to live without Primrose by her side, but she was determined to try.

There was a ringing sound outside her window, and Sera scrambled out of bed to find the source. Opening the curtains, she looked below to see Lady Sharp putting down a tray of food on the table that stood in the garden. As the head handmaiden moved back inside, Sera spotted a small silver bell hanging from one of her hands.

Sera picked a plain, canary yellow chemise to wear to breakfast. It flattered the ample curves of her chest. Walking down the ornate halls, she moved gracefully as she crossed the threshold to the garden. In the center of the palace, the royal garden was full of lavish flowers and a large willow tree. Wide hips swished towards the metal table set and Sera sat down, placing a napkin in her lap. *I can at least feign that I'm a proper lady.*

"Good morning, duchess," a deep but feminine voice came from the castle.

"Dame Tanaka, it's a pleasure to see you," Sera replied. She had only been duchess for a few weeks, but there were already visitors staying in the castle. This made things especially awkward for the two lovers, as they were unwed. Courting was fine, but sharing a room was not.

Haruka took Sera's fingers between hers and stroked them. "The pleasure is all mine."

"Is anyone else awake?" Sera whispered.

Haruka shook her head. "I don't believe so. Just our staff."

The sides of Sera's mouth quirked up. "I miss you. I miss your warmth, and you brushing my hair when I get out of the shower. Dare I say I even miss your morning breath?"

A hearty laugh left Haruka. She scooped some pudding, making eye contact with Sera as she deviously licked it off the spoon. There was heat in her dark, nearly black eyes.

Sera took a bite of a croissant, desperately trying to ignore the woman making sensuous expressions before her.

"When are those men leaving?" Sera asked through bites.

"The botanist from West-Terra? Or the animal behaviorist from South-Terra?"

"All of them. There's some other sort of scientist here, too. I'm tired of pretending to be something I'm not. I want to show the realm I'm with you." Sera pouted, freckles donning her rounded face.

"We can show them we're together, my flower. We just can't show them we're *sleeping* together. It would be this way if I were a man, too," Haruka reminded her.

Sera shrugged, taking in the muscular arms of Haruka's figure. They had mostly seen Haruka clad in metal armor as of late, showcasing her role to this dukedom, as guard. Sera was happy to see the woman's cut figure and feminine hips. It made her smile as much as it made her ache with desire.

"Here." Haruka stood and gestured a hand out to Sera. "Follow me."

Sera rose and took her lover's hand, walking with her towards the willow tree. Haruka donned a black tunic and olive-green trousers. The top was sheer and cut deep, showcasing some of her chest. It was just-decent-enough to be in the gardens, but not as modest for others to see. She had rolled up her sleeves, and Sera was sure the woman knew exactly what she was doing by that.

The usually vibrant green leaves of the willow tree had turned a bright orange, lighting up the surrounding space like fire. The lovers crept towards where it billowed down, hand in hand, and made their way underneath the cover.

Haruka grabbed Sera by the waist, pulling her in and planting her lips on hers in one swift motion. Sera gasped against Haruka's mouth. Sera's hands moved up to grasp at Haruka's shoulders and collarbones, reveling in their closeness. She was unsure if they were completely hidden, but she didn't care as their tongues danced against one another. This woman was giving Sera all her warmth, and yet she couldn't help desiring more. *Needing* more. It was cold under the willow tree, the billowing branches concealing the space from the sun. Still, Sera was surrounded by heat. In her mouth, around her waist, against her chest, and even coiling up below her belly.

Pushing Haruka against the trunk of the tree, Sera reached down, hands moving inside the waistband of Haruka's trousers.

"Let me give you what you want," she whispered, voice full of seduction.

"Duchess, I have a word about the crops," a man's voice rang from the other side of the garden. *Nothing could have ruined this moment more for me than a man*, Sera thought.

Pulling apart from one another, Sera made her way out from under the tree. "Lord Estrada, have you made a new discovery?"

"Yes, Your Grace. I believe your farmers have unknowingly chosen the wrong crops for Mid-Terra. Rice, sugarcane, these are crops that grow best in East-Terra and should be imported. We need to focus on growing roots, cabbage, lettuce, among other things. I've also brought some fruit tree seeds from my continent. You should plant them when winter ends." The man's light brown arms were carrying a small carton full of little paper bags. "I have labeled everything." He handed the box to Sera.

"Thank you. I deeply appreciate this." Though she was frustrated by the interruption, she was happy with the results. "What shall we do in the meantime? It's nearly winter."

"There *are* crops that do fine in winter. Kale, spinach, leeks. We can have your farmers grow them while we wait for spring," he replied.

A rustling came from under the willow tree, and Lord Estrada looked towards it.

"Must be a critter playing," she swiftly said.

"Must be," he said with an air of disbelief.

Later that same day, Sera and Haruka had a meeting scheduled with the scientists before they departed for their respective continents. The duchess chose to don a green gown to match her eyes, with sleeves that puffed at the shoulders before billowing down. The vibrant red strands of her hair cascaded onto her back, with the exception of two braided sections in the front. Though she didn't feel like a duchess, she appeared before them as one.

In contrast, there was nothing feminine or regal about Haruka's clothing. She had on full upper-body armor, with a green surcoat coming out from underneath the breastplate. Sera wondered if it was out of jealousy or pride that Haruka chose to match her. Either way, it delighted her. They were a united front.

The two women sat on one side of a long, rectangular table as they waited for Lady Sharp to escort the scientists in.

"Nice to see you again, duchess," Lord Estrada said, glancing over at Haruka. Sera nodded.

The three men sat down, and Lord Musa reached a hand towards Haruka, and they shook as he said, "Dame Tanaka, we haven't had much time to converse."

The men stayed in the Reditus Castle, but they spent most of their time out in fields with local farmers, as well as much time in Vero Village. Sera was grateful for the nights they spent at the Inn, though it had never lined up to where all three men were out on the same night. She appreciated their help, but she'd be glad when they were gone. There hadn't been this many visitors in the castle since she and Primrose were young teenagers. A tragic incident had left her aunt and uncle guarded, and with good reason, but she was happy to open the gates to the realm once more. The last two visitors they'd had were Lord Mercer, a perverted merchant, and Protego, the love of Prim's life. This was definitely a clear shift for the dukedom. *I can't believe the duke and duchess had never thought to invite professionals to come help save the land.*

"No, we have not," Haruka replied, jolting Sera from her thoughts.

Sera eyed the third man, who struck her as strange. Lord Orwell. He had white-blonde hair and ocean-blue eyes. She couldn't recall exchanging letters with him, much less inviting him here, but he showed up at the same time as the others, so she disregarded it as her own forgetfulness. Now that he stood before her, she was questioning whether or not she should have paid him more mind.

Lord Orwell smiled, a wicked grin of sorts, and an uneasy feeling flooded Sera's chest.

"Well, I'll go first, if that's alright with all of you," Lord Estrada began. Everyone nodded in response. "I have found a solution for the crop issue, and have provided the duchess with many resources to help in the meantime. Vero Village should be rich with food once more, and the people won't have to import as many crops."

"That is fantastic," Haruka replied. "Lord Musa?"

He shook his head, eyes weary. "I do not bear such good news. To be honest, the situation with the animals is dire. They aren't breeding, and they're dying off. There aren't many sheep, and there are only four cows left. I am embarrassed to say I made no progress during my time here."

"That's disappointing to hear." Haruka frowned.

Sera rose and made to shake hands with Lord Estrada and Lord Musa. "Thank you both for your time and efforts here, it is greatly appreciated."

She looked at Haruka, whose brows were furrowed, and winked. *Play along, my love.*

The two men said their thanks and exited the meeting room, leaving the two women alone with Lord Orwell.

"I didn't want to confront you in front of the others, but who are you?" Sera asked boldly.

The man's body shifted. His tall, muscular figure changed into a thin, boyish frame. The pale white of skin became a deep brown, and the white-blonde strands of his hair turned short and black, cut close to his head. Within a blink of an eye, he was a child.

"Who are you?" Haruka asked, unsure of whether or not to be afraid. Sera and Haruka had always been fond of children, but after their last experience with the sluagh, they were less inclined to blindly believe all children were... human. This child appeared very human indeed.

The boy let out a small giggle. "Kojo. I'm related to Abeni Umar. I figured if I disguised myself as a North-Terran scientist, I'd fit right in without risking Lord Musa recognizing me. He's friends with Abeni."

"Abeni... that's the sorceress Lord Zuberi is engaged to marry. Are you her son?" Sera asked.

"No, well... no. She's my older sister and caretaker." He was eleven, twelve at most.

Sera's head cocked to one side. "I hate to ask, but where are your parents?"

"They died in a shipwreck," he said, very matter-of-factly. *How odd.*

"As did mine. That's quite peculiar," she replied.

Haruka looked at them both with empathetic eyes. "If it's any consolation, my parents are both alive, but they're the worst."

"That doesn't make me feel better. I wish pain upon no one," Sera said. There was a brief moment of silence between the three of them.

Kojo stood, dancing around joyously in his now too-big clothing. "Can I tell you both an interesting fact?" He was an adorable child, with a wide nose and an even wider smile.

"Of course," Sera said. She was delighted to see such a youthful, joyous face.

"Every sorcerer and sorceress have mysterious circumstances that occur to their bloodline. A shipwreck, or other weird accident takes their parents or grandparents. Abeni believes it's because a magical entity interrupts the family tree," Kojo said quickly. He was full of energy.

"So Primrose interrupted my family tree, displacing my parents and I," Sera replied.

Haruka stood and gently reached for the child's hand, stooping down to meet his height. "Do you know if the magical entity in your family is still here? We had an angel and a djinn here not long ago, but they've left the realm," she said.

"No idea. Though I theorize it's a cousin of ours," he answered. "What do you need?"

Sera stood, moving over towards them. "We need help breeding our animals, as well as finding ore."

"That's easy! You're speaking to the second greatest sorcerer in all of South-Terra, don't you know?"

Sera let out a hardy laugh, bowing before the child. "We were not aware. Who is the best?"

"Abeni, obviously."

Haruka smiled, and Sera could see the tension ease in her body. "What've you got for us?"

"I brought a book with me. It's in my suitcase. Akil said I could let you two borrow it, but that you were both to be careful. It has brighter magic than the book you used in the past," Kojo informed them.

"Wait, if Lord Zuberi knows you're here, why didn't you just come as you are?" Sera asked.

Kojo smiled. "Then I would've spent the last few weeks with Lord Musa as a babysitter. What's the fun in that?"

Sera and Haruka stood in the hallway outside Kojo's guest chambers. They waited, with only the sounds of him digging through his bags to fill the space.

"Aha!" Kojo's voice came from inside the room.

Opening the door, Kojo stepped through the doorway and handed a book to Sera. "This is what you need. You are a sorceress, correct?"

"I am, but I've only just recently discovered my powers. I'm not positive I'm the best person to complete these spells," she replied.

"Nonsense. The best way to learn is to try, that's what Abeni always tells me," he said in earnest.

Sera shrugged her shoulders. "I want to try, but not at my people's expense. I don't want a repeat of what happened earlier this year."

Haruka's breath audibly hitched.

Kojo scratched his tiny chin. "Akil told me about it. Your cousin cursed the whole continent, right? That won't happen here. This is bright magic we're working with. It can't do much harm."

"Can you help me?"

"Negative." He shook his head. "I was told I can shapeshift, give you this book, and in absolute emergencies perform unbinding spells. Other than that, I am to explore and observe this continent peacefully and without much mischief. I believe that is word for word my sister's instructions."

"You're somehow extremely helpful and incredibly useless," Haruka said, causing Sera to gasp.

"Haruka, that was quite rude," Sera responded.

"She's right, though," Kojo said. "But Abeni knows best. Anyway, I will be staying at The Inn for the next few weeks. Come find me if you need anything."

Kojo bowed before crossing back through the doorway.

"What's our plan now, my love?" Haruka asked, rubbing Sera's upper arm.

"The scientists are leaving today. We should go visit Vero Village and form a council. A group of men and women in charge of different economicals sectors. Maybe our villagers can help one another in ways they didn't know?"

Haruka smiled. "You're a brilliant woman; I hope you know that."

Chapter Two

Upon arriving in Vero Village, Sera was both delighted and anguished by the sights she saw. There were many shops and merchants to buy things from, but everyone she spoke to expressed a struggle to make ends meet. Delicious baked goods and beautifully woven bags did well for tourists during the spring and summer season, but in fall and winter the shopkeepers were left depending on the villagers of Vero, who could not afford such luxuries.

Unlike her cousin Primrose, Sera was not raised to be a duchess. She didn't know the ins-and-outs of an economical structure, nor did she fully understand things like taxes. Sera was primed to be a maid, a servant to the royal court. She could cook and clean, and make the realm's best tea, but that was where her skills ended. Haruka was skilled in battle and strategy. This would be excellent if they ever went to war or if someone needed protecting, but it didn't help Vero now. Vero Village needed a strong leader or a quick solution, and Sera wasn't sure how she'd provide it. Though she wasn't skilled in ruling, she was smart enough to ask for help.

As the two entered the bakery, Sera smiled at Lisette, whose dark brown hair was tied back by a periwinkle-colored bandana with little flowers on it. She wore a matching chemise topped with a white apron. It reminded Sera of the outfits she used to wear to tend to the castle. Though it hadn't been very long since, it felt like ages ago.

"Hello there, Your Grace," the woman said with a white smile. Her skin was fair like Sera's, but free of freckles.

"It's so nice to see you. I'll have to have some dessert before we return to the estate," she replied.

Haruka, decked in nearly full-body armor, was silently standing next to the door, as if preparing for an attack. *It's cute how protective she is, but surely Lisette finds it strange.*

A little boy came out from behind the counter, with similar features to Lisette.

"Lady," he said in a cute, high-pitched voice.

"Yes?" Sera asked, amused.

He tugged on his mom's apron. "Can I ask?"

She nodded.

"When will Lady Primrose return?"

Sera felt her heart drop in her chest. She looked at Haruka, whose eyes flashed wide back at her. Sera had told her aunt and uncle that Primrose ran away with Protego to the Desert Isles. Though she had prepared the story well, she wasn't aware she'd ever have to clarify anything to the citizens. The Reditus family was not welcome by everyone in Vero, so Sera did not expect many to care about their departure, or about Sera's new role as duchess. Her coronation was held in private, and though she was working hard to improve the situation, few seemed grateful. Sera knew this was temporary, and that she needed to earn their trust, but it still hurt.

Sera crouched down to the boy's level and smiled. "Lady Primrose and her... husband went away to live where he's from. I don't know if or when she'll return, but please know that she's very happy."

He gave a small smile. "I will tell my friends. Thank you." He ran out the front door, nearly knocking into Haruka as he left.

Standing tall, Sera looked into Lisette's eyes. "Would you be a part of the Vero Council?"

"What would that entail?"

"Essentially, we would have meetings once or twice a season to ensure everyone's needs are being met, and to see how we can help one another. Ideally, I'd like to have a baker, butcher, shopkeeper, Lord Tobin, a farmer, and a few others join the council. You'll represent your profession," she informed the woman.

"Yes. That would be wonderful. When should we have the first meeting?"

"How about in a fortnight?" Sera looked over at Haruka, who nodded a confirmation. *It's all coming together.*

"Works for me!"

Crossing the threshold of the bakery door, Sera and Haruka made their way towards the center of Vero Village, where children danced around a maypole that had newly been put up in celebration of Sera's ascension. The queen had paid to have it done as a gift, and Sera was glad someone enjoyed it, though she'd rather the funds have gone directly into her people's pockets.

Around the maypole were two little girls with light brown braided hair and freckled faces, twirling around. They were tanner than Lisette's son, who danced alongside them. A few other children danced around with them, all clearly descending from different places. It reminded Sera of how Mid-Terra was such a conglomerate of all the continents, and she was happy her dukedom was here, in this magical place… she just needed to help her people. The other villages in Mid-Terra were rich in culture, and in wealth, so she knew it was possible to get there.

A little boy with deep brown skin joined the other dancers, swift on his feet as he shifted, pretending to be the other children.

"Ben?" a girl called out before Kojo transformed back into himself.

"Whoa!" another girl said, mesmerized by Kojo's magic.

He transformed into Lord Musa and scooped Lisette's son, who Sera now knew was called Ben, and tossed him into the air before catching him. Kojo put him down and shifted into Akil Zuberi, and Sera's heart grew in her chest as she stared at the familiar face, whom she missed so much.

"Transform back," Haruka said, sounding hurt. *She must miss Akil as much as I do.*

Kojo giggled, his true form revealed once more. "I'm really good, aren't I?"

"You are!" Sera smiled. "How are your clothes changing now?"

"I've been practicing a lot! Now I can shift the material alongside my biological structures. It takes some extra thinking, but it's not too hard." *Wow.*

"I'm impressed. By the way, who are those two girls, the sisters?" Sera asked.

Kojo looked back at the children still dancing around the maypole. "The ones with hazel eyes?"

She nodded.

"Those are Laurel and Jules," he said. "Daughters of Alexander Tobin... he owns The Inn, the local inn."

"I know Lord Tobin, he's a very generous man. He's always treated my family well," Sera replied. "Is he still here?"

"Yes, I saw him somewhere. Maybe try the farmer's market?" Kojo suggested.

"Thank you."

Sera walked the cobblestone and dirt streets of Vero, making her way with Haruka to the farmer's market, where local farmers sold their produce. Or at least, what little produce they had.

A man gawked at Sera as they walked by, and she became acutely aware of how desirable she was. She was curvy, with thicker thighs, a round belly, and a larger arse. In the safety of the castle, no one batted an eye. Here, however, it was strange. She felt objectified. Still, she smiled at the man, afraid of appearing impolite.

The man reached a hand towards Sera's behind before it was knocked back by the side of Haruka's blade. *He's lucky she's talented enough not to slice him.*

"What in the fuck do you think you're doing?" Haruka asked, face seething with rage.

"She was smiling at me, I thought she might be interested in what I have to offer," he said, spitting at the ground. He was older than them both, likely in his thirties. His hair was a white-blonde, similar to the man Kojo feigned to be. But unlike *Lord Orwell*, this man was not an innocent child. This man seemed anything but innocent.

"She isn't interested," Haruka bit out.

He laughed, seemingly unbothered by her rage. "She seemed amused, joyous even."

"She wasn't."

"And how are you so sure?"

Sera stood there, completely stunned at the coldness of this interaction. On one hand, this man's behavior felt predatory. On the other hand, Haruka's actions could lead to consequences. She didn't want the village to hate her guard, or potential consort.

Haruka flicked her sword up in one swift motion, and it rested just underneath the man's chin. "Because if the duchess is happy, I am happy. If she feels fine, I feel fine. But if she is upset or uncomfortable? You should start running."

He raised both arms as a sign of truce. "My apologies, Your Grace, I didn't mean to offend or cause discomfort. I shall go." He backed away, quickly darting the other direction.

"That's what I fucking thought."

"Are you okay?" Sera asked, brows furrowed.

"Are *you* okay, my flower?"

Sera nodded. "I'm fine, really. He's just a pervert; I don't want you to get so worked up."

"The reason I'm even here is because of what happened to Primrose. I'm sorry if I overreacted, but I can't have something like that happen to you," she said, pure empathy in her gaze.

"I understand. Thank you," Sera replied. "Let's go talk with Lord Tobin."

The two continued down the path, now arm-in-arm, as they walked to the butcher shop. Inside, Lord Tobin and Lord Al-Azmi were speaking about the lack of goat and lamb in the area.

"I prefer lamb, but we have more goats available... though we need to be careful, I'm going to have to start rationing the meat," Lord Al-Azmi said.

"Hello," Sera said, and the two men smiled.

"Haruka, it's been a while." The butcher looked at the sword sheathed in her hilt. "I could put you to work with that thing. Teasing, of course. I'm sure it's not sanitary."

"Very funny," Haruka said.

"Lord Tobin, I just saw your daughters. They're both lovely." Sera's grin grew even wider.

He nodded. "I think they made a new friend, too."

"What brings you here?" she asked.

He moved his wheelchair in a circle, showcasing colorful ribbons that were tied into bows on the back section. "Oh, you know, the girls thought I needed a makeover."

Everyone laughed. He had a thick beard and a deep, burly voice, which made it extra wonderful to see him embrace his girls' fun antics.

"I needed to do some stocking up on supplies anyhow," he admitted. "What are you doing here, duchess?"

"I have a question for you. Well, actually, it's for both of you." Sera glanced at both men. "I would like to extend an offer... would you both like to be a part of the Vero Council? You'd be representing your... sector? Your...." Sera trailed off, unable to word things how she wished.

"You'll be a representative for your job's contribution to our society. Obviously, for some, you're only representing yourself, and for others there are more than one of you, but Sera has chosen you both," Haruka chimed in.

"Thank you. Precisely what Dame Tanaka said," Sera replied.

"Of course, I will represent all of the wonderful inns available to stay in," Lord Tobin said, pink meeting his cheeks.

"You're so funny. The Inn is the *only* inn we'll ever accept here." Sera looked over at the other lord, who nodded.

"Yes. When are we meeting?"

Sera felt giddy with joy and said, "In a fortnight."

Chapter Three

Sera had spent the last few days since arriving back from Vero Village in the library, attempting new spells with the bright magic book. They had given seeds and advice to the farmers, which would help both agriculture and their local seamstress, but animal breeding and finding good ore was another issue entirely. In the book, Kojo had bookmarked a page containing a location spell. Having successfully completed it, Haruka was out near the edge of the continent, using her sword to find ore. Sera was hopeful they would be able to tell the miners and blacksmith about its location, so that at least could provide *some* good news during the very first council meeting.

With the two goats that Lord Al-Azmi provided, Sera was able to go outside and test a love potion of sorts.

"Affigere vosmetipsos in caritate," she said, making sprinkling motions with her fingers at the two creatures. The goats made obnoxious noises as she stood there, yelling spells at them.

"Teipsum mihi adiunge," she said, feeling strong arms wrap around her from behind. "In amore." The last two words formed naturally, not having been read off the page, and Sera dropped the book.

Haruka bent over to pick up the book, handing it to Sera. "I'm going to head in and shower, but I did find some promising rocks out there. The sword dinged and everything, like you said it would. Any word on the animal breeding?"

"Nope." Sera pouted.

"I'm sorry." Haruka kissed her forehead before heading for the inside of the castle.

Within a second, the two women were catapulted into one another, an invisible force dragging their bodies back together.

"Did you just run into me? It felt like I'd been pulled backwards," Haruka said.

Sera shook her head. "No, I didn't move. Something... moved me."

"That doesn't make any sense."

"You're right. It doesn't make any sense at all. Here, walk backward and look at me as you walk away."

Haruka had gotten hardly a few steps away before their bodies were slammed into one another's once more.

"The fuck is happening?" Haruka asked, looking towards the sky. "Did we sin too much and piss off The Committee?"

"I don't think this was caused by a deity," Sera confessed. "I think this is my fault."

Haruka's brows furrowed, and she crossed her arms, elbow still in contact with Sera. "How so?"

"I misspoke the spell when you touched me. I'm not blaming you, but it distracted me, and...."

"You're teasing... you sound like Primrose, now." Haruka looked at her with disbelief.

Sera scrunched her mouth up, embarrassed. "No. I'm almost confident this was me."

"Shit. Well, we can fix this... we can totally fix this. Let's head inside, we'll devise a plan together."

"Okay."

"There are worse things to be, my flower." Haruka smiled. "Many worse things to be than stuck to me, I can assure you."

The two young women walked while holding hands, giggling over the mess that was their situation.

"How ironic. I'm physically attached to the most beautiful woman in all the realm," Haruka said. "My body literally can't stand to be away from you."

"Oh, stop. Now you're just being silly."

Haruka stopped in her tracks. "What if this isn't a spell at all? What if I'm so attracted to you I manifested a physical bond between us?"

"You're not a sorceress, Haruka. It would've been me that manifested the bond," Sera laughed.

"Wow. I'm that appealing to you, eh?"

Sera could feel her face flush a bright red as they continued down a corridor to her bed chambers. "Yes, now shut up," she whispered.

"THE ROYAL DUCHESS–" Haruka yelled before Sera's hand came over her mouth, muffling the sound.

"Shut the fuck up, Haruka." She lowered her hand off Haruka's mouth, steam practically radiating from out of her ears.

"Put something on my mouth, and I will," Haruka winked and her words made Sera weak in the knees.

Sera wobbled the doorknob to her chambers open with one hand, the other hand still intertwined with Haruka's. She closed the door, and Haruka turned her so they were facing each other, their lips colliding as Haruka stripped off her armor.

"I thought you were going to shower," Sera whispered between kisses.

"Later. I have more important matters to attend to."

They kissed with a fervor that Sera hadn't felt in a long time. It was somewhere between love and desperation. Once Haruka's armor had clanked against the floor, and she was only wearing her pants and surcoat, she pushed Sera onto the bed and spread her legs. As hands moved up Sera's thighs and teeth bit at her undergarments, she felt that rush of heat and desire reach her once more.

"You have the prettiest pussy," Haruka said, kissing up Sera's inner thigh. Haruka used her tongue to lick around Sera's opening, teasing her with every movement. Sera's legs shook with anticipation, before Haruka dove in for the kill.

Tongue lapping against Sera's most sensitive parts, she moaned out in pleasure. Haruka's tongue moved in languid motions as her fingers caressed Sera's thighs. Haruka used one hand to spread Sera's lips, and the other to gently move one finger inside her... ever so slowly. Once it was all the way in, she hooked it upwards, and Sera gasped.

"Fuck. Haruka, fucking Aeternus," she called out.

Haruka continued circling Sera's clit with her tongue while lightly pumping the finger inside her. Sera felt her pleasure building, and she teetered the edge as Haruka made slow, generous motions.

Haruka abruptly stopped, causing Sera to whimper.

"You're so soft. So wet," Haruka cooed. Sera could feel her warm breath against her opening, and it made her shiver. She wanted more, needed to finish.

"Please."

"I'll give you what you want, my flower."

Haruka put another finger in her, filling her, and Sera could feel herself widen at the touch. She was wet, likely dripping, as Haruka practically devoured her. Sera was full of love. This gorgeous, intelligent woman was practically worshiping her body, determined to please.

Tongue moving in swift circles, Sera built until she couldn't help but squirm, shaking with release as she moaned out. Letting go of Sera's legs, Haruka climbed up to face her.

"You didn't even let me take off my dress," Sera let out a soft laugh.

Haruka shrugged before kissing Sera on the forehead and wrapping one arm around her, nuzzling into Sera's shoulder.

"Tired," Haruka sighed.

"Good night, my love. We'll figure out this spell in the morning," Sera said before closing her eyes, drifting into the darkness.

Sera and Haruka had spent the better part of half a week trying to untangle the spell that bound them together. They had no such luck. Sera was ashamed to go ask Kojo for help, and Haruka was not going to force her to.

"What is your plan for the council meeting?" Haruka asked, breaking the silence at breakfast one morning. When they weren't trying to undo the spell, they were in each other's beds, and Sera couldn't help but blush every time they spoke, unsure of what filthy thing Haruka would say next.

"You were planning to attend, correct?"

Haruka nodded. "Of course."

"Then we'll just attend... close to one another." Sera was paler and redder than Haruka, and she could feel herself becoming a tomato as she shared her awful plan.

"Everyone's going to be suspicious."

Sera shrugged, the two playing footsies under the table to avoid being slammed. "We can just act a little bit more... romantic than we do in public? Feign that we're just so in love we can't keep our hands off each other."

"It's not feigning, I really am that in love with you... I'm just an adult, as are you. We don't need to act like giddy teenagers to show the realm we're together."

"I agree," Sera said. "But in this case, we can act that way so they don't become aware of the spell... situation."

"Then yes, we can do that. I'm going to be extra dramatic, though."

Sera rolled her eyes. "Of course you are," she said before taking a bite out of a waffle. Haruka stole the rest of it, causing both women to laugh.

"Can we go search for more ore? It'll be quick," Haruka suggested.

"That's fine. Will you go prepare Drusilla?"

Haruka scrunched her nose. "Really?"

"I forgot," Sera said. "Let's go get dressed and prepare the horse."

After both women donned trousers and brown long sleeve tunics, they made their way out the gates of the Reditus manor on horseback. Drusilla, their trusty mare, was tall and midnight black, with a shiny mane. As they galloped towards the nearest beach, making their way towards the ocean, Haruka's long black hair flew into Sera's face.

"Pth," came a sound from Sera's mouth. "Ever heard of tying your hair back?"

"I could tie it around your wrists," Haruka said.

"That isn't even close to practical." Sera laughed, reveling in teasing her lover.

Haruka looked back. "Okay, you're right. That one wasn't very good."

As they approached the shoreline, the wind picked up, causing both women to shiver. Sera hopped off Drusilla from behind Haruka, ready to help Haruka down, when Haruka's body fell onto her.

"Ow," Sera said.

"That was all you."

"I know, I know." The two women stood, heading towards what looked like a cave system when snow fell from the sky.

"Shit, we're aways from the castle," Haruka announced. "I don't have a coat on me."

"It's okay, let's keep looking."

Haruka shook her head, pulling Sera back towards the horse. "Absolutely not, we're heading back home."

Jumping back up, Haruka kicked and Drusilla headed full speed back towards the estate. Snow was falling rapidly, and they had to be careful. It became harder and harder to see through the white. Sera's teeth were clattering, and Haruka stripped off her tunic, wearing nothing but her beige stay. Haruka turned back to face her, wrapping the fabric around Sera's head and neck, ensuring her ears were covered.

Sera could feel nothing except the bitter cold. She had never been fond of winter, and with it almost there, she was dreading every moment.

How can I make the animals breed? I've got to figure out something... a love potion, maybe?

Drusilla was fast, and they were back at the Reditus castle before it was too icy to pass. The two jumped off, bringing the dark horse into the stable, and covering her with a blanket.

As they entered the castle, Haruka felt stiff to Sera's touch. She was quiet... too quiet. Sera dragged her into the kitchen, taking a hot kettle off the fire and pouring crushed cacao she'd recently had imported into two mugs.

Once their drinks were ready, they sat on a loveseat in a spare room and drank hot chocolate in front of the fire, nuzzled up under a blanket.

"Thank you," Haruka whispered, tongue moving quickly against her teeth. *Poor thing, now I feel awful. She really gave me her shirt.*

Sera kissed Haruka's cheek.

"Do you love me this much out of true love, or convenience?" Sera said abruptly.

Haruka gawked, sitting up. "What?"

"I'm sorry... I've wondered for a long time."

"We've only just become bound like this, Sera. I've loved you for longer than that."

Sera sat up too, staring into Haruka's dark eyes. "No, that's not what I mean. I mean, when you came here, there was just me and Primrose. We were the only single women around."

"Not women, you were girls. Weren't you both fifteen? Sixteen at most? I had only just turned eighteen myself," Haruka reminded her.

"Still... your options were limited. Do you think you would've fallen for anyone else?" She asked.

Haruka's face was neutral. "There were girls at Vero Village, which I did travel alone to on rare occasions, but I wasn't interested in them. In all honesty, I never sought out love. I came here running from it. My only job was to protect the two of you. But then you kissed me, and it was like the realm opened up, and the skies were a brighter shade of blue."

"I see," Sera responded.

Haruka sighed. "Please tell me you don't feel self conscious, my flower."

Sera shook her head. "No actually, it's more like... curiosity. Do you think our personalities are best matched for one another? Or do you think it's possible there's someone else out there, maybe even someone from your homeland, who is better suited to love you?" *I need to know if I'm ever to ask this girl to marry me.*

Haruka put her mug down on the table and kissed Sera's hand. "No, there is no one else. When you kissed me last year, that was it for me. You're the only person I'd ever accept."

"I feel the same. I am sorry you're stuck to me, though. Physically, I mean." Sera giggled, changing the subject. "Emotionally, I'm not sorry at all."

"I don't feel stuck," Haruka said.

Sera's smile widened. "Really?"

"To touch you–to *be* touched by you... is a privilege I never wish to live without."

Chapter Four

"Remember how Abeni told you that you could use your magic in an emergency?" Sera said to Kojo.

"Not exactly what she said, but sure. I remember."

"It's an emergency." Sera's fingers were interlocked with Haruka's, and the child eyed them suspiciously.

"Are you two stuck together?"

"Not the point. Can you please make these animals breed?" she asked, standing in a fancy blue gown, which was bright in contrast to the rustic wood of the barn they were in front of.

"No, that's super icky," he said. "I don't want to see animals breed."

"Can you close your eyes and do the spell?" Haruka suggested.

"Why can't *Duchess* Sera Reditus, sorceress and overall cool person, perform the spell?" he asked, voice silly with amusement.

Sera wrapped a fur pelt around herself. "Because I can't seem to get it right."

"Where'd you perform the spell?"

"At the castle," the two women said in sync.

"No, no." Kojo waved both hands in the air. "You have to perform it here, where they live. They'll be more comfortable, and it'll probably work better."

"Okay...." Sera tried to regain confidence. "I think it was 'affigere vosmetipsos in caritate,' or something." She flung her hand towards the goats, and their tails wagged. The goats screamed out, louder than they had before.

"Gross," Kojo said in response.

"What?" Haruka asked.

"They're starting. I'm going to go now, good luck with your meeting!"

Sera had a smug look on her face, proud she had more good news to provide the council.

The council members all made their way into a room that had a long table. Lady Murphy, their local seamstress, had generously offered up her space for the meeting.

There was Lady Ruiz, the blacksmith, as well as Lord Nguyen and Lord Kumar, who were both merchants as well as husbands. Lord Tobin followed alongside Lord Al-Azmi, and Lisette followed shortly after. Many faces showed up that Sera didn't recognize, likely invited by Haruka or Lord Sharp, upon request, and Sera was grateful for the extra minds.

"Hello," she started.

"Hello, Your Grace," multiple people replied, nearly at once.

She curtseyed. "I have gathered you all here today because I have good news, and I want to set a precedent that it is up to all of us to help one another thrive."

"Sure, what is your news?" Lady Ruiz asked. She had short dark hair cut at her shoulders, and a large nose. She was strong, though not as muscular as Haruka.

"I hired some professionals to come help, so this was not all my own doing, but the farmers have been provided with seeds and information on what crops will grow here, even in winter."

"That's amazing!" Lord Tobin chimed in. *He's my favorite.*

"Additionally, the animals have begun to breed, so we should no longer be short on meat or wool," she said.

Lady Murphy and Lord Al-Azmi looked at each other and nodded in agreement.

"I have news as well," Haruka announced.

Lord Kumar raised his hand. "Who is this?"

"Apologies, I thought you all knew her," Sera said. "This is Dame Tanaka."

"Is she your consort, or a knight?" Lord Nguyen asked. There was no judgment in his tone, merely curiosity.

"She's important to me, and to this dukedom," Sera said matter-of-factly.

"Sounds good to me," Lord Tobin said.

"Great," Haruka continued. "I have a map." She took a scroll from out of her surcoat and Sera helped her unroll it onto the table. "It provides detailed coordinates on where ore can be found."

"You're amazing," said Lady Ruiz.

"Our economy should improve greatly in the upcoming months," Haruka replied, still holding Sera's hand.

Sera's red hair was tucked behind her ears, and silver swirling earrings dangled from them. Sera wanted to show Lady Ruiz that she appreciated her craftsmanship, and that she had received her gift upon becoming duchess.

"I have also decided to lower everyone's taxes. I was able to do so by cutting spending at the castle, as well as on frivolous things like public celebrations," Sera informed them.

"Are you saying we won't have a festival for Nix Brumal, which is right around the corner?" Lord Nguyen asked.

"Lux Aestiva was so fun. We only have two seasonal celebrations a year, we've already cut down from four. Are you saying we'll have none?" Lord Kumar cut in as well, his long black curls billowing down his chest.

"No, I'm not saying we won't celebrate. I'm saying your taxes won't pay for it. Every year we hire merchants and shopkeepers, many from outside this dukedom, to create things for the festival. This year, it's all by volunteering. No outside workers will be welcome, though of course travelers can celebrate with us," she clarified. "I don't need people profiting off of my village when the people here are struggling to make ends meet."

Everyone made sounds of understanding and agreement. *This is going so well!*

"I think you should make a public speech. If we go and tell the townspeople, they might think it a rumor, but if it comes straight from our duchess, I think they'll believe," Lord Al-Azmi said.

"I agree," said Lord Tobin, cheeks red with cheer.

Oh shit. This is very, incredibly bad.

Haruka squeezed Sera's hand, a silent gesture of support.

Sera began, "I don't think–"

"You must," Lady Ruiz interrupted her. "This is too important, you must tell the village. These are *your* people."

Yikes.

"Alright, I'll do it," she said. *This is going to be a fucking nightmare. Although, I suppose, nothing could go as poorly as when monsters invaded the forest and tried to eat people's souls... it could be worse.*

Standing up on the platform in the center of the village's town square, Sera mentally prepared to give a speech, arm linked with Haruka's. The council had invited as many people as possible to come witness, but it had only been a few hours, and many had previous engagements.

Sera looked out at the crowd, which was a few hundred villagers, and prayed to The Committee for a miracle. A snow storm, a scary lightning strike, anything.

There were many familiar faces staring back at her. Her council members, Kojo, Laurel and Jules, and more. There were just as many faces lacking from the audience. Primrose. Protego. Akil Zuberi. Her aunt and uncle, and even Lord and Lady Sharp were missed. Some of these faces were at home in the castle, but others she wasn't sure she'd ever see again. She felt their absences deeply.

Sera blinked, and she was no longer in her body. She felt like a floating orb; space was everywhere and nowhere all at once. There wasn't a sky or ground, only air and spirit. Thought and soul. She blinked once more, and there she was. Everyone was clapping. The villagers cheered and hollered, so excited for... something.

"When should I speak?" she whispered to Haruka.

Haruka raised one brow. "You just did? It was brilliant, really. Say nothing else."

"Huh?" Sera was so confused, unsure if Haruka was kidding.

"No, really. I haven't spoken yet."

Haruka stared at Sera with subtle horror in her eyes. They could both sense it, Sera was sure, that overwhelming feeling... like someone else was there with them. Still, she said nothing else.

Chapter Five

The pair stopped at Lord Tobin's inn on the way back to the Reditus Castle for a night. Carriages didn't perform so well in the snow, and winter was almost there.

It was cold in the inn, and Sera's teeth were chattering.

"I heard there's an indoor spa? That's heated by magic. It's like a giant bathtub, essentially. Lord Tobin was telling me about it... a recent installation. We can go in there, just you and I," Haruka suggested.

Sera nodded, afraid her lips were soon going to turn blue. "Sounds lovely."

They made their way towards the spa room, where both women stripped out of their garments completely. Haruka's muscular, cut figure was on full display, and yet her supple chest was soft in contrast. Sera, however, was all soft curves and rolls, and Haruka couldn't seem to help but stare, holding onto each other's fingers.

"You're a goddess. You're quite literally ethereal," Haruka said, grinning.

Sera blushed before boldly saying. "I was just going to say you're fucking hot, but you had to one-up me with that sweet compliment."

"I'm just that good," Haruka proclaimed as they got into the water. They both chuckled, reveling in each other's company.

The two moved closer, Sera hooking both arms behind the back of Haruka's neck, and they kissed each other sweetly. Entangling with one another, Sera opened her mouth to welcome Haruka's tongue when a strange splash sounded.

"Don't mean to interrupt, but it's so cold in this place," said the voice of an elderly woman.

"I feel like there's a term for this... clam jammed? I can't believe this has happened to us twice recently," Haruka whispered.

Sera glared at Haruka, who promptly shut her mouth.

"No problem, ma'am. Sorry if we made you uncomfortable," Sera said in earnest.

"Don't apologize, missy. I was young once too, you know?" The woman was *old*. Possibly the oldest human Sera had ever seen. She had many layers of wrinkles, and Sera felt guilty for staring, but she was intrigued.

"How old are you?" she asked, surprised at her own boldness... and rudeness.

"One-hundred and seventeen," the woman replied. *What the fuck. Incredible. Someone surviving that long is unheard of....*

Haruka did not seem to be as enthralled in this revelation. Haruka's features were incredibly agitated in appearance, with furrowed brows, deadpan eyes, and mouth forming a thin line.

"Did you forget that we're naked? Or that we *almost* had a great time until this old lady showed up?" Haruka said in a hush.

"You're being impolite," Sera said into Haruka's ear. "Didn't anyone teach you to respect your elders?"

Haruka rolled her eyes. "Who are you, my mother? Actually, worse, you sound like Lady Sharp. It's cool that she lived this long and all, but I didn't ask to be naked in a bathtub with her."

"It's a heated spa," Sera corrected.

The old woman's eyes were closed, and she didn't seem to notice the quiet banter happening between the lovers. She turned away, leaning against the edge of the tub, and they both skittered out of the pool towards the towels.

"That was criminally awkward," Haruka said.

Sera shrugged, grabbing a second towel for her hair. "Oh, I don't know. I thought she was so cute. I'm genuinely amazed by that woman."

"I'm genuinely amazed by you, and that speech you may or may not have given," Haruka said, putting her trousers back on.

"I think someone possessed me."

"Is that possible?"

Sera's eyes grew wide, body still with thought. "Not a clue."

Sera and Haruka took a carriage back to the manor, grateful they hadn't gone to Vero Village on foot, and even more grateful to Lord Tobin for allowing them to stay in his inn. As they made their way through the gates, Sera felt an overwhelming amount of joy and love.

They entered the castle, and Sera guided Haruka towards the gardens, where she took Haruka in both hands.

"Haruka," Sera began.

"Yes?"

"Do you... do you wish to be my consort?"

Haruka moved swiftly, hands grasping Sera's jaw, drawing her into a kiss. When their lips parted, she asked, "Are you asking me to marry you?"

"Yes?" Sera answered unconfidently.

"Yes?" Haruka questioned.

She kissed Haruka again. "Yes!"

"I love you, my flower."

Sera's cheeks flushed. "There is no person I'd rather sort through this mess with. This mess called life."

Lady and Lord Sharp joined Sera and Haruka in the dining hall to celebrate their engagement. Lady Sharp cut the turkey, which had been freshly roasted, and served it to the others. "Is there anything I can do to help you both?"

"Yes, actually. Contact Lady Murphy about designing me a dress. Ooh! Also, please reach out to Kojo, or Lord Tobin, to have Kojo sent here immediately. I need his help with something magic-related," Sera replied, foot rubbing against the inside of Haruka's ankle.

"I'd also like Lisette and her husband to bake the cake, so you'll need to reach out to them as well," Haruka said.

"I can do all of that," Lady Sharp said.

"Lord Sharp, could you write a letter to Akil and Abeni? Thank them for all their help and ask when their wedding will be. We don't want to schedule ours too close to theirs." Sera brushed a strand of red hair behind her head.

Lord Sharp put his fork down and picked up a napkin, wiping his mouth. "Yes, Your Grace. I'll get right on that."

Laying in bed, limbs entangled after hours of tongues and bodies colliding, Sera let her hand drift down the strong panes of Haruka's abdomen. Caressing her, she kissed down Haruka's neck, licking her way towards her breasts. Placing a breast in her mouth, Sera sucked on her small brown nipple.

Sera took her thumb and used it to circle Haruka's clit. Her lover moaned, hips moving upwards to match the speed of Sera's finger. She playfully bit Haruka's nipple, and Haruka shook as she climaxed against Sera's hand for the second or third time that night.

"That's it, I'm getting you back for yesterday in the spa," Haruka said, voice sultry.

"Oh yeah? What're you going to do?"

Haruka reached under the bed and grabbed something. She placed a wooden box on the bed and smirked. "Open it," she commanded.

Sera obliged, fumbling with the box until it opened. Inside was a phallic-shaped piece of Jade tethered to leather straps.

"What is it?"

"An invention. I read about it in a book, and had an inventor from West-Terra recreate it. Lord Estrada brought it with him," Haruka replied, impressed with herself.

"What is it for?" Sera asked.

"Let me show you."

Haruka strapped the leather around both of her thighs, leaving the piece of jade sticking out from her pelvis. Sera had only been with a man, a boy really, once before when she was a teenager, but it looked similar, except it was Haruka. Gorgeous, strong Haruka. Her future bride.

Grabbing Sera by the hips, Haruka spun her around, making sure to stay in contact with her body so as to not upset the spell they both remained under.

"I have another surprise," Haruka whispered.

Opening the tub, Haruka dipped her finger into the lubricant before gently gliding it into Sera's opening. She took another small scoop and coated the jade with it as well.

Sera whimpered, begging to be filled. The new contraption intrigued her, and she couldn't wait to explore it together.

Slowly gliding the jade into Sera, Haruka started gently thrusting into her. As Sera moaned, she opened up, her body adjusting. Wetness dripped down her legs, and she wondered if Haruka liked it–liked seeing her from this new angle. She rolled her hips, wanting Haruka's devoted attention all on her. Her body.

Grabbing Sera's wrists, Haruka pulled her arms behind her back, thrusting harder inside her. "I love getting a full view of your arse, and that pretty pussy of yours, my flower." She sank deeper inside her. *So good.*

Sera felt filled, barely able to stop herself from screaming as Haruka continued to pound into her. She grinded back against her, chasing that need. This was the woman who gently kissed her forehead, the one who threatened men by sword for harassing her, and somehow that made it all the more pleasurable. *My future wife.*

"You take it so well, my good girl," Haruka practically growled.

Haruka shifted slightly, and Sera could feel the pressure building. Haruka had opened the dam, and her river was flowing, unable to stop as she climaxed hard. Feeling her legs give out, she fell forward onto the bed.

Removing the straps, Haruka crawled closer to Sera, making contact with multiple parts of their bodies. Sera wrapped her arms around her, kissing her softly. The warmth of Haruka's body against hers reminded Sera that she would never be alone. Even with her family gone, she would always have Haruka… and perhaps they could find a family of their own, together.

"You had that made for me?" she finally asked, ending the quiet.

"We're going to spend our lives together, I figured we could spend it trying all sorts of new things," Haruka smiled, kissing her nose.

"I'll try anything with you."

Sera and Haruka stood in front of the castle, arm-in-arm, waiting for Kojo's arrival. The small boy pulled up in a carriage drawn by two silver-colored horses. He tipped his hat at the coachmen, giving the man a wide smile. Kojo's teeth were large and pearly white, one of the prettiest smiles Sera had ever seen.

"I heard this was an emergency," Kojo said as he approached them.

"We can't seem to get unstuck," Sera admitted, cheeks flushing with embarrassment.

"Ah, I see." Kojo scratched his small chin. "What's in it for me?"

Sera shrugged. "Candy? Hot chocolate?"

"Do it or I'll tell Abeni," Haruka threatened.

"Whoa whoa!" He lifted his arms up in the air. "I was joking, watch this." Kojo spun around on one heel, making a show of it as he did a little dance and then snapped his finger.

The scent of magic filled the air, entering their noses, and Sera's face scrunched up. "Did you do something?"

"Test it out," he said with a smirk.

Sera and Haruka cautiously shifted away from one another, worried they'd be slammed into each other once more. When nothing happened, they moved farther and farther away.

Sera ran towards Haruka, jumping onto her, nearly knocking the woman over.

"We're finally able to be apart, and you jump all over me?" Haruka looked amused.

"I want the choice to be away, but I still want to keep you close," Sera confessed.

"By the way," Kojo said, interrupting the moment. "I got a girlfriend."

"Oh yeah?" Sera asked, the apples of her cheeks still red.

Kojo spun around again, unable to contain his excitement. "Her name is Laurel."

"Lord Tobin's daughter?" Sera asked.

"Yes! We're going to write to each other. She's even going to be my date to the two upcoming weddings," he said proudly.

"That's right. There are two upcoming weddings now," Haruka said.

Sera beamed with joy. "I cannot wait."

Epilogue

Standing behind the castle, Haruka helped as Sera draped wet clothes over the line, hoping they'd dry quickly in the summer sun. Sera threw a small hand towel, which landed directly on Haruka's face.

"That's it, I'm coming after you," Haruka yelled before chasing Sera through the fortress of hanging clothes.

Sera giggled, feet hitting swiftly against the grassy ground as she darted between gaps in the sheets, avoiding Haruka as best she could. It was no luck, Haruka had reached her. Sera felt her muscular arms wrap around her, and Haruka kissed Sera's cheek and neck.

"My flower... my duchess," Haruka whispered. "I'll never grow tired of saying that."

"You're just a consort," Sera teased, grabbing Haruka by her face and pulling her in. She loved the softness of her lips, and the way their bodies always perfectly fit together. The two kissed each other passionately, as they felt they always would. *Even when we're old and wrinkled, I cannot imagine not being this in love with her.*

They stood, basking in the sunlight and enjoying each other's company when Haruka said, "Do you notice those two birds perched on that tree?"

"Is that a crow?" Sera asked.

Haruka shook her head. "No, that is most definitely a raven."

Sera gasped, thinking of Primrose and Protego. "What is that other bird? I don't recognize it. The dark wings are almost iridescent. Such beautiful plumage."

"That's a starling," Haruka said as tears filled both women's eyes.

"I'll always remember," Sera said towards the tree. "Always."

About the Author

Still pretending she's a fairy princess and not a gremlin, Priscilla Rose resides in the magical swamps of Florida, where she writes Romances of the Fantasy and Monster variety.

When they aren't reading or writing, Priscilla spends their time at Renaissance Festivals and Anime Conventions, where she cosplays and socializes to her heart's content.

She is looking forward to showing the world her stories full of queer casts, magical creatures, and happily ever afters! Follow her journey by scanning the code below!

The Hidden Governess

THE BLOOD TOURNAMENTS BOOK 1.5

The Hidden Governess
THE BLOOD TOURNAMENTS BOOK 1.5

DANIELA A. MERA

Heat Level:
Smoldering

Content Warnings:
Sickness, blood, and brief mentions of child SA.

Islas de Arrebol

La Primera Isla
- Hacienda Rosa de Oro
- Ciudad de Rubíes
- El Palacio Viejo
- Cinturón del Fuego

La Segunda Isla
- Torrecillas de Magma

La Tercera Isla
- Ciudad de Cenizas

La Cuarta Isla
- Puerto Rojo

La Quinta Isla
- Puerto Dolores
- Casas Grandes

La Sexta Isla
- Agustín de Allende

CHAPTER 1
Time Won't Heal Me

It had been five days, three hours and sixteen minutes since they took Carmen Asbaje away from me.

She was my best friend. Practically my sister.

But she had Blood Magic, the kind that dazzled the world. She was... magnificent. But she no longer belonged to my world.

The lower classes did not have magic. We were isolated from wealth and mysticism. Our fear was our creed, and money was as good as some strange enchantment of health.

I was in a rehearsal for the Flamenco group I had danced with over the last three years. Though talented, Maestra Cecelia never put me at the front of the lineup.

A heavy sadness had settled over me like a thick blanket while I sat on the floor and waited for my turn to display the short routine Cecelia was using to audition us for the role of first dancer. Tension was thick all around me, but I couldn't seem to feel anything past the grief. We were learning a new routine in preparation for the Blood Tournaments Festivals.

I grimaced while Maestra Cecelia shouted at Aurora, one of the other dancers. "Have you been eating bread again? I swear on La Dama that if you can't fit in the costume I just had made for you, I will personally make sure that you don't eat for three days."

Maestra Cecelia was a generally kind person, but Carmen's departure had caused a nasty sourness to pour out of her at every turn. I knew that she believed Carmen had lied to her, betrayed her somehow.

But Carmen had just been trying to stay alive. She never asked for any of this. Even though some of the facts Maestra Cecelia believed were true, the context in which they were viewed was overtly negative. She was swimming in bias that made it impossible to exact a fair assessment of the situation.

Aurora, who I usually wouldn't feel bad for, was looking so pitiful, and it struck something inside of me.

Perhaps it was because I recognized her hurt, and I felt so isolated without my roommate.

Though not related by blood, Carmen and I were sisters in every other sense of the word. Both of us had arrived at the Bendiciones Orphanage around the same age, and we ran away together after a horrific series of bombings in our small town.

For most of our lives, we had been together. All of that changed when Carmen committed a felony and impersonated an Elite. She made her way to the Grand Hotel to return a stolen cufflink.

And was forced into an audition for the Blood Tournaments.

The music started again, and I closed my eyes. Aurora had been given the part choreographed for Carmen. It was so clearly made for her strong arms and wild-turns, the music spoke of her with every note. When I watched Aurora dance, I caught glimpses of my friend.

They were both so talented, though Aurora lacked the desperate passion that leaked out of Carmen with every move.

Closing my eyes didn't help apparently, because I still saw my long-lost sister.

The Blood Tournament happened every year around Winter Solstice. Usually they were fun, but this year, they were flushed with a sad ache that refused to quit.

It suffocated me.

"That's enough, Aurora. Why don't we give Magdalena a chance now?" Maestra Cecelia said.

What? I always went at the end.

My brows furrowed, and I opened my eyes again, only to find myself under the careful, critical gaze of our director. There was so much restless hurt seeping out of her, it made me want to cry. My sadness was matched with her anger, and seeing the familiar comfort of my former life dashed... this was a hemorrhaging wound.

Using every bit of strength I had, I snapped out of my trance and took my place in front of the other dancers. The routine still was no longer familiar, and I was shaking with emotion.

Alone, I contorted my body into the starting position and waited for the music.

When it came, my positioning was all wrong. After starting two beats two late, my steps were clumsy and rigid. That caused my practice skirt to get tangled between my legs, and I stumbled to my knees.

Shame burned across my skin, and I gritted my teeth together while I stared at the grimy floorboards beneath me. There was a chunk in the corner of one, revealing a compacted black substance, no doubt composed of dust, sweat, and dancing. The room around me came to life with a tangible silence. I knew what they were thinking, that I shouldn't be here. They were grateful that they weren't me.

That made me even more angry—I didn't need their pity. I didn't want it, either.

Maestra Cecelia cut through the silence like a hot knife through butter. "Again, Magdalena." Her voice was layered with carefully refined intensity.

To be honest, a small part of myself was frightened by the simmering quality of her words.

Rallying all of my strength through my belly and into my chest, I stood up while carefully avoiding Maestra Cecelia.

Facing everyone for the first time was just as painful as I'd imagined. The faces of my peers ranged from that odious emotion—pity—to cruel amusement. Any compassion I had for Aurora moments ago faded away the moment our eyes met.

She cared for no one but herself.

When at last my eyes locked with Maestra Cecelia, I found a harsh intensity I didn't recognize. The corners of her mouth turned down, and her eyes were narrowed. I could practically hear all of the dreadful things she wanted to say to me while I watched her eye me from toe to crown.

However, she seemed to swallow her words and stepped back to give me space to dance at the beginning of the room. Without another word, I took the starting position. Maestra Cecelia's eyes narrowed even further, but she motioned for the music to be played again.

Determination thrummed through my entire body, helping me to hit most of the beats correctly and keep my arms up high enough.

It didn't matter.

The music stopped halfway through, and Maestra Cecelia shouted, "Again!" loud enough for me to flinch.

The same tune played once more, and I started on time once more. But it didn't matter because the music abruptly stopped even earlier this time, and Maestra Cecelia demanded that I start moving once more.

Since this was my third time doing this, my anger, embarrassment and shaking muscles were starting to turn into personality traits. Maestra Cecelia was headed down the path to get her head bit off if she didn't let me finish this round.

We passed the half-point of the routine without problem.

And then the music came to a screeching halt once more.

"Magdalena Magaña, you will do the routine right, or you will sit the next show out."

Huffing, I angled my body so that I was facing Maestra Cecelia head on. My limit had been reached, and I would not tolerate anyone threatening me.

"No," I said simply.

Not my best comeback, but Maestra Cecelia looked absolutely floored.

Seconds ticked on and stared at her with hot defiance. Her mouth was still partially opened, and she looked absolutely bewildered.

"¿Perdón?," she started, and took a step closer to me.

Straightening my shoulders, I looked her right in the eye and said, "I will not dance again. I am not even interested in being the first dancer. So this endless torment is doing more to embarrass me than to help me become a better dancer."

Maestra Cecelia blinked. And then she drew herself up like a great, unknown creature. Like the moment in an old black and white movie that I got to watch a handful of Saturdays growing up where a bear stands on two legs, revealing its full, terrifying height.

Only, I wasn't afraid. I was tired, irritated, and lonely. If the mother bear mauled me, then at least I might have a little reprieve from my hellish reality.

She had gone still and scarily silent as she stalked toward me. "Vete a tu cuarto," she demanded.

"With pleasure." I did a mock curtsy, turned around, and walked straight out of the room. I would go to my room a thousand times over being subjected to whatever nonsense this was.

CHAPTER 2
An Outbreak

After being banished to my room, I sat down and tried to make sense of what had come over me. Unfortunately, the bed I slept in was often the bed that Carmen and I shared. The entire room smelled of her soap.

Carmen once told me that she needed to be near me while sleeping to prevent nightmares. She had made a joke. "I know I need you far more than you need me."

She was wrong.

I was born in a Night Merchant's brothel, and, aside from early-morning affections from every woman beside my mother, was mostly alone.

I was sure no one missed me when I left that poor substitute for a home.

Stretching out across the plain cotton cover, I tried to curl up in a ball and rest. When that didn't work, I grabbed the white pillows strewn about the bed —which were honestly more pale gray than white, now—and piled them high around me. Maybe if I could mimic the weight of my friend, the solid presence that had served to balance the flightiness that threatened to swoop me up into the sky and never put me back down.

I closed my burning eyes, took a few breaths, and then burst up from the bed. Pillows rained around the dusty room, and I was out the door in a second. Rushing through the hall, down the stairs, and out the back door.

Once outside, I took a deep breath and pushed forward to the street. My hands flexed and clenched as I walked through the streets, which had long since begun to fall apart.

I walked past the houses of the people I'd come to know in between rehearsals, eating, and sleeping. Carmen always kept to herself more than I did, but I still felt alone with her gone.

There was one place I could go. A person who could help me feel better; mi novio, Ronaldo. He was a year older than me, though we were of similar heights and builds, and his father owned a restaurant for Workers. We had been seeing each other for the last year or so. There was a comfortable, shallow rhythm to our relationship.

We saw each other, we kissed, had fifteen minute love-making sessions, and then he sent me back home with fluffy love letters stuffed in my pockets.

There were no promises between us, just ease. Nothing about him was threatening, and that was important to me.

Doña Filipa stood on her steps, sweeping off a day's worth of dirt with soapy water. She smiled at me and waved.

I waved back and tried to look less miserable.

I was coming up upon Ronaldo's parents' house. It was right around the corner.

In truth, his mother didn't like me much, and I didn't like coming here. But it was definitely the best place for me to be right now.

Mustering up a smile, I rounded the corner and walked up the short path to the building where his five person family was housed. In front there was a bush-green colored Guardia patrol car. Its lights were flashing. Directly behind that was the sanitized white of a hospital truck. Its red lights were also swirling around, seemingly straight into my eyes.

I blinked, realizing that there were several people around me. I recognized Ronaldo's downstairs neighbors, the Alvarez family. Three small children huddled around the parents, watching with thinly veiled horror.

That look on their face scared me enough to resist leaning over and asking them what was happening. It was at that moment that the door burst open. The first thing out was the tip of the metal bed housing a woman. I recognized her instantly as Ronaldo's mother, Ariadna.

The woman who didn't like me much.

My eyes widened. There was a tube hooked into her arm, and she lay oddly slack against the thin pad of the hospital stretcher. Her skin was covered in bright red sores, and enough rashes to turn her brown skin maroon.

Behind her was Ronaldo's father, Oscar, looking tired and desperate. His eyes were bloodshot, and there were deep purple shadows large enough to graze the tops of his cheekbones.

My heart constricted. Logically, there was only one answer for something like this to happen, but even then, I could hardly understand what it meant for life as I knew it in this small district.

Even if I had wanted to, I couldn't tear my eyes away from the scene in front of me. The pain in my chest intensified as my heart sputtered and galloped like a horse. It was seconds before Ronaldo's little sister trotted out of the house, looking confused as her head darted between her father and mother.

Then at last, the boyfriend I'd been seeing twice a week for a year appeared in the door frame. The wind picked up his yeasty-savory bread scent, mixed it with sanitizing chemicals, and brought it to my nose.

His thick, curly hair fell in his eyes, contrasting nicely with the light gray shirt he wore. There were grease splatter stains dotting the area around his chest, unsurprisingly absent from the spot where his apron would've gone.

Our eyes connected over the steps, and I froze. His normally brandy-colored eyes were nearly black. I blinked. I recognized Ash usage when I saw it. He was high. Where had he gotten enough money to make a visit to the Night Merchants?

Slow rage bubbled up inside of me. One of those men owned my childhood home, my drugged-up, unresponsive mother.

Even still, some part of me expected him to stumble over and fall into my arms. When he didn't move, I did. I wouldn't say anything to him just yet... but later, after we sorted what was happening to his mother.

The Guardia came to life, having been frozen on the sidelines. "Stay back," she barked, even going so far as to heave her body over into my path.

Ronaldo shook his head slightly, just as the Guardia said, "This area is now quarantined. I recommend you return home immediately."

"Quarantined" meant this wasn't the only case of the Withering in the area, and "recommend" meant this was an order.

The tight bun under the Guardia's brimmed hat seemed to stretch her face horizontally, making her severe expression that much more potent. I looked at

Ronaldo once more, realizing we wouldn't get a chance to speak for at least a month, and flinched when I heard the ambulancia's door slam shut.

The pain of separation kept piling on.

It had been so long since I had seen a breakout anywhere. Apparently, the preventative pills, pastillas negras, plus dozens of other safety measures weren't enough. And if someone healthy like Ariadna could get sick...

More ice flooded my veins.

With the expectation from the Guardia for me to leave still hanging in the air, I turned around. My brain fought to process what I had just seen, what I had just experienced, and I hurried right back to where I had come from.

Just as I had started to worry about where I was going, a familiar head of hair appeared in front of me.

I stopped dead in my tracks. Had he snuck past the Guardia? If he was caught now, they would throw him in jail. A flood of emotions went coursing through me, trying to understand what on earth I had seen, all while trying to read the expressions flashing across his face like flashes of subtitles on an old program.

"Amor," Ronaldo took a step forward and then shut his mouth. He took a deep breath. "Magdalena."

Dread curled in my stomach. Very few people called me Magdalena, but he absolutely never had. In fact, I didn't even know he knew that was my full name.

"Yes?" I asked slowly.

His left hand flexed before running fingertips over the outside seam of his pants. He always did this when he had something important to say. I'd seen it the first time he asked me to stay late after his family's restaurant closed, it had happened the first time he'd kissed me. The first time he met Carmen.

Intuition told me that this would not be a happy time like those other moments.

Very well, I thought. *My soul is already bleeding out, if he wishes to hurt me, there will be so little left to spare. Better to do it now.*

He took a deep breath. "I'm so sorry. With mamá... I mean, now I will have more..."

When he trailed off yet again, my brain filled in the blanks. He would have a lot more responsibility with his sister now, not to mention looking into the gaping jaws of death and grief.

I should have just let it go. I had already told myself it didn't matter, that there wasn't enough left to break to hurt me. I should have told him to go to hell for using Ash. For giving money to those monsters...

But I was in pain and needed someone, anyone. "Please," I said quietly. In contrast to the fierce little warrior who had stood up to Maestra Cecelia mere hours ago, I seemed so helpless. It would've been a Herculean feat to be that same level of courage and strength day in and day out. I know Carmen certainly expected that I was capable of those things.

However, I was not some mythical being from some faraway continent. The rumors of Faeries and Elves weren't real in Arrebol. I was no princess, and there was no Fae Prince coming to save me. I was an eighteen-year-old woman just trying to sort through life and grasp at glimmers of happiness anywhere I could find them.

Ronaldo looked at me with pity, and I recoiled. He shook his head sadly, standing his ground like some bronze statue. "The Withering would only get worse, more advanced as a sickness. Neither one of us thought this was really going anywhere serious. You said it yourself, your first true love would always be Carmen."

Another tremor wracked through me. I had said that once. And part of what he said had been true. But my heart was made to be used for more than just one person at a time. He didn't know where Carmen had gone. I needed friends, family, and sisters as well as lovers. A desire not to mess with the fragile passion between us had made me conceal how much I was really beginning to care for him.

I was funny like that—wild and carefree at a first glance, but not even revealing the depth of my emotions to those closest to me.

When I didn't respond, he continued, "Please, say something. Say you forgive me, that you understand."

At last I met his eyes. Those ugly, too-large pupils were straining to read my face. And yet, I had read his so easily. It was like he didn't know me at all. "You're right. This was nothing more than silly back-room kisses."

He visibly relaxed and my heart broke even further. In a moment of forgetting himself, he stepped forward and wrapped his long, lean arms around me. Heavy cast-iron pots and pans had given him an attractive muscle tone.

He never made me afraid, though. I could've put him in his place.

Sometimes, when he held me, it felt like he was strong enough to hold up all of my baggage as well. But not strong enough to hurt me.

It was that thought that made me back away first. Neither one of us was strong enough to continue in this situation, so it was time for me to leave. He kissed me one last time, a quick peck. A brush of lips that felt as lifeless as kissing a wall.

And then we were walking in opposite directions.

I felt like a brittle eggshell, crumbling across the sidewalk. Another step, another fracture. Every time I hugged myself tighter, another part of me chipped and fell to the ground.

"It only hurts this bad right now," I told myself and took a deep breath.

At least I still had my room at Maestra Cecelia's theater.

For now.

CHAPTER 3
Spinning Out

I stared up at the ceiling.
    One day passed.
Then another.

They brought me food and water. I would eat a few bites of the meals, and then leave the rest outside of my door. Apart from those rushed encounters, no one came to visit me. Apparently, Maestra was sick of the little orphans who had ruined her life so thoroughly.

My mind kept racing, trying to find a solution to the crushing grief that pressed down on me. It flipped through memories on repeat, but I could only focus on the worst of the worst.

Long ago, Carmen and I had escaped from the awful Bendiciones orphanage. There was a man who used to come by, always promising to adopt one of the children. The Niñeras would allow him to take some of the children into a back room for interviews so that he could speak with us, see how our personalities got along.

It was very much not that.

When he would take me back, he would ask me to strip naked.

I tried not to think about the rest. Actively not remembering was a muscle, but I had grown weak.

When the memories came flooding back, I tried to shut my eyes tighter.

But the images were stronger with my eyes closed. I was scared to hurt him then, but I wouldn't hesitate to kill him now. That's the thing about hatred, it wormed its way into the foundation of your soul and refused to leave.

So.

Staring at the ceiling.

Fighting with ghosts.

When the bombings that caused Carmen and I to run happened years later, I hoped that man died along with most of Puerto Dolores.

Since then, there had been other boys that made me feel better. I quickly learned that love was much different from abuse. Especially when I only chose men that I could win against if it came to a fight.

I was tough.

And then there was Carmen. I loved her freely, openly.

I wanted her to be happy, but I knew she was affected by things differently than me. That was why I never told her what happened. It turned out, if you held your tears in long enough, they stopped coming.

All of those walls, all of the pain was now breaking down. It was disassembled like sand falling through an hour-glass, one grain at a time.

One brick after another.

A full week passed, and it didn't stop hurting.

I never stopped seeing Carmen's face, never stopped remembering what it felt like to walk away from Ronaldo.

Sitting in front of Carmen's mirror, I looked at how gaunt the hollows of my cheeks had become. My hair hung in greasy strings around my face. I was disgusting.

It was hard to measure how much time I spent staring at myself, existing in a numb limbo that protected me from feeling anything.

The light cycling through my window—casting beams and shadows across the messy furniture that all smelled like a person who was no longer with me —pulled me to the surface of my thoughts.

The only thing that I could fix was my deeply smelly being.

When I stood up, it felt like I wasn't in my own body. I gathered my slightly musty towel that was hanging from the corner of my bed frame and walked out into the hallway. I had heard the girls coming and going, but everyone was probably downstairs.

Dancing.

If I was being honest, I felt relieved I wasn't with them.

When I shuffled into the communal bathroom, I took one look at the full-length mirror and cringed. I looked worse than I thought.

Taking a long breath, I peeled off the same clothes I'd worn the day Ronaldo had finished things between us, and climbed into one of the shower stalls. I turned on the hot water and waited for the temperature to turn nearly scalding before I stepped inside. There was a bar of soap sitting in a dish just outside of where the water stream hit. I should've been more concerned about sharing a soap bar.

While showering, I heard voices from the hallway.

I froze. Practice was over.

There wasn't a single ounce of will left inside of me, and I didn't want to see them.

It wasn't long before someone came inside and started to shower a few stalls down from me.

I continued in my spot. I was being wasteful, but technically, I had saved loads of water the entire week. A half-hour long shower was practically harmless.

More girls filtered in, and I recognized one particular voice of one of the other Flamenco dancers. She was by far the cruelest girl. She was younger than me, but had the attitude of some kind of quasi-Elite. She was just as devoid of magic as I was.

"Has she even come out of her room?" she asked with an annoyingly nasal voice.

A part of me considered answering, just to start a fight. But Carmen's voice sounded in my mind, reminding me to be quiet, not to start a fight.

She had spent a lot of time keeping us out of trouble. I had no doubts that she was the reason we had done so well for ourselves. Even though she was only six months older, she had this way of playing the role of my absent mother, of the older sister, that never really changed.

For a second, I wondered if she would help the other candidates in the Blood Tournament as much as she had helped me.

It wasn't uncommon for nearly a third of them to die. There was no doubt in my mind that Carmen would not be counted in those numbers. She was too strong.

I'd retreated into my mind too easily. I almost didn't notice when Aurora pulled back the curtain of my shower to peek inside.

"San volcán, if it isn't the little troll. Are you having a nice time?"

I didn't try to hide from her. It wasn't uncommon to see each other naked during performances because of all those quick changes. "I hope you get thrown right into the bubbly depths of the Doncella, small tits," I seethed at her while I grabbed the soap and began lathering my hair.

Aurora's smirk slowly faded. "Cállate fea," she said with venom in her words, and yanked the shower curtain closed.

It was my turn to smirk. Nothing quite got the endorphins flowing like telling Aurora off.

Since the other showers were now pouring water, the temperature of my measly drizzle was already plummeting. I finished rinsing off all the suds and stepped out. None of the other girls said a word to me as I passed.

What did I care? I felt like a new person. A person who was capable of taking on the world.

I hadn't brought another set of clothes with me, so I stepped out into the hallway. My damp feet stuck against the dirt-crusted floors. When I looked up, I froze.

Standing in front of my door was Maestra Cecelia. Her arms were crossed, and her expression was a cross between scowling and worried frown. Our eyes met. She straightened her back, wrapped her hand around the handle, and opened the door.

I hurried into my room after her.

Cecelia took no time before speaking. "Estos chavales ya regresaron."

Who had come back? I raised an eyebrow. "¿Cuáles?"

Maestra Cecelia bit her lips together. "The men who took Carmen."

My blood ran cold. Carmen was everywhere. A version of her, at least. Her face was painted in a way I'd never seen, and they tamed her curls almost completely. She looked older, and healthier, than she'd ever been. Maybe some of the other dancers suspected, but I hadn't heard anything.

To be fair, I hadn't been anywhere to hear anything. The Elites had plastered her face on every corner, appearing in every televised interview. I had missed all of them.

Renata Bordón was a girl I didn't know.

Surely she was still alive. Right?

My heart sped up.

"Vístete, Magda. They are asking for you," Maestra Cecelia said.

My eyebrows furrowed. "They are... asking for me?" Somehow, the world was spinning slower.

Maestra Cecelia rolled her eyes. "Yes, now finish getting dressed and come downstairs."

I barely heard her. I certainly didn't hear her leave.

Suddenly, I was alone in my room.

You need to get dressed, I told myself. Those two brutes from before were here, and they were asking for me.

Carmen had to be behind this.

She just had to.

CHAPTER 4
She Who Shall Remain Nameless

When I walked into Maestra Cecelia's office, there was a thick silence coating the entire room. Two massive men filled the space with a menacing energy. It was... potent. I looked one straight in the eye, and he held my gaze.

There was a part of me that respected that.

"Buenas noches, señores," I said brightly. "You only ever seem to come at night. It's almost like you have something to hide."

They continued to look down at me.

"Buena noche," one of them said in return.

Maestra Cecelia took a deep breath. "Apparently, a mutual friend has sent for you." There was a quiet rage to her voice. She was too calm, too collected.

Emotions weren't something I was currently experiencing, mostly just observing from the distance. Somewhere outside of my body.

"A mutual friend," I said slowly.

She nodded, her hands clasped together beneath her chin. "So it seems."

The same man that had practically grumbled 'good evening' stepped forward and held out a note. It was embossed with gold letters, and sealed with red wax.

What the hell?

Had Carmen made this?

"We were instructed to make sure that you read this. Then we will leave."

I blinked. "You won't even let me get my things this time?" I asked.

The behemoth shook his head once.

"Bueno," I said quickly, and went to work breaking the red seal. When I opened the letter, the first thing I saw was, *From the office of Antonio Armando Castillas Morales.*

My brow furrowed. Everyone was watching me, but Maestra Cecelia was being careful to catalog my reaction.

I tried to ignore her.

This was supposed to be from Carmen.

The note read:

Señorita Magdalena Magaña,
A mutual friend has charged me with ensuring your safety. How she, who shall remain nameless, has any friends at all is shocking. But here we are.
You will be taken from the Naranja district and placed in an Elite's home as a governess. You will be a Working class institutriz for a very important family, and are expected to behave properly. The Flores Jimenez estate in the Primera Isla. This particular family owes me a favor. There, you will take care of their six-year-old daughter, Lirio. You are expected to tend to all her needs and demands.
I am also supposed to insist that you stop taking the black pills immediately. This will come with a form of withdrawal, but it will fade within a week. Make sure that you do not tell anyone.
-A

I looked at Maestra Cecelia incredulously, unsure of what I was reading. A governess? I had friends, Workers, who were servants for the large families of the Quinta Isla. Sometimes it was fine, sometimes it was... dangerous.

"What does it say?" Maestra Cecelia asked, relatively gently.

"It is for Señorita Magaña only," the man snapped.

There was an instinct inside of me to tell them off, to protect Maestra Cecelia.

But she had not done so for either Carmen or me.

I looked at her, really looked at her, for the first in a week.

She looked... sad.

That made my heart clench. It would have been unfair to leave with spite in my heart. "Maestra, thank you for everything you've done."

Her eyes flicked from the desk to mine. We stared at each other for a few long moments.

"Please, tell her that I am sorry."

My eyes burned. Would I really be seeing Carmen? It didn't seem like it.

But I nodded.

"Time to go," the massive cave monster said.

I looked up at the bodyguards. "Very well."

And they led me out of the room.

There was no fanfare this time, no one to say goodbye. No Fercho. No friends.

My gaze was glued to the ground, too defeated to take in the world around me.

The next thing I knew, they had opened the door to the car, and I slid into one of the seats.

"Buenas Noches," someone said. My head snapped up, and my eyes were instantly acquainted with a boy about my age. His long legs spoke to his height, and I could see his slender build up close and with alarming clarity.

I most definitely could not beat him in a fight.

His dark eyes stared at me with a mixture of curiosity and indifference.

The bodyguards settled in around me, as if they were an extension of the car itself.

"Señor Santiago Jimenez, this is Magdalena Magaña," the bodyguard on my right said.

The name rang a bell. He was competing with Carmen. I glanced up at the bodyguard. "So you do know how to introduce people?" I said snappily, suddenly feeling irritated that he hadn't told me his name.

The one on my right let out a huff that couldn't be mistaken for anything other than the beginning of a laugh.

I scowled at him. "What is so funny?"

He shook his head. "If you looked anything alike, I would've thought you two were sisters."

I froze, holding my tongue from speaking her name.

Instead, I turned my attention back to the young man before me. Santiago's gaze never left me, and I found it hard to look away. I thought I could see the hint of a smirk on his face, but I couldn't be sure. His expression made me feel uneasy, and I had to fight the urge to turn and run away.

It was unnerving to be observed while speaking with such intensity. I felt a chill run down my spine as we watched each other, my heart pounding in my chest.

San Volcán, I was being incredibly rude. I had been a Performer long enough to know a few things about addressing the upper class. "Mucho gusto, Señor Jimenez," I said.

He nodded. "Igualmente." Then that strange, blank expression twisted into something more pleasant. Kind even.

Still feeling uneasy, I looked up at both of the men. They were both so large, so muscly. How did men like this even exist? Did they spend every ounce of free time exercising? Even after years of physical labor, I was lean and small. Maybe they were better fed than me.

"Can I finally get your names?" I asked.

"Soy Javier," the one on the right grumbled.

"Me llamo Manuel," the one on my left hand side said, marginally more brightly.

"Excellent, now I feel less uneasy about being the filling to your muscle-sandwich."

Santiago laughed, but both of the men remained silent. I eyed him. "And no one calls me Magdalena. Magda will do just fine." I tried to give him a smile that was just as pleasant as the one he'd flashed. Santiago watched me, a faint flicker of curiosity in his eyes, but didn't respond.

Then we were off, speeding away into the night. The car started moving, and it was smooth. Not at all bumpy like a public bus, nor shaky like a train, and dozens of times faster than walking.

I realized just how tired I had gotten. My eyelids drooped a fraction of an inch.

Santiago Jimenez continued to study me from across the way, but I couldn't bring myself to care. If it meant seeing my friend again, I would do whatever it took. The time apart would feel like seconds if we could just be together once more. My world was a better place with her.

Scratch that. The whole world was a better place with her. There was a noble goodness to her that was rare in people. That was worth its weight in gold. I smiled, and now she was the golden girl. My last conscious thought was of Carmen.

CHAPTER 5
A Lovely Little Girl

The sun had already risen in the sky, its rays stretching towards the horizon as we arrived at the Flores Jimenez estate. This was the third leg of our journey, and, while on the boat, they had made me change into a proper Worker's dress. It was a pale blue dress cut in a flattering form, with gilded buttons, and a delicate ribbon serving as my belt. My shoes had small heels on them, but they were solid. Definitely good for running.

Or dancing.

When motion sickness soured my stomach on the boat, I was allowed to sit next to the window. They even told me I could keep it cracked open, despite the obvious chill. Women were generally colder than men, so I doubted that they suffered much.

When we transferred back from the boat to a car, I took turns sleeping against the chilled window and Javier's rock-solid arm. He never said anything, which was probably for the best because I was tired.

About an hour ago, I had woken up full of nerves and energy.

Santiago was awake as well.

No one objected when I rolled down the window even further so that I could feel the wind blowing through my hair. It was exhilarating.

We were in a stretch of estates just outside the capital, Ciudad de Rubíes. Every house was beautiful. I wondered if Carmen lived in any of them.

The houses slowly began to be built further apart, and the road gradually led up a hill. I could feel my heart racing with anticipation as we ascended. I wanted to know what awaited us at the top.

When we finally reached the peak, a gleaming white house rose over from the ground and seemed to pierce the sky. It was three stories high and had an imposing presence about it. You could tell from its intricate architecture and elaborate accents that it must have been constructed with wealth and luxury in mind.

For some reason, Santiago looked up and addressed me directly. "Welcome to our home, Miss Magda," he said in a voice that was as hard as stone. "I hope you will be happy here."

I held his gaze and smiled. "Gracias, Señor Santiago Jimenez." All proper and manners, but I couldn't resist using his first name.

Something about his expression softened, but I looked away again while I began running my fingers through my light-colored locks. I was so grateful I had decided to shower.

Sitting in a car with four men while smelling like a dumpster might not have been the most pleasant experience.

I didn't need Carmen seeing me like that, either.

We pulled up in front of the house, and Santiago got out of the car before anyone else had a chance. He strode up to the entrance confidently and opened the enormous front door without knocking. It was strange to see. Strange to think those doors ever opened for anyone but someone as important as the Chancellor.

This was how the wealthy lived.

Neither my wildest dreams nor the most elaborate pageant-like broadcasts could have prepared me for this.

The car started up again, and my brows furrowed.

"Where are we going?" I asked hesitantly.

Manuel responded, "To the Worker's entrance."

I nodded slowly.

When we pulled up to the side, Manuel helped me out of the car, and I walked inside.

Inside, it was even more beautiful than outside—the floors were marble, there were ornate fixtures everywhere, and luxurious furniture filled every available space. The walls were lined with exquisite works of art, and all around us was evidence that somebody with a lot of money lived here—or perhaps still did?

There was a line of people who were all waiting to meet me.

They each dipped slightly, and I had a hard time keeping track of their faces. I did notice that they were all wearing simpler clothing than my own. I felt awkward and out of place, as if I was a fraud. I wanted to explain to them that I was not what I appeared to be, but I couldn't find the words.

Manuel stepped forward and quickly took charge. He spoke rapidly, and I could not understand half of what he said. In no time, the people bustled around us, their eyes never leaving me––as if I was some kind of curious creature.

Just when I thought the situation could not get more uncomfortable, a group of extremely well-dressed people stepped in.

Santiago was there. Everyone fell silent at once, and then their voices united in saying, "Buenos días, Señor Flores y Señora Jimenez." The greeting extended to Santiago, who avoided looking at me, and a name I had only heard to this point.

Lirio.

I scouted the room for the girl I was meant to be governess for, but did not see her.

The Elites gave all of us a nod, then continued walking toward me.

I clasped my hands together and lowered my head, trying to not look too defiant. But inside, my heart was pounding. I had never been this close to the powerful families of Arrebol before.

I could feel the heat of everyone's gaze on me, burning into my skin.

"Señorita Magaña," Señor Flores said tightly. I looked up, not entirely sure what to do.

He had taken a step forward. Luckily for me, he looked kind enough. They all did.

My worries about Elite families might have been unfounded.

"We are grateful to finally have found someone to help us with Lirio. She is a darling girl, very eager to learn how to read." He smiled and held out his hand.

It was then that the curve of a small dress peaked out from behind Señora Jimenez.

It was Lirio, who had silently stepped in to join them. With extreme caution, she unfolded like a flower petal in the morning and looked at me with large, curious eyes. She was very pretty, with light hair just like her parents and brother. Just like me.

I curtsied. "It would be my honor to serve Lirio," I said.

He nodded in approval and turned towards the exit. As he left, he said over his shoulder, "Welcome to the Flores-Jimenez Estate, Miss Magda. I trust you will take good care of my daughter."

Señora Jimenez spoke next, having stayed behind. "If you would please follow me, I will show you where Lirio's room is. As governess, you'll have a room near hers, away from the servants floor."

I nodded, and fell into step behind the lady of the house. Both Santaigo and his father walked in an opposite direction, letting us be. It was only then that I looked back at the two bodyguards.

It was becoming more apparent by the second that I wasn't going to see Carmen while I was here.

The disappointment was hard to manage, but I trudged forward.

After all, this was my job now.

All I had to do was stay focused and help Lirio as much as I could.

I looked up at the sprawling white estate, and found myself feeling grateful.

Even if Carmen wasn't here, she was behind this. That made me feel... loved.

The small girl hung back with me, walking alongside and sneaking glances at me while we walked through hallways and up a set of stairs.

Señora Jimenez was an extremely talkative woman. It was nice that she didn't really wait for me to respond before she continued forward. "We are in the middle of redecorating. Can you believe it? We were asked to host one of the only formal dinners before the games. All of the people from the Quinta Isla will be coming to join us. Even that new girl. What do they call her? La Chica Dorada," she practically sighed.

My ears perked up. That was definitely Carmen. "I have heard so much about her."

"Who hasn't?" Señora Jimenez said with a wink. Then she was off, talking about the games, and how exhilarating they were. It was a little hard to follow.

Then, I looked down at my new ward. She was watching me closely.

When I smiled at her, she quickly looked away. I was already beginning to understand the little girl's quietness and apprehension.

We eventually came to a stop in front of a door that I assumed was her room.

Señora Jimenez opened the door and stepped inside. I followed behind.

The room was beautiful—it had richly colored furniture, an abundant closet, and a cozy bed. It felt comfortable, warm, and inviting. I could tell that I would be well taken care of here.

Carmen may not have been living in this house, but this was still her gift to me. I could feel it.

"What do you think?" Señora Jimenez asked.

I took it all in, the dolls, the wooden horse, the dozens of books stacked upon each other. They were unread, that was easy enough to see. But, the dolls and toys told me that this room belonged to a girl who was in love with stories, even if she couldn't read them yet. Even if there was no one who read them to her.

A girl who wanted to explore.

I could relate to that.

I looked down at Lirio, who was still peering up at me shyly. "It looks perfect."

CHAPTER 6
Fairytales And Flirting

The sun was beginning to dip in the sky, the colors of dusk painting the sky with a soft rose hue.

We had been at our lessons since morning, studying our letters while I read from books filled with fairy tales. A wood elf who raised a dragon by herself, a widow who married a fae trapped as a great white bear in order to save her family, and a princess who had been turned into a monster after killing her lover.

They were dark and delicious. Each one piercing me through the heart with their heart-wrenching tales of courage and love.

For Lirio, the stories were frayed, lackluster, and while I was enthralled by them, I saw her attention wander out the window.

I thought of how I had felt as a child. It was a struggle for me to focus as well. Something that always seemed to cure my racing thoughts was the outdoors. It was strange how the chaos of the natural world brought me inner peace.

"Let's go outside," I said, standing up and beckoning her to come with me. Elated, she followed me out, a wide smile playing on her lips.

I found a quiet spot beneath the tree; the shade protecting us from the heat of the sinking sun.

For a little while, she paid attention. Still, she was abnormally quiet for a young child. Then, all too soon, I could see her gaze wander again, and I paused.

"What are you looking at?" I asked her, trying to keep the exasperation out of my voice.

"Tiago," she said pointing to the distance, her voice filled with a layering of joy that I hadn't seen. I followed her gaze and saw her brother running. "He wants to be strong for the big tournament."

My breath hitched in my chest. The Blood Tournament was a bitter subject for me. He was tall, like Carmen... And strong. My heart raced as he took off his shirt, revealing a chiseled chest rippled with muscle. I had noticed his strength before, but now, seeing him with his bare chest glistening with sweat, his long legs carrying him through the wind, something stirred in my chest.

I don't think I'd ever seen anyone as beautiful as him.

I definitely couldn't beat him in a fight, not even if I stabbed him with a knife. The corners of my mouth quirked up at the morbid thought. My smile was a garden, but my brain was a graveyard.

"Tiago!" Lirio called. He was drawn from his intense, pensive state, and a brilliant smile broke out, softening the edges of his sharp face.

San Volcán, that just isn't fair, I thought.

As the last rays of sunlight bled from the sky, he jogged over to us. I felt Lirio tugging at the bottom of my dress to help her stand up. She ran over to him, and he picked her up in a fierce bear hug. They twirled in a circle while she kissed his face.

I watched the muscles on his arms ripple with movement.

He noticed my gaze and grinned harder, his teeth flashing white in the dimming light.

"I see you both decided to join me outside," he said, his voice not dissimilar to pure sunshine.

I hated him.

"¿Cómo vas con tus clases?" he asked while he set the little girl down. Instead of leaving her then, he kneeled down in front of her, meeting her at her level.

It was hard to be intimidated by him when he looked like this.

I watched with unveiled fascination. Then Lirio looked up at me and his gaze followed. He caught me staring at him square-on. His smile widened, and

I lifted my chin a bit.

The butterflies couldn't win me over.

"Mas o menos," Lirio said quietly. She studied my face, then looked at her brother.

A part of me wanted to laugh, but my mouth was a stone. I had nothing to really say to him. We shouldn't even be talking at all. I stood up, ready to go back inside.

"We should probably get back inside. We will resume tomorrow," I said with a hint of a smile. Lirio pouted, and I held out my hand.

Santiago nodded, gave his sister one last hug, and then looked up at me. "What do you think of your first countryside sunset?"

My eyes flicked up to the sky. The sun was nearly gone now, and already a few stars were peeking out behind the fiery air. "It's..." What could I say? It reminded me of the sunsets in Puerto Dolores. But I had been young then, and the seaside port town was a very different place to the large estates and sprawling hills. Lirio finally took my hand, and I realized I hadn't responded. "Beautiful," I finished lamely.

"You should see it like this more often," he said, standing up. I almost flinched when he drew to his whole height, and I hated myself a little. There were many reasons to be afraid in this place, but Santiago Flores Jimenez didn't seem like one of them.

I smiled, but my inner voice said, *I don't think I should.*

"Gracias," I said gently.

He smiled and nodded, as if he could sense my inner conflict. Then he told Lirio it was time to go in and she easily let go of my hand, running off towards the house.

He lingered behind for a moment, the light of the setting sun briefly painting his face golden.

"Enjoy your dinner," I said, our gazes meeting for a split second before I turned away, embarrassed. He knew who I was. As an institutriz, or governess, I wouldn't eat with the family. From the brief explanations detailed in a note with no name, I was instructed on the in-between nature of such a position.

I was afforded greater closeness with the family than anyone else, but it was mostly to be directed toward Lirio. My food would be delivered to my room, which felt isolating. Perhaps dining with the servants would be a mistake.

I walked back inside slowly, always a few paces behind Santiago. When we reached the doors, I wished him a good night and quickly hurried to my room.

As promised, there was a silver cloche sitting on a desk in the corner of the room. I sat down and picked up a book. Books were never so... available. I had heard some of the fairytales I'd read to Lirio told by different people, but it was a new experience entirely to read them.

There was more depth in reading them, more excitement. I wanted to re-enter that world of fairies and princesses, but my mind kept running away from the page.

I was just like Lirio.

For the next hour, I tried to focus on my studies as my mind continuously drifted back to the memory of him standing there. The way his eyes held so much understanding in that brief moment. His penetrating gaze made me feel like he could see everything I was thinking and feeling, and I'd never felt so exposed. There had to be some way to shake the memory of his eyes. With a snap, I slammed the book of fairytales shut.

Maybe it was time to sleep.

I stripped out of my clothes and put on the first thin white nightgown I could find in the ropero near my bed. After turning off the lights, I flung myself onto the cloud soft mattress. It didn't help.

Squeezing my eyes shut didn't help.

Growling, I sat up and looked around the room. There was a door frame peeking up from under one of the curtains. Something lightened inside of me. I bet the view would be beautiful. I turned on the reading lamp next to my bed. It cast impressive light throughout the entire room. Taking a deep breath, I walked to the set of glass doors which led to a small balcony. I had seen enough from the outside to know that these balconies were all over the house; I was far from special.

A cool breeze blew over me and I inhaled deeply. There wasn't any pollution, no smell of unwashed bodies or poorly discarded trash. Everything was... a little floral. Gooseflesh rippled across my skin from the chill.

Maybe I should've gotten a coat. Or brought a blanket.

Being exposed to the dark night air was better than thinking of Santiago's green eyes.

It... was even a little punishment. Punishment for how awful I felt. I was an imposter. This place was too grand, too beautiful for someone like me. I tried to picture Carmen in a house like this. The release of her outfits had already grown more extravagant by the day.

It had only been a week since she had left.

In my mind, Carmen could be just as much a comforting concept as she was a friend. Even though I was sad, her name made me feel better, safer. She had carried me for so long that a piece of her was ingrained in my heart. She had saved me from worse things than this while we lived in the orphanage. And she didn't even know what she was saving me from.

My skin started to crawl when I thought of cold, rough fingers grazing my skin. My insides tightened, and I started to sweat. It was freezing in the cool night air, making me feel worse.

Without thinking, I was moving.

Maestro Cecelia used to tell us that our muscles were our medicine. Exercise made us lighter, happier. Made our bodies strong. If getting lost in a routine could help me banish the frightful ghosts that were crowding all around me, I was willing to try anything.

Without thinking, my hands took the position of the dance Maestra Cecelia made me repeat over and over.

I tried to push away all the ugly thoughts with a memory of music.

Closing my eyes surprisingly helped this time.

It was good to focus on what I felt for a little while instead of what I looked like. As my heart sped up, my skin warmed, and the cool air started to feel nice. I turned once and then froze.

Someone was singing. It was a rich, tenor's voice trailing across the garden.

My moments stopped immediately, and I crossed my arms over my chest. Not that I was being indecent...

Well, maybe I was.

The singing stopped.

Leaning over the rail of the balcony, I looked around, trying to find the man who had been watching me. How could he even see me in the dark? I quickly turned around, and saw just how bright my room looked behind me. Anyone watching could've seen my little performance.

I quietly closed the doors, not wanting to wake anyone up, shut the curtains, and hurried to bed.

The lamp turned off with a click.

Damned thing.

CHAPTER 7
Sickness Didn't Become Me

Fever drew me from sleep. My stomach was roiling and my muscles were aching. One look at the curtains told me that it was still early morning. There was no light straining through the expensive cloth.

Whatever was happening was excruciating. I tried to lay still and rest, but no position was comfortable.

After stumbling to the decent-sized bathing room to throw up everything I had eaten the night before, I turned on the smooth, white bath. I couldn't bring myself to be a little more than surprised when water trickled down from the ceiling instead of the regular faucet. I'd heard of this. Like a rain shower.

Hopefully, it would help.

I didn't wait for the water to get warm, opting to step inside immediately. My head was pounding, so I leaned against one of the marble walls to keep from falling.

It was like my body was at war with itself. My heart raced, and my skin felt like it chilled to my core.

I stayed there for a minute.

Then two.

Instinct after all those years conserving water for other dancers had me soaping my hair even though it felt like my arms were falling off.

Then I remembered I wasn't in Maestra Cecelia's Theater, and that Elites could afford for me to use all the water I needed.

Slowly, I sank down. The steam from the hot water billowed around my body, and the pain began to subside. Not completely, but enough for me to breathe. I stayed there for a few more minutes, letting the water ease the acute pain all over my body and rinse away any trace of soap.

Finally, after what felt like an eternity, I switched the shower off and stepped out.

Wrapping a towel around my damp skin, I stared into the mirror. My eyes had lost the fiery spark of pain and my skin was ashen, but I didn't let my reflection dictate how I felt about myself. No one cared about how I looked as long as I was clean and properly dressed.

I had made it through the worst of it.

Though my body was still weak, I could stand tall for the rest of the day, even if I was mostly limping back to bed. I needed to get dressed, needed to go check on Lirio. She would be waking any moment.

Walking back into my room with nothing more than a towel, I tried to keep my back straight. I looked at a small array of dresses, pants, and button up shirts.

Pants and a clean-pressed shirt sounded nicer than a tight bodice or waist. I picked them out and carefully put them on. I still felt weak and nauseous, but having nothing in my stomach was actually turning out to be a positive.

Standing in front of the mirror, I started to do my hair, savoring the gentle sensation of a brush running through my ringlets. There were several bottles that looked similar to potions. I picked each one up and smelled it, getting a modicum of joy when I found aceite de lavanda. It reminded me of a friend called Silvia who owned something akin to a winery and apothecary.

She had always given me small samples. I added a little bit of lavender oil to the lengths of my hair, hoping it would make sense of my wild curls.

Looking down at myself with a critical eye I decided that I could do this. No matter what life threw at me, I would never surrender.

I was strong, I was brave, I was determined.

And today, I was going to show the world exactly what I was made of.

"¿Qué letra es esa?" I pointed to one of the words that I had carefully written on the paper in front of us.

After breakfast, I wasn't feeling much better, so I decided to go outside. The sunshine made me feel more alive. More energized.

Lirio looked at my carefully formed A, and squinted.

She was unnaturally still for a full minute before she said, "No se."

Then she looked up at me with wide eyes.

I let out a long-suffering breath. We had actually just finished the entire alphabet. She did well with repeating after me, but struggled retaining anything.

"Está bien, Lilita," I said gently.

She took a deep breath and looked away. Then, her face brightened as if she were pure sunshine. Every part of her woke up, and she was on her feet.

"Maestra, ¡mire!" Then she dashed toward a bush.

I saw what she was looking at immediately as dozens of butterflies fluttered off the bush. We were at a time of year where there were few flowers, and usually they migrated somewhere warmer.

It was unique. Special, even.

I smiled. It was hard to get mad when things like this happened.

While observing my ward, I noted how curious she was. How eager she was about the world around her. She was shy, but once she came out of that, she was a firecracker.

As Lirio ran around chasing the butterflies, I couldn't help but think about how different her life was compared to mine at her age. She had an innocence and naivety that I never had. But then again, I never had the luxury of being a child.

I was born into a brothel, and my childhood was filled with unspeakable horrors. I never had the chance to play or learn like other children. Instead, my mother spent the first three years of my life ignoring me. The other women were kind and devoted to hiding me from the Night Merchant who owned the brothel.

Mamá was always sick.

THE HIDDEN GOVERNESS

Always tired.

The women told me to stay hidden until after dark. Until the ugly sounds were finished.

I was never to go anywhere unattended.

It wasn't until my mother had died that I stumbled out of the only building I had ever known. I was only six, but I knew what an orphanage was.

But despite all the trauma and pain, I refused to let it define me. I was determined to make a better life for myself, and Carmen had helped me do that.

And now, here I was, teaching a young girl how to read and write. It was a far cry from my former life, and I felt a sense of fulfillment in knowing that I was making a difference in someone else's life.

As Lirio continued to run around and explore, I sat down on a bench and watched her with a sense of joy.

But my peaceful moment was interrupted when Santiago appeared out of nowhere and stood at my side.

"Buenos días," he said calmly.

I looked at him and repeated the greeting.

He had an easy smile that was hard for me to return. Just being around him made me feel nervous, tired. He was so large, so intimidating.

The worst part was that he was kind. Strong men were meant to be admired from afar.

He turned to me and motioned at Lirio.

"Se ve muy feliz," he said. His voice was warm, full of admiration.

I nodded and smiled softly.

"Hmm," I agreed.

He went quiet for a moment, then said, "She's doing well with you."

I looked up at him and raised an eyebrow.

"Gracias," I replied, my voice a little shaky.

He nodded, his eyes still locked on me. "You're not the first governess that she's had," he said. "She only opens up to people she likes."

I nodded slowly. "She hates letters, but she loves stories. She's definitely stubborn." It was almost too easy to picture her defying anyone who tried to tell her what to do.

She wasn't even loud.

She would just stare at them in silence.

The mental image made me laugh.

I could feel the warmth of Santiago's gaze on my face. "I'm friends with one of the other contestants, Isaac Monroy. He told me that Renata,"—he hesitated—"*Carmen* dances very well. I think you do, too."

Looking at him from the corner of my eyes and pursing my lips I said, "Come to one of my shows when your family was vacationing on my humble isle?"

His smile was too wide, too charming for his own good. "I attended a show much more recently than that. Last night, to be exact."

My face flushed instantly. Someone had been singing, watching me. But I thought it would be one of the Workers. I gritted my teeth together, and he seemed to like that even more. "Funny, I could have sworn there was a frog skulking about in the garden from all the croaking."

His eyes gleamed. "And can frogs not turn into princes with a kiss? There was something very enchanting about you twirling around in a sheer nightgown where anyone could see you."

Now I was angry. "It wasn't sheer." He looked like he was about to laugh. Fighting with him wasn't going to do me any good. I took a step forward, "Con permiso, Señor Santiago," and then joined Lirio in the dirt.

CHAPTER 8
I've Noticed

Nearly a month had passed, and the sickness wasn't getting better. I had considered pregnancy, but my menstrual cycle was regular. A part of me considered the Withering, but there was no rash, no physical sign yet.

Just pain and fever, day in and day out. Lirio wasn't in danger. Nor was Santiago, who never seemed to leave me alone for more than a few hours. He was persistent, too charming for his own good. When Lirio would go off to explore nearby, he would ease next to me and try to tease out my past.

Rich boys didn't understand how the world worked. I humored him, telling him half-truths. As far as he was concerned, I had been raised by wolves and danced naked in the moonlight as homage to my beastly parents.

He didn't need to know the truth. The sad story of an absent mother, an abusive almost-father, and a very lonely soul.

Having obeyed the ominous note from Antonio which instructed me to stop taking the black pills, I was feeling worse every day.

It became more and more plausible that Antonio Castillas had lied to me, and wanted me dead. Maybe they were poisoning my food. I tried to sneak snacks from the trays brought for Lirio, and picked at my own meals.

Maybe dying was better than whatever consequences could be waiting for me if they found Carmen was, in fact, not named Renata, nor was she an Elite.

Lirio was progressing in her studies very slowly, but I was dying quickly.

Today, she had actually requested to spend time in the library. Her parents had left on a shopping trip on the Tercera Isla, where exquisite artisan dishes were produced, and we were left alone.

Lirio, Santiago, me, and an entire house full of staff. I only seemed to find solace in strange fairy tales about lost princesses and heroines who find true love. I'd learned that a quick shot of brandy in the morning dulled my pain sufficiently. It was stolen from the kitchens by me, of course. It helped me to make it through the day, that was for sure.

Today was no different. Lirio and I were practicing basic letter sounds while playing a game of rewards. For every answer she got right, I handed her a small piece of turrón. It worked very well.

The door opened, and both of us looked up.

A part of me already knew who it would be; Santiago. He was just as constant as the sickness. Something akin to a very large shadow for the last several weeks. I would've thought that preparing for the upcoming tournament would've taken more of his free time away from him.

He smiled brightly at us. Santiago Flores Jimenez was a man much more prone to careful indifference than warmth. But that changed around Lirio, and by default, me.

However, I wasn't looking for kindness or honeyed words. Despite the unnatural closeness I was starting to feel around him, I knew he was dangerous. He flirted too much, and I just wanted to make it out of whatever this was alive. I cursed my tongue every time we spoke, and fought against my brain every time his attractiveness made me short of breath.

Maybe it was his privilege, maybe it was the fact that he was constantly around, but I was split clean in half between wanting him to touch me and begging him to leave me alone. Even just for one solitary day.

It was a futile hope for an institutriz, but it was my hope nonetheless.

Lirio, however, was enamored with the young man, and encouraged his presence. She lifted off her chair and hurried across the room to hug him as he said, "Buenos días."

Damn that adorable little girl.

After returning with my own half-hearted reply, I stood up. If he was here, then surely I could be allotted a few precious moments of alone time in a nearby wash room.

Lirio was already tugging him toward the table, but he didn't move with her.

He stayed there, as immovable as a mountain.

I took a long breath.

"Señor Flores, can I please just go for a moment? I promise I'll be right back."

He looked down at me, and I was extremely aware of how large and imposing he was.

He took one look at me and said, "I know you don't like me." Then continued to block the only exit.

I rolled my eyes. "Does that hurt your ego?"

He remained silent.

"I wasn't aware that was required of my current position." A stabbing pain went through my skull. For a moment, I squeezed my eyes. My eyes fluttered openly to see that he tracked the movement.

"Are you all right?" he asked, ignoring my snippy comment

That caught me off guard. "I'm fine." Unfortunately, my voice lacked every ounce of conviction.

He stared at me long and hard. "No, you really aren't. I've been noticing it for a while."

I scoffed, and another dull stab of pain went straight through my skull.

Suddenly, his hand was on my arm, steadying me. I yanked my appendage away, and he frowned. For a second, it was like the ever-pleasant and teasing statue came to life. There were deep lines in his forehead, which suddenly seemed much more important to look at than focusing on the throbbing in my head.

The midday sun was warm through the window even as the temperatures continued to plummet outdoors. I was suddenly so very cold, as if I had been doused in an ice bath.

The room tilted sideways, and a smooth, elegant hand reached out toward me, in my line of sight.

I was going down.

Santiago wrapped his arms around me before I hit the ground.

CHAPTER 9
You Had No Right

A Médico was standing over me when I gained consciousness. Familiar surroundings engulfed me, telling me that I was in my room. A fever was burning across my skin like a hot fire. I lay there stiff as a board as my eyes opened. It brought instant relief from the stewing heat that made them feel like orbs of jelly in my skull.

The Médico was shorter than most of the men I'd seen in my life, and his mouth was pinched together in a straight line through the plastic mask he wore to protect his stubby face. His features were washed out by the blinding overhead light, but I could see the curve of his balding head, and the wrinkle lines that came from a lifetime of inspecting those who were sick.

Reason flooded back into me as I wondered why the hell he was here. Was I still in the Flores Jimenez estate?

I shot upward, nearly knocking heads with the man. He staggered backward like a drunkard, and my chest heaved. It hurt to breathe.

"Where am I?" I croaked.

The door near the right-hand wall swung open, and Santiago walked in. There were no smiles this time, as he had seemingly gone to the impassive statue I'd first met in the car here.

He was holding a towel and a water jug with a basin. "It's all right, Magda." He spoke slowly, as if he were addressing a wounded animal.

"¿Por qué trajiste un Médico?" I hissed at him. The commotion was too much for my throat apparently, because I started coughing, and my body felt akin to what the asphalt must feel like unto a construction Workers jack hammer.

Santiago's throat bobbed. "Magdalena,"

I ignored his use of my name and continued. "I am not sick."

He opened his mouth to respond, but I was persistent. "You had no right to do this without me—"

The Médico interrupted me. "Enough. Señorita, it brings me no great pleasure to tell you this, but... You have the Withering."

My mouth hung open and my mind instantly was transported to Ronaldo's sick mother. Her sore-covered body. The letter telling me to stop taking these pills. Was Carmen really behind that? Or had this been a plot to kill me off all along?

If I had continued taking the pastillas negras, I couldn't be in this situation right now.

"No," I said indignantly. "There's no rash."

Santiago coughed, and the Médico's eyes went down. Well, shit.

I slid back the covers and found myself wearing nothing more than my regular slip. The air bit against my skin. How I had gotten to this state of undress without one of the maids helping me, I wouldn't know. The thought made a shockwave of electric fear travel down my spine. *What if I had gotten someone else sick?*

If, that is, I was actually sick.

I walked over to the mirror as quickly as possible, wobbling all the way. As I stared at the reflection in front of me, I saw a hollow figure with bright rash-like bumps all around her mouth.

I gasped and staggered back, right into Santiago. I looked up at him in horror. "Stay back!"

He looked down at me with a sort of sadness that reached deeper than a simple frown. "Magda, I can't get sick."

"Señorita Magaña, you really must come lay down again," the Médico said. He was spraying disinfectant on hands, and the whole room filled with the pungent scent.

Given few other options, I sagged into Santiago's support. For the second time, he steadied me before half-carrying me back to my bed.

The idea that I was weak in front of him was appalling. Much more so than the hideous bumps forming across my skin.

After I was laid back down onto the soft bed, Santiago carefully pulled the cover back over me. His touch was light enough that I shivered under it, little bumps of gooseflesh erupting all over my body in the most uncomfortable way. There were no more words for a few minutes until the Médico broke the gloomy silence.

"Señorita, lo lamento mucho," he said quietly.

I watched him for a moment, not envying his position one bit. How many times did he have to say that exact sentence to patients, to their families?

I looked up at him. "I haven't been talking the pastillas negras," I said quickly.

His expression clouded, and I was sure that he was going to give me a thorough tongue-lashing. Instead, he said, "That explains the rapid onset."

While I didn't understand his words entirely, I felt ten times worse, the fever burning hotter like some invisible being had decided to stoke the furnace fires lit inside of me. "I was... told to stop taking them."

The short man looked at me. "Señorita... the preventative pills don't actually prevent the Withering. They slow its progress." He looked away uncomfortably. Why wouldn't he meet my eye?

I blinked. Because I was dying.

"The person who advised you to stop taking them was more or less justified. There can be other side effects from the pills that are comparable to the Withering. Did you experience withdrawals?" the Médico said.

After taking a moment to think about the shakiness, the nausea, I nodded my head with a level of difficulty. The very instant I did, Santiago's heavy gaze was on my face. I didn't dare look at him.

The mystery of the pills had been solved... There was no one trying to poison me.

I was just sick.

That realization was a pit inside of my body. I grew more hollow with every second.

"How long do I have?" I asked quietly. If the pills slowed the speed of the sickness, that meant everything I knew about the sickness was likely incorrect.

The Médico looked right at me as he said, "About a month. Maybe longer."

The room stilled, including Santiago. Every part of me, even my heart, was immobile in my burning body. Steamy tears welled in my eyes.

I was never going to see Carmen again.

Everything I had worked so hard for crumbled to pieces.

The pain that had nothing to do with dying came.

"How long would I have had if I'd continued taking the pills?" I asked with closed eyes.

"Maybe six months."

His words felt like a series of daggers launched right at my heart. I could've seen Carmen again.

Of course she was going to win the Tournament. How could she not?

Large, burning tears started down my cheek.

A gloved hand touched my arm. "Señorita, let me take your blood."

I sobbed. "What's the point?"

"I can help make this next month more comfortable for you."

Comfortable? There was no such thing. But I kept my eyes closed as I nodded.

He tied a rubber band to my arm, and my eyes finally opened just in time to watch him prod my arm for a view. He took out the largest needle I'd ever seen and inserted it into my skin.

I gasped. It was a bit stronger than a pinch, but the sensation afterward almost hurt worse. It felt like cold metal was being poured into my bloodstream.

When I looked up, I found Santiago watching from the wall with the most peculiar expression.

Our eyes met, and I realized his nostrils were flared.

I smiled weakly, and he did not.

The time it took for the doctor to finish felt agonizingly long. When he was done, a part of me felt less fevered. Colder. After thanking him, I curled up under the blanket and fell asleep almost instantly.

CHAPTER 10
Two Seconds Away From Becoming Nothing More Than A Memory

"Magdalena," a rich tenor's voice said.

It drew me out of my fever-addled dreams of monsters and wild creatures, and into a world filled with pain and fever. The world was spinning. Maybe I was still dreaming, and the monsters had merely gone into hiding?

"Magdalena, wake up," the voice said again, this time much more commanding.

I obeyed, but not without regret. My mouth was dry and raspy, as if every particle of dust had landed inside of my throat and encrusted itself in the soft flesh of my throat. A part of me wondered if there had truly been a time before this awful pain.

My eyes focused, and I saw Santiago leaning over me. Upon opening my mouth, it became apparent that it would be impossible for me to speak. As my chest rose and fell laboriously, Santiago's eyes darted around my face, as if making sure I was still alive. He was so large, and I was helpless. If he tried to hurt me, I wouldn't be able to do anything.

He was so close. The clean white-linen scent of him was the only other thing that I could smell aside from my feverish body. There was a candle on the table reflecting his once-smooth forehead now crinkled with deep worry. My eyes traced the planes of his face to see the stubble just beginning to peek out along his sharp jaw and strong chin.

Assured that I was awake, he turned away from me. The sound of water being rung out a cloth alerted me seconds before he placed the cool compress to my forehead. The cool wash of water spread throughout my entire body, like an oasis in a desert.

"San Volcán, you look awful," he whispered. If I were in better health, I would've told him off. Or, better yet, slapped him. Even though he was right —death didn't suit anyone. He raked a trembling hand through his hair. "Shit. This is bad." It took several more nervous twitches before he said, "I don't know if you can speak, but I just need you to listen for a second."

I watched with half-moon eyes.

"Every Elite is taught about Blood Magic from a young age. We are told that we can't use this magic on anyone but ourselves. That means, if you are weak, then you have to be extra careful," he rushed through his words. It seemed like it was important for him to tell me these things, to express these thoughts to me even if I couldn't respond. "However, whispered in hallways and scribbled in old textbooks, there is a concept well-known but dangerous: the Sanguine Call. It's the idea that our blood… is desirable to another person sometimes. Blood bonds are as mysterious as they are rare."

He stopped, and I listened, completely immobile, but totally awake.

He took a deep breath. "When the doctor was here earlier, and he took your blood, he cut you and you kept bleeding for a while after he was gone. It was practically nothing, but the scent surrounded me. I—" He broke off. "Magda, you call to me. Your blood sings a song that only the wind can hear while brushing over a grove of flowers. I… I want to try to heal you."

He stopped. My thoughts were mostly blank. What did he mean that I smelled sweet to him? I looked like a corpse, and felt a great deal worse than one. While watching him, expecting him to hurt me, I realized what he was offering.

The defeatist thoughts from earlier were momentarily shoved away.

I could see Carmen again.

And really, that decided it for me.

One painful swallow later, I opened my mouth and told him yes.

His mouth parted slowly, intently watching me wince. "Really?"

I nodded.

He wasted no more time turning, reaching his hands into his pocket and producing a small knife. The lines of his throat bobbed as he took a nervous gulp. "Right, well. I think I need you to drink a little of my blood. Just a drop or two. Then I will... hurt myself. If this works, I can heal myself, and you will heal with me."

Hurt himself? Like, slice his palm? The thought scared me, but he didn't give me time to ask questions. There was a quiver to his voice, and I saw his hand fumble with the sharp weapon before pricking his index finger.

We both watched the blood well up for a few moments before his gaze slid back to me. He leaned over, his body weight shifting the mattress beneath me and causing the fine bed clothes to rustle.

I should've drawn away from him, reeking pig as I did, but I couldn't help myself. As his finger neared my mouth, I opened. He smeared the blood on the rough skin of my chapped lips.

"You have to swallow," he urged. I saw the tension in his face as I eyed him warily, yet I complied. I had expected it to taste like pure metal, but there was a sweetness to it—to him.

His hand drew away slowly, and then he took my hand. While we sat there, he closed his eyes and raised his hand with the dagger.

My brows furrowed, my mind too sluggish. Without warning, he rammed the dagger directly into his gut.

I screamed, and he reached over and covered my mouth with his free hand. The metallic sweet smell of the blood I'd tasted seconds before filled the room. His face was crumpled in an expression of agony, tears spring into my own eyes as I witnessed his pain.

"I'm... okay..." he ground out, trying to steady me.

With a unique burst of strength, I lifted my dying body up and yanked at the knife. It slid out of his stomach with hiss and exited the wound with a meaty click. If he started healing while the weapon was still inside, I shuddered to think what would happen.

No one but Carmen turned into a gilded statue when using blood magic, but I could feel a crackling on Santiago's skin. It echoed in my own. A warmth spread through me. It seemed like time suddenly stopped and an intense heat rushed all over my body.

The next thing I knew, Santiago's hands were on my face and he was staring closely into my eyes with intense concentration and focus. I felt his energy seeping through me, purifying every inch of my being with its thrumming power. His healing energy descended upon me like a gentle rain and continued to lull me in its cocoon-like embrace. I felt the bumps stop itching and burning. My pain was melting into a soothing abyss of blissful peace.

Before long, the hot agony that had been consuming my body disappeared completely and was replaced by a calming sense of stillness and serenity. I looked up at Santiago with wonderment in my eyes. A new kind of heat built up inside of me.

I tried to swallow, only to find my mouth dry. My heart was racing in my chest. Unnaturally acute senses listened to his breathing and watched every micro-expression on his face. He was so close, still leaning over me. His eyes were hooded as he watched my face, and I could feel the echo of his own racing heart through the sheets.

My fingers felt genuinely cold after what felt like an eternity of fever.

His long, smooth fingers touched my face. "You are healed," he said softly.

I had already known that from the way I felt currently. The way that there was a hot tightness in my lower belly told me that my body was ready to focus on something much different than fighting off illness.

Where was this coming from?

I pressed my lips together and held my breath. His eyes flicked down and watched.

The electricity between us crackled across my skin, and his fingers stroked my cheek once more before his thumb ran over my lips. Softly at first, and then more roughly. Possessively, almost.

My heart sped up, and my judgment clouded over with desire for… him.

Shit.

For the boy I had spent more than a month avoiding. I'd wanted him to go away, but he had healed me. Given me a second chance at life.

And the healing made me burn for him in a way I had never felt.

His head dipped, and my head jerked away out of instinct. He was dangerous. Kissing him wouldn't be harmless. The movement had brought me back to the glaring, filthy state of my body. Aroused or not, I was caked with sweat and grime that came from a sickness and infrequent bathing.

"Wait," I said breathlessly.

He stilled. Then leaned back.

I wished that the pull, the heat would've stopped. The gap between us only stoked the flames.

My strength had returned completely, so I pushed myself off the bed. The thin nightgown was wrinkled and stained with sweat. It took every inch of restraint not to peel it off as I walked to the washroom. Energy was pulsing through me, intensifying every sensation.

It wasn't until the door was closed that I loosened the strings and let it all fall to the floor. After turning on the water, I sunk into the still filling bathtub.

The warm water soothed my aching muscles, and the steam enveloped me in a serene atmosphere. I closed my eyes and let myself be transported to another world where there was no illness, no war, no need to fight for survival. It was a world where I allowed myself to think of Santiago without any fear of repercussions.

I knew that he wanted me. Boys had always wanted me.

But... the thought of him wanting me was both exhilarating and terrifying. I had never desired someone with such intensity that it bordered on obsession. But now, with Santiago's touch still burning on my skin, I couldn't help but crave more.

As I soaked in the tub, I heard a knock on the door. Santiago's voice followed, muffled but undeniable. "Do you need help?"

I hesitated for a moment, but the pull was too strong. The burning refused to ease––I needed him, his touch, his heat. Then I blinked. Despite the adrenaline coursing through my veins, my muscles were still relatively sore. Floral-scented soap bubbles coated the surface of the water like an opaque lace blanket.

After taking a deep breath, I said, "Come in."

Everything moved in slow motion as the door inched open, and his sandy brown head came in first, followed by his entire body.

Hungry eyes landed directly on me. Even though I knew he couldn't see anything, my skin flushed. Deciding to break the tension in the room, I said, "Can you help me with my hair?"

Santiago stepped forward, his nostrils flaring as he took in the scent of the floral bubbles. Without a word, he crossed to me and knelt beside the tub. That strange awareness took over again as I watched his hands reach for the shampoo bottle. There was a strength in his movements that translated as grace. The tone of his body made him elegant, powerful. His strong fingers massaged my scalp, sending shivers down my spine. I closed my eyes and leaned back, biting my tongue just before letting out a soft sigh of pleasure.

The tension between us was palpable, and it was only a matter of time before it erupted into an irresistible explosion of passion.

Santiago's fingers trailed along the curves of my neck, sending goosebumps down my arms. "You're so beautiful," he whispered into my ear. "If you couldn't tell, I didn't want you to die. And I am glad my half-crazed plan worked."

I was trembling as his words washed over me. Whatever this was between us was hard to track, damned near impossible to understand. It was impossible, but in this moment, the boundaries fell away. I turned around to face him. Even I didn't know if I would kiss him or send him away.

"Tiago." The word fell off my tongue before I had a second to reconsider, and his mouth spread into the widest grin I'd ever seen. It was the pet name that I'd heard Lirio call him over and over again.

Apparently, it had stuck.

"Yes?" he said slowly, reaching out to brush away one of the hair strands plastered to my cheek.

"I think you should—"

"No. Don't send me away, Magdalena. Tomorrow we can go back to bickering in front of Lirio, and you can keep pretending that me following you around like a puppy dog annoys you, but tonight, please don't send me away."

His eyes were dark with passion, and my body was responding in kind. I knew that I should push him away, tell him that this was a mistake, but I couldn't. I was stuck in orbit around him.

"All right. Stay."

Without another word, Santiago leaned forward, digging his arms into the warm water, and scooped me up. The bath water sloshed under me, and I watched the fierce determination in his face as he brought me to the door, opened it with one hand, and then barreled toward my bed.

This should've terrified me. Being with someone bigger than me was giving them power to hurt me.

But I didn't feel that way right now. It felt like I could hurt him just as much as he could hurt me.

And neither one of us wanted that.

After placing me on the bed so that I was sitting with surprising gentleness, he started ripping off his shirt and undershirt, which were stained with water from where he had held me. He was... stunning. It was overwhelming to senses with the pace at which he went. The grace and elegance of his arms, his hands, his fingers, extended to every part of him.

"Shouldn't I do that part?" I asked with more bravado than I felt.

His smile was wild. "You didn't let me take yours off," and then he stood right in front of me.

He took my hand and kissed it gently. Then trailed kisses up my arm. "You must promise to be quiet, Magdalena," he said gently, and then pulled me up. At last, our lips met.

Then, our bodies were connected from head to toe as if we had become one person sharing the same breath and beat of heart. My hands found their way around Santiago's neck as his arms held tight against my back. He continued to kiss me as the world faded away along with the night.

CHAPTER 11
Kisses On The Balcony

I didn't know what they had told Lirio or anyone else about my sickness, but I never saw the doctor again. The next day, when Lirio pushed into my room, begging me to feel well enough to come play with her, I smiled.

The night before was still burned in my memory, and there were glowing embers scattered through my insides as my insides recalled everything I had said. Had felt.

I sat up slowly, but Lirio's face was filled with concern and I knew that she was too young to understand the full extent of what I had just gone through. All that aside, she was an Elite. She didn't understand what it meant to fear for her life.

I gave her a warm smile. "I'm feeling a bit better. Let's go for a walk in the gardens."

"Yes!" she screamed with joy.

We stepped outside, and I inhaled deeply, taking in the crisp air. The sun was so bright it almost blinded me and the sky was a deep blue. I felt liberated, as if a heavy weight had been lifted off my chest.

As we walked, Lirio chattered about the different plants and flowers that filled the garden. She gestured at each one with excitement, making me laugh at her young exuberance.

Burning ash, I am so glad to be alive, I thought. The way that Lirio played as we walked reminded me of how Carmen and I used to play together. I was so reserved until I had her.

There was a sense of wholesomeness in the moment as I twirled and ran with her.

As the day wore on, I thought about Santiago. He was going to wait for his parents' boat, which would be docking today.

My skin pebbled and heated at every stray thought to him.

I would just need to be patient.

It was night when Santiago's parents arrived. I wasn't present to see them, but there was an odd sense of normalcy. As if I hadn't been dying in my bed last night. I could hear the servants bustling, but I knew I wouldn't be required for any of it.

After eating my dinner, I laid in my bed, wondering if I would see Santiago today.

Tiago.

I had called him that more than once last night. It had been difficult to tell where one of us ended and the other began.

I couldn't believe how careless I had been. It wasn't like me to openly show my emotions, but something about Tiago made me feel different. I tried to push him out of my mind, but every time I closed my eyes, his face would appear. And with it, the memory of his touch.

Suddenly, there was a knock on the door. I bolted upright, my pulse picking up like a gelding horse spooked by a snake. It took me a second to realize it hadn't come from the regular door.

He was standing at the window of my balcony door, highlighted by the evergreen jessamine vines and soft outdoor light.

How had he done that? Did he climb all the way up? He was dressed in a crisp white shirt and black trousers, his hair neatly combed back. He looked so handsome and sophisticated that I was momentarily taken aback.

"May I come in?" he asked, his voice deep and rich.

I nodded, unable to speak, and he stepped into the room. His eyes roved over me, taking in my thinnest nightgown. The air bit against my skin, suddenly making me self-conscious in something so indecent and sporting my messiest hair.

Tiago's intense gaze made me feel like he was seeing right through to my very soul, making me shiver in both excitement and fear. But before I could think further, he suddenly strode towards me. I could feel his warm breath on my face.

"I missed you," he whispered in a low voice, causing goosebumps to form all over my body.

"I'm sorry," I stuttered, feeling an intense surge of guilt building up inside me like a wave about to crash. "I shouldn't have been so foolish with you last night."

He chuckled darkly; the sound sending a thrill down my spine. "Foolish is such a subjective term, Magdalena linda. I thought you were quite wise and delightful."

My skin heated as I remembered how he touched me, gentle and protective. "How did you even get here? Did you climb all the way up here?"

He smiled enigmatically, making me feel like I was missing something crucial. "I have my ways."

I decided not to pursue the matter further, not wanting to spoil the moment. Instead, I let him take charge, and he closed the distance between us, tilting my chin up with his fingers before sealing his lips over mine in a deep, passionate kiss.

As we broke apart, breathless, he murmured, "I won't let anything or anyone hurt you."

He didn't know the full extent of my past. Didn't know how much it meant to me to hear him say that. I was slowly giving everything to him. His words sent a shiver of pleasure and fear down my spine. I knew what he was capable of, and I couldn't help but be drawn towards him, like a moth to a flame.

I was in a lot of trouble.

Thank you so much for reading The Hidden Governess! If you enjoyed the novelette, please consider leaving a review and mentioning Magda's tale. You can read more romance, pining, danger, Blood Magic, (not to mention our lovely Magdalena) by checking out The Gilded Survivor.

About the Author

Daniela A. Mera was born into a royal Fae family in Scotland. She was a free spirit who loved traveling and cloud watching while laying velvet-soft grass. When she came of age, her mother forced her to travel to Las Vegas in order to kill a dragon and conquer a neighboring kingdom.

The dragon turned out to be a man, whom she fell wildly in love with. The couple ran away to the gentle hills of Mexico where Daniela ate lots of tacos and fruits the size of her head.

Something along those lines, anyway.

She writes whimsical tales full of lore all around the world, full of emotionally available men and women who run the world. She can be found listening to sappy romance ballads while writing scenes meant to emotionally damage her readers.

When not writing, Daniela can be found doing yoga and playing video games. Join her newsletter for freebies at: http://danielaamera.com/

FROM STEEL AND STONE

From Steel and Stone

DANIELLE M. HILL

Heat level:
Hot

Content Warnings:
Alcohol, attempted murder, blood, death, grief, misogyny (not MC or LI), murder, profanity, consensual sexually explicit scenes, and violence.

NORTHERN PLAINS

ISLE OF AVALON

CAMELOT
CITY

Prologue

Two hundred and seventy-five years ago

A tall man stood on the balcony of the Great Hall, his hands covered in blood and a frenzied expression on his face. Gongs rang from the top of the castle, resonating the sounds of war and carried by the wind to the farthest parts of the kingdom. The ministers in the Great Hall gathered around the bodies of the King and Queen, who had been ruthlessly murdered by their greatest advisor, Merlin, the most powerful sorcerer in the Seven Kingdoms.

One of the ministers ordered the Royal Guards to kill Merlin. They ran towards him but were too late. The sorcerer raised a closed fist to his mouth, whispering several words before blowing in the direction of a little boy who stood behind one of the curtains, hiding from view. Tears stained his face as he stared at the spot where his dead parents were lying in a pool of blood at the foot of their thrones.

Merlin's magic flowed through the air and etched itself into a ring, which landed on the little boy's finger. The green stone of the ring pulsated with energy and sparkled in the darkness behind the crimson curtain. The boy looked at the ring and then at Merlin, who smiled at the boy before jumping from the balcony.

As the soldiers watched, Merlin fell from the balcony, turning into a beautiful blue bird and flying up towards the sky.

The Kingdom of Camelot burned as the humans and mages fought through the night. Blood flowed through the streets as magic spells were cast on the soldiers, who retaliated by shooting poisoned arrows at the unarmed magical beings.

Even though the mages were extremely powerful, the humans overthrew them with their numbers. So many lives were lost that night due to a single man's betrayal. The last magical survivors ran and hid somewhere they hoped would never be discovered. Magic was banned in the kingdom as a small boy was seated on the throne of his father.

When King Roland outgrew the ring he wore on his finger, he wore it on a chain around his neck. Even though he didn't know what the markings on the inside of the golden band read and had forgotten how he had come to acquire the ring, it became a symbol of hope for the royal bloodline. It became a token of their victory and proof they would come out victorious no matter the odds.

Seventeen years ago

Even though magic had been forever banned from the Kingdom of Camelot, there had been whispers on the streets of a certain race of sorcerers who were still alive in the mountains of Isgaard. When King Uther Pendragon, the seventh king to have ruled Camelot since the war between the humans and mages, found out about these rumours, he felt the same rage course through his veins as his ancestor, King Roland, felt when his parents were murdered in front of his eyes.

King Uther initially denied these rumours, but he knew such a claim could not be left to fate. He decided to wage war on the rebel magic wielders who might still be hiding in the kingdom. As his wife, Queen Igraine, was a skilled warrior as well, she and seven hundred warriors accompanied the king up the mountains.

A great battle was fought, fiercer than any human war. By the time more soldiers were sent their way, King Uther and Queen Igraine had defeated the sorcerers, but at the price of their lives. When the news of their deaths reached the castle, history had repeated itself once again.

A child orphaned at the age of two. This time a princess. A princess who would one day become the greatest warrior the world would ever see. A princess who would unite the world which the naked eyes saw and the world which existed beyond the consciousness of the human mind. A princess named Princess Ariella Pendragon.

Chapter One

Nearly seventeen years had passed since the death of my parents, King Uther and Queen Igraine. My name is Princess Ariella Pendragon. My father's advisor, Mordred, had accompanied my parents into the mountains and had been one of few survivors. He had been appointed my guardian that day, as well as Regent of Camelot until I grew old enough to wear the crown and take on the responsibility and honour of becoming queen.

When Mordred returned from the mountains, he brought with him the jade ring my father wore on a chain around his neck which had been passed down from generation to generation. Even when my fingers grew large enough to fit the ring, I chose to wear it around my neck on the same golden chain my father had.

There was no one else to lay claim to the throne; I had no other relatives. Everyone knew I would be the rightful queen of Camelot before I could even say the word Camelot. Unlike my ancestor, King Roland, I was not allowed to be seated on the throne until my eighteenth birthday; I would then be crowned and bestowed the responsibility to protect and serve my people. I understood at a young age what a true ruler must do for her people, and for that purpose, I began my training.

I aspired to embody the best qualities of both my parents, or at least those ascribed to them in the history books I studied. My mother had been a powerful warrior queen who did not just fight alongside the royal guard in battles, but often led them. My father was knowledgeable, wise, and just. With a peace agreement we still abided by today, he had united the Seven Kingdoms. The two of them were adored by the people of Camelot, and I longed to be as cherished as they were.

Great at my studies, I absorbed all that I could in hopes of being half as great as my parents once were. My favourite subject of all was history, where I could learn about all my ancestors. They listed every member of my lineage as far back as hundreds of years. I wanted to know everything; they were a part of me, my blood. Aside from my parents, I was especially fond of the stories of King Roland. The first Pendragon to slay giants, dragons, and monsters. I dreamed about doing just that; not only keeping the peace within Camelot, but fighting to protect it.

Unfortunately for me, Mordred would never allow me to train in any sort of combat. He wanted me to be more feminine. I always tried to reason with him; surely if my mother were a great warrior herself, you can be both feminine and still fight for your kingdom. He never listened and told me I needed to focus on more important things, such as cooking and stitching and other ways I could take care of my future husband. Every time we had this same argument, I hated him for saying such things, but through it all, I still loved him because he had raised me with care and affection in the absence of my parents.

It was a week before my eighteenth birthday, and we were to be having a dinner with the council members shortly. I stared at my reflection in the mirror as one of my handmaidens brushed and braided my hair. It was hard to believe that in just one short week I would be queen. I would make all the decisions about my life and Camelot. Tonight's dinner would be difficult to get through without bringing up my plans to start my training the day after my coronation. I didn't want to start an argument in front of the council members, so I would wait until after my coronation to tell Mordred.

The handmaiden finished my hair and helped me dress. I practically held my breath as she pulled on the back of the corset to tighten it. Another thing I would be changing once I was queen; no more too-tight dresses with corsets. I was not ashamed of my body and did not think anyone else should be telling me how I needed to look or dress. Mordred always told me I needed to impress possible suitors, but if they didn't want me the way I was, that was their issue, not mine.

After the handmaiden left, I took one last glance in the mirror. Pieces of my light brown hair were braided back, while the rest fell freely to just below my shoulders. I breathed heavily before making my way towards the door. As I opened it, my eyes immediately landed on the guard standing at attention, waiting to escort me to the dinner. For as long as I could remember, Sir Lance Alott had been one of my personal guards. In addition to Mordred, he was one of the few constants in my life, and I adored him for that.

When I arrived, everyone had already gathered around the table. The counsellors were all male and had been working here since before I was born. They stood and bowed at the waist as I entered the dining hall. I nodded, and they waited for me to sit before taking theirs once more. Lance pulled out my chair, and I took the seat at the head of the table. With Mordred to my right, he and the rest of the council members took theirs.

Quietly eating my dinner, I fought not to roll my eyes as the council members droned on about how great they were, in an effort to impress whoever was actually listening. I knew many of them had sons and were trying to push for me to marry theirs over the others. I knew I would have to marry for Camelot and not for love, such was the life. I would do anything for my kingdom, but I had time. With my coronation next week, that was all I wanted to think about. Courting potential suitors could wait. Besides, I had what they wanted: the crown. Though they would only be King Consort, they would still gain more power; power they wanted. I was the one who was going to pick my own husband from the list of eligible lords.

"So, it is decided then." Mordred clapped his hands together once as a smile pulled at the corner of his mouth. My gaze darted around the table as the counsellors muttered their agreements. Usually, all important decisions were discussed and made after we finished eating, so what had I missed?

"Excuse me," I interjected, and all eyes fell on me. "I am terribly sorry, but I was just so overcome by how delicious this meal was; what exactly has been decided?"

Mordred cleared his throat as he glared at me. I glanced around the table, but no one had noticed as their gazes were still fixed on me.

"You will wed Lord Wallace Barnsley's son one week from today. Your coronation will be postponed until after your wedding."

"What?! Why?" I stood abruptly, knocking the chair out from under me. All of the counsellors looked at me with wide eyes and gaping mouths after my outburst and the subsequent loud clang of the chair. In the past, I had never publicly opposed or even questioned Mordred, especially not in front of the counsellors.

"You must be married to take the throne. It is law." Mordred pinned me with another pointed stare, but I didn't care. Normally, I would never behave like this, especially with so many guests around, but this didn't make any sense.

"We have never followed this law before. My father had not wed my mother before he became king; why should I?" I challenged.

"Because *he* was a man." I flinched at his words, like they'd struck more than just my heart.

"What difference does that make?"

"He was born to be a king. Born to rule." Silent murmurs began around the table, but I ignored them as I continued to attempt to reason with Mordred.

"I was born to be queen," I insisted, raising my chin to emphasize the point.

"You were. However, the council and I believe you should wed before your coronation. You will still be queen, just sometime after you are married. It is what is best for Camelot."

It is what is best for Camelot. Anytime he used this phrase, it meant the discussion was over and not up for debate. I sighed, nodding my head once in agreement before returning to my seat. A servant had already fixed my chair from earlier, and I tried not to scowl as I finished my dinner.

I always had Camelot's best interests at heart. But I didn't understand why I had to be married to become queen. Mordred would never have had this discussion in front of the other council members. I should have waited until after dinner and spoken to him privately in his office about this. I still would. I had to marry eventually, and I would. But I wanted a say in who would be my king consort, and Geoffrey Barnsley was not *it*.

Tonight was the night which would change everything. I had to convince Mordred to cancel the wedding tomorrow. He had avoided me the entire week, knowing I would do exactly what I was planning to do now. This was my last chance.

I waited for the perfect moment. Lance would be briefing the next guard on duty outside my door. They always stood several feet away. If I was quiet enough, I might be able to sneak past them and corner Mordred alone in his study. I knew if I spoke with him one on one, I could reason with him. He was never like this; he always took what I had to say into consideration. So, why was something which affected me so directly not brought to my attention? Why was it not up for discussion?

Once I reached the door to Mordred's study, I immediately froze. He wasn't alone. Muffled voices came from the other side of the door. I pressed my ear to the thick, wooden door, not daring enough to open it.

"The plans have changed," Mordred whispered, and I blinked in surprise. Perhaps there wouldn't be a need for me to speak with him tonight. Perhaps he finally realized how absurd this situation was and agreed to postpone the wedding in favour of my coronation.

Just as I was about to step away from the door, another voice spoke.

"So, you want me to do it tonight?" The deep, unfamiliar voice said.

"Yes, I cannot wait until after Ariella marries Geoffrey. It would be too risky. If we waited until after they wed like we originally planned, he would come after the throne. I can't have anyone standing in my way. I need her dead tonight."

My body went rigid, and I felt a tightening in my chest. Everything slowed down while simultaneously accelerating. With trembling legs, I backed away from the door. I tried to block out the words with my hands over my ears, as if that would make them go away.

Mordred intended to have me killed. Tonight.

He had hired someone to do it. *Tonight.*

Stumbling back towards my own chambers, I no longer cared about going unnoticed. Tears streamed down my face, further blurring my already hazy vision. He was one of the people I had trusted most in this world, and he wanted me dead.

Mordred had been like a father to me. He was all I had; he had raised me. Had this been his plan all along? I would not have believed it if I didn't hear it for myself. What was I going to do? Who could I trust? The guards worked for me; but could I trust them, or did he have them under his thumb?

Chapter Two

Just steps away from my chambers, I lost my footing and tripped. A strong set of arms caught me, steadying me. Lance was standing before me; his mouth was moving, but all I could hear was a loud buzzing in my ears. Wiping and squinting my eyes, I tried to read his lips, but I could only make out my own name.

Lance looked down the corridor behind me, searching for an answer to why I must look as horrified as I felt. He wiped a tear from my cheek and pulled me into his arms. I cried into his chest, even harder than before. Aside from Mordred, Sir Lance was the closest person I had to family. He had always been there for as long as I remembered, but what if I couldn't trust him either?

I pushed him back at an arm's length; the concern etched into his face couldn't have been faked. I wasn't sure who I could trust anymore. Then I remembered all the times growing up that Lance had been there for me and had gone against Mordred's orders. He was the one who let me be me. He was the one who taught me to ride a horse—and not side saddle like Mordred had demanded. Lance tried to teach me fencing behind Mordred's back, and Lance was the one who was punished after we were caught.

Had this been why Mordred never wanted me to learn? Because he didn't want me to be able to fight back? I didn't want to believe it, but I didn't know what to believe anymore. The ringing finally stopped inside my head as I looked up at Lance.

"Are you hurt? What happened?" Lance asked as he carefully searched me for wounds.

Lance was the only person in the world I could trust now. I always believed Mordred to be like a father to me, but the truth was it had always been Lance. He had been there for me when I needed him in the past, and I knew he would always be there for me.

"He—he's trying to kill me," I said in between harsh breaths, uncertain of the clarity of my words as I continued to sob.

Lance did not hesitate, shoving me behind him and drawing his sword from its scabbard in a single, seamless motion. With his blade in the air, Lance slowly made his way down the corridor.

"Wait!" I cried as I placed a hand on his shoulder to stop him.

"Did you see their face? How did they get inside the castle?" Lance mumbled the last part to himself as he shrugged my hand off his shoulder.

"No, it's not what you think." I struggled with how to word it, the conversation I overheard replaying in my mind once more. I was still fighting to accept the reality of what happened.

Lance shot a look over his shoulder at me briefly, before returning his gaze to the corridor before him.

"It's Mordred," I whispered. "He wants me dead."

Lance's eyes widened as he turned back towards me. "Shit," he cursed, "are you sure?" His eyes searched mine, seeing the truth behind them, before flicking back to the empty corridor as a wrinkle formed between his brows.

I nodded. "I overheard him. I don't know who he hired, but they are planning to kill me tonight." A burning sensation stung my throat, and I fought back more tears which wanted to fall.

Lance grabbed me by the wrist and ran back towards my rooms. Throwing the door open, he pulled me inside with him, then did a quick sweep of the room to ensure we were alone, checking every inch of the room for some unwelcome intruder. Once he was certain the room was clear he handed me a bag from my closet.

"Pack lightly and quickly," he whispered before making his way back towards the windows to close the drapes.

"Where are we going?" I asked, frantically packing clothes and bread and dried meat left on a platter from earlier.

"As far away from the capital as we can get. Let's go." Immediately after peeking his head out the door, he grabbed my arm and dragged me back into the corridor.

We were too loud, our footsteps shuffling down the stone halls. It was hard to keep pace with Sir Lance as we weaved through different pathways. We finally made it to the servants' quarters, and he opened a passageway only they used.

Stone slid against stone as an opening appeared in the wall. He reached for a lit torch inside a sconce which hung along the wall just inside the opening. He jerked his head down the dark passageway. Seconds after I stepped inside, the stone wall slid back into place.

I followed behind him as he led the way, sword in one hand, torch in the other. The passage was dimly lit, the lustre of the other sconces hung every several feet the only light. A faint dripping sound echoed from within the darkness.

We made it to what seemed like a dead end, when Lance placed the torch in his hand in an empty sconce and pushed the stone next to it. The wall slid open just as it had when we entered the passageway and opened to the exterior of the castle.

As I stepped outside, a cool breeze kissed my skin, blowing the loose strands of my hair around me. I wished I had time to properly braid back those pieces that had fallen out, but I didn't have time. And if I had a wish, I would use it to not be in this situation at all.

The moon shone brightly in the sky above us, and the stars danced around in its silver glow. The trees around the grounds swayed in the breeze as Lance directed us towards the stables.

He saddled up a horse which was not his, then opened the stall guard for several horses, encouraging them to run free in different directions. Grabbing me by the waist, he lifted me onto the waiting horse before climbing up and mounting behind me. He caged me in his arms as he grabbed hold of the reins, just like he had when I was a child first learning to ride, and he flicked the reins.

We left the city of Camelot behind as we headed north through the outskirts of the Forest of Ascetir. The night was long, but Lance wanted to ride for as long as we could under the cover of darkness. It was hard to keep track of time while we rode in silence. We hoped we had gotten out of there before Mordred's assassins got wind of our escape, but we still didn't know who they were.

Suddenly, Lance let go of the reins, and he wrapped his arms tightly around me before sliding off the side of the horse, his body cushioning my fall. His arms cradled my head and neck while we tumbled down the rough road.

A dagger whizzed past the spot his head had just been, barely missing the horse. The mare whinnied loudly before galloping further into the forest.

"Get behind me," Lance shouted as he turned back the way we had just came, a sword in each hand.

Three shadows appeared on horseback from within the forest, slowly creeping towards us.

"Run!" He commanded without looking back at me.

"I can't just leave you here to die!" I cried.

"Go!"

"Not without you!"

Lance groaned before he picked me up and threw me over his shoulder and ran. We didn't get far before he stopped abruptly.

"Fuck!" he cursed.

"What is it?" I pushed out of his arms, falling to my feet. He jerked his head behind me, and I turned to find we were at the edge of a cliff. "What do we do?"

"We fight." He faced the assassins again as they persisted in their pursuit.

Before I could argue or come up with an alternative plan, he ran straight for them, sword raised, ready to protect me at any cost, but we were severely outnumbered as even more figures stepped out of the shadows.

Lance fought the original three at once. His sword clinked against theirs as he deflected every one of their blows with ease. The three men he fought stopped their advances, but something about it did not seem right. An arrow shot out from the darkness and landed in the center of his chest.

He stumbled back, and I ran forward to catch him.

"No!" His blood coated my hands, and I sobbed as I struggled to hold him up.

"It's okay; you need to take a leap of faith." His eyes darted to the cliff's edge then back to me once more. "It's your only chance. If you jump, you can swim away and hide. Just like when you were younger, remember? You always wanted me to play hide and seek, but you only ever wanted to hide."

Holding him close, I nodded. Tears and snot dripped down my face as I sobbed.

"They're coming, g-go," He pushed me back, but he had nothing else to support him and collapsed to the ground before me.

As the assassins drew closer, their taunting laughter reached me. Another arrow sailed through the air; this one striking Lance in the side of his head. As I staggered back, a frightened cry escaped my lips. However, I was too close to the cliff's edge and fell. I screamed, my arms flailing in the air while I fell rapidly towards the deep waters below.

Black tipped arrows flew past me as I fell. When one of them nicked my arm, I felt an agony like I'd never felt before. Black tendrils formed from where the arrow had pierced. They grew up and around my arm underneath the skin. Everywhere these lines touched, they burned.

Seconds before I hit the water, I took a deep breath and held it as the water's force pulled me under. I tried to swim, but between the water's fast-moving current and the pain in my arm, I couldn't reach the surface. My lungs burned, and I wouldn't be able to hold my breath much longer.

This was it; I had survived the assassins' attacks to drown here within these waters. As soon as I took in the breath I was desperate for, it would be the end. I fought against the need, but it was too strong. Finally, I took in a breath. Everything blurred and then went black.

When I awoke, I wasn't exactly sure where I was, how I had gotten there, or why I had survived. I was laying on the shore of a beach. Sand stuck to every inch of my body, and my hair was plastered to my face. The sun shone, and the waves of the water lapped around my feet.

Thinking back to what happened last night, I rinsed my hands and arms in the water in case the poisoned arrow had done any further damage to my arm. Except, my arm was completely normal. No dark tendrils, no blood, no pain, nothing.

What happened?

As I looked around for any sign of life, a single blue bird flew from the treetops behind me and out into the open water. The assassins were bound to come looking for me, and I didn't know where I was or if it was safe to stay. All I knew was that I had to leave the city of Camelot behind me. I had to forget who I was and become someone else entirely, or else death would follow me here as well.

Chapter Three
TWO YEARS LATER

"Ella, could you possibly stay until close tonight?" Cynthia's melodic voice sang from the kitchens.

"Of course," I laughed, as I took the cups of ale from her and made my way through the swinging door into the main tavern, where I set them down in front of the waiting patrons. Cynthia walked out behind me, placing their food on the table for them.

"You're a lifesaver." She patted me on the shoulder.

There were just about two hours or so left before we shut down for the night. The tavern was where I liked to remain most nights. My nightmares had become more frequent, and I found being alone was something I tried to avoid. There had been nights when I'd woken up to find the ring around my neck was glowing a faint green light and was warm to the touch.

The crowded space filled as more and more people entered, hoping to temporarily forget their worries and escape their troubles, just as I did. Only a dozen or so tables could be found inside the Ye Olde Sword Tavern. The bar counter was lined by wooden stools. The room was filled with laughter, shouting, and whispers from those who didn't want to be overheard. As far as I could tell, the tavern had been overrun by its usual customers. I knew their orders well and brought them to each person with ease. As I delivered a table's food, the cool kiss from the ring against my chest heated.

Instantly, my hand rushed up to where it was tucked under my dress, and a tingle of unease crept up my spine. I frantically searched the room, unsure what exactly I was looking for. My eyes narrowed as they wandered the dimly lit room for answers.

A loud whistle pierced my ears. Flinching, I turned to find Ector shaking his empty glass at me. I took the glass from him with a tight smile, then headed back to the kitchens to fill it.

When I was alone in the kitchens, I pulled the chain from around my neck to inspect the ring. Nothing seemed out of the ordinary. I touched it; the warmth I had felt seconds ago had vanished.

The rest of my shift went smoothly. After we kicked everyone out for the night, I locked the doors and began cleaning. I told Cynthia I didn't mind finishing up on my own, so even she was gone. I was completely alone, but somehow felt as if I were being watched.

Walking over to the door, I triple checked that it was securely locked. My hands curled restlessly on the ring around my neck as I nervously glanced at the clock. I made a concentrated effort to clean up the tavern much more quickly than usual. Once everything was done, I grabbed my cloak from the kitchen and slipped out the back entrance.

It was a moonless sky tonight, and my eyes darted around the shadows. Not much happened here on the Isle of Avalon. My arrival two years ago had been the biggest news for a while. They did not get many visitors here. Some sailors would stop by Avalon every other week to deliver goods from the mainland, but they would only stay for a few hours before returning home. It was such a lovely island, but it was small and quaint. Everyone knew everyone here. They welcomed me warmly, and, although it had taken me a while, I had finally found my place here.

A voice whistled in the wind.

"Only the rightful heir will lead this kingdom to glory. She will rise, forged from steel and stone."

I turned back, but no one was there. Cautiously creeping towards the source of the voice, I recoiled at the sound of a rustling in the night. A bird swooped out of the shadows. I didn't live far from the tavern and raced back home.

Once I arrived at my tiny upper-level home, I ensured I was truly alone, as I did every night. Then I locked all the doors and windows before heading to bed, hoping I would have a peaceful sleep for the first time since that horrible night.

A couple of days passed, and I hadn't had the same feeling; nor had I been attacked by any more birds.

I was working the early shift, which meant it was a slow shift. There were two men drinking at the bar and one couple seated at a table.

The bell above the main entrance rang, alerting me of another customer. I grabbed the drink I had just poured for Henry and brought it to him before welcoming our newest guest.

Scanning the entryway, I realized they had already seated themselves. A man sat alone at a table in the corner of the room. His brown, messy hair fell over his face, shielding his eyes from view.

The moment he finally looked up, his mouth parted slightly, and his green gaze widened as it locked on mine. My chest warmed as the ring around my neck heated, my hand instinctively shooting up to touch the spot where it seemed to burn beneath my dress. I turned and headed into the kitchens.

Tugging on the hem of my dress, I peeked down at the ring as a faint green glow emanated from it; yet, the ring was already cooling against my skin.

Who was that? Was he a royal guard? He seemed to have recognized me. The way he had practically flinched as our eyes met—he had to have known me, hadn't he? Not only that, but my ring had never felt as hot as it had when our gazes held. I couldn't risk anyone discovering it on me, especially if he worked at the castle.

The door to the kitchens swung open, and I jumped before realizing it was only Cynthia.

"You really need to get back out there. A shipment just arrived, so we're getting a bit of a crowd now." Cynthia tipped her head toward the other room before placing down the sack of potatoes she was carrying.

I nodded before heading back, still a little stunned by that man. With any luck, he had mistaken me for someone else and already left.

Cynthia wasn't lying. Within seconds, the tavern must have filled with every single person who had been on that ship. I did not waste any time as I went from table to table to take orders. There were a couple of men at one of the tables who had clearly already been drinking before coming here. I painted on my best smile and tried not to roll my eyes at their unwelcomed comments.

Chancing a look in the direction of the man from earlier, I noticed he was still seated alone in the corner. Watching me. His eyes seemed to follow me around the room, his stare deepening as I tended to the other guests. I was unsure if he knew who I truly was, or if he was just angry I was completely ignoring him and taking others' orders. I couldn't risk going over there, not if he knew.

"How can I help?" Daphne asked. Cynthia must have asked her to come in early, and it could not have come at a better time.

"Can you help the gentleman in the corner?" I nodded in his general direction, trying not to make it too obvious, as I was certain he was still watching.

"Don't mind if I do." Daphne winked before heading over to him. I sighed in relief and continued with what I was doing.

Just as I walked past the already too drunk table, one of the sailors gripped my wrist, twirling be towards him. "Refill, honey." He didn't even try to hide the way his eyes wandered over my body.

Jerking my hand free, I laughed lightly as if I didn't want to stab him with the butter knife on the table next to him. "Coming right up."

After refilling his mug at the bar, I hurried back, hoping this would be the end of the interaction. But, just as I placed the mug in front of him on the table, he grabbed me by the waist.

"Why don't you join us for a drink, hm?" he slurred.

"Why don't you keep your hands to yourself?" A rough voice called from behind me. Glancing over my shoulder, I noticed the man from the corner had been the source.

He swung his hand down over the inside of the drunken sailor's elbow, breaking his hold on me.

"What was that?" The sailor pushed to his feet, eyes narrowing on the corner stranger.

"Keep your hands off her, or you'll lose them." The strangers' eyes flicked to the tiny bulge in the sailor's pants, then back to hold his glare. "Among other things."

"Oh, yeah?" The sailor chuckled mockingly.

The scowl the stranger wore intensified as he towered over the sailor, nearly a head taller in height. The sailor's head swung towards me as he looked me up and down. "She isn't that attractive anyways; I was doing her a favour." He chuckled again, and the others at his table joined in.

The stranger took another step towards the drunken sailor, his fists clenched at his sides. The sailor winced and turned sharply, staggering out of the tavern without another glance in our direction.

As if asking a question I couldn't answer or understand, his gaze returned to mine. My ring warmed once more. I carefully reached for it, his eyes tracing the path of my hand as it settled on my chest. Even though I knew he couldn't see it, I couldn't help but get the feeling he could sense it.

Most of the sailors and merchants who had been here mere moments ago had now departed, and the place was nearly deserted once again. Still, heat rose from my chest; as I reached for my ring again, I realized it wasn't the cause.

"Thank you," I quickly bit out, then left before he could respond or follow.

Chapter Four

Every morning, a small blue bird perched on the bottom windowsill of my home. It had become my new routine to bring him seeds or stale bread on my way to work, and today was no exception. He ate seeds from my hand before taking to the sky, circling above several times. As I walked to the tavern, he seemed to follow from above.

The tavern had already been open for an hour, with Cynthia working the first shift today. Over the past few days, the stranger had established himself as a regular. According to Daphne, his name was Ambrose, and he had always lived on the isle but departed a couple of years ago, before my arrival. He was very popular among the people of Avalon.

Although he tried to keep to himself, I couldn't help but notice how everyone who came into the tavern appeared to hold him in such high regard. All the locals that came in ordered drinks to be sent to his table. When I questioned Cynthia and Daphne, they said everyone was simply happy to see him again after such a long period. I, however, had the impression there was more going on. Everybody was whispering, and they all stopped talking when I got close. There was nothing particularly unusual about this happening in the tavern, but it was happening more regularly.

Ambrose sat in his regular spot in the corner of the room. He was the only guest inside the tavern, but there was nothing on the table in front of him. I walked over to take his order, hoping he hadn't been waiting long.

"Can I get you anything?" I asked with a tight, wary smile.

"A cup of tea would be nice; thank you," he said as he held my gaze. I stood there for a moment trying to figure out what he wanted—aside from the tea, of course. He was up to something, and I did not trust him.

My necklace warmed again, but I was used to it warming and glowing faintly in his presence. My eyes narrowed before I finally pulled them from his and left to get him his tea. I placed the large cup of tea on the table and turned without a word.

"Thank you, princess." I froze, slowly shifting back to face him.

"Excuse me?" I whispered in a harsh breath.

"I said, thank you." The corner of his lip twitched.

"And after that?"

"I said nothing. Why? What did you hear?" Ambrose didn't even attempt to hide the smirk which pulled at his mouth that time.

"I don't trust you," I muttered.

"Well, that isn't very nice, now, is it?"

"I don't like you either," I said, squaring my shoulders and raising my chin as I glared down at him where he sat.

"You will." He picked up his cup of tea and took a sip from it.

"That's a little presumptuous," I laughed dryly.

"We'll see." He shrugged, and I decided to leave him to his tea.

After an hour of him not ordering anything else he had finally left. An early lunchtime rush was beginning to fill the bar. Lots of regulars, including several sailors and businessmen, hung around all day drinking excessively and eating very little.

As I was grabbing an order from the back, a loud commotion started, and I ran out to see what was happening. Two large men were standing and arguing; their speech slurred. Soon enough, more and more people were taking part. The men began to pound their fists on the tables and shout even louder. The fight quickly became physical as more people began to cheer them on. Fists flew, and I panicked.

This had happened many times before, but never while I was alone. Cynthia was out running errands and was due back any minute. My mind raced as I tried to come up with a plan until she arrived.

One of the men drew a dagger, and the room soon fell silent. Seconds ticked by before the man with the dagger attacked; the moment he struck, the room scattered. Shouts and cries echoed around the room as everyone headed towards the doors.

I couldn't abandon the place, so I hid under one of the tables in the far corner. The two men who had started the fight were the only others left as the one dodged the bladed man's attack, ducking low and catching my eyes with his just before the other man kicked him in the back of the legs and stabbed him in the side of the head. His dark gaze held mine as he fell to the ground.

My hands shot to my mouth, muffling the scream I tried so hard to hold in. I scooted farther back into the corner, my eyes stinging with tears as I squeezed them shut, silently praying he wouldn't see me.

The man's footsteps carried to me before the chime of the bell at the door sounded. He must have left, but I couldn't be sure. I waited a few moments before peeking around the corner to ensure he was truly gone.

My eyes widened as the room around me burst into flames. Thick clouds of smoke swirled around, making it impossible to breathe. He had killed someone and now he was burning the evidence. To avoid the smoke overhead, I crawled across the floor toward the exit.

The tavern's interior and the structure itself were both constructed almost entirely of wood. The fire spread everywhere I looked, with flames engulfing everything in its path. I had to be fast. I pushed myself to my feet, covering my mouth and nose with my arm, and made a run for the door, just as part of the roof came crashing down, blocking my way to the exit. Fire roared towards me in every direction. I was trapped; there was no way out.

Green sparks swirled in the air. Was this it? Had I already passed out from the smoke and was hallucinating? A body appeared, and, after a moment, I recognized his face; Ambrose. Amidst the green lighting, he was suddenly before me.

"We need to go!" he shouted, grabbing hold of my wrist and pulling me into his chest. He held me tight, one arm around my waist.

As my eyes widened, I focused on him. I fought off the impulse to cough. My throat burned and it became even more difficult to breathe.

"We need to go!" he repeated through gritted teeth. I noticed he had one hand held high. From that hand, an emerald glow illuminated. Since the fire had grown so rapidly, we were engulfed in a sphere of fire. I knew whatever Ambrose was doing, it was the reason the flames didn't touch us.

"How are you doing this?" I said between coughs.

"Magic," he replied. The fire around us disappeared, and the same green sparks from before whirled around in a gust of wind. I closed my eyes and pressed my face into Ambrose's chest as the green light became too bright. His grip on me tightened, and it was like the floor beneath me collapsed just as the roof had a moment before.

Within seconds, my feet met with a hard surface, and the light dimmed before vanishing altogether. Opening my eyes, I pulled away from Ambrose; his hand tightened for the tiniest of moments before letting go.

We were inside another building; one I had never seen before. It seemed to be a small cottage. The hearth was lit; something was cooking over it, and the smell carried to me, making my stomach grumble. There was a small circular table next to it with only two chairs seated around it.

The aroma of whatever was cooking mingled with the smell of sandalwood and pine. There was nothing else in the room save for a chaise in the middle of the seating area and two pots of herbs on either side. The house was bare, but it was bigger than the one I currently lived in. I wondered who lived here.

Glancing at Ambrose, I assumed this must have been his house, but how did we get here? *'Magic'* he had said. But this didn't make sense. Sorcerers were evil; magic was banned.

Taking a step away from him, I stumbled. He was evil; he had to be. I needed to leave. He had saved me from the fire just to bring me here to do something so much worse.

Ambrose opened his mouth to say something, probably an incantation to trap me here, but I didn't give him the chance to start it—let alone finish it—before darting for the door. I pulled it open, but it wasn't an exterior door; inside was only a bed and a small table made of wood. I cursed under my breath before slamming it shut and running for the other door to the right of me.

"What are you—" Ambrose called as I sped out the door.

The house was in the middle of a forest. The woods were vast and thriving. Its canopy was overshadowed by pine and cypress, yet enough sunlight filtered through their branches to encourage an abundance of saplings to take root in their soft, rich soils below and an assortment of flowers bloom, scattering across the woods.

Birdsongs echoed from above, overpowering the trickle of a stream in the distance. I ran toward the sound of the flowing water, hoping it would lead me to someone who could help.

The path I'd taken led me to a clearing where the waterfall cascaded into a lake of beautiful blue water. I kneeled before the edge of the water, my reflection clear. My hazel eyes appeared sunken and tired as they looked back at me. Cuts and ash covered my face and arms. I rinsed my hands in the water before splashing some over my face.

A branch snapped from behind me, and I whirled around to find Ambrose stepping into the clearing, hands raised in surrender.

"You need to trust me; I'm not going to hurt you."

I scoffed as I rose to my feet.

"I mean it. I just want to help you." Hands still raised, nodding to the cuts on my arms.

"How do I know you won't make them worse?" I asked, taking several steps back, right into the cold, shallow water.

"Like I said, you'll have to trust me." Ambrose took a tentative step closer; I didn't back away this time. He did save me from the fire, after all. Maybe he wouldn't hurt me.

When he stood before me, he motioned for me to take a seat. I made my way to the shore and sat down slowly. Out of nowhere, Ambrose materialized a washcloth in his palm. I flinched at the sudden use of his magic, and he chuckled lightly.

"You don't have to be afraid." He tried to assure me as he wet the cloth before dabbing it on my face and arms over the cuts.

"Easier said than done. Magic wielders killed my parents and ancestors," I mumbled.

"I want to tell you a story," Ambrose said, as he continued to clean my wounds. "Will you listen?"

I nodded.

"Hundreds of years ago, many innocent mages were forced to leave their homes and run for their lives. They lived peacefully with the humans for centuries. Until one day, one corrupt sorcerer who craved power betrayed not only the king and queen, but his own people. They did not have any choice;

they fled and hid in fear. If they ever used magic openly, they would be executed. Many of them went to the mountains, where they were safe, living in peace, but still afraid to be their true selves. Until one day, they were chased out of those homes as well. Now, the last place where they live, again in peace, is here on the Isle of Avalon."

"No, the magic wielders started this. This is all their fault. They started this war."

"No, they didn't. They wanted to live in peace." He sighed, staring into the water.

"But—but—" I didn't know where I was going with that sentence. I had never thought of it like that, I had always read that it was a war brought on and led by their leader Merlin, that they chose this war. "They never had a choice. They didn't want to start a war. All of this was because of Merlin."

"All of this because of *one* evil sorcerer, yes."

I didn't have anything to say; I didn't know what I could say.

"We've made this island our home. We live here in peace, and we would never hurt anyone who did not deserve it." He paused briefly, his hand on my cheek, the cloth no longer in his palm. My face flushed, and I thought about that drunken sailor at the tavern who he threatened. "Avalon is full of mages and sorcerers. Some you know quite well."

After giving it some thought, I realized that there was only one person on the island to whom I felt any sort of familial or emotional connection.

"Cynthia?" I whispered, and he nodded.

Chapter Five

We sat in the clearing in silence as I tried to process everything which Ambrose had told me. I had lived among mages for two years and had no idea. I worked with them, served them their meals, and I was friends with them. Even though I was a stranger to them, they welcomed me in and made me feel at home. Although my family had been killed by mages, it was a human–the person I had come to consider a member of my own family–who also attempted my own murder.

Things weren't as black and white as I had once believed. Mordred had continued executions of anyone he had suspected of witchcraft and magic use, but it shouldn't be this way. Maybe we didn't have to live like this anymore. Merlin was the one who had been behind the betrayal. My parents had been killed in a war that should never have even started, not to mention so had many innocents.

"I want things to be different," I said, finally breaking the silence.

"I was hoping you'd say that, princess." He smirked and stood, extending a hand to help me up.

As I accepted his hand, my pulse raced as he dragged me to my feet. My lips parted as he continued to hold on. My necklace warmed against my skin, and a bright green light burst out, illuminating the clearing we stood in. I hadn't realized how dark and late it had gotten until the light of my ring shot out around us.

Ambrose looked down at me, grabbing hold of the chain, drawing me and the ring closer. My chest brushed against his as he held the ring between us. "Where did you get this?"

"It's been in my family for generations," I answered as I reached for the ring, but he held it up higher, the side of his lip twitching as I struggled to get it back. "And I'd like to keep it that way."

"Do you know what it is?"

"A ring." As my brows crinkled, he rolled his eyes.

"Do you know what this inscription is on the inside?" He finally placed the chain back around my neck.

"It's just a bunch of weird symbols."

"It's a prophecy." Ambrose stated, his warm fingers still resting on my.

"What...what does it say?" I questioned in shock as I inched closer to bridge the gap between us.

He moved in close and whispered, *"Only the rightful heir will lead this kingdom to glory. She will rise, forged from steel and stone."*

"I've heard that before. In my dreams." My eyes shifted to his mouth briefly before returning to hold his gaze. "How can you read it?"

Ambrose pulled back slightly, and the feeling of warmth in my chest and from my necklace vanished instantly.

"They're what you may call witch markings. Only those of us gifted with magic can read them. A mage or sorcerer must have given this to someone in your family."

"That doesn't make any sense," I muttered to myself.

"Because you're a Pendragon?" Ambrose shrugged, and I flinched.

"How...how did you know?" I went to take a step back, but he stopped me. Heat radiated from where his hand rested on my arm.

"This ring was given to King Roland; it holds great power within it, can't you feel it?" I nodded, and Ambrose's other hand came to rest on my shoulder. "This is how he was able to wield superhuman strength. This ring was the reason he was able to fight against monsters and magical beings like no other human."

"No... It can't be. He hated magic." I shook my head in disbelief.

"And yet, he had this ring. I doubt he even knew." Ambrose's other hand was on my other shoulder as he tried to reason with me. He gave me a look as if there was something more he wanted to say, but then he turned abruptly, his hand raking through his hair.

"What? What aren't you telling me?" I demanded.

"I think I've told you enough." He mock-laughed.

"I want to be different."

"Don't you get it?" He whirled around to face me once more.

"Get what?"

"The prophecy is about you, princess! You *can* make a difference; you're the rightful heir to Camelot."

"I don't want it to be! I want change, but I don't want to be the one that has to bring it!" I threw back.

"So what? You aren't going to fight for your throne?"

"No, I'm not. I'm not a princess anymore," I said, turning abruptly and running away from him again.

"You're the only one who can do this." He reached for my hand again, but I moved before he could grab it.

"No, I'm not. I'm not a princess anymore, and I need to go."

Ambrose called after me as I ran from him again. This time, he didn't follow. I still was unsure how to get out of the woods, but I figured the island wasn't that big; how long could it really take? In that moment, I would have rather wandered around for hours in the dark than stand there with him any longer. I knew it was childish, but why did it all have to fall onto me? I had given up on my big dreams of becoming queen and changing Camelot two years ago, and I wasn't going back.

I wasn't exactly sure how long I'd been roaming around the woods looking for a way out, when, through the darkness, a faint silver glow appeared. Just beyond the light was a figure in the shadows. I debated running, but then they called out to me.

"Ella?" Cynthia's familiar voice shouted.

I ran to her, throwing my arms around her neck and squeezing her tightly. She laughed, and I realized the silver glow had been a magical orb hovering above her.

"How did you find me?"

"Ambrose told me you may need some help getting out of the enchanted forest. Unless you are properly skilled in wielding magic, you can never find your way out. It is one of our defenses against anyone coming out here looking for us."

"He sent you?" I asked, somehow ignoring everything else she mentioned.

"Yes, he said you probably wouldn't want to see him again just yet."

"Or ever," I muttered, and she laughed lightly while she put one of her strong arms over my shoulder, pulling me close. Before I could even close my mouth, her thick, frizzy auburn hair was caught in it. I attempted to spit out her hair, but I ended up choking on it instead, which made her laugh even more.

"Come on, I'll take you home."

The Ye Olde Sword Tavern was back in business after Cynthia worked her magic on it. Still concerned, I was relieved to have knowledge of the island's magical practices. I'm not sure what other way they could have explained the fixes to me. Over the following several days, life seemed to proceed as normal, with the notable exception that Ambrose had not returned to the tavern. At least, not while I was working.

Cynthia had not brought up magic again, and yet, I began noticing things which I hadn't before. Knowing had opened something up inside of me, a sense I didn't know existed. Every magic wielder had a certain glow to them. It was faint, but they all had some colour emanating from them. Cynthia's was a golden hue, while Daphne's was a soft pink. The way that Cynthia had kept this place going in general was so obvious to me now: magic. The food was made far too quickly than any other tavern I'd been to before.

Despite myself, my thoughts kept returning to Ambrose; was he avoiding me? I should have been relieved, but my stomach turned every time I thought of him and the prophecy he spoke of. Whenever I closed my eyes, he was there, standing incredibly close, whispering the prophecy into my ear. Only this time, I arched into his touch, gazing up into his deep green eyes.

And when I finally opened mine again, I was alone. The ring around my neck felt unusually icy, the cold kiss biting into my skin a constant reminder of him and what he had shared.

Holding up the necklace, I examined the old witch markings inscribed. Was he right? Maybe he misread them. Cynthia stepped into the kitchen, and I decided there was no reason not to ask another mage about the markings. Her eyes instantly found the ring in my hand.

"Can you tell me what this says?" I asked, taking the chain from around my neck and handing it over to her. I didn't want to give anything else away in case Ambrose had been wrong.

She held the ring close, eyes squinting as she turned it over. "I can't read these markings, sorry."

"But they are witch marks, aren't they?"

"Yes, and only those with the witch or sorcerer's blood who wrote them can read them." She shrugged before heading back into the main room of the tavern.

That doesn't make any sense. I thought before voices from the other room caught my attention.

"Yes, he has completely taken over the kingdom, claiming to be the true heir of Camelot. He has increased executions for even the smallest of crimes, claiming everyone to be a sorcerer."

Were they talking about Mordred? Had he waited this long to start prosecuting everyone? He would have been the one in power this entire time. He wanted me gone to do exactly this. But why?

"We have seen many royal soldiers scouting the waters around Avalon; I fear they will try to come here next," the voice continued.

"I doubt they will be able to get past our defenses," another said.

A tightness in my chest reminded me of the betrayal of what Mordred had done. A desire for revenge burned inside me. He tried to kill me, and now he was killing even more innocents. Needing to take a walk to clear my head, I left the tavern and wandered around the isle. Could they have been right about the royal soldiers scouting the waters around Avalon? Could I risk staying here any longer? What if they were still searching for me? Was I endangering all those who lived here by staying here?

Without realizing where I had been going, my legs brought me to the beach. The same beach I had washed up on two years ago.

Though that night still haunted me, there were many parts which had become blurry, and I wondered if I had imagined some aspects. I remembered being struck by a dark tipped arrow, one which had sent some kind of poison deep into my skin, burning like no pain I had ever encountered. But, when I awoke on this beach, there was no trace of anything. No marks, no cuts. Had it all been something my mind had made up?

"I never expected to see you here again." The sound of Ambrose's voice stunned me.

"Again?" I asked, keeping my gaze fixed on the water far out in the distance, avoiding the temptation to turn around.

His footsteps drew nearer, then halted as he stood next to me, as we both stared out at the waves.

"I found you here that day. Two years ago."

"You what?" I whirled around, unable to resist after that revelation.

"You were in rough shape; you wouldn't have survived," he continued calmly, as if I hadn't just screamed at him. "The arrows they struck you with, they were poisoned arrows. The same ones they use on mages. It is hard to heal; it took all my strength to do so. That was part of the reason I had to leave for a while."

My head was already shaking before he finished. "I don't understand."

"They wanted you dead, Ariella." His head turned slightly, a pained expression on his face as lines formed between his brows and a sad smile tugged on his lips.

"I already knew that, obviously," I said, my head tilting low, refusing to hold his gaze as he pitied me.

"They would have succeeded."

"So what? You healed me and then just left me here on the beach?" My nose wrinkled, and I took a step away from him as my eyes narrowed. "They or anyone could have found me; you just left me here all alone, unconscious."

"No! Well, yes, but it's not what you think. I was watching over you from a distance. Before I left, I wanted to make sure you were okay. I told Cynthia to keep an eye out for you after you woke."

"So, you were stalking me?" I took another step back.

"No! I knew who you were. I didn't want anything to happen to you, and I didn't know how you would react. You are a Pendragon; you hated our kind. I wanted to ensure the people of Avalon were safe." He reached an arm out towards me but pulled back.

"I— I don't hate your kind." I muttered.

"Not anymore," Ambrose huffed.

"Right. I just... I need time."

"Right," he whispered, nodding his head once. Then he turned and headed back towards the forest.

I sat down with my knees pulled tightly to my chest, water splashing over my toes and watching the ocean once more. I sat at the beach for hours, letting my mind wander. Eventually, the sun began to set, and I watched as the sky filled with an assortment of shades from orange, pink, and yellow. It was beautiful; the reflection on the horizon set ablaze with colour. The chilled breeze was the only sound other than the waves as it continued to lap at my feet, much cooler than it was hours earlier.

In the distance, a ship sailed by, too far to notice much about it. Except for the colours of the flag. They were the royal colours of Camelot: gold and crimson. It was a royal ship. Were they coming here? Were they still looking for me? Did they want to finish the job, or were they coming for those who lived here? It didn't matter either way; I needed to do something, but what?

Ambrose.

Without another thought, I sprinted towards the enchanted forest. As I stood before it, I realized that once I entered, I wouldn't be able to leave without assistance. Though I couldn't see the barrier, I knew it was there. I took a long, shaking breath, then released it and ran inside. As I broke through the magical barrier, a warm sensation washed over me. Glancing over my shoulder, the village behind me had vanished. I was surrounded by the same overhanging trees and trunks I had seen before. There was no way out, no turning back. I raced froward, hoping I was going towards Ambrose's cottage.

A bird's chirping called to me. I tilted my head up to see the blue bird which had perched on my windowsill many times.

"I'm sorry; I don't have anything for you today." It circled around me before taking off in another direction.

When I didn't move, the bird flew back and circled around me once more. *Does it want me to follow it?* I hesitated for a moment, then gave in, rushing to keep up with the small creature as it flew faster and faster.

When it stopped, we were in a clearing, much smaller than the one I'd seen by the lake. It was more overgrown, barren of signs of human or animal life. Grass and vines grew everywhere. In the center of the clearing, there was a large, smooth stone with an old, rusted sword embedded in it. The sword called to me, drawing me closer, a siren singing to a sailor on the sea. The blue bird sat atop the pommel, chirping proudly.

As I slowly extended my hand toward the grip, the bird took flight, flying off into the sky beyond the treetops. I jerked back a moment before reaching for the hilt once more, but a voice spoke, halting me.

"You found it."

Whirling around, Ambrose stood in the clearing, smirking down at me.

"I was looking for you." My shoulders tensed as he stalked closer.

"You found me." He held his arms out as if I hadn't realized who I was talking to.

"Actually, I think you found me," I countered. "What is it?"

"A sword." Ambrose shrugged as the corner of his mouth tipped up.

"I can see that; why is it here?" My hand gestured back to the sword in the stone.

"She will rise, forged from steel and stone." He took a step closer, then kneeled before me.

"I don't understand." My eyes darted from Ambrose to the sword and back.

"I told you the prophecy was about you. I was right; you found the sword, and now you must pull it from the stone and take your rightful place as queen of Camelot." His green eyes shone as he watched me expectantly from where he knelt.

"I need your help," I blurted, trying to ignore his claims. "The isle does. They're coming; you need to stop Mordred."

He finally rose, his gaze fixed on me the entire time. "No, you are the only one who can stop him. I am not strong enough."

"But I am?" My laugh was hollowed.

"You can be." Ambrose tucked a stray piece of my hair behind my ear, his fingers brushing lightly against my cheek.

"How?" My question was a breath against his lips as he leaned in.

His fingers slid behind my neck and tangled in my hair as he tilted my head back to hold his gaze. His eyes flicked to my mouth and then back as he waited for me to take the final step toward him. Without a second's hesitation, my lips crashed into his, my arms circled around his neck, drawing his chest flush against mine.

His hands trailed down my back before gripping my ass and hoisting me up. My legs wrapped around his waist instantly, and I deepened the kiss. I could feel his smile against my lips before he suddenly broke away. He watched me as I fought to catch my breath. Ambrose's lips twitched for a moment before his mouth met my throat. My head fell back, giving him more access as he trailed kisses down my neck to my collarbone. My pulse quickened as heat crept through my body each time he kissed me.

His mouth made its way back to mine. This time his kiss was slower, softer. He lowered me, my feet reaching the ground. He placed one last kiss on my lips then pulled away completely.

"This will make me stronger?" I panted.

He chuckled. "No, you have to pull out the sword for that."

"What?" My gaze was drawn to the substantial bulge in his trousers. I already missed the feeling of it pressed against me.

"Though I do love where your mind went, I meant the sword in the stone," he said as his head jerked towards it behind me.

"Then why did you kiss me?" My head shook slightly in confusion.

"Technically, *you* kissed *me*." He smirked, and I wished I could wipe it off his smug face.

"Well, you kissed me back!" I countered.

"Because I am drawn to you just as much as you are drawn to that sword." His eyes dipped to my mouth, and I wondered for the briefest of moments if he was about to kiss me again. That was, until I remembered why I'd come back here in the first place.

My chin raised as I spoke. "You need to help make me stronger, strong enough to save everyone on the isle and the rest of Camelot."

"Then you need to pull the sword from the stone."

Chapter Six

I hadn't pulled the sword. Ambrose told me I had to wait until I was ready. As the days passed, I didn't leave the enchanted forest. Ambrose assured me everyone on the isle was safe, but I needed to get to work if I wanted to help them and the rest of Camelot. I had been staying at his cabin with him while we trained. He had slept on the floor in the main room, offering up the bed for me. We hadn't spoken about our kiss at all since it happened; a part of me wondered if I'd dreamt it. I had to force myself not to stare at his mouth every time he spoke. I thought about it all the time, but I didn't want to be the one to bring it up. There were far more pressing issues that needed attention.

Ambrose told me that although I could not wield magic on my own, I would be able to harness the power of the ring just as King Roland once had. Every day, I focused on the energy I felt humming inside of the ring. It called to me just as the sword had. A warm wave of something swept through me every time I called to its power, but aside from that feeling, nothing else had happened. I needed to be able to control its power before I could remove the sword from the stone.

Today, much like every other day, Ambrose wanted to get up early and train. Every morning since I had been staying here, he made me get up before the birds sang to train my mind, and, after lunch, we would train physically.

He had been trying to teach me hand to hand combat as well as fencing. He'd said if I wanted to pull the sword, I needed to know how to wield it first.

Pulling myself from bed, I braided my hair and changed into the leggings and tunic I wore for training before heading into the main room, where I knew he would be waiting for me with breakfast made. However, when I opened the door, he was still passed out on the floor.

Sighing, I made my way to the kitchen. I supposed this once I could make breakfast. As I prepared our meal, I focused on my mental training. Calling on the power inside the ring, it warmed against my chest, a low humming sounded as a faint green light shone. I repeated the same mantra in my mind as I did every morning. *I call upon the magic inside. Your power will become my power. We are one.*

The heat of power inside the ring rushed through me. I closed my eyes, tipping my head back. This felt like nothing I had ever experienced; it felt as if a part of me had been missing until this moment. My entire body tingled with the overwhelming power, begging to be wielded. Ambrose said I wouldn't be able to wield magic on my own, only harness the power inside the ring, and yet, this felt as though it were mine. It was probably supposed to feel this way, but my instincts were telling me otherwise. With this magic flowing within, I no longer felt powerless and weak. A blaze ignited, demanding to be set free. My body no longer felt tense, and I felt a renewed surge of energy and alertness.

A groan sounded from the other side of the room, and my eyes shot open, spinning around to find Ambrose waking. His eyes squinted; arm held over his face to shield him from something. Me, I realized. The same green glow which radiated from the ring was shining off me. I gasped, clutching onto the band. The moment my hand wrapped around the warmth of the ring, the light faded. Ambrose lowered his arm as a grin formed on his lips.

"You did it." He ran to me, lifting me off my feet as he spun me around. I couldn't help but join in his laughter as he spun me. He stopped; our eyes locked as he continued to hold me. Slowly, he lowered me back to my feet, never removing his gaze from mine. When I extended my hand, reaching to brush my fingers along the hard lines of his jaw, his smile faded just as the light around me had. He pulled back so quickly, I nearly toppled over from where he had been holding me mere seconds ago.

This was how it had been the last several days. He had been avoiding touching me; this was the only contact we'd had since our shared kiss. Why did he pull away? Had he not felt what I had felt?

He cleared his throat. "Now you can free the sword. We will use that with our training from now on so you can get used to the weapon you will need to wield."

I nodded, unsure what to say in that moment. How could he not have felt what I had—a raging fire ignited within me every time we touched? I knew it wasn't from the ring or the sword. There was something between us.

Ambrose made his way to the tiny dining table with both plates. He laid them out and sat, staring at his food absentmindedly as he ate. I sighed before joining him at the table. I watched him while I ate, curious as to what was going through his mind. His brows pulled together, looking down at his plate intently while he chewed. After we ate, Ambrose told me he had to go into town to check on things and that he wanted me to stay here to continue practising harnessing the ring's magic while he was gone.

I had no intention of doing that.

I waited several minutes after he left, ensuring he was really gone, and then I ventured out into the woods. I was, of course, going to practise harnessing the ring's power, but I didn't see why I had to do so inside his cabin.

Racing through the trees, I felt a hum of power deep inside of me. Something was calling to me, beckoning me closer. Since I'd been staying here, I hadn't gone beyond the cabin on my own, as it was far too easy to get lost within the enchanted forest. My heart raced with every step. The ring's magic seemed to spark to life, guiding me in the direction I had to take. I knew where it was taking me, destiny pushing me forward.

When I first saw the sword, it had been covered in vegetation, lichen clinging to it, but now the sword gleamed brightly. The sun was shining through a break in the tree canopies, illuminating the blade. The rust from before was gone, and the golden hilt with the dragon engraving beckoned me.

Time slowed as I inched closer and closer to the blade, as if the whole universe were waiting with bated breath to see what would happen. The chirping of the birds faded, and the gentle air which had made my spine tingle only moments before had gone. Not a sound was to be heard as I reached for the hilt.

Unlike the warmth of my ring, the metal of the blade was cold to the touch. As I touched the sword and the ring, I could feel their pulsating energy.

After a light tug on the blade, it released from the stone with ease. An emerald beam burst before my eyes as I held the freed sword in my grasp.

"What did you do?" Ambrose's scream caught me off guard, and I whirled around to find him staring at me at the edge of the clearing, a frightened expression on his face.

"I pulled out the sword like *you* wanted." I waved the sword in my hand to emphasize, surprised by how light it felt compared to the practise swords I had been using.

"Not now!" He cried. Ambrose ran towards me but stumbled, the ground around us beginning to shake.

"What?" I breathed; my knees felt weak, and I fought to catch my balance.

Thunder boomed, and green lightning illuminated the skies above, striking directly on the stone where the sword had just been. Heavy grey clouds blocked the sun that had shone through moments ago, leaving us in darkness save for the occasional flashes of green lightning. The trees surrounding the clearing rustled in the strong wind.

"What's happening?" I called to Ambrose, his hand extending as he reached for me.

Another tremor sent me falling to the ground, and I crawled towards him while attempting to dodge the crashing branches and other debris all around us. I was only a few feet away from Ambrose when he was knocked off balance by another bolt of lightning which struck the ground between us.

"Ambrose!" I cried as I lost sight of him in the darkness.

The same swirling green magic that Ambrose used that day in the fire appeared next to me. Just as a massive branch came crashing down towards me, his power encircled me, pulling me in with him. In less than a second, we were standing in front of his cabin. The woods here were not nearly as shaken as the clearing had been, but still, it did not look as it should. The trembling started again, and Ambrose jerked his arm up, pulling the ring from around my neck, snapping the chain as he did so. As soon as he had the ring in his hands, the shaking and storms in the distance vanished.

"What the hell was that?" I screamed, pushing Ambrose's chest. This was *his* fault; *he* told me I had to pull the sword; *he* told me it was fated. With my throat burning, I gripped my fists in his shirt and forced back the tears that were welling up in my eyes. My accelerated breathing only worsened the pain in my throat.

"You were not ready." As he looked down at where I was still holding his shirt, he sighed in a steady, composed voice. "You can not wield one unless you can control the other's power."

"I can control the ring's power!" I shoved him again.

"You cannot; it controls you." His voice calm, he reached to place his hands on my shoulders.

"It does not!" I argued like a child, pushing him a third time.

"Would you stop that!" he demanded. He grabbed hold of my wrists, his eyes glaring into mine. "I told you to stay here."

"I didn't want to; I don't think I could have even if I did. It was like the sword pulled me there, it called to me." I felt my face soften as I held his gaze.

His eyes narrowed slightly. "Did it really?"

I nodded and drew nearer to him, feeling the same pull into his embrace as I had previously felt towards the sword. As my chest lightly touched his, something ignited within me. His eyes quickly landed on the spot where he held my wrists; then he released them with such suddenness that I wondered again whether he felt the same internal fire I did.

"Why?" I asked him.

"Because it just further proves that you are the chosen one but—"

"No," I interjected. "Why did you pull away? Why do you act like nothing happened between us? Why do you act as though you do not feel the same burning desire inside you that I feel every time we're near? Just...why?"

"Because there are more important things to worry about at the moment," he said, turning his back, refusing to even look at me.

"That is just an excuse! Why can't you just be real with me? Why can't you let yourself feel what I know you are feeling? I don't understand!" My hand shot up to his shoulder, trying to force him to hold my gaze.

"How don't you understand that this is all for you? Everything we're doing is about you and your kingdom." His arms flew up dramatically as he yelled. His eyes were dark for the briefest of moments before they softened, and then he turned from me once more. "If I had you the way I wanted you, I don't know that I'd be able to think of anything else. You already occupy my mind far too frequently as it is; I need to focus on what needs to be done."

"And how do you want me?" My fingers gently brushed against his arm.

Ambrose whirled around, barely giving me a second to think about what was happening before his lips were on mine. The last time we kissed, it was like a hunger inside of us needing to be satiated, yet this time, it was somehow even harder and more demanding than before. My mouth moved against his in an act of desperation, as if I required his kiss to survive. Every touch, every taste, lit a spark of burning need inside of me. I responded with a faint groan which was equal parts agony and desire as he bit down on my already bruising lip.

Titling my head back, his lips trailed down my jaw and neck as he kissed his way lower. My hands frantically pulled at his shirt, needing to feel the warmth of his skin against mine. I undid the final button and pulled his shirt off, my fingers brushed down his shoulders and back, nails digging in as his shirt slid off his arms. His head lifted from my collarbone, pulling my tunic over my head, freeing my breasts. He took in the sight of me, his lips twitching up before I pulled him in for another kiss. He smiled against my lips, his hand wandering down my neck and to my breast where he began to tease my nipple between his fingers.

My thighs squeezed together as the need inside me grew more and more. He broke our kiss, his mouth moving lower, and stopped to tease my achingly hard nipple. His hand had moved, pulling my leggings down to my knees before he slowly slid his hand up and down my thigh.

His legs moved between mine, parting them as he lifted me up, just as he had last time. I wrapped my legs around him as he carried me into his cabin. He kissed me again, not breaking it the entire time he held me. He kicked the door open, and we went tumbling inside.

Ambrose's arms wrapped around me as we fell to the wooden floor. His body tense as he kneeled above me, his bare chest against mine, his knees straddling me while his hands were placed on either side of my head. The crackling of the fire in the hearth and the panting of our breaths was all I could hear in that moment.

His eyes swept over me. "Are you sure?" he asked, still struggling for breath.

"Yes," I pleaded, needing more.

Ambrose's hands were on my inner thighs once more. As he brushed his hand slowly up them, a shiver of need went throughout my entire body. His head dipped between my legs, and before I realized what he was doing, his name escaped my lips in a loud moan as his tongue circled the very spot where I'd been aching.

My spine arched at his touch, while he explored my body. His one hand still rested on my thigh, while the other found its way back to my breast, tormenting it once more. A coil of searing heat built inside of me, begging to be released as his mouth moved again, sucking and licking my clit. My fingers fisted in his hair, his laugh vibrating through me as he pushed two fingers inside of me.

"Ambrose," I sighed. The sound of his name on my lips had him groaning his own desire while he continued to pump his fingers inside of me. So close to finishing, my body started shaking and twitching with pleasure.

"Say my name when you come," he commanded, his lips against my body, and it was my undoing. Moaning his name as I fell over the edge of ecstasy. My body shook with pleasure before losing all its strength. I sank into the ground, panting as I struggled to catch my breath.

He kissed me forcefully and passionately before drawing back and whispering, "*That* is how I want you." His breath was warm against the shell of my ear.

"Is that all?" I challenged. The glint in his eyes as his mouth kicked up told me he was more than up to it.

Ambrose tugged his pants off, then slowly pulled mine, kissing his way down my thighs as he did. I was already needing more. He hitched my knee over his hip as he lined himself up and pushed inside of me, inch by inch. He was slow at first; his eyes held mine in a silent question, and I nodded, my hips meeting his, urging him to go faster—so he did. Faster and harder.

Heat was already pulsing through my body again. I slid my hand down to where our bodies met, rubbing my clit. Ambrose noticed what I was doing, and he smirked down at me before reaching between us. He grabbed my wrist, pinning it above my head and holding me at his mercy while his other hand took over massaging that perfect spot.

I moaned each time he thrust into me. My free hand moved to his back, digging in again, positive it would leave marks. His heart pounded against my chest in a frantic rhythm.

He leaned down, capturing my lips with his as he cried out in pleasure, "*Ariella.*"

And with that, I came for him once more.

Chapter Seven

"You need to be ready," Ambrose said, raising his sword. "You need to master both the ring's power as well as the sword's before you can claim your kingdom back from Mordred." We had been training for several hours, and my body was aching in pain, my strength depleting—though I would be lying if I said it had been entirely from training.

Ambrose held on to the jade ring anytime I practised with Excalibur, King Roland's legendary sword. He had told me that for over a century people had come from all over the Seven Kingdoms to try and free the mighty sword. Eventually, people gave up and believed it would never again be wielded in battle. But the people of Avalon knew. They knew that it was destined to be freed by the chosen one from the prophecy.

Me.

"You're distracted," Ambrose teased as he pushed his blade towards me; I barely had time to block, the blow forcing me backwards several steps.

"And you are not?" I countered.

"I am always distracted when I am around you; that is the problem." He spun around, hitting me in the back gently with the sword before sweeping his leg beneath mine, knocking me to the ground. "However, that is not the issue, as I already know how to fight and work through it."

Huffing out a breath, I pushed the loose strands of my hair that had fallen out of my braid back out of my face. Forcing myself back to my feet, I readied my sword once more, trying to anticipate his next attack. He struck from above, and I just managed to block the attack again. This time, however, I did not stumble. This time, I was the one to kick out at him. He dodged the kick with ease as he tried to stifle his laugh.

"What is so damned funny?" I asked through gritted teeth, striking my sword towards him again.

"You." He shrugged. "Perhaps you need more motivation in his fight."

"More motivation than stopping a psychotic, power-hungry monster that stole my throne and tried to kill me?" I stopped my advances, arching a brow at him.

"Indeed. If you can land one blow on me, I will reward you with a kiss."

"Ha! That sounds like it is more for your benefit than mine." I rolled my eyes but resumed my strikes at him.

"It would be mutually beneficial." He shrugged again. The grin on his face did not fade as he continued to dodge and block every one of my attacks. This only intensified my need to strike him and wipe the smug look from his face.

Though Ambrose's technique was far greater than mine and would probably always be so, I was faster. At least I was when I wasn't as physically and mentally drained as I was currently. We had spent the morning working with the jade ring's powers and the afternoon working on my balance and the different techniques I had learned thus far. I was exhausted, but I was determined.

Timing was everything. It was the entire reason we were still here training instead of storming the castle. I knew this to be true from years of studying my ancestors' histories of great battles. But studying it and mastering it were two different concepts.

Without concentrating on really hitting him, I kept coming at Ambrose from various angles. All my focus was truly on my footwork as I calculated the ideal time to strike. On the one hand, he might relax his defenses if he believed I wasn't giving my attacks any consideration, if he thought I was just blindly slashing my sword at him. On the other hand, I had to act quickly enough and time it perfectly.

I gradually slowed my advances, and he did the same without realizing. Not only did I strike out with a decreased ferocity, but my assaults were becoming noticeably slower overall. I wanted him to think I was far more fatigued than I was. The chances of this really succeeding against Mordred or anyone else were limited; I knew they would not hesitate to kill me at the first sign of weakness. In this case, however, I just needed to wipe that smirk off Ambrose's face.

With each successful block, his arrogant smirk widened. He feigned yawning, covering his mouth with one hand while his sword met mine with his other. He was far from exhausted. He wanted me to know I was boring him. But that was my intention all along.

High, fast, and hard—I swung my blade. The shock in his eyes told me he hadn't bargained on me having so much energy left. As he brought his sword up to block mine, I whirled around and kicked his legs out from under him, sending him tumbling backwards onto his ass.

I stood over him, pointing Excalibur at his chest. Letting him know exactly who had just won. My lips twitched up while I held in my laugh at the sight of him on the ground beneath me. As my eyes met and held his, I raised my chin high. His emerald gaze only seemed to sparkle brighter as I did so.

The smirk I had desperately wanted to fall only intensified as he said, "Well done."

The enchantment emanating from Excalibur seemed to course through my veins, giving me the strength I needed. I no longer felt exhausted from my training with Ambrose; I was energized, ready. Prepared to take on anything or anyone.

My ring, which Ambrose wore around his neck, began to glow as it lifted and hovered between us. As I watched, my jaw hung open and my eyes widened. My stomach fluttered and my chest tightened as he unclasped the chain and let it fall, the ring slowly moving towards me. My hand trembled as I reached up, brushing my fingers against the ring as it continued to float before me. The ring gently found its way into my open palm. As I closed my fingers around the ring, both it and Excalibur warmed. My grasp tightened around them, and the light around the ring faded. As their power merged within me, a wave of molten heat swept through my body. The ring's green light emanated from me for a brief moment before it slowly faded.

"You're ready," Ambrose whispered.

My gaze lifted just as his eyes darted between my sword and ring.

They thought I was ready. There was no thunder, no storm or earthquake as I held both. I had the power of Excalibur and the ring now, just as King Roland once had.

"And for the record, I do believe you to be ready. And I'll be there with you." Ambrose winked before turning and heading back toward his cabin.

"What are you doing?" I asked as I struggled to match pace.

"Getting my things so we can go," he replied without slowing.

"Wait," I shouted as I pulled his arm. Finally, he halted and turned towards me. His brow quirked up, silently questioning me. "You can't be serious. What are we just going to go storm the castle?" I huffed a laugh.

"Precisely." Ambrose nodded, then continued on his path.

"That's ridiculous!" I called out, but he didn't look back. I groaned as I ran to catch up once more.

Ambrose left the door to his cabin open. When I entered, he was packing everything into a satchel. It had to have been some other kind of magic. I watched him warily as he threw clothes, food, books, water, and more into the satchel without it ever expanding. It seemed to be bottomless as he shoved items that were far larger into it with such ease.

He finally turned to me after a few moments. "Are you ready?"

I swallowed and nodded nervously. "Yes." I hoped that saying it aloud would make me feel more ready.

Ambrose shot me a wicked grin and grabbed my hand, pulling me out the door. As we walked through the enchanted forest, his hand never left mine. We weaved through the trees, and I was glad he seemed to know exactly where to go, because it felt like we were walking in circles to me. I would have been lost in the enchanted forest without him, and I knew that was the point. Without magic, one would be lost inside, roaming around endlessly with no way out.

A tingling sensation washed over me when we left the magical barrier. The sun had set and I looked up into the moonless sky as we stood on the beach where I had washed up when I first arrived on Avalon. Where Ambrose had found and healed me.

Ambrose's hand finally slid away from mine, and he began to move them around rhythmically in front of him. Green sparks swirled around, and a portal opened before us. He stepped towards it, but I hesitated. Was I truly ready? I had been training all day; shouldn't we wait until I was well rested? Didn't I need to train even a little more?

"We have to go; it won't stay open for long. This will take us right to the castle grounds." He reached for my hand again, but I jerked back out of reach. "You are ready."

"No, I'm not." I shook my head, taking another step back.

"We can do this. Together." He smiled softly, his hand remaining outstretched. My eyes looked at his hand then moved up to his eyes, where I could see the sincerity in his words. I didn't believe I was ready, but maybe he was right, maybe we could do this together.

"Together," I said, finally taking his hand before we stepped through the portal.

Chapter Eight

After passing through the portal, we found ourselves on the castle grounds. In an instant, I was taken back to that terrifying night: Sir Lance Alott guiding me across the castle grounds and into the surrounding forest, saving me and losing his own life in the process. And now I was back. My eyes lowered, and my arms wrapped around my stomach as the guilt set in. He gave his life to protect me. Tears welled up in my eyes, and I fought them back despite the pain that spread to the back of my throat.

The cool wind howled around us; the night sky seemed so much darker here than it had on the isle. The full blood moon shone brightly overhead, seemingly providing the sole light as it bathed the castle in a soft red glow. Had that much time passed while we walked through the portal? I didn't think so, but it was hard to tell. Not only was there no moon on the beach when we left, but the blood moon was almost too telling of the blood I knew would be shed tonight.

"I—I don't know the way." I looked to Ambrose, realizing he was probably counting on me to lead us inside. "Last time I had help escaping," I admitted as the tears I had been struggling to hold in finally began to fall. Ambrose raised his hand, gently brushing the tears from my cheek with his thumb as his palm cupped my face.

"It's okay; I know the way. Do you trust me?" I nodded, and his lips brushed mine. "I love you, Ariella," he whispered against them before I pulled back abruptly.

"What?" I asked, my eyes wide.

"You don't have to say it back, or even feel the same. I just needed you to know in case I don't make it out alive tonight." I resisted at first, but his words overcame me, and I let myself be pulled into his embrace, where my arms wrapped tightly around his waist and my fists clenched into the back of his shirt.

"We both must survive. I don't want to live without you." I cried into his shoulder as we continued to hold one another.

"I will not hesitate to sacrifice myself for you. You are the one that needs to survive. You are the rightful heir to this kingdom, and Camelot needs you," he said, pushing me back at arms' length, his eyes pleading with me to understand.

"But I need you." My voice broke. I grabbed hold of his shirt and pulled him close. My mouth crashed onto his, desperately needing this to not be the end; it was only the beginning. It had to be.

His arms snaked around my waist as he tugged me flush against him. Heat rose within me seconds before I realized that the ring squished between us played a major part. We pulled back at the same moment and watched as the ring's light faded.

"We should go," Ambrose said, and I followed his lead as he started towards the castle.

He directed us to a stone exterior wall. When he pressed his palm onto the stones, a magical emerald flash of energy shot out and into the cracks. The emerald lights pulsed between the cracks as he pushed on them. The sound of rocks scraping against each other reached me while they slowly slid open, revealing a hidden doorway. When I escaped with Sir Lance Alott, we used the servants' tunnels. I remembered we had exited through a different doorway than this. I assumed there were many tunnels for the castle's servants and wondered how Ambrose knew his way around them. Was he being led by his magic?

As the doorway slid shut behind us, it took the little bit of light which the blood moon had provided with it, leaving us in complete darkness. Ambrose murmured something in a language I couldn't understand, and, within seconds, a small ball of golden light appeared and floated before us. It was the only source of light within the passages and seemed to lead the way as we followed behind. The echoes of our footsteps and my racing heart were the only sounds as we walked.

The light which Ambrose had cast led us to what seemed to be a dead end. The light vanished, and I took in a sharp breath as we were once again cast into darkness. "It's okay," he breathed just ahead of me. The same emerald light sparked to life as he pressed his power into the stone wall again. The wall parted once more, and as we stepped out of the passageway, I realized where the light had led us.

The Great Hall.

Mordred stood alone in the center of the Great Hall, his back to us. A golden crown encrusted with rubies sat upon his head. The crown of Camelot. Moonlight, in its crimson hue, streamed in through the open windows, lighting up the large space. Mordred's shoulders were relaxed as we slowly approached. The mocking tone in his laugh had told me he already figured out we were there. It was as if he had been anticipating our arrival. We had not seen a single guard stationed outside; he didn't want them to see me.

"Ironic that we meet here once again," Mordred spoke, yet he still hadn't turned.

My mind whirled with what he could have possibly meant. Of course, we had been in this very room many times before, but why was it ironic? What was he talking about? Ambrose shifted beside me, and I watched as his eyes flicked back between Mordred and myself.

"You must really hate your lineage to be standing here with him," Mordred continued when neither of us said anything.

"What are you talking about?" I demanded, and he finally, slowly, turned to face us, a sneering smirk spreading across his face.

"Yes, what am I talking about, Merlin?" He spat the name, and I flinched at the accusation. "Well, do not keep her waiting." He smiled cruelly, and I looked to Ambrose for him to deny it. But he didn't. Ambrose's jaw clenched as he glared back at Mordred.

My head shook in denial, and my throat burned, holding back more tears which wanted to fall. Ambrose was Merlin. He lied to me. He killed my ancestors and started this war. He was the one responsible for my parents' death. But how? Had he really been alive for all these years? I needed answers. I *deserved* them.

Before I could even begin to process all the thoughts swirling around in my mind, Mordred struck.

Chapter Nine

Crimson light flashed towards me. I didn't have time to process what was happening, let alone counter the attack. I was frozen in place. The reality of who Ambrose truly was and Mordred somehow casting a magical attack on me were too much. I was not ready for this fight. My eyes squinted shut, as if it would somehow shield me from what was about to happen. I was going to die.

But nothing happened.

I cracked one eye open, wondering if it happened so fast, I hadn't felt the pain. Ambrose kneeled in front of me, hands raised, as his green magical shield surrounded us.

"I don't know how long I can hold this. You must defeat him," he gritted out as he gave so much power into his shield.

I shook my head. "I can't win."

"You can and you will," he promised.

My entire face seemed to harden as I watched him.

He lied to me.

He was a murderer.

He was the one behind all of this.

He must have noticed the change as he looked up at me. "I cannot deny who I am. Merlin is my surname. But the history books have it wrong. I never betrayed the king and queen. Mordred did in this very room. Mordred was born of two mages, and yet, he possessed no power of his own. He grew jealous and sought out other forms of magic he could control. Dark magic. But even with this dark power, he wanted more. He was power hungry. He wanted my position within the castle, to work for the king and queen so he could climb the ranks. They knew of his dark magic and banished him from Camelot. That night he entered the Great Hall from the same passageway we arrived in. He killed the king and queen while everyone knew I was with them. I managed to save Prince Roland and gave him the same ring of power that you wear around your neck now. All the mages who fought then and even now know that it was not I but Mordred who had murdered the king and queen and started this war between our kinds."

My body shook as rage coiled inside of me, and my wrath roared in my ears as I fixed my gaze on Mordred. My hands clenched and unclenched around the hilt of Excalibur, which hung in its scabbard at my hip. He was the mastermind behind it all. This war and every innocent life lost were because of his corrupt need for power. He plotted to have me assassinated because he wanted to rule Camelot. He had been alive for hundreds of years, planning. He told me that all magic wielders were evil, when he was one of them. He was the true villain.

I finally drew Excalibur, squaring my shoulders as I stood. I pointed my sword towards Mordred as he continued to cast his crimson magic my way, attempting to penetrate the barrier. "Surrender now for all the crimes you have committed."

"You think you can defeat me?" He laughed menacingly. "Merlin doesn't have his great power that he once possessed, and you... you're just some foolish girl."

"I am your Queen, and you will bow before me." I took a step forward, freeing myself from the protection of Ambrose's barrier. He let it fall seconds after I stepped out and stood next to me. My necklace warmed against me, its own emerald barrier shimmered tightly against my skin.

"I may not have the same powers I once had, but that is because Queen Ariella Pendragon has them now." His gaze flicked between the ring around my neck and the sword I held before returning to Mordred. A wicked grin pulled at Ambrose's mouth as Mordred's eyes flashed with fear, so briefly I almost missed it.

I did not waste another second before swinging my blade for Mordred's neck. At the last moment, my sword met with a clank against the red barrier which Mordred cast, similar to the one my ring had just produced around me. I screamed my anger as I continued to strike at him with the same ferocity I had in my training with Ambrose.

The ring glowed and hummed against my chest, giving me all the power it had to win this fight. Mordred chuckled mockingly at me while his shield continued to block every attack.

"Take the rest of my power," Ambrose shouted from behind me. My body shone even brighter with the same green light I had learned to recognize as his magic. I felt his power inside of me, urging me on as I kept trying to land a strike. When I dared to look back at Ambrose, he was a beacon of bright light that flooded from him all the way inside me.

His power raced through me, illuminating Excalibur as I pushed it down against Mordred's shield with all the strength I had. All the rage, the grief, and the loss I had experienced because of him poured out of me and into my sword. His shield cracked, and he gasped in horror just as I plunged the blade into his chest.

He laughed, a maniacal smile twisting his mouth. His body collapsing, a black shadow left his corpse as all the dark magic he had consumed over the years disappeared into nothing. I watched, eyes wide and panting for breath, as I too collapsed.

Ambrose kneeled next to me and pulled me into his arms. "I'm sorry," he whispered as I cried in his arms.

Finally, guards burst in, their faces etched with bewilderment and disbelief. They were trying to help me up while they spoke, but I did not hear them.

Even though Mordred had betrayed me time and time again and was the one responsible for everything, he was still the man who had raised me, and as much as I hated him, it was still something which would not be so easy to forget. I breathed a sigh of relief as Ambrose held me wordlessly. I was finally at peace.

Epilogue
FIVE YEARS LATER

Today's the day. Ambrose and I are getting married. He will no longer just be High Advisor to the Queen, he will be my King Consort. He had always been so much more than my advisor, but I wanted to ensure Camelot was truly happy and ready.

It was difficult to bring him in as my councilor after my coronation, but I knew he was the right choice for me and my people. It was the first step to mending the peace between those with and those without magic. Although it took time, the people have grown to love him just as I did. Well, maybe not *just* as I did.

My chambermaid styled my hair while I sat in front of my vanity. Already in my dress, I ensured this one was comfortable, wielding my own magic to create this stunning white ball gown, which held no corset. Ambrose had refitted the ring I once wore around my neck, which was the same ring I now wore upon my ring finger. I looked down at it happily as a smile pulled at my lips.

Only the rightful heir will lead this kingdom to glory. She will rise, forged from steel and stone. I supposed the prophecy had come to pass.

When my maid finished my hair, she curtsied low, and I dismissed her, needing a few moments alone before the ceremony. I slipped the ring from my finger and studied the old symbols which lined the inside of the band.

"Having second thoughts?" Ambrose spoke from behind me, and I jumped in surprise.

"Never." I laughed, stepping forward. and placed a gentle kiss on his cheek. "I was just looking at the runes on the band again. How could you read them?" I asked, though I was pretty certain I knew the answer. He was Ambrose Merlin. That I knew, and only the sorcerer who had placed them there would read them.

"Because I put them there." His lips twitched as he fought to hold back his smirk, and I rolled my eyes.

"Yes, but how did you find the prophecy?"

"I didn't." He shrugged, and my eyes narrowed as I waited for him to elaborate. He laughed, "I created the prophecy. I could feel your soul bound to mine the night I shared my powers with that ring." He nodded to that very ring I wore on my finger before he continued. "I knew that the Pendragon legacy would come and conquer the world with me by her side. I knew that woman would be mine and I hers. Forever. And together, we would write history," Ambrose smiled as he touched his forehead to mine. Our energies flowing through one another because of the common link which we shared. Our love.

About the Author

Danielle Hill is an Amazon Top 10 author of drama filled, swoon worthy and magical contemporary fantasy novels. Danielle first came up with the idea for A Kingdom of Sun and Shadow in late 2017 and began publishing chapters on Episode shortly after. After a warm reception on Episode, she decided to expand the story and began writing the manuscript in February 2018.

Danielle resides in a small town in Ontario, Canada and spends her free time creating remarkable worlds full of magic and being a mom to her daughter and dog. She loves Marvel, anime, binge-watching TV shows and cheesy hallmark movie marathons.

For more content from Danielle, go here:
https://linktr.ee/Daniellemhill

A Fate of Feathers & Fae

A Fate of Feathers and Fae

MIMI B. ROSE

Heat Level:
Hot

Content Warnings:
Consensual and explicit sex, murder, blood, misogyny (villain), and violence.

Chapter One

Princess Nerya pinned her black hair beneath the fine net and prayed her mother had persuaded Prince Lutin to sign the peace treaty. Lutin's nearby kingdom had been threatening war for several years. Queen Isabella had called for diplomatic negotiations to settle their differences, so she could work on the internal conflicts between the peoples of her own kingdom. Strife surrounded them. Nerya had returned home less than a year ago, hoping to remain in the background of her mother's court until she could retire to the local nunnery at a respectable age.

But it was not to be. She would follow her mother's bidding and show up to support the queen's political ambitions. Nerya left her chambers and followed the bright red uniform of the Yeoman through the Queen's Gallery, with its bank of bright windows and dozens of servants cleaning and polishing the honeycomb colonnade. Sucking in a big breath, she smoothed down her silk mourning robes with her brown-skinned hands.

Skirts swishing as she strode through the Great Watching Room, she passed the members of the lesser court, who strutted and pranced along the tiled floors. They had watched her, silent and waiting, when she returned as a widow four years after her wedding. Not sympathetic. More like...curious. They regarded her at a distance, like a pet or an oddity. Steeling herself, she held her head high and trained her eyes above the crowd.

Her husband had died of the sweating sickness a mere eleven months ago. The role of a princess was to cement alliances and make connections with other royal families. They didn't choose their spouses, they simply did as they were told. She had been relieved–guiltily so–when her husband had passed. Thankfully, they didn't have any children, so she quickly returned to her mother's kingdom.

Nerya followed the Yeoman's scarlet coat as he walked through the small doorway leading to the Presence Chamber. Her mother, Queen Isabella of Ishbilliya, Defender of the Fair Folk and Sovereign Ruler of the Cinque Ducados, sat upon an ornate throne, flanked by elaborate tapestries and imposing marble pillars. Beside her was Nerya's older sister, Sultana Lynnara, every bit the Queen's heir in her saffron, gossamer robes. Nerya's breath caught in her throat as the two women's Fae wings shone brilliantly at their backs. Her own wings had never grown in, her gift of foresight only provided occasional flashes, and she had never mastered the long sword, preferring the short and precise *navalla* blade.

Lynnara, by contrast, excelled at everything. She would make an exemplary Queen someday.

"Her Grace, Princess Nerya, royal daughter to Her Majesty, the Queen," the Yeoman announced.

She curtsied in front of the dais. "Greetings and salutations, Your Royal Highness."

The grandeur of the Presence Room, its walls festooned with yellow and blue tiles in ornate geometric patterns, always set Nerya's heart pounding. A memory sparked of a small child waiting anxiously for a kind word from her mother—the beautiful, distant, dark-skinned Fae Queen on the throne. Although Nerya may have been taller and older, she still felt like that little girl. Would she ever be good enough?

The Queen, looking more hopeful than she had all week, gestured for Nerya to join them. On the other side of her sister sat Lutin, Prince of Nain, his light skin gleaming and elongated ears twitching. Lutin had showered attention on Nerya's sister this week, throwing practised white, toothy smiles in her direction. Nerya wanted to punch his face every time he did it. Prince Lutin's people had declared war against the Fae folk, regularly invading the border villages and killing and capturing the Ishbilliyans. In addition, his kingdom's sanction of child brides and corporal punishment for wives and daughters violated her kingdom's egalitarian values. Nerya clenched her fists at her sides and turned her grimace into a diplomatic smile.

The treaty negotiations with the Prince of Nain and his uncle, the Chancellor, had been strained, but the look on the Queen's face suggested something had changed. The kingdoms were far apart on the issues. Nerya's mother worried they wouldn't make a resolution by mid-month, when the cease-fire ended. Lynnara had argued that every piece of negotiation brought them closer to agreement. Nerya wondered if they should give up and go back to war.

The Yeoman called the court to attention with a flourish of trumpets.

A hush fell as the Queen rose and looked out over the assembled group, shoulders back and head high. "We thank you for gathering with us." Her voice rang out loud and clear. "We are pleased to announce that Prince Lutin of Nain has pledged his troth to our daughter, Sultana Lynnara, and we have accepted on her behalf."

Nerya gasped and glanced quickly at her sister.

The Heir to the Throne sat upright on the edge of her seat, her face neutral, wings relaxed and folded behind her: the picture of composure. Nerya's heart caught in her chest. Relief wash over her. She had escaped being married off again. Then a pang of regret hit. She was losing her sister. Queen Isabella held out her hand and Lynnara rose and clasped it, poised and perfect. The Prince stepped out from his seat. He strode toward the princess, his bright, beady eyes fixed on her.

Nerya's whole body shook. The memories attacked her and her pulse thundered in her ears. Five years ago, Nerya had been in the same position as her sister, married off for political reasons to a stranger. She had protested and threatened to run away. Her mother scolded her and doubled her guard. In the blink of an eye, she went from a lively young woman to a colourless Duchess going through the motions.

Did the same fate await Lynnara?

When the applause died down, Nerya rose and approached her sister. They had never been close. Lynnara sided with their mother in many decisions, arguing that tradition was most important, while Nerya wanted to see change—more cooperation among the Fae and the shifter communities, greater transparency in the High Council, and more responsibilities given to the courtiers who shirked their duties in order to gossip and watch the entertainments.

Though she and Lynnara had different ideas, she still wanted to connect with her and tell her it would be all right. She had to give her sister something more than the speech their mother gave her five years ago. "Princesses are peace-weavers" was a favourite saying of the Queen. "It is the role you were born to play."

Nerya pushed through the throng of Lynnara's well-wishers. She yearned to tell her sister not to lose sight of herself in all the layers of expectations. Did she know this already? Or did Lynnara do everything for their mother and not for herself?

At that thought, Nerya stopped two paces away from her sister. Maybe they weren't as different as she had always believed.

Feeling the hair prickle on her neck and a swirl of air around her, she turned around. Duke Alonso, ruler of the Caliphe of Mursiya, stood stock still in the centre of the hall, while the other courtiers milled around, smiling and laughing. Glossy black hair framed his handsome, tan face. He had grown since they had spent the summer together at his home. She had been sixteen years old, he was eighteen–it felt like a lifetime ago. For one glorious year, they had been betrothed to each other, until her parents had broken off the engagement and sent her overseas to marry a man twice her age. Since that time, his physique had changed. He had gained more height and brawn.

His eyes met hers. There was a question in them, but she couldn't decipher it.

After a moment, he turned to the woman beside him. Lady Camila, the Prioress of Estrella del Mar Abbey, inclined her head and laughed at Alonso's words. A stab of jealousy coursed through her, though she knew it was irrational. She'd had a crush on Alonso when they were engaged, but it wasn't serious, of course. They had been very young. And then there was the night they had spent together some months ago after she had returned home, but she had been lonely and seeking some kind of connection. It hadn't meant anything.

Nerya shrugged her shoulders. She was glad Alonso was friends with the Prioress. Camila was not wearing the turmeric-coloured linen robes of the Prioress, but instead wore the Stella Maris Order's warrior uniform, white *sarral* pantaloons and green *juvva* tunic, a long sword buckled around her waist. Was her friend expecting trouble? Nerya scanned the crowd for more worried faces.

Nerya closed her eyes briefly and let out a long breath. She had the overwhelming urge to get out of the crowd. Her nascent wings itching between her shoulder blades, Nerya took a few steps back and moved toward the edge of the dais. She wished she could soar out of this uncomfortable situation.

Catching her gaze again, Alonso walked towards her, his gait lithe and graceful. Her heart skipped a beat at the smoulder in his eyes. She wanted to talk with him, but she was afraid she might slip up and want more. And she didn't need the complication of whatever this thing was between them. Not that there was anything between them.

Then chaos erupted.

Chapter Two

The sounds of a zing and a thud rang out. Alonso whirled around. An arrow jutted out from the Queen's throne, where Nerya's mother had sat only minutes before. Alonso's warrior training kicked in and he dropped to the floor. He crawled to a pillar for cover. From his vantage point, he scanned the room for threats, homing in on the princess, Nerya. It was still like a punch to the gut every time he saw her, but he couldn't let his emotions gain control. He had to ensure her safety. For that, he needed a clear mind.

Someone had fired a crossbow in the Presence Chamber. The Queen was bleeding on the ground. Lynnara struggled with the Prince. Nerya, grim determination on her face, wove her way through the crowd to reach her family. Alonso calculated the easiest path to meet her. She was his goal.

Pandemonium reigned. People ran in all directions, screaming and crying. Nerya crouched beside her mother and conferred with the High Mage next to her. Several paces away, Lynnara screamed. Prince Lutin pulled her by the arm off the dais, two of his guards in tow. The Prince's uncle followed behind, slashing with his dagger at anyone who approached. Then Lutin ran his hands around the edge of the silk brocade tapestry and released a hidden mechanism behind it.

Alonso hesitated. Should he help Nerya or stop Lutin? A split second and he pushed toward Lynnara—Nerya would never forgive him if her sister was lost.

Lutin pushed open a camouflaged door, one of many hidden passageways in the palace. Nerya reached the door at the same time as Alonso did. Her hands and dagger were stained red and Alonso's pulse raced. Her scent was still the same, persimmons and figs, and as he sucked in a breath of relief, it slowed his beating heart.

"Is that your blood?" He searched her for wounds.

"No," she said. "I killed Lutin's uncle, the Ambassador."

Pride blossomed in his chest. Her fiery spirit still burned inside of her.

Prioress Camila pushed her way to the door just as Nerya and Alonso breached the entry.

She opened her mouth to speak, then cried out. "I've been hit." She grimaced, an arrow lodged in her leg. "Alonso, get her out of here."

He stepped forward and took Nerya's arm, his heart pounding.

Nerya wrenched her arm free and turned to Camila, who had fallen to the floor. "I don't need him. I have to find my sister."

Frowning, Alonso opened his mouth to protest. Two of the Lady Prioress's warrior sisters appeared beside Camila, one short and one tall.

Camila waved at her charges. "Sisters Alma and Elena, go with the princess and the duke." She turned to Alonso. "You can trust them."

"But—" Nerya protested.

"Don't argue. You have to escape the palace." Camila put her hand on Nerya's leg and whispered, "Do it for me."

Nerya sighed and nodded. When she gave Alonso her arm, his chest filled with warmth. He would ensure her safety, keep her close by his side. Nobody would stop them, not even Nerya's stubbornness and pride.

The warrior sisters closed the secret door after they had entered. As it swung shut, the sounds of people shouting and crying faded.

Silence descended. Clattering and clunking noises came from down the passageway.

Nerya tugged at his arm. "I can hear them."

Alonso cleared his throat. "Nerya... Your Grace, I must keep you safe."

"We find my sister first."

"We will follow your sister's path, then," Alonso said. "But my first priority is you. Any danger and we leave immediately." He had to get her moving. They were vulnerable as long as they remained in the palace. If they found her sister and her kidnapper, then they would help. If not, they would continue through the passage and get Nerya to safety.

Nerya clutched Alonso's hand as the four figures wound down the stairs. When they reached the bottom, two tunnels presented themselves.

"Left," Nerya said.

That passage led to the east side of the palace. A good enough place for their escape. They crept through the winding tunnels, keeping on the main path. Dark stone glinted off the torches held by the sisters. Nerya held her dagger in her free hand.

They met no one. The noises died away as they drew closer to the exit. Alonso racked his brain for ways to ensure Nerya left, even without Lynnara.

Soon they reached another staircase that led to a small gate to the outside of the palace. The exit was private and little-used, a useful escape route.

"Do you think he took my sister through this door?" Nerya asked. She opened the door and peered outside. "I don't see her. We should go back."

"We can't," Alonso said. "There are too many false tunnels in the passageways. And too many other exits. We'd never find them." He took a deep breath and prepared for an argument.

"I have to find my sister." Nerya clenched her fists.

"I agree she's in danger. But my first concern is protecting you," he replied, keeping his voice level.

"What about Lynnara?" She looked up at him, eyes shining.

"Your kingdom needs you," Alonso said. "We have a chance to escape."

She shook her head. "I'm not important. My sister is."

"You don't really believe this, do you?" He frowned. "You're worth three of her."

Nerya blinked. "But—"

"We'll argue about that later. For now, think of it politically," he said. "If you're separated from your sister, then it increases our chances that at least one member of the royal family will survive." He pushed down his annoyance at her family for making her feel useless. They could deal with that once she was out of danger.

Nerya took a deep breath in and blew it out. "I don't like it, but you're right." Her hands trembled as she pushed open the door. "Lead on," she said.

Alonso told her to wait there while he fetched horses. The shorter nun followed him, while the taller one waited with the princess. The sister-warriors had already shown their value and he was glad Camila had sent them. Nerya was a brilliant fighter, but they didn't know what they might face ahead.

They saddled two horses in the stables and found some day-packs with provisions stashed under a pile of hay.

The nun spoke up. "The Lady Prioress left the packs in case we were deceived by Lutin. She left orders that we are to take the princess to your califate. Stay off the main roads and protect her at all costs."

"Camila is always prepared." Alonso put his shoulders back and took the reins of his horse.

They led the mounts back to Nerya and the other sister by the side gate. Nerya stepped forward and her beauty knocked the breath from his lungs. She was luminous in the moonlight. It was a wonder she didn't know how precious she was.

When Alonso approached her, the princess stopped moving. She stood stock still only a few steps from the gate.

She doesn't want me. His stomach lurched.

Her eyes betrayed her. Too much had already passed between them. Their broken betrothal, their night together after she had returned to the castle. Their silence since then.

He approached her slowly, like he would a skittish foal, though she would hate that comparison. "*Princesa,*" Alonso said. "This is our mare." He checked the straps and then mounted the horse. "Climb up in front of me."

Please, he thought.

He reached for her hand. When she touched him, a spark jumped between them. She pulled back.

Shouts echoed from inside the palace walls. Nerya looked back, eyes wide. "I can't make my feet move," she said.

Alonso took a deep breath. "We don't have much time."

He bent down and grabbed her around the waist. She was solid and muscular, but he was strong. Even though she might struggle, he would win. And win he must, for her life was in danger.

She squeaked as he lifted her up and set her sidesaddle in front of him. When he held her close against his muscular body, she shivered and pressed herself against him. He put his arms around her and grabbed the reins.

Her reluctance to mount the horse gave him pause. He had hoped they might rekindle their friendship, at least, even if their night together didn't lead to a romantic connection. Perhaps he had to give up his expectations and accept it wasn't meant to be. Lock away his feelings and focus on the present.

"We must go right away," Alonso said, his voice breaking. He settled her hips in front of him, brushing his hands gently along the small of her back before turning the horse around. Their mount whinnied, and they rode away.

He had dreamed of getting her in his arms again, but not like this.

Not on the run, fearing for her life.

Chapter Three

Nerya was being held in strong arms. A gentle rocking movement soothed her senses. She revelled in the warmth until she came fully awake and the events of the last day crashed down upon her.

Alonso and two of Camila's warrior sisters had helped her escape the palace last night. The women had ridden ahead and would meet up with her and Alonso at his Califate, the largest duchy in her kingdom. His falcon shifter clan was a formidable ally, but the relationships between the Fae and the shifters had been tenuous for many years. Her betrothal to Alonso had been meant to ease the tensions, but when her parents broke the engagement they maintained an uneasy truce with the shifters through gifts of land and positions on the High Council.

She wished she could have stayed with Alonso and his family. They were warm and loving. She felt like she belonged when she was with them. Her husband's family had been cold and distant, in contrast. They had bullied her parents into accepting their marriage offer and then treated her like a piece of property.

Alonso held her body close against his, one arm around her waist. His well-built form sent tingles through her core. She couldn't stop conjuring up images of him naked in his bed, her underneath him, above him, in front of him. All the delicious ways she'd had him that night.

Stop thinking about the past!

Sitting upright, she tried to shake off his hands and place some distance between his thighs and her ass. She tensed up, her thoughts racing.

"You're awake," Alonso said, wrapping his arm around her waist again.

"You're observant," she snapped, standing straighter. She regretted her words as soon as they were out.

Why was she angry? If she was honest with herself, he wasn't to blame for what had happened. She had tried so hard to close herself off and not feel anything. And now his presence reminded her of the disappointments and resentments swirling inside her.

"How much farther to your home?" She shifted in the saddle as another stab of desire shot through her.

"We'll be there by midday. Only a few hours now."

"Thank you for your assistance." The words were too formal, but she couldn't take them back. "I'll be fine once we get there."

His arm tensed around her waist. "There's nothing wrong with needing your friends."

"Princesses don't have that luxury." She wished things were different, but they couldn't be.

"Why do you close yourself off?" He kicked the horse to increase their pace.

"Not everybody had your loving family," she said. If she'd grown up with the support of her mother and sister, perhaps she would be more flexible. But what was done was done. Her strength had helped her survive difficult situations before.

"I know you're independent," he said. "But being self-reliant and isolating yourself are not the same."

She tensed. It was like he was reading her mind. "Princesses are isolated. They are set above their court. We can't allow anyone to get close."

"That's a lonely life."

She had been alone for a long time. She was used to it. Nothing needed to change.

"You haven't been lonely, have you?" She snorted.

"What are you talking about?"

"Nothing," she said. "It doesn't matter." Her heart fell. She'd heard the stories of his bedding all the ladies in court, one after another. It shouldn't have bothered her. He had his own life to live. But it did. That lover wasn't the Alonso she remembered. What had happened?

She sighed and changed the subject, willing herself to let go of her sorrow and regret.

"Do you remember how we used to go riding with your brother?" she asked in a soft voice.

"That feels like another lifetime. Do you still love horses?" His body relaxed slightly.

"I still love them, but not like that." Her lips turned up at the corners as she thought about her obsession with the filly they had let her ride when she stayed with his family.

"You used to roll your eyes at me when I taught you how to communicate with horses." His breath puffed the top of her head and she breathed in his scent, citrus and cloves.

"I remember your lectures about showing patience and gaining your mount's trust. You loved to talk about the 'nobility of the four-footed beasts.'"

"Was it that bad?" he chuckled.

"No, I was just a spoiled girl." She relaxed her posture, settling her back against his front. "But when I got married, my mare became my best friend. She was my only confidant in my new home."

They rode in silence. She had thought of Alonso often when she was married. She had dreamed of him sometimes, too. In one particularly vivid dream, they had gone riding in the woods, then made love under the trees for an entire afternoon. That dream had spawned several fantasies over the years.

She had locked away her passionate side when she didn't produce an heir and her marriage went sour. It was a loveless existence, turning into a pale grey wife, and then a widow whose heart had gone cold. She'd let out her fire for one night with Alonso, but she feared that if she did that again she might not be able to control it.

"Were you happy in your marriage?" he asked, interrupting her thoughts.

"It was a political alliance, nothing more."

After another silence, Alonso spoke up. "Did I ruin things when you came to my bed? I'd hoped it would bring us closer..." he trailed off.

She settled her head against his chest, suddenly unafraid of the question. "I needed comfort from someone I trusted. I had lost myself." It was a mistake, going to his chambers, but if she was honest with herself, she didn't regret it.

Her mother, though, had made it clear her daughter could not "consort wilfully with members of the court." The Queen had told her if she visited the Duke's private chambers again, she would have him sent to the farthest reaches of the kingdom.

"Since you returned, I haven't seen the Nerya I knew when we were younger. Marriage changed you."

She cleared her throat. So much had changed. "Yes, it didn't agree with me."

"Did I do something wrong that night? I want to know." His hand tightened its hold on her.

She sighed. "You did everything right. That was the problem. I—"

A falcon's cry pierced through the sky. Nerya shaded her eyes from the morning sun. It was Alonso's brother, Enrique, in his shifter form.

"What is it?" she asked, her heart pounding.

"Nothing good." Alonso stopped the horse and dismounted.

Nerya hopped down into his waiting arms. Another spark pulsed between them and she jumped back.

Another raptor's cry, this time right above them. Enrique took a pass over them. He was in his large form, the size of Alonso's horse, dark brown feathers on his head and wings, lighter brown on his breast. This shape was faster and stronger than the smaller form his clan members could take—useful for delivering messages or making trips quickly. That he had shifted into the large falcon form to seek them probably meant trouble.

The large raptor flew down and came to a stop beside them. Enrique shifted quickly into human form, putting on the clothes secured in a bag around his neck. His grim face made Nerya's stomach clench.

"There are three warships bearing down on the bay," he announced. "They will be here within the hour."

"We need to get the princess to safety," Alonso said.

"We've also spotted riders pursuing you on the ground." Enrique added.

"I'm ready to fight," Nerya said. Her heart raced. It was time to get revenge on her enemies.

"Absolutely not!" Alonso turned toward her.

"Don't coddle me, Alonso. I need to be ready to defend my kingdom with my life."

He shook his head. "You don't need to put yourself in danger needlessly. It's just like that time you got lost looking for the missing lamb."

"I found her, didn't I?" She pursed her lips.

"And my whole family spend the night searching for you. I had to fly you back home—"

"It's not my fault my wings never grew in!" Nerya's face grew hot.

"I didn't say that. I want you to think before you act."

Enrique interrupted. "There's no time."

"Your brother is right. We need to find them right away," Nerya said.

"I beg your pardon, Your Grace, but you will have to finish this argument after you are safe at the castle."

She blew out a breath. "You always sided with your brother."

Enrique gave a low bow. "Your Grace, I appreciate your desire to fight. My mother, the Duchess Dowager, has asked that you be escorted to her. After you are secured in the castle, you are invited to convene an Adhoc War Council and plan your battle strategy."

Nerya nodded reluctantly. "I accept your mother's invitation."

"May I offer to fly you to her?" Enrique held out a hand.

Alonso pushed his way between them and took Nerya's hand. "You won't take her. I will."

"For the Goddess's sake, Alonso, stop posturing." She rolled her eyes. "I'll go with you."

Alonso's smile spread warmth down to her toes. She shook it off as Enrique took their day packs and set their horse free. Her breath caught when Alonso shifted to his large falcon form. His regal posture was enhanced by the sunlight catching on his feathers. His piercing call summoned her closer. She drew toward him and her heart skipped a beat. She would fly with him. She had dreamed of this a hundred times.

He spread his dark brown wings and scratched his grey claws on the ground. Alonso gave a soft chitter and put his beak close to Nerya.

Sweetling.

Love.

Mate.

The words floated into her mind as though Alonso spoke them aloud. A mental picture formed of her on his back soaring high above the clouds, his wings fluttering in the wind. It was night and they were one, their magics combined into a joyful power that healed the land and their peoples. Tears coursed down her cheeks as relief washed through her.

The vision ended, and she blinked.

He chittered again, rubbing his beak in a soft caress along her side. As she climbed on his back, his soft tawny feathers tickled her face. When he spread his wings, she held tight to the sinewy muscles of his neck. They took off and gained altitude as they caught the eddies.

She remembered the first time she had flown on his back—the exhilaration of flight, the sense that she was a part of him, that together they could change the world. Would it be the same this time, or had she fabricated the connection they had shared in her memory?

Her whole body tingled as they made their ascent. She caught the rhythm as he banked and glided higher. She anticipated his moves, leaning forward and to the sides as he flew up.

The limestone ramparts of Mursiya Castle came into sight below them. One of the largest castles in the kingdom, the imposing structure had been built atop cliffs on the seashore, one side accessible only by ships or birds. They approached from the other side, which connected the castle by roads to the rest of the Califate. The sea was choppy and dark, but the warships advanced steadily toward their location.

His brother let out a wail and circled around them. Dark creatures flew toward them from the bay.

Over-sized ravens?

No, sea eagles, their white underbellies a clue. They were bred by goblins for strength, size, and ferocity. She trembled. Goblins would be riding these birds of prey. Would their foes meet them before they reached the castle? The eagles' wing-spans were gigantic—even bigger than the Duke's and his brother's in their large forms—and they were gaining quickly. Yet Alonso and Enrique had the speed advantage when they dove.

Nerya held on tight as Alonso urged his powerful muscles forward. She looked at the sea eagles as they closed the distance. When he chittered at her again and pumped his wings, she flattened herself against him. A flash of satisfaction surged through her as they rose higher, then turned and stooped, drawing in his wings and pointing his beak to the ramparts below. She held on tight in anticipation of the rapid descent.

The golden cloak of the Mursiya Mage, Dama Porphyria, was visible on the curtain walls that formed the first line of defense of the castle. The Mursiya Mage was powerful, having served many years as Chief Mage for the kingdom before retiring to her shifter village last year. Porphyria was a welcome sight to Nerya.

Alonso aimed for a landing near the imposing figure, the eagles' cries behind them. Nerya breathed a sigh of relief. She prayed they would make a landing before the goblins could attack them.

As they neared, the Mage threw up her arm. Golden lightning flickered in the sky as Alonso and Nerya came within a stone's throw of the rampart. Porphyria pointed her staff behind them and a screech sounded above Nerya's left shoulder. She chanced a quick look. The eagle was wounded, but still flying. It was too far away for her to reach it with her dagger. She hunkered down against Alonso's neck as he landed on the castle walls behind the ramparts. Beside them, the Mage continued to target the eagles as lightning charges rocketed through the sky.

Enrique landed beside them, the flight feathers on his left wing broken. Nerya jumped off Alonso's back as another eagle swooped down. She set her jaw and grabbed a nearby sword, swinging it in a large arc. The eagle banked and avoided the blade. Nerya reached for her dagger and threw it high. It lodged in the eagle's breast, but the bird shook it off and it clattered somewhere below.

Alonso took flight and aimed for the eagle, bringing his claws up to slash at his opponent's wound. The Mage sent a flash of light that knocked the eagle's rider off. The goblin screamed as it plummeted to the ground outside the castle. Screeching, the eagle retreated to the harbour, along with several of its companions.

Alonso returned to the walls as Nerya dispatched another rider who had landed beside her. Nerya looked at the surrounding melee, then noticed the warrior sisters who had helped her escape the palace. The shorter one pulled out bandages and herbs from a leather pouch. She went from one warrior to the next, assessing their wounds and sending the serious cases with medics down into the castle.

Nerya drew a breath, and Alonso shifted. A servant appeared and gave him clothes. Alonso quickly dressed and rushed over. "Are you hurt?"

She shook her head. "I'm fine."

He whooshed out a big breath and looked around. The commotion on the ramparts eased up. The Mage held two of the eagles inside golden energy cages. They were shrieking while the others fled. Mursiyan guards lined up along the ramparts or tended to the wounded.

The fighting had ended. They had held off their attackers.

Nerya looked at Alonso. When he smiled, her heart leapt.

"I should have been terrified when you dove for the palace, but it was exhilarating!" she said.

"That's my Nerya. My brave *princesa*." Her body flushed with warmth when he wrapped his arms around her.

Nerya's hand went to reach for her dagger, but it wasn't in its scabard. "My blade!" Her stomach clenched.

"I'll get some to look for it," Alonso said.

She nodded, eyes bright. "My mother gave it to me for my last birthday."

"We'll find it." His hand lingered on her arm, spreading another flush through her form.

A tall, striking woman with long, silver hair approached them. Her features resembled Alonso's, and she wore the traditional brown cloak of the falcon shifter clan. Her circlet of brown gems was twined with falcon feathers. It was Alonso's mother, Zaida, Dowager Duchess of Mursiya.

Alonso embraced her and she held him tight. Then she pulled away and swept into a graceful curtsy in front of Nerya.

"Your Grace," she said. "Welcome to Mursiya Castle. We are yours to command."

Chapter Four

Nerya curtsied to Zaida, the woman she had considered her second mother, and then was enveloped in the Dowager's embrace.

"We missed you," the older woman whispered in her ear.

"I'm sorry I wasn't allowed a proper goodbye," Nerya wiped away the tears from her cheeks.

"My little *eyas*, I have held you in my heart these many years. There was no need for a goodbye. I knew we would see each other again."

Nerya's vision blurred as Zaida steered her toward the door and the staircase into the castle courtyard. Alonso and Enrique followed close behind.

She gazed around at the marble floors under the honeycomb colonnades, the lush gardens, and the gleaming armoury entrance. A pang of sorrow shot through her.

"It looks the same. Just as warm as I remember it," she said, with a half smile.

Alonso looked around. "I suppose you're right. I haven't been back in a while." His face betrayed a mixture of nostalgia and regret.

Duchess Zaida led Nerya and Alonso toward the main building.

"I was sorry to hear you lost your husband," Zaida said.

"Thank you. It was difficult being away from my people. Nobody in my husband's kingdom used the skies. They all travelled on the land."

"That must have seemed strange."

"Did your wings ever fill in?" Alonso asked after a pause.

"No," said Nerya, her shoulders slumped. "The High Mage gave us a story about how I needed to discover my *joyel* first and then love would spread my wings. It was nonsense."

"It is true that joy leads to the exhilaration of flight," Zaida said.

"But I don't see how feelings could make your wings develop." Alonso cocked his head.

"In our clan, children must wait until puberty to grow into their bird forms. There are stories about late developers with rare gifts, and sometimes mating can help a shifter achieve full transformation if they had difficulties previously," Zaida said.

"You are perfect with or without wings," Alonso said, pink colouring his face.

Before Nerya could answer, they reached the Great Hall, portraits of dour Dukes and Duchesses staring down at them from the brightly coloured tiled walls. Alonso had told her he hated this room, but she always thought it was cozy, not imposing. Perhaps it was the people who made her feel that way.

The cavernous fireplace at the end of the room roared with flames to ease the chill in the seaside air. Zaida led them past the large benches and tables toward a group of chairs set near the dais. She gestured Nerya to a high-backed chair, and the others arranged themselves around her. Nerya's heart had almost resumed its regular tempo after the mad race to the castle.

The servants brought refreshments—ale, marchepain, and cold pheasant. She took a sip from her goblet. Several nobles were led into the room.

She looked around the room. Alonso and Enrique sat to her right. She trusted them with her life. Camila's warrior nuns, Sisters Alma and Elena, stood behind Zaida's sons. The women made an odd pair. Sister Alma was tall, lean, and serious, while Sister Elena was short, round, and had a kindly face.

The Mage, Dama Porphyria, sat on Nerya's left beside the Dowager Duchess. Two of her mother's most trusted advisors, the Countess Sofia and Lady Catalina, came next. They lived in the neighbouring calife and it was likely Zaida had summoned them. Sofia's long grey hair was fashioned in a simple plait down her back, but, despite her age, Nerya knew the tall warrior was a force to be reckoned with. Catalina was younger, Lynnara's age. She had distinguished herself in several battles against Nainian troops and would be an asset.

Nerya took in a deep breath. They were at war. Her mother was dead. She didn't have time to grieve properly, but she would do so when the crisis was over. She blinked her eyes. *Focus, keep it together.*

The group settled in their chairs and looked expectantly at her.

"Update. Who shall start?" she asked.

Countess Sofia cleared her throat. "A fourth warship has anchored in the harbour. A small barque from the flagship is nearing our drawbridge."

"We are preparing both for an attack and a siege," said Nerya. "Lady Zaida, is your castle ready?"

"Yes," said Zaida. "We've increased fortifications and laid in additional supplies in the stores."

Nerya's stomach settled a little. "Can we expect reinforcements from the Queen's Palace?"

"They won't arrive for another day or so," Elena said.

"Any word from my sister?"

The taller warrior sister, Alma, spoke up. "Lady Prioress Camila has sent word. She is still trying to find your sister."

Nerya wiped tears from her eyes. *No time, blast it.* "What about the Prince?"

"When the barque arrives, we expect Prince Lutin will be on board," said Sophia.

"Are any of Nerya's ladies-in-waiting coming?" Alonso asked.

Her heart skipped a beat at his concern.

"Lady Marjita is on her way with Her Grace's lady's maid," Alma replied.

"Countess Sofia and Lady Catalina have stepped in as advisors," Zaida said. "I have hand-picked the staff who will wait on Her Grace."

Alonso nodded and crossed his arms, apparently satisfied with the arrangements, and her heart skipped another beat.

Nerya nodded. "How about siege preparations?"

"Sister Alma is taking the lead, assisted by Lord Enrique," said Elena.

Nerya started when she heard voices in the hall. A messenger entered and approached the group of advisors. He held out a scroll affixed by the dark green seal of Prince Lutin. Nerya held out her hand, but Alonso stood and intercepted the messenger to take the scroll. He inspected it and handed it to Nerya, bowing low.

She broke the seal and read it out loud. "Prince Lutin of Nain, Heir to the Supreme Ruler of the Western Shores, requests the immediate surrender of Princess Nerya, Heir to the Throne of Ishbilliya, and her kingdom. He awaits Her Grace at the harbour landing, where she will join him on his ship and travel with him to the Queen's Palace. If she refuses, then she must prepare for war."

There were gasps around the table.

He's come to take me by force if I reject his ultimatum. She steeled herself for the coming confrontation.

"Send a message that I will meet with him now," she said. Over the murmurs of her council, she added in a loud voice, "We will discuss his terms and then I will make my decision." She didn't know if she could be the leader her mother was, but she had to try.

The messenger retreated quickly to find a scribe and deliver the message. The door secured behind the herald.

Nerya closed her eyes and took a deep breath. Alonso's arm touched her shoulder gently. "I know what you are going to say," she said.

"That this is foolhardy?" he sputtered, as he took his seat. He put his head in his hands and slumped forward.

"Well, maybe not the exact words, but the sentiment, yes." Nerya's heart was pounding.

"I will go with you. You can't stop me." He looked up and his eyes sparked. A ripple of desire coursed through her.

"I know. But I can defend myself." *I'll feel better with him there, if I'm honest with myself.*

"Yes, of course," he grumbled. "But there are too many unknowns out there. I would be happier if the Prince had to meet in the castle."

"You know he wouldn't have agreed to that," Sister Alma intervened. "Besides, we have to keep him off-guard, make him think he has the upper hand."

"He does," said Alonso, bringing the heels of his hands to his eyes. "We need to come up with another plan. Something that keeps Nerya away from this man."

Nerya put back her shoulders and tilted her head up. "Duke Alonso, I need your support, or you can leave the Council Room."

He looked at her, deep furrows creasing his brows. Shaking his head and pursing his lips, he ground out, "You know I'll stay."

Her stomach settled and she rested her hands in her lap. Turning to the rest of the group, she asked, "Who else will join me?"

The rest of the Nerya's adhoc council argued, finally deciding that Countess Sofia would also accompany her. Sisters Alma and Elena would go as well, disguised as Nerya's personal attendants.

Lady Zaida sent the others away and brought Nerya to a nearby antechamber, where a host of servants dressed the princess in a striking gold, silk brocade dress. They fixed her black hair long and loose, pinning a fine golden netting over it.

Zaida took her own sword and scabbard and wrapped them around Nerya's waist. She held her at arm's length and pronounced, "Now you are the warrior princess we knew you would someday be!"

Nerya's cheeks grew hot, but she smiled at the woman. If only things had been different. She took a moment to indulge her thoughts, then took a deep breath.

"We are ready. Duchess Zaida, what is the best means of transport to the harbour?"

Alonso and Enrique had explained to her long ago that their castle defenses relied on difficult terrain of the sea cliffs. Falcon shifters could fly up and down the steep inclines, but humans and other land-based creatures would not gain access so easily.

"By wing or basket. We have arranged for you to be flown down in a litter." The Duchess signalled and four handsome, brown-skinned shifters approached and bowed to Nerya. Holding fastenings and ties in similar fabrics to her outfit, they escorted her to a nearby balcony. A golden litter waited, the rectangular platform festooned with brocade cushions and fine netting curtains hanging from the posters. Nerya sat on the platform, joined by Sisters Alma and Elena, in their handmaids' robes.

As the shifters got into position and transformed into their falcon forms, Alma passed Nerya an object in a piece of cloth. Nerya unfolded it to find her dagger.

"I thought it was lost!" she said.

Alma smiled at her. "The Duke found it for you and asked that I return it."

She reached through the slit in her robes to find her thigh holster, sheathed her dagger, and rearranged her clothing. A warmth settled in her chest.

The flight down to the landing ended too quickly. Nerya wished she had the ability to enjoy the experience, but there was too much on her mind. Soon she was schooling her features and donning her best warrior princess posture.

Countess Sofia approached, jaw set and shoulders back. She curtsied and spoke quietly. "The Prince will try something. Provoke you, back you into a corner, set some impossible conditions. Try not to overreact, Your Grace."

"I'm always calm," Nerya said.

Raising her eyebrows, Sofia exchanged a glance with Alonso, who had taken his place beside Nerya.

"I will try to help her," he said, sighing. "Wait and watch, *mi reina*."

Nerya was aware of the small space between her arm and Alonso's body. She could reach out and touch him if she wanted to, but to show that kind of weakness in front of the prince would be a disadvantage.

Prince Lutin waited on the dock by his barque, in a small tent. He was flanked by two advisors in formal garb. Four guards scowled and postured outside the tent, hands on their weapons. They looked like they were ready to knock the whole tent to the ground.

The Prince had a very different energy, holding himself aloof, lips curled in disdain.

Countess Sofia came forward and formally greeted the Prince. He ignored her, homing in on Nerya, and made a grand bow. "Your Grace. You are still as beautiful as a doe in the spring meadow." The Prince's hawk-like eyes scanned her form.

Alonso tensed up beside her and she tried to will him to remain calm.

"Your Highness," Nerya said. "Are we here to discuss my appearance or the acts of war you have committed?"

Prince Lutin's eyes narrowed. "I have the castle surrounded. You are at my mercy."

"We are well prepared for a long siege," Nerya replied. She was not surprised at how quickly he showed his true colours.

"Trust I will have my warriors ravage the country while you hide behind the castle walls." Lutin sneered.

This was her greatest fear. She couldn't let it happen, but she couldn't bow down to him either. "We will not be strong-armed, Prince Lutin." Nerya's lips pressed her lips into a thin line.

He paused for a moment. "We don't need to fight," he said, his mouth turning up in a smile that didn't meet his eyes. "This misunderstanding can be solved easily. I will stop everything when we are wed."

She drew herself up and fixed him with a glare. "Misunderstanding? What misunderstanding? You attacked my country, killed my mother, kidnapped my sister. You may think the blood will only flow from my side if you engage us, but I guarantee you, the land will be stained red with the blood of your people as well."

"You seem to labour under the delusion that you have some power here," he said.

Nerya fingered the hilt of her dagger under her robes. Alonso put his hand on the small of Nerya's back to steady her. She took a breath. "Before we continue our discussion, you need to answer a question. Where is my sister? Why did you break your engagement with her?"

"She was deemed...unsuitable and dispatched. I regret this action had to occur."

Nerya's blood boiled. Her sister had deserved better. "I *regret* it as well. You will pay for your actions."

"My dear, you will not continue with this petty insolence," Lutin said, his voice turning cold. "You will accompany me to my ship, where we will be wed. Then we will sail to the Queen's Palace, where we will be welcomed as the new King and Queen of Ishbilliya."

Frustration built in Nerya's chest. She started to speak and the Prince stopped her.

"If you do not follow my orders, I will slaughter everyone in the castle," he said. "Then I will sail to the Queen's Palace and cut down anyone who opposes my coronation as King. You don't want to be responsible for all those deaths. You are kind and compassionate." His mouth turned into a sneer as he said the final words.

Every muscle in Nerya's body went rigid. She was trapped, again. Everyone made decisions for her and left her suffering for them. But she couldn't refuse.

She sighed. "I will accept your... proposal, Your Highness. I beg your indulgence to prepare a suitable wedding ceremony and feast to celebrate the occasion of the joining of our two kingdoms. May we propose the hand fasting take place in the morning?" She fluttered her eyelashes. "Then we can take our leisure on your ship as we sail to the Queen's Palace at midday."

The corners of Lutin's mouth twitched. "My sweetling, I know women make a big fuss over such festivities."

She shuddered inwardly at his words, but kept her expression blank.

He paused and looked her over again. "Yes, this is acceptable. We will retire to our ship while you make the arrangements."

He swept out of the tent, his advisors and guards trailing behind him.

Nerya swayed, her knees buckling. Alonso reached for her arm and steadied her, while Alma and Elena helped them to the litter. Her vision grew blurry as the shifters began the ascent to the castle courtyard.

Chapter Five

Alonso sat beside Nerya on the litter. He clenched his fists. Everything was slipping away. "There's got to be something we can do."

"We're surrounded by his knights." Nerya's shoulders sagged. "He's given me an ultimatum: sacrifice myself and save the kingdom, or he will destroy our people."

Alonso wanted to take her pain away. Make the Prince pay.

Sister Alma spoke gently. "The parley is not the end of the battle. The Prince wants you to capitulate before the fighting can begin."

"I can't let him become King. He will change our way of life and oppress our people." Nerya put her head in her hands.

"We have to stop him," Alonso said, putting an arm around her. *I'll kill the man myself if I have to.*

"Your Grace, do you wish to convene the council later today?" Alma asked.

"Yes," Nerya replied. Her eyes looked hollow and she was pale.

"She needs some rest first," Alonso said.

Alma nodded. The litter swayed and bumped. They had landed on the balcony. Alonso held Nerya's arm and they stepped onto the marble floor. He fought the urge to yell, taking in a steadying breath instead. His mother appeared and spoke with Alma and Elena while Nerya took off her head covering and pulled off her shoes.

"Alonso," his mother said. "Please show Her Grace to her quarters. We have set her in the North Wing's ambassador's quarters. You are staying in the suite of rooms opposite the princess."

Alonso's chest swelled. Did his mother place him near the princess because she knew of his feelings for Nerya? Or was she relying on his warrior training and understanding of the court to help ensure the princess's safety? Zaida usually knew what was in her children's hearts. It wouldn't surprise him if she was doing both. He bowed to his mother and held out his hand to Nerya.

He kept quiet as they walked short distance to the North Wing. She kept her eyes on the ground and the touch of her hand light in his. He thought his heart might burst, but he wanted to wait until they were alone to talk. It had taken them so long to find each other again, so many false starts. Could they make up for lost time? Would it matter when the morning came?

They reached the doors to the Ambassador's Chambers. They were the most luxurious rooms in the castle, prepared for visiting dignitaries and decorated with bright colours and soft fabrics. Servants had freshened up the rooms and left fruits and nuts on the large trestle table in the antechamber.

Nerya surveyed the rooms, opening windows and patting furniture, while Alonso confirmed the guards' schedules and looked for holes in the security configurations. When both of them were satisfied with the arrangements, Nerya dismissed the ladies' maids, shut the door, and rested her head against the frame.

Without thinking, he took a step forward. Emotions bubbled up inside him. He reached out a hand and stopped just short of touching her shoulder.

"Nerya—"

"I know." She sighed, her shoulders sagging.

"That summer, I never told you how I felt." He wished he had connected with her properly when she returned last year.

"We were so young then." She kept her back to him.

He lifted his hand again and placed his fingers lightly on her back. "I wish things had been different."

"Maybe it was meant to be—I knew nothing about the world. We're older and more experienced now."

He smoothed down her hair. Her locks were still mesmerizing—shiny, soft, reaching down to the small of her back. He ached to hold her in his arms, but his breath caught in his throat. Would she reject him? Did she feel the same way?

"I'm here for you," he said. There was so much more he wanted to say.

"You've always been there." She stretched her arm backward to catch his hand. "I'm sorry I've been distant. I couldn't—" She broke off.

His heart thudded in his chest. He squeezed her fingers and closed the distance between them.

His firm chest pressed against her soft back. He skimmed his hands along her torso as he nuzzled his face in her hair. Persimmons and figs, her signature scent, filled his nostrils. She relaxed, melting into his front, leaning her head back on his shoulder. He held her tight and pivoted them so his back was against the door, while she faced the room.

"There's this thing inside me that wants to claim you." He nuzzled her neck and she reached back to run her hand through his hair. "Mark you all over with love bites. Rub my scent all over you. Fight anyone who looks at you." He murmured in her ear as she sighed. "I don't know how to stop it." He nipped her ear and she rubbed against him.

His hands roamed back up to the swell of her breast, traced down to circle her belly button, then out to her hips before moving down to the V between her legs. The heat from her pussy warmed his fingers through the layers of fabric. She moaned and gyrated against him.

His hands came alive and pulled up her skirts, seeking to touch her flesh, brand her, possess her. She reached inside his breeches. When her fingers found his swollen cock, he gasped and thrust in her hand. He sought her bare thighs with his hands and found her already slick.

He paused for a moment. "I take my herbs to prevent conception and the pox. Do you?"

She nodded. "I still use the Mage's spells, even though I can't have children."

"I'm sorry," he said.

"It's okay," she replied. "I didn't want them before."

He touched his nose to her cheek. Then he adjusted his stance, moving into a semi-squatting position with her sitting on top, facing away from him. Her delectable, fig-coloured skin of her thighs and backside was exposed to his gaze, looking good enough to eat.

He reached his hand forward and slid his fingers to her pussy, probing gently at her entrance. His thumb moved up her slit to find her button. She moaned and wiggled her generous ass against his hard cock when he rubbed her juices on the cluster of sensitive nerves. He wanted everything. Here. Now.

They fumbled with skirts and breeches until his swollen thickness lay naked against her buttocks. She rubbed against him, humming with satisfaction. He moved his cock down along her lips. The tip of his head reached her hood and she shuddered.

"Take me," she moaned.

He was lost in her.

He shifted as she arched so they could find the right position. Inching his cock into her wet pussy, he nipped her ear and whispered, "You are mine, right here and right now."

She gripped him with her muscles. He thrust himself further in, sliding slowly.

"Yes," she gasped.

"Nothing else, nobody else matters." He was in to the hilt now and stilled for a moment, relishing their intimate contact.

"Mmm," she whimpered.

She fit him like a glove. It was perfect.

Then he began with a slow thrust, grunting. "It is only you and me. Just you—and—me...."

She cried out and braced herself with her powerful legs, bouncing up and down on his lap. He picked up the pace, taking them up higher. Sliding and thrusting, his cock throbbed inside her tight, hot channel.

He growled. "I want to feel you squeeze me, pulsing around my hard cock."

She lifted herself up so only the tip was still inside her. "Give me all of it," she moaned.

He thrust in as she bore down. He held her mound in his hand, keeping her as close as he could to him. "Are you ready? I'll fill you up so our juices mingle and overflow your sweet pussy."

Her scent filled his nostrils. His cock plunged deep inside her pussy. Another thrust in and out.

"I'm almost there." She thrust her hips in a frenzied rhythm, driving him to the edge.

"Come with me, mi arma," he said, pinching her clit and holding her waist. Gasping as her walls constricted, he was coming with her, her sweet pussy milking his hard cock. He couldn't stop bathing her womb with his hot seed. It felt so right. He didn't want it to end. He held her close, showering her with kisses.

She panted and rested her back against his chest. He held her on his lap and sank to the floor, allowing his muscles to turn to jelly. She turned and sat sideways on his lap so she could wrap her arms around him. Emotions overwhelmed him. He took her face in his hands and kissed her.

As their lips met, a wave of magical energy coursed through his body. It reminded him of shifting into his falcon form, but it swirled around him and Nerya—just for a moment—before it dissolved into sparks of light like fireflies.

"Did you see that?" Alonso asked.

Nerya's eyes were half-closed already as she murmured, "No."

Alonso put one arm around her shoulders and the other under her knees. He held her close as he knelt and then stood. "You should rest now, Your Grace."

Her eyes fluttered and she kissed him, brushing her lips to his. "Stay with me."

"I'll be here for you." He laid her gently on her bed, pulling up the linens around her beautiful form.

She clung to him and he settled beside her, resting her head on his shoulder. He could take a few more minutes alone with her. To dream of being together before the real world crashed in on them.

Chapter Six

Alonso found his brother Enrique on the ramparts, surveying the Prince's encampment outside the castle walls.

"We're outnumbered three to one," Enrique reported.

"I'm glad the Queen sent two infantry units to our duchy before the peace talks," Alonso said. "I hoped we wouldn't need them."

"Will there be reinforcements from the Queen's Palace?"

"They have to. Nerya can't be forced to surrender." Alonso raked a hand through his hair.

Enrique searched Alonso's face. "You've fallen for her, haven't you?"

"I've always loved her." His heart raced. "I locked away that piece of my heart when her family took her away all those years ago." He felt free saying it out loud.

"And now?"

"I can't lose her again," He clenched his fists. "This is worse than the first time. I didn't know anything back then, but now I know she's my true love. I can't live without her."

"How do we help you?" Enrique pursed his lips and grasped Alonso's shoulder.

"I will do anything," he said, trying to control his breathing. "Kill the Prince and the guards by myself, if necessary."

"That can be the last resort. And I'll be by your side the whole time."

Sisters Alma and Elena appeared and called them to the Council. They walked in grim silence to the room that had been set up for their meetings. Cold marble contrasted with warm yellow curtains and red upholstery on the benches. The large trestle table was topped with an inlay pattern made of ivory, mother-of-pearl, and bone. The intricate surface reminded Alonso of the puzzles he and Nerya had loved to solve when they were younger. She had told him there was always an answer, sometimes it was just obscured until the right time. He hoped that was true in this instance as well.

The faces at the Council table looked grim. But there was an energy, a desire to fight, that he hadn't seen before. Nerya inspired loyalty and strength from her people. His heart leapt to realize they were facing this challenge all together.

Nerya swept in the room and sat at the head of the table. "What is the update on the Prince's troops outside the palace?" she asked.

"They are getting restless and noisy," Enrique said. "Our warriors are setting up lanterns and torches along the ramparts and preparing for a long night watch."

"Do you think the reinforcements could be here by midnight?"

"Not likely," Elena said. "When they do arrive, rest assured the Order will fight to its last breath."

"Will we have enough warriors to defeat the Prince by morning?" Alonso asked.

"We may need to stall for a few hours," Elena said.

Alonso grew quiet. What if they couldn't stop Lutin?

Nerya spoke up. "We have to go along with his plans until then."

"You mean you'll have to marry that *gilipollas*?" Frustration mounted in Alonso's chest.

Nerya turned in her chair and stared him down. "I can go through with the handfasting ceremony."

He loved her for her courage. But he hated that she was putting herself in danger.

"The wedding feast will be our opportunity then," said Sofia.

"It's not safe. I—we can't protect her suitably," Alonso said. His shoulders tensed.

Duchess Zaida caught his gaze, kindness in her eyes. "We will arrange Her Grace's bridal party to be our best hand-to-hand fighters."

"Alma and I can serve as attendants," Elena added. "All of us will be armed."

"No, I forbid it!" Alonso exploded. As soon as the words were out, he regretted them. Yet his protective urges couldn't be controlled.

Nerya's voice was sharp. "Duke Alonso, I value your opinion, but don't push your luck. You can't let your personal feelings—"

"Personal feelings? This is ridiculous." He looked around the table. "Do you agree with the princess?"

"We may be able to prevent all-out war by pretending to go along with the wedding," said Sofia. "If we can arm most of the wedding guests and servers with concealed weapons, we may get the upper hand." She looked at Alonso. "Duke, you and Enrique can wait in the kitchens and hallways with additional warriors. If we can subdue the Prince and his retinue without them alerting the troops outside, then we could stall until the reinforcements arrive."

"I won't be a part of this madness. Nerya, you can't do it." His heart thudded. He couldn't believe what he was hearing.

"Alonso, are you trying to contradict your ruler?"

The tone in Nerya's voice made him pause. Her lips were pressed together and there was fire in her eyes. Despite his fears, he wouldn't want her to be any other way. "I will follow you to the ends of the earth, Your Grace. If you choose to go through with this plan, I will support you unconditionally. But don't make me do it." He put his head in his hands.

He was startled by a movement at his seat. The scent of persimmons and figs wafted around him. Lips that had travelled over his body now whispered in his ear, "Please do this for me."

"You can't go to his bed. It will kill me," he said, turning his head and locking her eyes in his gaze.

She reached a hand and caressed his cheek. "I will slit his throat first."

His heart skipped a beat. She loved him, he knew it. She was his passionate, fierce, and loyal mate. And he would defend her with his life.

Alonso permitted himself a small measure of hope. Together, they could stop Lutin.

"What about the warships?" Nerya stood up and returned to her seat.

"When our reinforcements arrive, we will have an even fight outside the castle," said Sofia.

"We just have to hold out until Camila and the knights arrive?" Nerya asked.

Sofia nodded.

Nerya put her head in her hands. "I'd like to be alone," she said. "I'm going to rest and think a while. Sister Alma, please meet with Duchess Zaida to discuss wedding preparations. We'll need food and entertainment. I'll speak with you later."

She drew up her skirts and swished out of the room. Alonso started after her but Alma stopped him. "She needs some time. You can check on her later."

Alonso looked at the nun, seeing only kindness in her face. He took a deep breath and nodded. "I'll discuss the defenses with my brother."

Alma smiled up at him, squeezed his arm, and let go. He felt strangely lighter because of her touch. Magic? No, only compassion. He took a deep breath and left the Council with Enrique.

Chapter Seven

Nerya read for a while, but she couldn't stay calm enough to sit still. She tried praying, gentle exercises, and taking deep breaths, but nothing worked.

How was she going to get out of this mess?

She could take matters into her own hands and throw herself on the mercy of the Prince. Offer herself to him on the condition that he allow her people to be free. She would be his, and she would love him willingly.

It would be worth it, wouldn't it? She could make that kind of negotiation and know that her sacrifice would make the lives of her people better—or at least not worse.

She heard a door open in the hallway. Someone entered Alonso's chambers. Would he come and see her? She waited for him to knock on the door.

Her heart pounded as the minutes dragged on and the noises stopped. She would have to seek him out. She stood up and pulled on a robe. No time to put up her hair, but he had seen her in undress before.

She didn't know what he was thinking. She only knew she needed him, now more than ever. She padded to his door and pushed it open a few inches. He was standing in the middle of the room, shoulders slumped, head down.

"*Mi amor,*" she whispered.

He turned. The devastation in his face almost broke her heart.

It took him only a moment to cross the room and pull her against him. He closed the door behind her. Crushing her in his arms and showering her with kisses, he backed her up against the door. When he stopped for a moment, she wiped away the tears on his cheeks.

"You're mine," he said, his eyes glossy.

"I'm not an object." She tried to push him away, but her arms listened to her heart, not her head.

"I'm yours, you're mine. Tell me I'm wrong." He was stubborn, but he was right. She knew it in her heart.

When she pushed his doublet off his shoulders, he shrugged out of it. Running her hands up his chest, she soaked in the feel of his hard muscles.

"Alonso—" she whispered.

He loosened the string of the linen camisa at her neck, pulling the fabric down to the top of her breasts. His hands cupped her mounds, caressing, squeezing them, rough and desperate.

She arched her back as his head dipped down to feast first on one breast then the other. His tongue worked magic, making her nipples pebble through the thin fabric.

It felt so good. "You're mine," he whispered against her skin.

She shivered, then the answer burst forth. She couldn't hold it in any longer. "Yes. Since I was a foolish girl, I have always loved you. You are the only one for me." Joy bubbled in her chest. It felt right to tell him the truth.

He lifted his mouth to hers and greedily devoured her. Spices and salt, his tongue intertwining with hers as they explored each other. His hands roamed over her back while she nibbled his neck and shoulders. Her centre began to ache, her breasts tingled.

He pressed her against the door, rubbing his body along hers. She was throbbing, her pussy damp with need.

Stepping back, he breathed, "I want to look at you." He pulled down her shift until it pooled on the floor. Licking his lips, he took in her lush breasts and the swell of her hips. Under his gaze she felt beautiful.

It felt too good to stop.

She pulled him closer and kissed him, their tongues twining as they explored each other. He gripped her hips, bare hands on her skin, burning it like a brand. Droplets trickled from her mound down her thighs.

She pushed up against him, feeling the fabric of his breeches against her bare skin.

His hands traced circles on her buttocks as he pulled her even closer. His cock was thick and hard against her centre.

She wanted him. Wanted this.

"I need you in my bed." He pulled back.

She whimpered, missing the feel of his body against hers.

He took her hands and pulled her through the antechamber to the bedroom. A fire flickered in the hearth near a large bed half-hidden by gauzy curtains. The safe and quiet space calmed her senses.

She lay down in the middle of the bed. The satin fabrics soft against her skin, she stretched out, her skin tingling and hot.

"Stay right there. Don't move." He returned with some candles from the other room. Standing beside the bed, he pulled off the rest of his clothes. She marvelled at his muscular chest, broad shoulders. As he pushed down his breeches, she followed the vee of his stomach down to a dark thatch of hair. The big, hard cock springing free from his clothes made her gasp. She wanted to touch it. Lick it. Feel it deep inside her.

His heavy-lidded eyes raked over her body. "So beautiful."

When he climbed beside her on the bed, she reached out and caressed his member, moaning at the soft feel of his skin.

He kissed her lips, her neck, and breasts. She arched into him, luxuriating in his touch. His mouth and hands were flooding her with sensation. She could hardly think, only feel.

When he moved further down to her navel, she moaned. Her centre ached as he licked her belly button. He made larger circles with his lips and tongue over and around her belly.

Nibbling a path to her mound, he gently pushed her onto her back and spread her legs with his hands. He looked at her exposed sex and licked his lips. She shivered and his eyes snared hers. "I can't wait to taste you."

She whimpered as his fingers reached the apex of her thighs, slick and wet. He traced her pussy with his fingers, reaching up to spread her lips and reveal her clit. When he breathed lightly on the sensitive bundle of nerves, she shuddered. Then he put his tongue on her button and swirled it around.

"It feels so good," she whispered.

He chuckled and looked up. "I've fantasized about feasting on you. Making you hum until you come all over my face."

She almost climaxed from his words. Then he was sucking her clit, and she didn't want him to stop. If only they could shut off the world outside and stay like this forever.

He licked and sucked as she moved her hips. When he inserted a finger slowly inside her pussy, she felt like exploding. Then he put his thumb on her button and moved his tongue to lick her folds as he thrust inside her channel.

She was getting close to an orgasm, moaning as he pleasured her.

He shifted again, reinserting his fingers deep in her pussy. She groaned as he licked and sucked her centre.

He worked her hard and fast until she gripped his head with her thighs and bucked off the bed in ecstasy. Her pussy walls pulsed around his fingers as she moaned. She didn't think it would ever end.

When the aftershocks drew quieter he made lazy circles with his fingertips on her folds. Soon, she was throbbing again.

She cried, "More?"

"Yes. I want to be deep inside you, your sweet pussy sheathing my thick yard until we come together."

"Yes, I want it too," she sighed, trembling from his touch.

He climbed on top of her, rubbing his cock against her thighs, bringing it to her wet entrance. He thrust in hard and fast. She gasped, but it felt so good when he filled her up.

He was relentless, pounding into her as he groaned. It didn't take her long to crest again, and she used her legs to pull him closer on each thrust.

"Ohhhh," she wailed. "It's time, come for me."

He grasped the sides of her face, bringing his eyes level with hers. Looking deep into her soul, his dark eyes were on fire, burning just for her. And he was coming with her, shooting his hot seed deep inside her. It felt so right.

When they came down from their heights, he collapsed on top of her, supporting himself on his forearms. He caught his breath, then held her tight and rolled them to their sides.

Lying on a pillow beside her, he caressed her like she was the only thing in the world. She felt the same for him. She knew it might not be forever, not even for a little while, but it was perfect for now.

She sighed. He looked in her eyes and smiled, brushing hair off her face, leaning in to kiss her again.

"*Mi arma*," he whispered.

She rubbed her cheek against his hand. *This is heaven.*

"We can't stay too long," she said.

"I know." He smiled–a sad little smile that reached his shining eyes. "Just stay a little longer. Then we'll get up and face our problems."

She nodded.

He sat up and leaned back against the cushions on the headboard. Pulling her into his lap, he stroked her hair as she leaned against his shoulder. She was sated and happy, relishing the quiet, safe, little world they had made in his bed.

Then she felt a flush of magic course through her, from her head to her toes. She started tingling, golden shimmers emanating from her arms, her legs, her skin.

What is happening?

When she put her hands on Alonso's chest, he groaned and nearly knocked her off his lap. The shimmers surrounded them, coursing through both bodies. As he clutched her to him, his body trembled and his wings pushed out between his broad shoulder blades. Large, dark brown feathers fluttered, pushing them forward until their bodies settled in the middle of the bed, with his wings cocooning them. She clung to him as the changes rocked them both.

"This has never happened to me before," he gasped, his wings unfurling to caress her skin. The feathers brushed softly against her body, and she snuggled in. The shimmering sensations continued as she wrapped her legs around his waist.

She reached forward to feel his back, her touch tentative. "Your wing muscles are powerful. I don't know what will happen if you shift back, but this form is strong…and sexy." She ran her hands over the feathers on the wings, feeling another rush of tingles spreading through her torso. "You don't usually have a half-form?" Her thighs rubbed against his waist.

"No," he said. "This has never happened before, but it feels really good. Like it's supposed to be like this."

"I like it, too," she said, snuggling into his chest while enveloped by his soft wings.

He held her tight. "Just before I shifted, I had this urge. An urge to claim you as my mate."

When he said the word mate, the golden magic shimmered again, stroking along their forms. His wings stroked her back, her legs, her arms as she straddled him. His feathers soothed her, while the shimmers pulsed around them. He nuzzled his face in her hair and held her close, making little bird-like cooing noises in her ear.

She felt completely relaxed and at peace. As the golden magic entwined with Alonso's wings and folded around the pair, she felt an itch between her shoulder blades.

"Something's happening," she gasped. There was a pricking sensation at the base of her spine.

Alonso stroked and cooed, rubbing his palms against the small of her back. Then a burst of pinpricks fanned out along his touch. Alonso started, but held on to her.

"I can feel feathers, and something else," he said. "Right where..." He used his fingers to probe her backside, pulling her flush against him, his hard muscles taut against her flesh.

When he stopped and poked in the centre of the strange sensations, she asked, "What is it?"

"There's something hard. It's shaped like an oval or an egg." He prodded for another moment. "Hold on," he said. He scooted them to the edge of the bed, held her buttocks, and used his wings to lever them to a standing position. Turning around, he lay her on her stomach on the bed. She felt the loss of his touch, but soon he was straddling her and looking closely at the changes.

He breathed deeply. "It's the most beautiful jewel I have ever seen. It's mostly translucent, or crystal, with brown and green tones. There are bevelled facets on the surface. And there is the most beautiful starburst of brown and tan feathers. Near the bottom of the jewel the feathers are longer and point down, sort of in a heart shape."

"What? Am I turning into a falcon shifter?"

He chuckled and ran his hands down her sides. "No, I don't think so. It looks like a falcon's cloaca--but I've never seen a bejewelled one."

She tried twisting to see, but couldn't make it out. "A clo—?" It didn't hurt, but it felt strange.

"Female raptors have a cloaca on their backside, at the base of the spine. It's how we mate in our bird form. It's a spiritual and physical bonding. Usually it is reserved for married mates among our clan."

Her heart caught in her throat. "How can this happen?"

"*Mi arma*, I don't know, but it feels right inside my soul to see it. I can't explain it."

She tried to twist around, but could only see the feathers. "Have you ever seen anything like this before? What does it mean?"

"It means we are mated. I've heard legends about pairings between Faery folk and bird shifters. My people say great power comes from these matings." He showered her with kisses on her shoulders and back.

"But what do we do?" His attentions soothed her, but her heart still pounded.

"This means you are mine, and I am yours. We are meant to be together."

"Wait, don't I have a choice?" She stopped as she felt a wave of pain from between her shoulder blades. "Oh no, something else is happening." As she lay under him, waves of golden magic washed over her again. She felt something shift, then unfurl within her.

Alonso gasped. "*Mi amor!*"

"What is it?" she asked, panic rising.

"It's beautiful! Your wings, they are sprouting from your back. The feathers are brown with a rainbow sheen." As the sensations continued he soothed her. "They match your cloaca. And they are gorgeous."

"They're not like my sister's or mother's then." Tears came to her eyes.

"No, they are exactly, perfectly you."

She breathed a sigh of relief and wiped the moisture from her cheeks. Alonso came and stretched out beside her, easing her up and into his arms. "What do we do?" she asked in a small voice.

He said, "We are meant to be together. Nothing can stop us."

"But what about the Prince? The kingdom?" A queasy feeling passed through her.

"We will fight him together," her mate said, but the feeling didn't pass.

She had to do something to save her friends and her kingdom. It might involve a terrible sacrifice, but she couldn't sit back and wait for the Prince to discover she was already mated to someone else.

Chapter Eight

It was dark when Alonso woke up. He reached for Nerya, but her side of the bed was cold and empty.

Where is she?

He sat up and looked around the bedchamber, shoving down his worry. All was quiet. After putting on a robe, he left his quarters and knocked on Nerya's door.

A lady's maid answered and curtsied.

"Where is Her Grace?" he asked.

She stammered. "We...we thought she was with you."

A shiver of fear passed through him. Had she done something stupid? Or was she simply preparing for her morning wedding? He had to find her.

He marched to Sisters Alma and Elena's chambers down the hall and knocked.

The shorter one, Alma, opened the door. "Your Grace," she said.

"Have you seen Nerya?" He willed his pulse to slow down.

Alma shook her head and invited Alonso into their chambers. She went to one of the bedchambers and returned quickly. "Elena is missing too."

"Maybe I'm worrying over nothing," he said.

"What does your heart say?"

He blinked. That was where the bad feeling was coming from. He wondered if he could use their mating bond to find her.

"Let me try something," he said.

He closed his eyes. Thought of his mate, her soft caress, her smile, the love they shared. A light touch of her wing grazed along his soul.

"She's not in the castle. I see dark water and the bow of a ship. Lutin's flag." He opened his eyes, his stomach clenching. "The harbour."

Alma furrowed her brow. "I hope Elena is with her, at least." She called an attendant and asked them to assemble the Council.

Alonso hurried to his brother's chambers, quashing down his growing anxiety. He shook him awake. "Nerya's gone."

Enrique sat bolt upright. "Gone?"

"We have to find her." His voice broke.

"Of course." Enrique got dressed. "Are we meeting the Council?"

"Alma can take care of the Council. I need you to fly with me to Lutin's ship right away."

His brother nodded. A wave of affection flooded through Alonso. He could always depend on Enrique.

They padded out to the balcony. Enrique shifted into his large falcon form. Alonso concentrated for a moment and reached for his half form. Could he make the transformation consciously? Use it to save his mate?

He shuddered as bones and feathers protruded from his shoulder blades. Waves of magic surged through him, more powerful than ever. His hands and legs remained human, but they were supercharged, full of more-than-human strength. He was ready to take on the world.

Enrique gave a shrill cry.

"I have some things to tell you," Alonso said. He made a low chuckle as he took off. Enrique followed him and they flew toward the bay.

The harbour was quiet. Dark waves lapped against the shore, their crests reflecting the moonlight. Lights flickered on the flagship. Low voices carried across the water.

Suddenly, the flagship was rocked by an explosion. The percussive sounds echoed down the bay. Debris flew in the air and landed in the water. Flames shot up the hull of the ship as it rocked on the waves. Alonso struggled against the blowback, but he was far enough away that they were not seriously impeded. The vessel broke into pieces, flames licking the sections above the water.

Enrique beside him, Alonso sped up his approach. His pulse raced. Was Nerya on board? Was she alive? His heart told him yes.

He flew closer to the debris. Several soldiers held onto the sinking prow of the ship. As their shouts echoed on the surface of the water, the other ships started to respond.

He scanned the area. No Nerya.

Reaching out again with his subconscious, he searched for her. Would he sense her presence? His nerves jangled.

No. But he did hear something several paces to the north. A barrel bobbed in the sea and something splashed beside it. Was it two figures or just pieces of the ship? Alonso approached cautiously. One shape in white and green robes treaded water by the barrel, while another clung to the cask. The second figure had long dark hair and...wings! Beautiful white and brown feathers.

It was Nerya. His heart soared.

Alonso pointed for his brother. "Go tell the Council I've found them. And if Lutin's ship has been destroyed, then we can exploit the situation and force them to surrender."

Enrique turned in a big circle, heading back toward the castle.

Alonso went in the opposite direction and landed on a nearby section of the ship's hull, pulse racing. Alma and Nerya floated in the water. His mate's eyes were closed and the warrior nun held onto her. He cried out.

"She's all right," Alma called. "We weren't far from the ship when the blast hit. It knocked her unconscious, but she's not seriously injured."

Relief course through him. He sucked in a breath and dove into the cold water, coming up beside Nerya. Alma kept her hold on the barrel.

He held her inert body in his arms. Her head lolled back as he kissed her on the mouth, willing her to awake.

"Nerya, my sweetling," he cooed. "*Mi reina*, wake up."

She stirred in his arms. He wrapped his wings around them, trying to warm her up.

"What did she do?" He looked at Alma.

"I found her sneaking out of the castle. She planned to gain entry to the Prince by offering herself to him, then she would kill him in his bed."

"Like Judita, in the story?" He was angry, but his heart was filled with love.

Nerya was as fierce and brave as Dama Judita, who had surrendered herself to her enemy, Oloferne, and then ran a sword through him in his chambers.

"I couldn't dissuade her, so I insisted on going with her by posing as her handmaid."

"*Mierda*," he said.

"You would be proud of her. Nerya didn't hesitate to cut off Lutin's head when he made advances upon her."

Nerya breathed deeply. Then she tossed her head back and forth for a moment before opening her eyes.

"Alonso?" She whispered, cupping his cheek with her hand.

"Yes, *mi amor*," he said. "My brave, foolish, stubborn mate."

"I'm sorry I didn't tell you. But you would have stopped me."

"You're right." He held her close. "You're supposed to lead us, not run away. Not leave me."

"It's too much responsibility," she said. "I can't be the person they want."

"You are meant to rule. Everyone else can see it, why can't you?" His breath quickened. "You are kind, wise, compassionate, and fair. You listen to your advisors and make well-informed decisions."

"I can't do it without you, Alonso," she said, eyes wide. "You are my rock, you always have been."

His heart soared. "I will always be here. You can depend on me." He showered her with kisses.

As they embraced, the goblins raised an alarm.

"We have to get you out of here," Alonso said. When he glanced at Alma, she nodded.

"Leave me," Nerya said. "You have to warn the others."

"I'm not going without you." He blew out a frustrated breath. "Can you fly?"

She smiled wanly. "I think so. Can you help me take off?"

"I'll get you in the air." He turned to Alma. "Then I'll come back for you."

The sister nodded. "I'll be fine until you can return. I won all the swimming competitions at school."

Alonso scooped Nerya into his arms and pumped his powerful wings. It took only a moment and they were airborne. He pivoted so she was on top of him as he flew upside down, allowing her to set her feathers right and take wing.

His heart swelled with pride. She was beautiful in flight. It didn't take her long to get used to her wings. While they resembled his, they also had an ethereal quality to them. Likely her fae ancestry played a part in this marvellous combination. She had an advantage over him as well, since she didn't need to expend time and energy on shifting before she could fly.

He could feel her presence inside him. They were connected as mates. Sharing their love and joy together in flight.

Joy.

That was what the prophecy meant. The jewel in her cloaca, the joy they shared together, the love in their deep bond. It was her *joyel*—her joy and her jewel. Their love.

Why didn't he put that together earlier? He shrugged. It was only now, in the fullness of her power, that she was turning into the Fae Queen she was meant to be. And his love was the ember that lit her fire.

They were living out the prophecy in this very moment. His cheeks ached from smiling.

The couple flew across the harbour, aware of the falcon shifter warriors fighting the dwarf soldiers in their galleys. As word that their Prince's ship had sunk, Lutin's troops turned tail and fled. Still, Enrique and his knights kept up their assaults as the ships retreated from the harbour.

Alonso followed Nerya back to the ramparts, where a dozen warriors and most of the Council waited. When they landed, Alonso called for dry clothes for them both and sent one of his brother's warriors to fetch Alma.

His mother approached and wrapped Nerya in wool blankets, tutting as she patted her dry.

Sister Elena waited with bated breath for her companion to appear. She took a robe and some blankets from the waiting attendants. Once Alma arrived, Elena set to helping her friend recover.

In the meantime, Nerya dried herself off and conferred with Zaida and Sofia. Alonso joined them and his mother put her arm around him.

"You make me proud, my son. They will sing songs about you and your mate for many years."

Alonso's heart nearly burst. He had everything he wanted. Now they had to do the same for their kingdom.

Chapter Nine

Nerya couldn't believe she was still alive. She had thought the explosion was the end of her, had fully expected not to live. But her sacrifice would have been worth the cost if she neutralized Prince Lutin and stopped his invasion.

Then she had woken in Alonso's arms. Reborn, ready for a new life.

Now she stood on the ramparts while Alonso's mother, Duchess Dowager Zaida, updated her on events in the castle. Lutin's army on land wasn't giving up. The giant, General Orgoglio, remained on alert, giving orders to his warriors. The falcon shifter troops lined the curtain wall, watching their enemies, and polishing their weapons. The Mursiyans may have been outnumbered, but their determination was larger than life.

A warrior sister approached with Elena and Alma. She had ridden all day to deliver the message that Camila had sent a squadron of warriors by sea. They would arrive by mid-morning. Hope fluttered in Nerya's belly.

"We only have to withstand the assault until then," Zaida said.

Nerya nodded. "We can do it. The head of the snake has been cut off. The rest of the slithering body will not live for long."

Enrique and Alonso walked down the sea-facing rampart and returned to report. "The ships have withdrawn from the harbour," Enrique said. "I've left a small watch in the harbour and sent the rest of my troops to the north wall of the castle. We'll keep Lutin's warriors from gaining entry to the castle."

"Your Highness." Alonso looked at her with admiration. "We await your command."

She was as ready as she was going to be. To become the Warrior Queen her mate believed in. To take on her mother's mantle and make peace for her kingdom. To rule her people her way.

She took a breath.

Then everything changed.

The castle's foundations rocked. The sound of boulders crashing against the curtain walls pounded in Nerya's eardrums. The cries of injured warriors and the clash of battle weapons spurred her into action.

"My love, *mi amor*." She grabbed Alonso's hand. He shifted quickly into his half-falcon form and they took to the air. His face was grim, but she could feel the love he had for her. Warmth spread through her chest, despite her fear.

Devastation awaited them when they reached the curtain walls on the north side. General Orgoglio had launched his trebuchet, an imposing wooden structure capable of tossing large boulders with no more effort than one might toss pillows. Large sections of the ramparts had been demolished. Bodies and blood were everywhere.

Nerya's heart lurched as dozens of enemies scaled the walls, seeking to gain entry to the castle. The Mursiyan troops responded by pouring buckets of boiling water, hot sand, and the little oil they could spare onto the climbers. Most of the dwarves were stopped, and those who made it to the top were dispatched by falcon shifter soldiers. So far, they were able to contain the assault.

Dama Porphyria had joined the battle on the north-east castle tower, hurling lightning bolts from her staff down upon the invading warriors below. Falcon shifters worked in pairs, circling in the air and pitching heavy iron bolts on their enemies. Archers and warriors with crossbows—and the larger versions called ballistas—hunkered down along the battlements.

Nerya's eyes brimmed with tears as she thought about the consequences of her actions. She had not surrendered. Instead, she had committed her own act of war and brought retaliation upon her people. Yet she was not sorry, not one bit. Princesses might be peace-weavers, but they could also wield the sword of justice. Her people would be free, despite the cost.

Dama Porphyria appeared at her side in a puff of smoke. The Mage raised her arms and lit up the sky with golden lightning. Her voice echoed across the ramparts, after she uttered an incantation to magnify it.

"Her Highness, Queen Nerya, Defender of Ishbilliya and Sovereign Ruler of the Cinque Ducados, will lead us to victory!" The Mage stepped aside with a flourish and gestured Nerya forward.

Nerya unfurled her wings. She raised her arms to the sky. Alonso stepped up beside her and linked his hand in hers. Golden magic shimmered around them, surging through their bodies in an endless loop, sharing their passion and drawing on the energy to make them both stronger.

"Lutin is dead!" Nerya cried. "Reinforcements arrive mid-morning. Hold the castle until then and they will aid us in defeating our foes." She set her lips in a firm line. "And we will win!"

A loud cheer rang out among the warriors. Squadron leaders issued commands. Heavy wooden springalds were set up on the corner towers and loaded with bolts to launch at their invaders.

Enrique landed beside them and made a quick bow. "Your Grace, the general has taken lead on their trebuchet. Do I have your permission to engage him in combat?"

Alonso stepped forward. "I will assist him, my Queen."

Nerya's heart thudded. They were warriors through and through. But they were her family, too. Could she put them in danger to save their kingdom?

She paused only briefly. Then she put her hand on her mate's arm and looked at the brothers. "Come back, both of you."

Their jaws were set with determination. Fire glinted in their eyes. She sent out another pulse of golden energy to Alonso and nodded.

The two shifters turned and flew toward the enemy troops. She sent a prayer after them. She had to allow them to do their job, to lead and inspire their people, just as she did. Trust, faith, and love went hand in hand.

Nerya located Porphyria on the nearby tower and flew to her side. "Where can I be of most help?" she asked the Mage, who was still raining down golden lightning below.

"Beside me, so I and my assistants can keep guard over you," Porphyria said. "Did the emergence of your wings bring other powers?"

"Let me try something," she said. She drew her hands together and focused the magical bonding energy she and Alonso shared. Pushing it out to her palms, she visualized golden spheres appearing in her hands. Nothing.

Porphyria put a hand on her shoulder. "Try again." She handed her staff to her assistants, who continued the attack.

With a gentle nudge from the Mage, the spheres took shape easily in Nerya's hands. Porphyria guided her through the process of discharging the magical orbs, showing her how to project them toward a target. After two more attempts, Nerya could complete the action herself. She lobbed the projectiles upon the enemy warriors, concentrating on the area underneath their tower. Porphyria had the experience and capacity to send her lightning further afield, ranging across the battlefield. A glow of pride spread through Nerya, as she helped her people defend themselves against the invaders.

Then she spotted two falcon shifters near the enemy's trebuchet. The giant general faced them. Her heart leapt into her throat as the first fingers of dawn crept up the horizon.

Chapter Ten

Alonso's heart raced as he and Enrique dodged the buffets of the general's mace. The giant was twice as big as they were, a hulking mass with beady, cunning eyes. The giant's leather armour was coarse and tough, giving him a layer of protection that Alonso envied. He and his brother fought with every ounce of their strength.

They had already dispatched the ginours who worked the trebuchet. Three on each side, he and Enrique had dealt the death blows quickly. But the giant was a force to be reckoned with. If Alonso didn't believe in his brother's strength and courage, he might have given in to despair.

Orgoglio pivoted—slowly, as his weight made him less than nimble—and Alonso could see the wheels turning in their enemy's head. The large creature brought his mace above him, intending to finish them. The first blow landed mere inches from them. They ducked from the next stroke. Alonso wiped at the sweat on his brow.

He called out to Enrique. "Undercut!" They had practiced the two-pronged attack sequence when they were younger.

Alonso dropped to the ground. Rolling toward their foe, he brought his saber above his head and swept it in a graceful arc. He connected with the general's shins, steel slicing through leather, flesh, and bone. At the same time, Enrique lunged at the general's torso. He aimed his curved sword at the unprotected portion under the breast plate, exposed when Orgoglio had raised his weapon.

The two-pronged attack caused the giant to buckle, crying out in pain. He glanced off the trebuchet and his corpulent mass landed on the ground, making the earth beneath them tremble. Alonso staggered to his feet, chest heaving. The knot in stomach eased when he saw the siege engine was in pieces.

But the fighting was not finished.

General Orgoglio struggled to his knees. Alonso and his brother attacked again, concentrating their blows on the parts of the giant that had already been compromised. Their foe grabbed his axe and thrashed it around erratically.

Alonso pumped his wings and landed on top of the giant, seeking a weak point on the edge of the leather helm. He aimed for the side of the neck, under the ears, but Orgoglio flailed and Alonso nearly fell off. He wished he had Nerya's nimbleness, her ability to stay seated on her mount no matter the commotion. At that thought, a touch of her golden magic seep into him, helping to steady himself on top of the general.

Emboldened by this injection of power, he struck at the giant's neck. He made contact and pushed his saber down further into the general's body. The giant scrabbled at him, but Enrique held one arm and the other flailed underneath, unable to grab hold. Alonso expelled a pent-up breath and said a prayer that Orgoglio would stay down.

As the general grew weaker, his followers attempted to intervene. Enrique signalled to two shifters flying overhead. They landed and helped him fend off their attackers, keeping the dwarves at bay. Alonso remained on top of the giant until their foe ceased moving. He collapsed for a moment, his chest heaving.

Exhaustion set in as the sun peeped over the horizon. Enrique hailed him and climbed up to join him on his perch atop the dead general. They nodded at each other, eyes wide. This had been the largest enemy they had conquered in their lives. Relief washed over Alonso and he patted his brother on the back.

Together, they surveyed the battlefield. Pockets of warriors continued the fight. Falcon shifters circled in the air, seeking targets for the projectiles they carried. The dwarf troops continued strong.

"The battle is not yet won," Alonso said, his heart sinking.

A few moments later, a cheer rang up from their warriors. Falcon shifters flew above the castle with warrior sisters on their backs. The reinforcements were being brought in. Their ships must have been close enough to the harbour that Mursiyan shifters could transport them to the battlefield. Alonso's pulse raced. They could have a chance.

While the reinforcements arrived, Alonso and Enrique climbed down from their perch to rejoin the fight. A renewed sense of determination spurred their actions. Alonso was intent on his mission: cut down as many enemies as he could and get back to Nerya. He glanced up and located his mate on the ramparts, throwing balls of golden fire on the dwarves. His heart swelled with pride. Everyone was inspired by her courage and resolve.

Soon the fighters turned the tide of the battle. The nuns were fierce combatants and assisted the shifters with making short work of the remaining dwarves. As the fighting wound down, Alonso roamed over the battlefield identifying injured soldiers. Falcon shifters brought in healers to help with the wounded.

Alonso found Enrique when the battle ended. Covered in battle grime and blood, his brother swept his gaze across the scene. "I didn't think we could do it. But we won."

Alonso closed his eyes and took a deep breath. "We did, didn't we?"

"After the battle, can you show me how to shift into the half-form?" Enrique asked. "It's proven convenient today."

Alonso nodded. "You might need to find your mate first."

The brothers chuckled and then made ready to fly back to the ramparts. Back to their family and Alonso's mate.

Chapter Eleven

Nerya waited in the Great Watching Room while the Presence Chamber filled with courtiers, guests, and dignitaries. The space buzzed with excitement as the kingdom looked ahead to a joyous future.

The Nainian invasion had ended a fortnight ago, when Camila's warrior sisters helped push out the enemy troops at Mursiya Castle and the Lady Prioress had routed the remaining dwarven soldiers from the Queen's Palace. There had been casualties among her people, but the kingdom had rallied behind their new ruler. They were proud of her courage and the way she had defended them.

Nerya let out a big sigh and said, "I'm ready."

Lady Prioress Camila, Countess Sofia, and Lady Catalina fussed over her veil. She adjusted her bright red silk robe, decorated with borders worked in golden thread. The Council had planned a momentous occasion celebrating both her Coronation and the installation of Alonso as her Consort. The High Mage and Dama Porphyria would officiate, at her and Alonso's request. And Lady Zaida, Duchess Dowager of the Califate of Mursiya, would bestow the crowns upon both their heads. It was a fitting tribute to her love and unconditional support for the couple.

Sofia addressed the attendants. "Tell the Mages we can begin the ceremony momentarily."

Nerya's heart was full. Her life couldn't get any better than it was at this moment. The day after the battle ended at Mursiya Castle, they had celebrated her mating with Alonso in a small hand-fasting ceremony. After professing their love for each other and toasting their family and friends, they made an appearance at the harbour dockyard. Scores of soldiers and locals cheered the union of the fae and shifter peoples of the kingdom. Everyone had celebrated long into the night, while Nerya and Alonso enjoyed their first bedding as spouses.

"Look at your mate," Zaida said, her chest puffing up. "He's so handsome."

Nerya peeked into the Presence Chamber. Alonso sat in the left-hand throne on the dais, in a sapphire blue silk kaftan with a double belted golden sash. He looked every bit the Consort of a Fae Queen: regal, handsome, and fierce. His love buoyed her up. He had helped her make sense of the tragedy of the last moon's events. It wasn't an easy task ruling a kingdom which had violence in the recent past and examples of oppression and inequity in its longer history. But it was her responsibility—with the help of her mate—to set things right and make her lands safe for all. Her dedication to Alonso, his family, and his clan reminded her every day of the importance of this duty.

Lady Zaida had already reminded her of another important obligation of a Queen and her Consort: babies. Heirs to continue their dynasty and live their legacy. Nerya and Alonso had consulted with healers in the falcon shifter clan, who had pronounced the Queen's transformation miraculous and assured them they could conceive if they wished. When the time came, the healers would monitor the incubation and nesting period to ensure the health of the parents and babies. Nerya found herself looking forward to the preparations and to sharing this new phase of her life with her mate.

The Yeoman signalled they were about to begin. She put her shoulders back and Lady Catalina squeezed her hand. Nerya smiled at the women surrounding her. She had felt alone for most of her life. Now her heart—and her life—were filled with family and friends. With a community that loved her unconditionally and wanted her to succeed as their leader. She wished with all her heart she could be worthy of their trust and faith.

A flourish of trumpets sounded her entrance. The guests in the Presence Chamber hushed and rose from their seats. Alonso stood and clasped his hands in front of his kaftan, eyes shining. The magical sparks of their bond twinkled above the crowd like golden stars. The audience gasped in wonder and clapped at the sight.

Nerya took the first steps into the next chapter of her life, filled with joy and love.

About the Author

Mimi B. Rose is a dreamer and arm-chair adventurer. She loves to get lost in captivating worlds peopled with strong women, their partners, friends, and families (found or otherwise). She reads and writes stories that resonate with our contemporary experiences, even though they take place in worlds and times different from our own. Mimi lives in Toronto, Canada, with her family and a menagerie of pets--furry, feathered, and scaled. Join her as she chases the moon and chooses love!

https://linktr.ee/authormbrose

BE CAREFUL WHERE YOU BLEED

Be Careful Where You Bleed

E. MILEE

Heat Level:
Steaming

Content Warning:
Blood, drugs, themes of religion, and violence.

IT IS A CRIME TO TAKE TWITCH
Anyone found under the influence or in possession of twitch will be punished to the full extent of the law,
up to and including fines, imprisonment, and execution.
Report users, smugglers, and suspicious activity to a Toltana City Enforcer.

When I was asked to write about the night that Scourge's blood dribbled down the hill, I didn't know where to start. Does the story begin when my mother placed me in a basket and left me on the steps of an orphanage? Maybe it's when the orphanage ran out of beds and no one searched for me after running away. By all means, a childhood of living like a feral street cat prepared me for that fateful night.

Perhaps we should go back a century before I was born, when the first settlers arrived at the bottom of the hill. But you already know how they polluted the river, then built Toltana further up the incline, where their sensitive noses never had to smell the miasma. Is there a record of when the smog emerged or the initial sightings of Scourge? I'm sure there is, but forgive me for not studying the monster's history in depth. When he stomped our streets, all we knew was how to hide. For years after he fell, I spent my time rebuilding everything he destroyed. Now, I try not to think about him at all. Besides, you're not interested in my thoughts regarding how Scourge and his smog came to be. No one ever is. If someone asks me for a story, they want a tale of blood and debauchery.

When I think about that night and all the events leading up to it, I always come back to the flyers posted throughout the city—IT IS A CRIME TO TAKE TWITCH—and how they taunted me as the love of my life begged me not to smuggle the contraband. Bear with me, because although my account begins with two women simply sharing supper in a seedy tavern, it's not long before I start cutting throats.

Aria was many things, but never subtle. She took one look at the tattered burlap wrapped around my package and burst into tears. I had anticipated her being upset but hoped she might compose herself better, considering our booth in the corner of the crowded tavern offered little privacy. I would have preferred to disclose the details of my latest assignment behind the closed door of our boarding house room. That offered little more privacy than the booth, with its thin walls and vagrants plopped throughout the halls, but we had already planned to meet for dinner after her shift—cleaning the townhome of a family four blocks up the hill—and I had to be on my way down the hill after this.

"This isn't part of your arrangement!" Aria said.

"What am I supposed to do? Refuse?" I tucked the package back into my cloak, away from Aria, who looked as if she had half a mind to tear it open and scatter the contents all over the floor. That wouldn't have stopped anyone from consuming the drug. I had seen twitch addicts on their hands and knees, lapping from a puddle where a single leaf had been dropped.

"Make someone else do it." She slammed her fist on the table, rattling our glasses.

I had considered that. I was one of Luther Penn's many lackeys, running around Toltana on various errands. Tasks ranged from picking up his laundry to killing whoever's debts had gone bad. We all wanted the same thing: to pay off the man who owned us. I had been doing this since he bailed me out of prison (without my consent) when I was twenty-eight years old. Seven years later, I had climbed the ranks and got the first pick of his assignments. I excelled in shakedowns and murder, usually going on one or two assignments a week, and left the smuggling, petty theft, and laundry delivery to the newbies.

Maybe that made me a ruthless killer, but it was kill or be killed. Penn was going to make sure these people died either way. At least I got to them first and put them down with a quick bullet through the brain. If he instructed me to keep them alive, I broke as few bones as possible.

I passed Aria a handkerchief and checked our surroundings for eavesdroppers. Any guests who weren't invested in conversations at their own table stumbled around on drunken knees. The barkeep couldn't hear us over the noise of clinking glasses and loudmouths seated around the bar. The owner, Shelly, kept a watchful eye by the back door, but they didn't concern me. I had broken up plenty of fights and chased down countless patrons who tried to skip out on their tab. They needed people like me to keep things in order when the crowd got too rambunctious. If anyone was watching, Aria and I looked like we had been caught in a lover's quarrel.

"Penn gave this to me personally. If I give it to one of the kids and they fail or run off with the money, I'll be the one to pay. I have to go." She didn't pull away when I took hold of her hands, letting her mousy blonde hair fall around her face. With each tear that splashed onto the table, my gut twisted tighter.

Aria could not take my nighttime escapades for much longer. The fear of me not returning weighed heavily on her, but she never told me not to go. Never got angry or threatened to leave me. She only cried as she helped me get dressed, then paced across our room so diligently her path was embedded into the floorboards. I hate myself for admitting this, but her tears kept me focused. I would have bottled them up and drank them if I could, a reminder of how everything I did, I did it for her.

"You promised you'd never smuggle," she whimpered. She could handle murder, breaking and entering, robbery, and coercion, but delivering twitch was too much.

It was a line I had not crossed since my arrest. Not since I ended up as Penn's glorified indentured servant, stealing and slaughtering my way through the nights. Smuggling the leaf was the only crime city enforcers actually enforced, and the consequences were steep, especially for as much as I carried in my cloak. It thudded against the revolver on my hip as I stood from the booth. "Come with me," I said, gently pulling Aria out of her seat and towards the back door. Shelly nodded and held it open as we stepped into the alley.

The stench of sewage and too many people living in proximity almost made me double over and heave. Aria kept a straight face much better than I did. I scowled at the thought of what messes she encountered in her job as a housekeeper that would accustom her to such filth. Then I noticed the sticky residue on the ends of her hair.

"You weren't cleaning a townhome today, were you?" I reached for her locks, but she turned her back and stomped away. I chased after her. "Aria, wait!"

"I have never asked where you go, so what right do you have to pester me?" She trembled under the faint light of the streetlamp, terror and shame written on her face.

"How long?" I approached slowly, drawing her back into the alley.

She stared at her feet, and I could not hear her over the sounds from the street. Carts rustled down the cobblestone, vendors called out from their stands, heels clicked and clacked against the pavement, and in a flat above us, a baby's wail echoed through the passageway.

I squeezed her hands, and she spoke up. "Two weeks. But I've only gone three times, on days when no one needed their house cleaned. Everyone is so frugal now that the smog is getting closer. They save their coins like they can pay Scourge to stay away—"

"Do not speak his name!"

Her eyes widened at my outburst. Aria, my love who cried for me and made herself sick with worry, who was always patient and kind, my rock to stand on when I felt myself slipping away. But she thought superstitions were full of shit and had no problem saying the name of the terrible creature that tormented every part of our existence.

I brought her hand to my lips and kissed each knuckle between my admonishments.

"You should have told me." Kiss.

"What if you got caught?" Kiss.

"People die in the lab." Kiss.

"You can't trust anyone." Kiss.

And last, "Never again. I love you too much."

Her cheeks turned a fierce shade of red under my scrutiny, but I leaned forward and pressed my lips against hers before she could protest. It wasn't fair. I had no right to get upset with her for engaging in illegal activity, but she hummed when I twisted my fingers in the hair along her scalp, demanding more, more, more.

"At least tell me you stole some for us," I said when she paused for a breath. She smirked and unwrapped her arms from around my neck, then withdrew her own contraband from her satchel.

Aria had stolen a milk bottle full of clarity, enough for our window and plenty left to trade with others. The landlord would give us two weeks of rent for this paste. Aria handed it to me. I shook it up, mesmerized by how the gooey, brown sediment mixed with the oil. Bright green bits of crumbled twitch leaves floated around.

And then I smelled it, the fetid mud and river water that formed the goop. The potion was one part mud, one part river water, and two parts cottonseed oil with two to four twitch leaves, depending on the potency and cost of the final product. It smelled like a carcass baking in the sun. How Aria managed to stand in a stuffy, dark room and work with the ingredients, I would never know.

She laughed when I shoved it back to her and stowed it away, as if she weren't walking around with a product someone could kill her for. The demand for clarity was higher than production, and the cost for a vial of diluted solution was exorbitant. Aria must have found work in a ghost lab. Government labs charged more, paid less, and supplied everyone at the top of the hill first. If there was any left for people living below Fifth Street, it wasn't worth more than a copper, but they often charged ten or more. So we started making clarity for ourselves. Aria and I lived on Ninth Street, and I knew of three ghost labs near our boarding house. Working in these labs was risky, because if enforcers raided, everyone could be charged with possession of twitch. Addicts got bold and attacked them, burning down entire buildings just for a handful of leaves. Production supervisors were known to undercut paychecks.

All of this over twitch, the little green leaf that grew upriver, where the water was clear, the land was not in constant shadow, and the air didn't smell like an overflowing toilet.

Twitch. The drug wealthy settlers fed to peasants in Toltana's infancy. It dulled their senses and left them so dependent on it, they didn't notice they were building an empire but would never be invited to the palace. Those settlers' descendants banned consumption of it decades later, when addicts became more of a burden than a blessing. When all of a sudden, *they* needed twitch. If people used up all the twitch to get high, how could they protect themselves from the smog?

"Take this." I placed three coppers in Aria's palm. "Apply a layer of clarity around our door. Then pay someone outside to scale the building and seal our window."

"Our door?" Her mischievous manner was short-lived. We had never sealed our door to the hall. The owner may have been a slumlord, but he always made sure the lobby openings were protected. Probably only because he had to live there, too, but I wasn't taking any chances.

"I don't think the smog will reach us tonight, but it might get close," I said.

Her tears glistened as they streamed, lips quivering as she opened her mouth to say something, but she only stifled a sob. I felt my own eyes welling up, and my chest felt as if someone had reached inside and squeezed my heart. I pulled her toward me, resting my chin atop her head as she shook and cried into my shoulder.

"Please don't go. I'll sell it to the ghost lab in the morning before you report to Luther Penn. They will pay more than his client, and we have more than enough saved up to get on the next ship out of here. Please come home with me. *Please*."

"He would have us both killed. I'm sure he has spies in the lab, and there'd be a price on our heads so high that none of the captains would take us onboard." A cold breeze sent a shiver down Aria's spine. I squeezed her tighter and nuzzled my mouth near her ear. "You know I can't leave Toltana as long as I'm bound to Penn."

Aria looked up at me and shook her head, conveying what words could not explain. We never acknowledged how Penn owned me. If we didn't talk about it, maybe it would go away. The circles under her eyes looked darker than they had been in the morning. I had done this to her. When I pondered how her face changed over the years we had been together, I couldn't help but wonder if she aged quicker because of me. But everything I stole, every shopkeeper I coerced, and every life I ended were all so I could give Aria the life she deserved. It was almost over—the tears, nightmares, and pacing.

"Penn gave me something else." I pulled the leather cord out of my pocket. A dingy brass tag dangled from it, engraved on it: my name.

Winnifred Thomas.

Aria gasped and took it delicately between her fingers, handling it as if it might disappear in a puff of smoke. She had never seen it before. I met her four years after I was forced to give it to Penn. The day he bailed me out of prison, then marched me to his office, where I had to cut open my palm and bleed into a vial. My blood hung from this cord on his wall, along with dozens of others in his retinue. I knew I had to be getting close to paying him back, but I had not expected it to be for another year or so. I tried not to let my expression reveal my uneasiness, but of course, Aria saw through me.

"How much is the package worth?" she asked.

"Don't worry about that. Just go back to the room, take care of the door and window, and sell the leftover clarity to the landlord. For coin, not rent. This is our last night in Toltana. Pack our things, get our money together, and as soon as the smog clears, I'll finish up with Penn, get my blood, and we will head to the wharf."

Aria stood on her toes and kissed me. She clutched my collar and tugged my bottom lip between her teeth, stumbling over her skirt as she shoved her knee between my legs. She tasted like lemon tea and smelled like lavender soap. My senses were full of her, despite the rats pilfering through nearby heaps of rubbish and the layer of soot and grime that coated every surface of the city. I pulled her scarf over her head, then pressed her into the wall and cradled the back of her skull with one hand, and with the other, laced my fingers between hers. She squeezed my hand, nails digging into my flesh, and I winced but didn't stop kissing her. With each swipe of her tongue over mine, I imagined laying her down on a feather mattress far away from the straw-stuffed mattress we had been sleeping on.

She moaned softly, and I kissed harder, not caring if anyone saw us, because all I could think about was the noises she'd make when we had a proper home. Maybe we would live in a house on a farm and never be interrupted by strangers stomping up and down the stairs or gawking at us from the sidewalk ever again.

I opened my eyes, and Aria was staring back at me. In her eyes, I saw the world. Every sparkle was a glint of hope—for my safe return that night, for a ship in the morning, and hope that, for the rest of our lives, we'd fall asleep together and wake up knowing we escaped from Toltana—that we could conquer anything at all. This twitch delivery was the final test.

"It's just a simple drop. I'll be back before you know it." The warning bell began to toll as I pulled her toward me.

"I'm still angry you broke your promise never to smuggle. Hurry home so you can beg me to forgive you." Aria's voice was raspy. If it were not for the bell, I would have dropped to my knees right there in the alley and kissed my way from her ankle to her navel, biting, sucking, and leaving my mark.

Ding.

Watching her cry made my mouth dry out, made me feel like I'd die from thirst, like drinking her tears was the only remedy. But she clutched my shirt again, resting her cheek against my bare chest before I could catch them on my tongue. Her tears trickled between my breasts, and I swear, they were absorbed by the flesh just below my heart. If I couldn't drink her, I would settle for her melting into me.

Ding.

"Listen to me." I tilted her face up. "If I'm not back by sunrise, take our savings and leave the city. Don't wait for me. Penn will take everything we own if I don't report to him. He will take *you*. Promise me, Aria."

The fourth bell toll and Aria's slap across my face happened at the same time. "Take it back, Winnifred. Take it back!" She trembled with such ferocity, I had to hold her up as she cursed and spit.

"I am better off knowing you're safe, that this time tomorrow, you will be on your way out of here." I waited for her to slap me again, but the bell rang for the fifth and final time, at least until the watchman spotted smog. Five tolls for the first warning—time to pay your tab and head home. Four tolls for run, beg someone to let you inside if you're far from your own shelter. Three for it's too late, better pop that twitch leaf on your tongue if you have one. Every night we heard the bells, and lately, there was hardly any time between warnings.

I kissed Aria quickly, then shoved her toward the street. Before she got swept away in the panicked crowd, she turned and said, "Never again. I love you too much."

She didn't promise anything.

And then she was gone.

I wanted nothing more but to sink into the ground and sob, but I had work to do. My shifts began at the first warning. When everyone else was running away from the smog, I ran toward it.

MY PISS TASTES BETTER THAN TEARS FROM THE GODDESS.

There was a joke that went like how do you know someone doesn't believe in the goddess? Answer: they will tell you at every opportunity. If you were in Shelly's tavern, you would see them writing their blasphemy on the walls. I suppose it was only considered blasphemy to those who believed the goddess cried from the sky and her tears were what made twitch leaves grow. In the days before Scourge fell, only fanatics believed that.

Why would she only cry over one area upriver—were the raindrops over Toltana not her tears?

Why would she give us a drug, then punish us for taking it?

Why did she put twitch here for men to find? A believer would say she did it because someday she would come to Toltana. Something about how people who still followed the goddess before she came would be righteous enough to be saved. That sounded like a scam. What about the people who tried to believe but couldn't? What about me? A loving goddess would not have made us suffer just so she could save us.

And in the end, it was not the goddess who saved us.

"I saw what you're hiding under your cloak. Are you trying to get yourself sent to the gallows? People swing for half that amount." Shelly yanked me into the corner when I reentered the tavern.

"Don't be ridiculous. They'll send me to the rack if they catch me with this much twitch." I winked and gave them my last coppers to pay for Aria's and my meal.

"If I saw it, who knows if anyone else did. Your arrogance will be the death of you."

"I invite them to try and take it from me," I mumbled, then squeezed my way through the horde of patrons trying to get out the front door. This crowd was on edge, more so than usual. People shoved and grabbed one another, everyone rushing for the exit, desperately trying to spare each second. We all sensed it. The smog would be especially bad tonight.

For months, it had not risen past Twentieth Street. Every night, it stayed at the bottom of the hill between Twentieth and the river, and for a while, people still lived in that area and we could visit during the day. Two weeks before this, it rose to Nineteenth. Then Eighteenth. It had reached Twelfth Street the night prior. No one dared venture below Fourteenth even in the daytime when it was clear of smog. The people who had been poisoned by it were not limited to prowling at night.

Finally, I got outside and sucked in a lungful of mildewy air.

I hated this fucking city.

"Winnie!" I knew who was calling and did not turn around. He sounded far back, swimming against the crowd. I planned to lose him by turning down the next alley.

"Winnie, wait for me!" He was practically on my heels before I reached the corner. He would have just followed me if I tried to escape. An inconvenience, but I had taught him how to track people in a crowd, so I couldn't be angry he was so good at it.

"I told you to stop calling me Winnie," I said when Antony caught up to me. We stood in the alcove of a bank's entry. It stank. A fresh coat of clarity wafted around us, the brown goo lathered thickly in the crevice of the door. That foul paste would keep the smog from seeping inside.

"Can I borrow some money?" He bounced up and down on his feet, full of nervous energy.

"What happened to the coins I gave you yesterday?" My head began to ache. Antony could not have picked a worse time to be a thorn in my side.

He did not say anything, but looked up and revealed the mess that had been made of his face. Two black eyes, a bloody nose, and a busted lip.

I wiped away the blood crusted on the corner of his mouth with my thumb. "Oh, Antony, you *must* start sticking up for yourself."

"I will after tonight," he said quietly. Poor kid. He reminded me of myself when I was fifteen. The streets of Toltana would chew you up and spit you out every night until there was nothing left of you.

I searched my pockets but only had spare bullets. "You can stay with me and Aria." He almost knocked me over from the force of his hug. *So much for begging her to forgive me.* But I liked the idea of Aria having company. Antony would chew her ear off and be annoying enough that she wouldn't have to worry about me all night.

"Run before the landlord barricades the door." I gave him a quick squeeze before sending him away.

"Thanks, Winnie! I'll pay you back someday!" His voice echoed down the street as he ran up the hill. The crowd had already thinned out. All that remained were stragglers rushing home, homeless people who had no choice but to find whatever shelter they could, and people like me who lurked in alcoves and shadows.

"My name is Winnifred," I shouted back.

The warning bell rang again when I stepped onto the street. Four tolls—I still had time to reach Halle's House of Blessings. If I had to, I would spend the night there. I knew Aria would not actually leave if I wasn't back by sunrise. I had spent many nights sleeping on the floor of Halle's shop when I first ran away from the orphanage. That was where I met the crew who introduced me to smuggling. The irony of it being my last stop before leaving Toltana forever made me laugh as I ran down the hill.

The steep incline worked favorably. I felt like I was flying, and when I arrived at Halle's, the air was foggy, but the poison hadn't reached me.

Welcome To Halle's House Of Blessings.
You are safe here.

I still wonder if Halle would have survived Scourge's rampage. Maybe it's better I will never know. Humans are simple creatures—I can rationalize why they painted her blood on the walls. But Scourge? I cannot comprehend what he was or why he wanted to destroy us.

I cocked my revolver and opened the door just enough to listen inside.

"Halle?" I called into the darkness. On a night like this, her shop should have been full of people sleeping on the floor, but it was silent. I kicked the door open all the way and stepped inside.

"Drop the package on the table in the center of the room. Then leave. Walk slowly. No one else has to die." A voice I vaguely recognized, deep and raspy, like he spent his days in the cigar lounge.

"Who's there?" I growled and braced for someone to launch from a dark corner.

I didn't have to see Halle to know she was dead. The sharp smell of blood burned my nostrils. After all the years of protecting people who had nowhere to go, she died at the hands of robbers. The injustice of it filled me with rage, but I stifled it. I would unleash it as soon as they revealed themselves.

"Put the package on the table. It's directly ahead of you." He sounded about ten paces to my right. I reached for my dagger and took a tentative step toward him.

"I wouldn't do that if I were you," a woman in the furthest corner said. *Shit*. I had no idea how many there were. Had someone seen me leaving Penn's office? No, Shelly was probably right. Someone had seen me show it to Aria in the tavern, and they gathered a crew. I was close to the door. My best chance at escaping would be to turn and bolt. My rage bubbled up at the thought of letting Halle's killers get away, but she would have told me to flee.

I took one step backward, then froze. A whimper I could decipher in a chorus stopped me in my tracks. "Aria?"

"Put the package on the table, and you can both walk out of here. Last warning." Oh, I was going to kill whoever that was on the right.

"Okay," I said and crept further into the darkness. I had two options. Drop my revolver on the table and hope the darkness fooled them, or place the twitch there and make sure Aria was safe, then chase them down to take it back. Leaving without it was not an option.

It had been a while since I had a gunfight in the street. My last night in Toltana would go out with a bang. I placed the package on the table, then backed up to the door.

"Claudia, check on it," their leader commanded. *Claudia.* She was one of Penn's lackeys. She had tagged along on a couple jobs with me when she was new. I helped her learn the ropes. Did she think she would get away with this?

She confirmed that it was, in fact, one pound of twitch.

"It's been a pleasure doing business with you, Winnie." The man to the right, I knew who he was now. Antony's older brother, Xavier. He had recently paid his debt to Penn but still took side jobs from him. I never expected anyone besides Aria to have my back, but knowing it was other lackeys who were robbing me made it worse.

"Let. Her. Go." Aria was all I cared about.

Xavier shoved her away, sending her staggering toward me. Her hands were tied behind her back, and a dirty scrap of cloth was tied around her mouth. She limped on an injured ankle and a dark bruise colored her cheek. Aria yelped when I tugged her arm, leading her out of the shop, my blood close to boiling over. But I had to stay focused. If they got away with the twitch, it wouldn't matter that she survived the night. That package was worth more than my life. Penn would claim Aria as well.

We crouched behind a newspaper stand as I cut her hands loose. "I'm alright," she said as soon as I released the gag. I didn't even have a second to kiss her before the first person exited the shop.

"Stay here. Keep low," I said, then moved toward Halle's. The dense fog limited my view, but I was still breathing. The final warning bell hadn't tolled. I could still get Aria and myself out of this.

I charged and threw my entire body into the person outside the shop, sending us both flailing inside. Whoever shot at me missed, their bullet going into the skull of their partner I had just tackled instead. I tossed his body off me, then crawled to the center of the room and hid under the table.

"Someone get the lights!" Xavier was at the back of the shop, realizing the windows were bolted shut. Fools. Their only way out was through the front door, where I kept my gun pointed. After a minute of fumbling around, someone found the cord for a lightbulb in the corner. The moment they pulled it, I fired. Claudia went down screaming and spasming. I flipped the table over and pointed my gun at Xavier.

"You didn't think Penn would actually let you go, did you?" he asked, showing no remorse for his fallen crewmates.

"Just give me the twitch, and you can be on your way," I answered.

"You have your assignment, and I have mine." Xavier flashed a crooked, toothy grin and slowly approached. I put my finger on the trigger. He knelt in front of me, inches away from my revolver, and whispered, "You won't do it."

No, of course I wouldn't. Killing Xavier would kill Antony. Xavier had forced Antony to drink his blood, binding himself to the boy. Everyone in Penn's retinue loved Antony. Everyone except his own brother. It was Xavier's selfish collateral—no one could touch him without risking Antony's safety.

"What do you want? Money? I've got lots of it. Just give me the twitch and you can have it all." A pointless offer, but it was the best I had.

Xavier clicked his tongue. "No, money is useless these days. Look around you. These are end times."

In the distance, the bell rang.

The final warning.

"Uh-oh." Xavier cackled. "Looks like neither one of us will make it out. Perhaps we will team up in the smog."

I shoved the table up, knocking him over, then pinned him to the ground. "You can stay here if you'd like."

I wrapped my hands around his throat, squeezing just enough for him to lose consciousness. But he overpowered me, bringing his knee to my stomach and throwing me to the side. I grunted under his boot as he pressed into my lower back, bones screaming from the pressure. He'd paralyze me, then leave me to be consumed by the smog.

"I was supposed to leave you alive. But I'm sure the boss will be content with Aria." Her name on his lips sounded like a curse. I tried to turn and face him, but my vision was quickly turning to black. Of all the ways I had imagined I might die, this was certainly the worst scenario. I only hoped that Aria started the trek up the hill when she heard the bell. That she would make it further than the smog.

I heard bones crunch and thought it was my spine, but Xavier collapsed beside me. Aria tossed the pipe she had used to knock him out and rolled him onto his back. "Where is your dagger?" she asked me.

"My hip." I could barely speak.

If Xavier's boot had been on my back a second longer, I would have been dead. I blinked, and when I opened my eyes, Aria was straddling Xavier, carving open his chest and reaching inside him. It was not a quick death. He stared at me as she took hold of his heart, then pulled. Maybe it was a spasm, or maybe I was seeing things, but the image of him smirking as she cut the arteries is burned into my memory.

I tried to get up. Aria was in bloodlust, stabbing and squeezing the heart. "It's done," I croaked. "Aria, stop. You saved Antony."

When a person drank another's blood, the only way to be released from the bond was to cut out their still-beating heart. Antony was free from his brother. At least he would survive the night.

Xavier's blood oozed and gushed out of his chest, spilling across the entire floor. Aria's face was splattered with it. My clothes were soaked in it.

And the package of twitch was saturated in it.

"No," Aria gasped.

I forced myself up. We had a bigger problem to worry about than Penn's lost goods.

"The door." I pointed to how it hung loose from the hinges. We must have broken it when I crashed inside with the thug. "Check the woman," I said as I dragged myself toward the first man, then searched him hastily for any twitch. Nothing.

For a moment, I thought we could outrun the smog. My strength was returning, and we'd run for our lives, but wisps of it swirled into the shop. We had nowhere to go.

"I have one leaf." Aria crouched beside me and held it in her palm.

I closed her fingers around it and guided her hand back to her. "Take it. Please, do it for me."

"I'll cut it in half. We can share—"

"If you love me, you will put the entire leaf on your tongue right now," I wheezed.

The smog was up to our necks and after only a few breaths of it, I felt myself slipping away. I didn't know what would happen next. There were varying reports of what you would experience if you got stuck in the smog without a twitch leaf. Some people said you would simply suffocate and die. Others said you would become Scourge's puppet, wandering through the poisonous fog every night. I didn't plan to find out. I would turn my gun on myself as soon as Aria took the drug and passed out.

"Before I met you, I was never afraid of dying. There was no time to fear, not when there was so much danger in life. But you've always protected me from life and death, and I know you will come back for me." She spoke frantically, coughing and choking between words.

"You are the only reason I bother staying alive. I can't go home without you." In the seven years I had been working for Penn, I thought I had encountered everything—had a plan for everything. But I had never prepared to convince Aria to take the last twitch leaf. I had so much more to say.

"You can, and you will." She shoved her fingers into my mouth the next time I coughed and pressed the leaf onto my tongue. I tried to spit it out, but she held it there until it dissolved. Every ache and pain in my body dissolved with it, my consciousness following. I tried to scream, tried to regurgitate the drug, but Aria pressed me onto the floor and devoured my mouth with hers. I kissed her ferociously, savoring everything before I blacked out. The smog had her struggling to breathe. The twitch had me struggling to stay awake. But we kissed until thunderous footsteps broke the silence that had fallen over the block.

"He's coming. You have to hide." My eyelids lost the battle to stay open, but I had just enough strength to hand my dagger to Aria.

"I am not afraid of Scourge." She didn't try to hide. What was the use? With the broken door, the shop was completely open for the smog to find us and alert its master of a fresh, sober human. I opened my eyes just enough to see how the wisps solidified and wrapped around Aria's limbs. They had not become solid enough to stop her from slicing her palm and bringing it to my lips. "Drink," she commanded.

I obeyed, drinking as much as I could before fatigue defeated me. I felt her blood mixing with mine. She became part of me.

"I was waiting for the right moment to do that. It doesn't get much more romantic than this, does it?" Aria hovered over me, planting sloppy kisses all over my face and neck. Just when I thought I would pass out, she hauled me up and pushed me toward the door. "Go home and rest. Come back for me when you wake up. That's an order."

The bond was complete. I was no match for how every bone and muscle in my body pulled me away from her.

The last things I remember were the smog swirling around Aria like an impenetrable, black cloud and how loud Scourge's stomps were from a block away. I got a quick glimpse of him before turning to drag myself up the hill. Downhill, he loomed over the buildings. He was more terrifying than any description ever spoken, a nightmare coming to destroy us all.

Be careful where you bleed or monsters you will feed.

Growing up, I had a terrible fear of accidentally feeding a monster. If I got even the slightest cut, I wrapped it in layers of bandages, not risking a drop of blood ending up on the lips of some foul creature. Now that Aria's blood flows inside me, the monsters take us both in my nightmares.

If you were born after Scourge, if you have never lived in terror that he might lick your wounds and claim you, then you cannot understand how terrible the blood bond was. It brought me peace knowing Aria was still alive, yes, but at what cost? I could not see her. I had no idea where she was or if she was in trouble. My heart would continue beating as long as hers did, and with each beat, Scourge grew stronger.

I woke up two days later in my own bed.

"Miss Winnie?" A girl brushed the tangled hair away from my face. "Antony, she's awake!"

He burst into the room and jumped into bed with me before I had fully opened my eyes. "Winnie, wake up. I thought you were dead."

"My name is Winnifred," I groaned and swatted him away. Antony sent the girl to collect breakfast. "What happened?" I asked. There had been some wild dreams in the two days I slept, and for those first moments awake, I thought maybe the blurry memories of what Aria had done were a dream as well.

"You don't remember walking to Shelly's and collapsing outside the front door? They found you in the morning, convulsing and covered in your own urine and vomit. Don't worry. I helped you back here before anyone else saw you."

Lovely. I did not recall any of that.

"You were twitching," Antony said.

"Yes, I was."

"You took twitch?"

"Yes."

"You're doing it right now." He pointed at my eye.

The withdrawal was not as bad as I expected. I struggled to keep my eyes open, and my arms and legs jerked occasionally, but I wasn't frothing at the mouth or scratching my skin.

"I need to find Aria." I sat up too quickly, blood rushing to my head and making me sway. I felt her. She was alive.

The girl returned and placed a tray of toast and bacon on the bedside table. She could not have been older than sixteen, but behind her eyes, I saw an old soul. Beneath her dress, a round belly. I nodded my thanks and asked for a moment alone with Antony.

"How could you? I told you how to avoid getting a girl pregnant. You can't afford to take care of yourself. How are you going to take care of her and a baby?" There were too many problems to deal with at once. Aria. My withdrawals. Penn. The smog. Scourge. Unfortunately for Antony, he took the brunt of my pent-up rage and fears I had been sleeping on for two days.

He scurried off the bed with a look of horror. "It wasn't me! She was like that when I met her. I am like you and Aria…" He blushed and turned away.

I should not have laughed at Antony. He scowled and stomped toward the door, but I laughed at more than the bizarre timing of his proclamation. I couldn't contain it, and soon I was curled up, laughing, crying, and twitching as the weight of all my emotions unleashed. Antony stared at me like I was a madwoman. Maybe I was. But laughing felt better than screaming.

"Are you saying you're a lesbian?"

He threw a pillow at my head and collapsed beside me, joining my fit of giggles. I wondered what emotions he released. Did he know his brother was dead? Was he happy about it?

"Her name is Annie. I met her a couple weeks ago. She had nowhere to go the other night, so I invited her to come with me. I knew you and Aria wouldn't mind. But Aria never came, and I was going to look for her at Shelly's, but the smog got to Tenth Street—"

"*Tenth Street?*" My jaw dropped. At the rate it was progressing, it would reach the top of the hill in a week or two. And when his smog got to First Street, who knew what Scourge would do.

"It was outside our window last night." Antony peeked over his shoulder. I sat up and looked out the window above my bed with him. Grime usually coated the pane on the exterior, but an additional layer of gunk stuck to it now.

I slid back onto the mattress as a sudden, sharp pain in my side had me writhing. Flashes of memories from Halle's House of Blessings spun through my mind.

The moment I heard Aria's whimper.

The brain matter of that thug falling into my mouth.

Aria's fingers in my mouth, forcing me to consume twitch.

"Annie, she needs help!" Antony cried for his friend as he tried to steady me. I thrashed and screamed between visions.

The first whiff of smog. How it clogged my throat.

You've always protected me from life and death.

Aria reaching into Xavier's chest and pulling out his heart.

I am not afraid of Scourge.

"Easy now, drink this." Annie held a mug to my lips. One sip of the spicy tea, and my muscles and mind relaxed.

"That's twitch," I said.

Annie nodded. "Just a little bit. Enough to stop the tremors and bad thoughts."

She told me her mother was a nurse at a sanctuary on Twenty-First Street. She had been helping twitch addicts at the bottom of the hill since before Scourge appeared. Her mother made the revelation that a person could not be poisoned by the smog as long as they were on twitch. In the early days of the smog, many people were convinced that like called to like, and because addicts could spend a night in the poisonous fog seemingly unscathed, they must have been wretched and dirty as well. But Annie's mother realized twitch was not a curse, it was a cure.

She hadn't seen or heard from her in three months. When the trolley stopped running and the postal service stopped delivering below Twentieth Street, they were cut off from everyone living on Nineteenth and above.

"Is it true the smog corrupts them?" I asked. Rumors about people who got caught in it without twitch spread like wildfire throughout Toltana. Tales of cannibalism and savagery. Stories about turf war and torture. Descriptions of how they clustered together near the river during the day, then wandered aimlessly at night. Accounts varied, but we knew one thing for a fact: once you were poisoned by it, you could never leave the smog. Fresh air became a venom to your lungs.

"I don't know what the smog does to them. They tend to stay between Twentieth and the river, even though they have at least ten more blocks they could come up when the smog is thick." Annie rested a hand on her womb and sighed. I wondered if the father was stuck at the bottom of the hill with her mother. I thought about Aria and hoped she had found her way to them. They seemed like they would help her.

"There's something else." Antony handed me a folded note.

Come see me as soon as you wake up.
  -L.P.

By signing here, you agree to this contract's terms as described, as well as any amendments deemed necessary by the employer, Luther D. Penn.

For how much blood he had on his hands, Luther Penn was a docile man. Average height, slim frame, unremarkable face. But his voice would haunt you the rest of your days. I still hear it echoing in the back of my mind. It scratches the walls of my memories on good days, reminding me of a debt I never returned. I fear I may never be free from him, not even in death.

Penn's office was located on Seventh Street. Close enough to the wealthy families at the top of the hill but still in the midst of the middle class who did all his peddling. He had a suite on the top floor of a seven-story building—the tallest in Toltana. From there, he watched over his domain. The governor, council members, enforcers... none of them mattered. There was only one who had more influence in the city, and he was a monster contained to as far as the smog reached. If Penn worried about Scourge reaching him, he didn't let it show.

"I saw him!" I said. Penn declined to look up from his newspaper.

"Yes, yes. You and everyone else on Fourteenth Street." He shoved the paper toward me. The front page featured quotes from people who had seen him.

Taller than the houses. Correct. The brief glimpse I got was of his head towering over the buildings. But as I thought about it, perhaps that was an illusion. He was walking uphill as I was looking down. That would have made him look taller.

Eight legs like a spider. I couldn't agree with that. I never saw his legs, but I heard his footsteps. They were slow, like two long limbs dragging his feet along the street.

Translucent skin. Absolutely not. I would have remembered that.

"Everyone describes him differently." I scanned the page, eager to satisfy

Penn's irksome requirement for small talk before getting down to business. Whatever emotions he tried to stir by stalling, I would not give them to him.

"Why do you suppose that is?" he asked.

Seated across from him at his desk, I shoved my hands under my thighs, a miserable attempt to hide the twitching. "The smog plays tricks on your mind."

"Quite the contrary. The smog shows us the truth. It is a consequence of the truth." He poured a cup of tea, then tore a small piece off the end of a twitch leaf and crumbled it over the mug. He stirred it with his finger and slid the drink toward me. "Drink."

That sharp pain in my side returned as I recalled how Aria had made the same demand. The mug trembled in my hand as I brought it to my lips, tea spilling over the side and staining my khaki trousers. I drank it all in a few big gulps, then relaxed into the seat. The pain subsided, replaced by a feeling of euphoria. That lasted for no more than a second. When I saw Penn's smirk, I remembered where I was.

"Xavier tried to rob me. Send one of your scouts to Halle's. They'll find his body along with Claudia and one of the brutes you recruited last month."

"There would be no need. I believe you." He leaned back in his chair and crossed one leg over the other. I arched a brow, trying to determine what game he wanted to play.

"You knew." It dawned on me when Penn took a bite of one of the gourmet chocolates he always had on his desk. The man could never be bothered by anything. His office was a throne room tucked safely away from the battles he waged in the streets. "You sent Xavier to rob me."

"Careful, Winnifred. You don't have much leverage in this situation." Penn licked his fingers and stared me down.

I stood up and slammed the cord with my name tag on the desk. "I did what you ordered. I took the twitch to Halle's. Now give me back my blood."

He jerked forward and snatched my wrist. "Not as quick as you usually are," he said as I tried to pull away. "You've lost some of your strength as well. I had been told the leaf was not affecting you, but there are other side effects beside twitching. Tell me, what did you dream about during your recovery?"

I had dreamed about Aria hiding in an alley, sleeping with the rats and begging for scraps. She cried until her tears ran out. Each night she wandered up the hill as far as she could make it before the smog thinned out and she couldn't breathe.

I had a dream about what I'd do when I found her. Aria would have to take twitch for the rest of her life. We could never leave Toltana—the leaf only grew here. We had enough savings for a month or so. If all my earnings went to Penn and Aria was too sick to work, I would be forced to borrow from Penn.

"I dreamed that you gave me my blood and then I never saw you again." Sweat formed on my brow, another convulsion threatening to surface. I'd be on the floor pissing and throwing up if Penn did not let me go soon. He followed my gaze to my empty mug.

"I'll give you a discount," he said with a smug grin.

"You bastard! This is your fault. You did this to me!" I swiped at him across the desk. I would have clawed his eyes out, but he shoved me down and pressed his arm into the back of my neck, then crouched and brought his face inches away from mine.

"You have two options. Pay your debt willingly, or I force you." He opened the top drawer and withdrew a vial.

My blood.

"Please," I moaned and reached for it. He pressed into my neck more, cutting off my airway as I kicked and flailed.

"I have never lied to you, Winnifred. Our arrangement still stands. Settle your debt, and you can have it back." Finally, he released me. I gasped and slid off the desk, collapsing to the floor.

"How much do I owe?" Everything hurt from my neck to my toes.

He took his time walking around the desk, then stood over me. "Halle had agreed to twenty platinum coins, but for you, I will settle for eighteen."

No. That was more than I had owed when he bailed me out of prison. It was twice as much as Aria and I had been saving up for three years. I had sworn I'd never cry in front of him, but my despair could not be contained. I wiped a tear and stared up at him, hoping that maybe any humanity he had left might empathize with me.

"Eighteen platinum, plus the remaining ten gold coins from your bail." The asshole smiled wider than I'd ever seen.

"Xavier killed Halle. Wait until her clients and everyone in the neighborhood finds out. They'll have your head on a spike," I seethed.

"And Aria killed Xavier."

"Because he was trying to kill *me*! He forced Antony to drink his blood—"

"If you don't calm down, I will make a snack out of your blood." Penn grabbed the vial and removed the stopper, tilting it toward his lips. Time froze. I forced myself to be rational. If he wanted to risk binding me to him, he would have done it by now. I think he always knew I would kill myself if he did. I'd sacrifice myself and take him down with me.

"What are you going to do when Scourge gets to the top of the hill?" I whispered. Penn set the vial down. "What will happen to you when he reaches the temple?"

"We will find out soon enough." He looked over his shoulder out the window, where a crowd had gathered in the plaza across the street. Execution day.

"You will die a slow and miserable death." I winced as I stood up. My blood would stay with Penn, but I retrieved my name tag. At least I could keep something.

"Likely so, but not today. Take my advice, Winnifred, and worry about today."

I scoffed and turned toward the door.

"I have a job for you."

"Not today." Antony was waiting for me outside. I had to check on Shelly. I wanted to see what I could find at Halle's. And I needed to plan for how I'd rescue Aria.

"You'd do well to remember who is in charge here." Penn picked up my blood again.

What choice did I have? Penn and I would play this game forever. Next time I was close to paying him back, he'd find a way to trap me into remaining in his service.

"Visit Father Marcus. He is too far behind on payments." Penn wasn't going to make this easy for me. "I want him dead."

The boss stepped up and placed half a dozen twitch leaves in my hand. "My treat."

MISSING: Aria Stewart.
Thirty-two years of age.
Approx. five feet three inches, stout.
Dark blonde hair, hazel eyes, pale skin.

The poster was all wrong. Aria is five feet four inches. I would have described her as soft—the right amount of flesh to protect every part of her, and there is no part I cannot cuddle and hold on to. "Dark blonde" doesn't do her hair justice. It is the color of coffee with the perfect amount of cream, the kind where you take a sip and know it will be a good day. She corrects anyone who says her eyes are hazel—they are grey. She isn't pale. Her skin is fair enough that she burns in the sun, but moonlight suits her.

I would have mentioned the tiny scar Aria has to the right of her mouth and how it lines up with the tip of her brow when she smiles. How I like to count the seconds they stay lined up. The longest she has smiled is seven seconds, and it was after the first time she said she loved me. The memory of that smile carried me through the hours we were separated.

Half the city must have gathered in the square to watch the hangings. A young couple who had tried to break into a pharmacy. The elderly man who hired them to steal the medicine. His wife, who needed it. Four bodies hanging from the gallows as a horrified crowd gawked.

"When did they start arresting people for thievery again?" Antony asked.

When I was a kid, I had to hide from enforcers posted on every block. They'd chase people down for the smallest infraction and either toss them in prison or beat them in the middle of the street. When the smog began, they were quick to abandon the fallen blocks. It wasn't long before blocks that hadn't been touched by smog became a land of lawlessness as well. Sometimes, a few unfortunate enforcers got assigned to patrol streets downhill for smugglers and twitch users, but I hadn't seen any in weeks. Why should the government risk their dwindling crew of law enforcers when there was a terrible monster and poisonous fog that would take care of the riffraff?

"They tried to break into a place on Third Street," Annie said. Far enough away from the smog and in a wealthy neighborhood, where the enforcers still enforced things. Annie couldn't peel her eyes away from the bodies. I gripped her shoulders and turned her around.

"How are you feeling?" she asked me.

"I'm alright," I lied. The tea I drank in Penn's office had worn off, and every time I lifted my feet to step forward, they twitched before coming back to the ground. A dull headache formed behind my eyes. It would be throbbing before I got back to my room, but I still had to go to Shelly's tavern and Halle's House of Blessings.

We moved with the crowd downhill. The mid-morning sun was already sweltering, cooking up all the filth that coated the city. I think the reason why the stench of Toltana bothered me after thirty-five years of living here was because I refused to get used to it. I never wanted to become one of those people who didn't smell the filth and grime.

"You should rest. I'll go to Halle's and stop by Shelly's on my way back." Antony squeezed my hand when he noticed how my arm jerked.

"I don't want you going down there. The smog might still linger," I said. There had been whispers of how it did not completely disappear during the daylight. And I didn't want him to see his brother's mutilated body.

Antony squeezed my hand again. "Let me help you. I would have died a dozen times already if it weren't for you and Aria. I want to get her back, too. I know she'd come for me."

Before I could insist that Antony stay in the room, a man climbed to the top of a light pole up ahead. He swung his legs over the lateral rods and banged a wooden spoon against a pot. "Repent! Repent! Scourge is coming, but it's not too late. The goddess loves you. Let her save you. Repent and open your heart to her."

I muttered a curse and looped my arms between Antony and Annie's elbows. This crowd was already riled up from the executions, and I did not want to get stuck in the mob that would form if this fanatic didn't shut up.

"Repent! Don't fear the poisoned mist or its master. Let the goddess claim you and protect you from Scourge."

Their definition of repentance was bleeding into a fountain in the temple on First Street. They believed that when the goddess came to Toltana, she would go straight there and drink it all up, that everyone whose blood she tasted would be spared. If the wrong person gained access to that fountain and took even one sip, who knows how many people they would bind to them. I stayed far away from that place. It felt haunted, like desperate people had left behind their last hope.

Someone threw a stone at the man on the lamppost. Someone else shook it. Antony, Annie, and I were caught in the middle of a sea of people. I pulled us forward, battling against the current. We turned at the next corner a moment before the enforcers showed up where the man had fallen from the lamp. Shots fired into the air as the enforcers ordered everyone to clear the area. But where could they go? Many of those people had come up here seeking refuge from the smog. Every boarding house and inn was full, and unless they wanted to bleed into that fountain, the temple would not shelter them.

"Antony," I panted when we finally reached a quiet area to catch our breaths. "Go now. See if you can find anything at Halle's. Then tell Shelly I'm awake but won't be there tonight."

"Where are you going?" He draped my arm over his shoulder as we finished walking to the boarding house.

"To the temple." I sat on the bottom step once we got inside and withdrew the twitch Penn had given me. Six leaves. If I was careful, that would last me a couple days, at least. Antony said something else, but I wasn't listening. I wanted so badly to shove all six into my mouth, but I only needed a taste to get through the tremors.

I'd need a lot more to get through the smog.

The goddess made you. She filled you up with her own blood and sent you here for a reason. Who are we to question her? All she asks is that we trust her, that we believe in her love and mercy.
All she requires is a little cut.

Father Marcus was a teacher at the orphanage before he became a priest. He taught me how to read and instilled my love for stories. He was full of tales about monsters and heroes, magic and mayhem, and history. My favorite was about an orphan who ran away and joined the circus, discovered they had magic, and saved the kingdom from a terrible dragon. When Marcus left to join the temple, I left to find a circus. Instead, I found a crew of smugglers and discovered my knack for sneaking in and out of places, and I didn't care about saving anyone but myself.

I wonder if Father Marcus found what he was looking for. For a long time, I was angry at him for leaving, but now I understand. Some of us believe in stories so much they feel real, and it isn't until we've lost everything that we realize we were wrong.

"Oh, Winnie, you look frightful."

I did not correct Father Marcus for calling me Winnie. He was the only person I didn't mind using the nickname, and it felt good hearing it. I felt like I was a girl again, sitting at his feet and listening to one of his stories. For a moment, I felt safe. Then I remembered why I was there.

The temple was the oldest building in Toltana, a behemoth of a structure at the top of the hill. It consisted of one cavernous chamber that could fit a thousand people or more and a few smaller rooms off to the side for meditation. The priests and priestesses lived in the back wing, never leaving, always watching over the blood.

I met Marcus at the fountain in the center of the main chamber. A dozen others strolled around, everyone speaking in whispers, as if too much noise might summon something terrible. Gooseflesh formed on my arms, and I tried not to fidget when Marcus motioned for me to sit next to him on the fountain.

It was unnatural how the blood flowed and sprayed from the marble rose. How much blood was there? How many people had cut themselves on the spikes and bled into the pool? My mouth tasted like copper. My muscles tensed up, like my body begged me to flee. But the temple was perhaps the only clean public area in the entire city. The marble floors sparkled under faint ceiling lights, the grout between tiles on the wall was pure white, and the blood certainly didn't smell good, but at least it didn't stink.

"What brings you here?" Marcus placed a hand over mine. He already knew why I came—I could see it in his eyes.

"Why don't you let the families who have been displaced from the bottom of the hill stay here?" I stalled.

"Is that really what you'd like to know?" He tilted his head. I nodded. "Do you remember the story about the fish who got lost?"

Yes, it was a favorite bedtime story in the orphanage. One day, a young fish did not listen to his mother's instructions and wandered away from the school. When he realized he was lost, he asked an octopus for help. The octopus said she would help in exchange for one of the fish's scales. Horrified, he swam away and found a turtle. The turtle wanted two scales. Then the fish met a shark who demanded three scales. Realizing he had to make a sacrifice if he wanted to find his mother, he returned to the octopus and agreed to give her one scale. But the octopus said it was too late, his mother had already come through there. When the fish asked if she told her she'd seen him, the octopus said why would she have helped him if he didn't trust her? The turtle laughed in the little fish's face when he returned, and the shark gobbled him up.

"Those families are like the lost fish," I mumbled more to myself than to Marcus.

"They had their chance. They thought a small blood sacrifice was too much, and now it's too late. Our first obligation is to protect the blood, and we cannot do that if people are living here." He sounded clinical, like he was talking about characters in one of his stories and not real people.

"There was a man at the plaza telling everyone they still had time to repent," I argued. I loved Father Marcus. I wanted to believe he was the same compassionate man who raised me, but his apathetic approach to people who had fled from Scourge terrified me. What had happened to him?

He sighed and trailed his fingers across the surface of the pool. Of the blood. I inched away from him.

"People can still come and make their sacrifice, but they'll have to find somewhere else to stay or return home. If they trust in the goddess, if their sacrifice is genuine, they wouldn't worry about such things."

"*Such things?*" My jaw dropped. "Things such as food and shelter?"

"Don't be so surprised. You've heard it all before. Everyone in Toltana has. More people chose not to believe it and chose not to trust in the goddess until now. Now it's obvious how much we need her, and she still asks for so little. Today, food and shelter seem like a crisis. How many more days until the smog reaches the top of the hill, when everyone is displaced? That's when the goddess will return—when we need her the most."

I wanted to scream. I wanted to shove him into the fountain. I wanted to burn the temple down.

"Penn sent me to kill you. Will the goddess protect you from my bullet?" I reached for my revolver on my hip.

Marcus smiled and scooted closer. "My dear, I've been waiting for Luther.
"

I withdrew the gun and pressed the barrel into his chest. No one else in the room seemed to notice or care. "I don't want to kill you."

Father Marcus had supplied twitch leaves to countless people who needed it most. When it had been banned a few years prior, he coordinated his own network of smugglers to deliver it to anyone sleeping on the streets where the smog rose, and higher up, addicts who wanted to quit. A person couldn't simply stop taking it—the convulsions would turn to deadly seizures. I had come close to experiencing that myself after taking just one leaf. Many people were suspicious of how the temple spent the money it received from donations, but I was aware of how much twitch they bought. They were Penn's biggest customer, and they did more to protect citizens from the smog than the government.

"Help me kill Penn," I said. Marcus took my hand and pulled me up. He led me to one of the meditation rooms.

"What I'm about to tell you is a secret. You cannot share it with anyone." He helped me lie down on a plush sofa as my entire body trembled. I started to take a leaf out of my satchel, but Marcus stopped me. "Enough of that. I have something better." He removed a vial from a cabinet in the corner and handed it to me.

"Clarity?" I held it up to the light. He could not expect me to drink it. The potion worked for blocking smog from seeping inside, but it was made from mud and river water that came from where the smog originated. From Scourge's home. He retreated to the river during the day, hiding under the water and waiting for the sun to go down to reemerge and retry his attempt to get to the top of the hill.

Marcus shook his head. "It's not clarity. This is made from mud and river water from upstream. It's clean. And not for drinking." He dampened a scarf with the concoction and held it over my mouth. At first, I thought he was trying to smother me. But after a deep breath, the tremors subsided, and I relaxed into the cushions. "Wear the scarf on your face when you enter the smog. It will protect you. Your partner will need more. I suggest she keep a scarf over her face for a couple days as the poison leaves her body, but she should make a full recovery." He tucked the bottle into my satchel.

"How do you know about Aria?"

"Luther Penn is not the only man with spies." Marcus winked.

"What are you going to do about him? If I don't kill you, he will come up here and do it himself."

"He's coming up here tonight regardless of whether or not you put me down. But we will make him believe you followed his orders." Marcus returned to the cabinet and took a pair of large garden shears. He handed them to me. "Cut my hair."

I didn't question him. The long ponytail he had been growing since he left the orphanage fell from his head with one snip. I stowed it away in my satchel and would take it to Penn as soon as I finished up in the temple. Let him believe I had killed the priest.

"He has a private service with his men on the tenth night each month. I'll stay in this room, out of sight. On your way out, I need you to give this to Cal," Marcus said as he scribbled a frantic note. "He's the young priest standing at the door. These are special instructions for how to prepare the wine."

I nodded and accepted the note. He wrapped his fingers around my wrist and held me tenderly, staring into my eyes with all the compassion I remembered as a girl. He made me question everything. Maybe he was right. Maybe I should make a blood sacrifice before I left.

"You could save yourself and Aria," he said. My gut twisted. How could he know? I hadn't told anyone I drank her blood, not even Antony. "If you're going to do it, do it now," he said, squeezing my hand.

"Why do you say that?" I whispered.

"Because I love you and I want you to be saved."

I hurried out of there before Marcus scared me into doing something I'd regret. I wouldn't be sacrificing only myself. I had to think about Aria as well. *You don't believe in the goddess...* I said to myself over and over as I ran to the front door. I shoved the note into Cal's hand and kept running to the boarding house. I didn't know where Father Marcus got the concoction he had saturated the scarf with, but whatever it was, it worked. When I got back to the room, my vision was clear, and I felt no symptoms of a pending convulsion.

"Get ready," I told Antony and Annie. "It's going to be a long night."

Father Marcus was right. Food and shelter became the least of our worries.

News of Penn's death spread quickly. A touch of nightshade, and suddenly everyone who reported to him was free. Everyone who had feared him was safe. The atmosphere throughout Toltana shifted between relief and uneasiness. The temple had wiped out Penn's entire leadership and left the streets unguarded. What happens when a city is finally released from under the thumb of their oppressor? Well, in this city, they rioted.

They smashed the lobby windows as Antony and I got our weapons ready. My revolver and dagger for me, an ax for him. Annie would stay in the room preparing bandages and medical necessities. "Do not open this door for anyone but me or Antony," I ordered her. She nodded and caressed her belly. I got out of there before the guilt of leaving a heavily pregnant teenager alone in a boarding house currently under siege overwhelmed me.

"Go to the temple. I'm sure Father Marcus could use your help," I said to Antony when we got outside. Penn's warehouse across the street had already been pilfered, men fighting to the death over packages of twitch, weapons, and money. Two blocks down, the ghost lab burned, its fire quickly spreading to every building on the block. One street up, a mob was stringing up a crew of enforcers from the streetlights. At this rate, we would destroy ourselves before Scourge made it up here. We had about an hour left of daylight, and then we'd be helpless against the smog. I gave Antony a twitch leaf. "Take this only if it's your last option. Don't let anyone steal it from you, understand? Kill anyone who tries to hurt you. Tonight, the only rule is to stay alive." He hugged me, then ran up the hill. I watched him disappear into the crowd, hoping he would make it and that Father Marcus would let him inside.

I prepared my face covering, pouring just enough of Marcus's potion over the scarf, and tucked it into the breast pocket of my cloak. My gun stayed in my hand. And then I ran down the hill.

. . .

The block where Halle's House of Blessings was located was deserted. I sensed no sign of smog yet, but I imagined everyone had relocated up the hill out of fear it wouldn't go away one morning and they'd be trapped. Houses had been broken into, carts lay in pieces in the street, and I passed at least three bodies that had been thrown into the gutter. The difference between just a couple streets was astounding. This was what all of Toltana would become: a wasteland. I had to find Aria and get out of the city. I had no idea where we would go or how we'd get there. My plan was for her and me to leave with Antony and Annie. Travel would be difficult for the girl, but if we were quick, maybe we could catch one of the last ships.

Someone had boarded up the front door of Halle's. Wilted flower bouquets decorated the path leading up to the shop. I hoped I wouldn't have to see her. The night she died, everything happened so fast and in the dark that I never saw her body. Fortunately for me, Halle and the others had already been cleaned up. Blood stained the floor where Aria had carved open Xavier. Just above where the puddle had been, a note was written in his blood.

Come to the place where we first met.

I hadn't been to Lavender Park in over a year. It was right along the river and one of the first places we considered lost when the smog got bad. I took off immediately toward the river, imagining every terrible scenario possible. Why would Aria go there? You couldn't get much closer to Scourge's domain than Lavender Park. But when I arrived, the scene was further than anything I could have imagined.

Hundreds of people scurried about, preparing what looked like giant cannons. Tents were set up to provide food and medical care. Even children ran throughout the crowd, chasing each other or carrying things for the adults. They weren't the lost, wandering husks of people I had been expecting. These people were alive, maybe even more so than everyone toward the top of the hill.

It was the potion Father Marcus had given me. They had it too. Everyone kept their scarves over their mouth and nose, protected from the wisps of smog that were forming. It wasn't thick enough for Scourge to come out, but I saw how calmly and efficiently they worked, and I knew they would be safe once the smog did become thick enough to poison them.

I had so many questions. Why didn't everyone in Toltana know about this special potion? There was no need for anyone to take twitch, not when we had this clean version of clarity. Why did all these people stay down here, so close to Scourge? My head spun, but I couldn't think about those things. I had to find Aria. Maybe our face coverings would protect us from the smog, but I had seen Scourge, and his giant feet could squash a person. His long arms could grab you and launch you three blocks away.

I zigzagged through the crowd, checking every face, peeking in every tent, and asking everyone who would listen if they had seen Aria. Finally, someone pointed me to a cart near the library. My body begged for rest, but I couldn't, not when I was so close.

"Winnifred!" Her voice carried over the sounds of everyone hustling about. We ran to each other, then met in the street and collapsed to the ground.

"I'm sorry I couldn't come sooner," I sobbed between kisses.

"It's okay," she said, cupping my face. "I'm okay."

I scanned her for any injuries, but it was true. She seemed fine.

"I'm sorry I couldn't come to you." She helped me off the ground and pulled me toward her cart. "After you left, I tried to get uphill. I only made it two blocks before I passed out. Then I woke up down here, and I wanted to tell you I was safe, but we had to keep this operation a secret."

"Quite an operation you've got here." I spun around, trying to understand everything around me. I couldn't believe it. They were preparing an army. "All of this has been going on since they closed the block?"

Aria explained that they had been getting ready for battle for six months, when someone had smuggled the first bottle of Father Marcus's potion to them. They sent people out only to gather more ingredients for it. Everything else, they had available near the river.

"We're taking down Scourge. It ends tonight." The ferocity in her eyes terrified me. I had never seen her wear such an expression. I tugged her arm, but her feet were planted to the ground.

"You've done enough. We need to leave. Now." The smog had thickened in the few minutes we'd been reunited, and the river rose over the docks.

"Will you let me protect you just this once?" She kissed my knuckles. No fair, that was my move.

I opened my mouth to argue, but the ground began to shake.

"Scourge?" I whispered.

"No, that was something else." Aria looked around. Everyone else was equally uncertain. A disturbing silence fell over the park, followed by another tremor.

"Father Marcus," I said. "The fountain."

Sometimes, monsters are not the most terrifying creatures.

It's been twenty years since Scourge fell. At this point, I have heard so many accounts of what happened that night, I often question if my memory is accurate or if it has been skewed by what someone else said. I don't think we misrepresent our stories on purpose, but how can we know with certainty who is telling the truth? Is it considered lying if we forget a detail or misremember something? That's why I waited twenty years to share my experience. Every time I tried, the anxiety of saying something wrong and leading people astray stopped me.

So here is the part you've been waiting for. Now that you know what happened in the days before the battle, I hope you understand that we were at battle with more than a monster. Scourge can never return, but the men and oppression we tackled before going up against Scourge? I already see the seeds of their return. Be aware—they will not be as obvious as a giant, insidious monster, or poisonous smog.

Aria and I made it ten blocks uphill before we had to rest. Behind us, the crowd shoved carts full of guns and ammo, swords and people. They took turns pushing and riding, everyone trying to beat Scourge to First Street. He trailed a couple blocks behind them, his stomps echoing throughout the city.

"You have to keep going. I need to help with the harpoon cannons," Aria said.

"*Harpoon cannons?*" I pulled her with me as I continued my ascent. Whatever this group was planning, I definitely did not want her near any harpoon cannons.

"You will be more useful in the temple. Father Marcus will listen to you. Let us deal with Scourge. We are ready for him."

As if on cue, he roared from the pit of his stomach, a deep, terrifying sound I felt in my bones. No, no, no. Aria wasn't going anywhere near him. After everything I did for us—the years of assignments from Penn and then facilitating his murder—I was not going to lose her when we were so close to escaping.

Another roar, this one even worse. I looked toward the source, and there he was. Scourge, towering over the buildings as he slowly moved uphill. His arms were almost as long as his legs, and he alternated between walking on all fours and standing upright, swinging his arms and smashing the structures he passed by. The smog followed him, leaving a trail so thick behind him I couldn't see anything more than a block behind us.

Aria grabbed me by the shoulders and forced me to face her. "You will go uphill, and I go down."

"Downhill? What are you going downhill for? *He* is downhill!" I tried again to drag her with me, but she pulled her hand out of mine.

"The harpoons. They'll only work if we fire from below him. When he gets to the top of the hill where it's steepest, that's when we fire. You need to clear the area. If anyone is in the temple, they need to evacuate. Now!"

"Aria." I begged her to come with me. We had only been reunited for a few minutes. How could I leave her so soon?

"I am not afraid. I'm not afraid for myself or for you. We've survived so much. It won't end here. You and I are going to make it through the night, and then we are going to live the kind of life we've always deserved, and when we are old ladies, we'll remember this moment and be thankful we were brave. Because if you don't get to the temple right now, something more terrible than Scourge could kill us all."

She pulled in for a kiss before I could argue, before I could ask what she knew. Father Marcus had implied something similar, that Scourge wasn't the worst that could happen. I shoved the thought out of my mind and kissed Aria back, savoring as much as I could, drawing from her as much courage as she could give me. She started moving away, but I wasn't ready to let go.

"I think you're the one who will have to beg for forgiveness." I held her tight for a second before Scourge released another roar upon us.

"Deal," Aria said, then took off down the hill.

When I reached the temple, it was empty. It had been turned into a ruin, with the fountain destroyed and all that blood flooding the chamber, but only a few people patrolled. A few people and bodies—so many bodies.

"Winnie!"

I jolted my head toward the back wing, hoping to see Father Marcus, but it was Antony. He was covered in blood and limped toward me.

"It's not my blood," he said when I met him in the middle of the room.

"Where is Marcus?" I scanned the area. Antony nodded to the fountain, and there was Marcus, a crumpled corpse lying under the rose where blood had once flowed.

"He had a vial of Scourge's blood," Antony said.

Oh, Marcus. I wish he would have told me. If I had known that's what he wanted from Penn, I would have found another way to kill him.

"He drank it?" I asked. Antony nodded and held up his ax. Blood coated the blade. He dropped it and fell into me, sobbing into my shoulder and shaking until we both sank to the floor. I couldn't comfort him or tell him he did the right thing, that I would have cut Marcus down if he drank Scourge's blood in front of me, because the earth shook so violently, dust rained down on us from the ceiling. The monster's roar was deafening even inside the building. He could not have been more than a couple blocks away.

"We have to get out of here." I pulled Antony up and ran into the street.

Scourge had made it to the temple, but Aria and the rest of the army got there just in time. They fired their harpoons into his back, dragging him back down the hill as he thrashed and swung his arms, smashing buildings and shattering the pavement.

The people who thought they were safe at the top of the hill were the ones who lost the most. Scourge tried to resist the blades and bullets, but all those people who had been trapped by his smog attacked him like an army of ants, hoarding and pulling him down. When he collapsed onto his belly, they sliced into every inch of his flesh, spilling out all his blood even after he finally died.

His blood dribbled down the hill, mixing with the usual filth of Toltana and carrying it to the river.

Went to the market. You'll probably still be asleep when I return and never see this note.
But anyway, I love you.
-A

Settling into a quiet life is one of the hardest things I've ever done. I had never known what it was like to sleep in, to not have work or to have a quiet bed worth staying in. Aria and I argued a lot in the beginning, mostly over silly things. I wanted to stay home, but she wanted to go out. She wanted a blue quilt, but I wanted tan. It was the first time we *could* argue about silly things, and so we squabbled over everything.

We got the feather-stuffed mattress we had always wanted and hated it. It unsettled me how I could sleep so soundly on it, how I wouldn't hear if there was danger. But we agreed to keep it for a few more months and try to get used to it since it was such a pain getting up to our room.

We stayed in Toltana. We own the boarding house now and live on the top floor. Antony and his partner are here, too, as well as Annie and her family. Scourge's destruction allowed us an opportunity to rebuild, and we decided to try something new. Before, life was everyone for themselves. Now, we live in communities and support each other. It's the kind of life I always wanted but was scared to dream about, and sometimes, I'm scared it could all be taken away. But for now, we are safe. When I hear whispers of misguided religious orders and crime bosses, I'm glad my story is finally written down and that it can be remembered long after I'm gone.

About the Author

E. Milee writes stories about women who would go through hell and back for each other. She lives in the Midwest with her cat, in an apartment that may or may not be haunted. When she's not writing, you can find her curled up peacefully with a book or kicking and screaming in front of the TV over a video game.

twitter.com/writtenbyemilee

instagram.com/writtenbyemilee

LORD OF WEBS AND WHISPERS

FAE COURT OF CASAKRAINE #3

Lord of Webs and Whispers

ALISYN FAE

Heat level:
Hot

Content Warnings:
Kidnapping, coercive breeding, violence, frank discussion of SA.

Chapter One

GAREN

A truce.

A truce by blood or seed.

Was the female mad? Had the High Lord of Casakraine city tripped over the invisible demarcation between powerful High Fae into insane Old One?

A truce, by my ass.

"You object, Lord Garen," Lord Issahelle said in her cool voice, not bothering to turn. Or to make it a question.

On my knees in the mud, I eyed the vicious monsters she cooed at and petted as she fed them bits of still quivering flesh.

I searched my mind for the correct response, as I had no intention of becoming swan fodder. I'd been House Lord of Anteyan for a trifling quarter century, my rise due to the deaths of Lords stronger and more powerful than I.

But not cannier. They'd perished; I'd survived.

I would not die by bird.

I inclined my head, expression pleasant, posture complacent. Issahelle liked her males pretty and cooperative—I offered her what she wanted.

"No, Lord. I have no objection." I wasn't an idiot.

Unlike the male at my side.

Lord Narazah seethed, his twitching shoulders a disgrace. Despite being several hundred years my elder, he couldn't control his reactions—he would be dead in another few centuries. I was amazed the fool had survived this long; but then, he sent his warriors to die in his stead. I fought beside mine, though I'd come reluctantly to the role of warrior and High Lord.

I fought because the insult to my halfling cousin would not be borne by my House and the only option besides war was annihilation. House Anteyan hadn't asked for a blood feud, but we were Fae. We'd answered the call.

Consign Narazah Gisleyan, and every blight in the realm that carried his bloodline, to the Darkness.

"I serve," Narazah said through gritted teeth.

I knew better than to show my derision. Even base pretense was beyond him. Any random faeling yanked off the streets would possess better acting abilities. A five-year-old human could obsfucate with more conviction.

Lord Issahelle set down the small wooden pail of swan feed and turned to us, her fingertips bloody.

She was an exquisite female. Tall, dark of hair and blue-gray of eye, a countenance that could morph from maternal to chilly faster than the fleeting thought it might take her to end one's life.

Her Heir bothered with the majority of the day-to-day rule of Casakraine city these days—she called it training rather than her retirement—but at times she stirred herself to take matters into her own hands.

I thought fleetingly of a distant cousin, Constin, a Sahakian Casakraine vassal and favorite of the Heir Andreien and his consort. I'd let the relationship lapse, and that wasn't the soundest strategic decision.

One of the swans wandered too close. I didn't twitch; it was hard. On the other hand, maybe it would pay dividends to befriend the monsters.

I smiled at it as if I found it as adorable as a kitten or a plump, well-read mortal, remaining still as it stepped closer.

Maybe when this was all done, I'd pursue a career in theater rather than resume the diplomat's path I'd left behind because of this feud.

"So which is it to be, my Lords?" Issahelle asked. "I'm in the mood for a quiet century or two now that my son has settled into his bonded life, and you two are among the loose threads I must tie—or snip."

Yes, because this infernal idiot, Narazah, had struck and killed one of her mortal dancers during a strike against several of my warriors. She hadn't remembered we were feuding before that incident. That it had been unintentional collateral damage didn't matter.

Issahelle was enraged.

But in her anger, she was reasonable enough. We were still alive, after all.

Slowly, I lifted my hand and let the colorless beast peck at my empty palm. Flicking my gaze towards the High Lord, I waited as her brows rose. But she shrugged, and set the bucket of...feed...next to me.

I thought of cheery things—evenings free of damage reports, Maggie reopening her flower shop, Narazah crucified in the middle of Anteyan District square—so the spawn wouldn't scent my revulsion as I began to feed it morsels.

A thorough scrub under my nails would be needful this evening.

"By seed," Narazah said. It had taken him time to come to the conclusion Issahelle desired.

It mystified me how the Darkness granted someone with his lack of even average mental faculties so much power. I didn't resent any longer that Anteyan wasn't a powerful House in terms of our affinities and Skills—clearly, raw power wasn't everything.

We'd had to become powerful enough to survive the last century, my own rise—from private High Fae citizen reputed as a fine negotiator, to House Lord—a startling example of such.

"That pleases me." Issahelle clasped her hands together. "It's been some time since we've had a formal High Court marital alliance. And who shall you offer up to the slaughter?"

It wasn't a jest. The unfortunate bloody end of her own marriage was legend. Another idiot who'd fallen victim to her wrath.

"I have a daughter," Narazah said.

I continued to smile at the...swan. It plucked another morsel from my fingers, eating almost delicately. Issahelle watched us like a mother monitoring a not quite trusted acquaintance with a child. As if I would beg for execution by upsetting the creatures.

If Narazah offered his daughter, I could not insult him or displease Issahelle by offering a male of any lower rank from my own House.

Unfortunately, the majority of my House was comprised of Low Fae youths under five centuries; our Lords had succumbed to the feud and we had not been a robust House prior. I was the only one left, and the responsibility weighed on me.

"I'm the only Lord of Anteyan of suitable standing to wed Gisleyan's Heir," I said.

It took me three seconds to know I had no choice. No, the best strategy would be to tie the marriage contract up in years of negotiations. Maybe the female would die in the interim.

Maybe I would arrange an accident.

...but no, I couldn't do that to Maggie. "Unless the Gisleyen Heir prefers a wife and not a husband." It pained me to abandon subtlety, but needs must.

"My daughter will wed as she is commanded," the blockhead said. "But I believe her preference is for a husband."

This intellectually stymied parasitic one-celled monstrosity didn't know his own daughter. Typical.

I relaxed my jaw into an easy smile, projecting an aura of pleasure. Issahelle eyed me—not fooled, but she would appreciate the effort.

"I would be honored to take Gisleyan's eldest daughter to wife. It is high time I wed."

Because I would be pleased to end this damn feud and return to my life. And because I was in possession of vital facts this kobold-brained lackwit wasn't. I could almost plot strategy for the next three years in the time it took him to struggle through a single concept.

"Excellent," Issahelle said. "I am gratified my Lords are determined to be examples of obedience worthy of the High Court. We must learn to resolve our differences with diplomacy, and not bloodshed."

She paused, frowning a little. She must be taunting me. "Or so my Heir insists. I have told him we will do it his way for a few centuries and compare results." She shrugged. "What can it hurt in the long run? Diplomacy. Such an interesting concept. I used to think all diplomats blathering fools."

She was most assuredly taunting me.

"Well?" my halfling cousin asked as soon as I emerged from Court.

I waited until we were in the coach and a District block away before replying. "A forced truce. The feud is over."

Maggie narrowed her eyes. I mourned the girl she'd been, bright-eyed and able to see the good in everything. But that was the way of our people, to devolve with time and experience.

"How will the High Lord enforce a treaty?" she demanded.

"By marriage."

Her eyes widened and she paled. "Marriage," she stammered. "Whose?"

I leaned forward, taking her hands in mine and squeezed. "I'm sorry, Mag. I'm sorry. But I've been ordered to wed the eldest daughter of House Gisleyan."

She stared at me, eyes disbelieving. "But she can't. You know why you can't."

I squeezed her hands again and released her. "It's not the disaster you think. I'll wed her, and she may do as she wishes." I paused. "Take any lover she wishes. I've no need for monogamy if her lover is loyal to the House."

Maggie closed her eyes briefly then opened them, exhaling. "You'll need an Heir."

"There are methods that don't require contact, if she prefers to shun my bed. The humans are skilled in such things." I arched a brow. "You may even have the consummation."

Maggie lurched forward, grabbing my hands again. "Cousin, we would be in your debt forever."

I smiled at her, my mood lightening. "Everything comes full circle. The bloodshed will end, you will be with your lover and after enough decades have passed you may be with her openly without fear of Narazah's retribution."

She pursed her lips. "Not until after your Heir is born. We'll be safe then."

"You'll be safe now." I kept my voice firm and infused with the hopefulness Maggie had once been known for. Perhaps she'd be known for it again. "Did not I promise when this began everything would be well?"

Her eyes shimmered. They were the most expressive part of her, her eyes. I loved her, and if a part of me had wished. . .no, best not entertain those thoughts.

A simple female, a quiet life of harmless pursuits and intellectual challenges. My dreams were modest.

But despite seven centuries of life, I hadn't been able to achieve them, and now. . .well. I would reframe my thoughts, and paint new dreams. With the feud technically over, there were possibilities to explore.

Technically. The war might be leaving the battlefield, but Anteyan and Gisleyan would always be enemies at Court—bound by marriage or not. But politics was where I was my strongest.

"It's not going to be that easy," she said. "Narazah doesn't give in to anything, and he's a liar."

I took her words to heart. "We will plan. Contact Valyah, discreetly. See what she can tell us. It's in her best interests now to aid us and she doesn't appear to have inherited her father's intellect."

Chapter Two

VALENCIA

Ten months later

I entered my apartment, the walk in a nearby park that was supposed to have been time for productive thought leaving me more frustrated than ever.

It was too cold for the beach, and that always put me into a foul mood. I needed sun and sand, not city streets and chilly breeze.

Tossing my keys on the couch after I shut the door, the jingle of the little self-defense gadgets on the key ring alerted my boyfriend I was home.

Gary appeared in the hallway. "How did it go?"

We'd been living together for four months, and he'd yet to get on my nerves. Mostly because he was a quiet man, kept to himself, and filled his time with harmless pursuits.

He was a unicorn.

When I'd left him for my walk he'd been nose deep in a thousand piece puzzle, a landscape from one of the Fae realms. He let me help from time to time, but I'd learned that he took his puzzles seriously. The few times I'd tried to engage, he'd stepped back and. . .looked at me. Saying nothing.

Gary wielded polite, pointed silence like a poisoned stiletto.

I shrugged and headed into our small kitchen to finish a jug of horchata. "I don't know. I'm still feeling unsettled. This isn't a decision I'm going to be able to make in a few days."

"It's not a decision you have to make in a few weeks," he pointed out, entering behind me and leaning against the counter. "You're in burnout, mi cielo. You're allowed to change careers. Or even take a vacation. When's the last time you had one?"

About twenty years ago?

"I appreciate that you're advocating for my well-being so strongly," I said, pulling the jug of soaking rice, almonds and cinnamon from the fridge to strain. "But you know my concerns."

"You have an overdeveloped sense of responsibility. I understand. It's one of the things I love about you. But your first responsibility is to yourself."

He pulled out my small blender and set it on the counter next to me.

He said all the right things. All the time. When we'd first become friends it had set me on edge because no man in this day and age was that perfect. But my spidey sense hadn't gone off.

My spidey sense always went off in the presence of a threat. Even if it only gave me at max fifteen minutes warning, it never failed me.

No, I'd accepted I was jaded. Owning and managing a women's crisis shelter for the last eighty years, I'd seen too much of the dark side of humanity, and of men in specific. I didn't trust easily, though I understood my perspective wasn't balanced.

He'd helped me with balance in the last several months by being so relentlessly harmless and well-intentioned.

"I do agree with you," I said, adding milk to the mixture and blending some more. "I think we're going to have to accept this decision will take me some time to come to terms with."

Emotionally, I wasn't ready to walk away from the shelter. But I was exhausted.

I needed something different. Something lighthearted, adventurous in a way that didn't involve life and death. The problem was what I needed, and what I thrived on, were often on different sides of a battlefield.

After blending, I added sugar and vanilla and poured into a chilled glass, then faced him. Gary reminded me of a slightly more muscular Cary Elwes, Farm Boy version but a tad more earnest, and more talkative though he could go into long stretches of contemplative silence.

It was one of the things I loved about our relationship. The utter peace of it.

Gary stepped forward and slid an arm around me. I stiffened, a brief instinctive reaction, then relaxed. He leaned his chin on my head as I sipped my drink.

"I arranged a surprise," he said.

I hated surprises, but knowing he was trying to cheer me up, I could endure one for his sake.

"Oh?"

"I booked passage to Casakraine."

I almost choked on my horchata. "You did what?"

Gary pulled away from me a little, looking down with earnest brown eyes. "I hope I didn't overstep. But you've been saying for so long how much you want to travel, and it's one of the cities that's on both of our lists."

He smiled, a tinge of pink on his cheeks. High boned cheeks, the kind of slashing structure that when glimpsed in the right light made me think of ancient sorcerers, and immortal warriors.

"That's. . .so thoughtful of you. Yes, I would like to visit Casakraine. But that's a major expense, Gary. I wish you'd discussed it with me beforehand."

He took the mug out of my hands and set it on the counter. Uncharacteristic of him. Gary was the opposite of take charge, commanding, or forceful. He was almost rabidly cautious of my boundaries.

He lifted my hand to his lips, brushing a kiss against my knuckles.

My abdomen tensed, but not with desire. Not that he wasn't handsome, and attractive, but we didn't have a sexual relationship. I'd assumed he was asexual, and that suited me well enough. A man pleased to call himself my boyfriend with all that entailed, but he wasn't gay—though I wouldn't have cared if he was—and was content with surface physical affection? The king of unicorns.

And he wasn't cheating on me. I had ways of finding out that sort of information. I wasn't the director of a women's shelter without having learning some investigative skills.

Moving him in as a roommate had been a monumental decision, one I hadn't made lightly, but I had trusted him. Our personalities meshed well.

I noted a new tingle of tension, internally hesitated, and slowly set it aside.

"There's another reason I booked the trip," he said.

I smiled. "Because you're a Faeophile and a geek?"

Gary pursed his lips. "I thought that was one of the things you liked about me, Val."

"Oh, it is."

He knew things about the Fae only someone with a lifelong obsession would. It was a relatively harmless hobby. For a man who was so well adjusted, I would have been more suspicious if he hadn't had a few unreasonable obsessions. Me and my Kpop, him and his Fae.

Besides, I'd suspected for decades now I was a halfling.

If being close to twelve decades old but possessing the body of a 30-year-old woman could be considered a mere suspicion.

My mother was long dead though, and her siblings and parents. There was no one left in Spain for me to grill about the circumstances surrounding my birth. She hadn't wanted to talk about my father, and when I'd begun to miss that connection, it was too late. So I was learning about that side of my heritage through Gary.

He tucked some hair behind my ear. "I thought it would be not only a good couple's vacation. . .but an enjoyable honeymoon as well."

It was a good thing I wasn't still holding the horchata.

I stepped out of the arm that felt a little too restraining, increasing the distance between us in a deliberate cue that it was time for us to both step back and do some slow thinking.

"Are you asking me to marry you?" He'd been teaching me negotiating skills in the last several months—another of his hobbies. Hostage negotiation. So I knew how to wield a fine stalling tactic.

His eyes narrowed, and I thought I caught a flicker of something. . .else, but then it was gone. He slid his hands into his khaki pockets.

"I am," he said.

"Why? That's not a discussion we've had. Ever. We're not that kind of couple."

Maybe there had been times I'd wished for something more, but. . .he was so relentlessly normal, *harmless*, quiet—I doubted he could give me the kind of sex I wanted, and I valued our relationship as it was now enough that I couldn't quite bring myself to broach the subject. I didn't want him to think he had to change his sexuality for me. Besides. . .I'd never been a woman who'd enjoyed initiating.

"We've been together for almost a year now, and I haven't regretted a minute of it," was the quiet, even reply. "I know I want to spend the rest of my life with you."

I stared at him. "As husband and wife?"

His lips thinned, another flash in his eyes. "I have said so."

"Gary, we don't have a romantic relationship. Why get married?"

"You mean a sexual relationship. There's a reason for that. It isn't because I don't want you."

I frowned at the dry, almost crisp intonation, subtly altered from his usual soft, diffident tone. It was like watching a spider carefully weave a web in its quiet corner; you'd ignored the small creature, mistaking it for a harmless thing, only for it to now reveal dangerous markings.

"This. . .this is. . ." I gathered myself. "Then why? We haven't even talked about this."

"There are things you need to know first. It would be dishonorable to take you to my bed before we discuss certain matters. I'd intended on broaching the subject during our marriage negotiations."

To say I was floored would be putting it mildly. "Have you been taking assertiveness courses?" Another thought occurred to me. "Are you on drugs?" Also, marriage negotiations? Did he mean a prenup?

He sighed, glancing away from me. "Being in your presence has been relaxing, perhaps too relaxing. I've enjoyed simply being, for once, for the first time in a long while. Maybe I've enjoyed it a little too well. But I wanted to have this time together without external complications intruding on our relationship."

Another deeper, stronger tingle in my abdomen, this time reaching tendrils up through my body to hit my temples on either side, like ice picks.

I forced myself to relax, keeping my expression open but concerned. "Well, I feel the same way about our time together. But a proposal is something that needs to be negotiated beforehand."

His lips quirked, then firmed. "Yes. I know how much you loathe surprises."

Every muscle in my body tensed. Instinctively, I placed a hand on his chest, my heart rate jackknifing.

Gary lifted a hand and cupped my cheek, searching my eyes. "We can discuss it. A discussion isn't a no."

He said something else, but only half of me was paying attention. Well, less than half. A fourth of me was nonplussed because not only was he touching me, inserting himself into intimate physical space—but now he was lowering his head, his brown eyes deepening to something like agate, the well-shaped lips closing in on my own.

The hand on my cheek slid around the back of my neck and he pulled me closer, flush against a body surprisingly strong for the golden retriever-like personality it contained.

But there was nothing golden retriever about how he was kissing me.

Tipping my head back, his mouth brushing across mine with unexpected skill, confidence.

His tongue slipping into my mouth, his other hand sliding around the small of my back with possessiveness he'd never displayed before.

"Gary," I tried to say, tried to twist away. "We need to—"

"Shh, Val," he whispered, arm tightening, voice deepening, taking on an inflection, an intonation I would have thought was playacting if it didn't sound so real. "Shh. I won't hurt you the first time."

And through it all, the other, colder part of my mind was assessing the new threat.

In almost a year, he hadn't set off my spidey senses once.

Now, every single one screamed in unison. It overrode the spark of desire deep in my core, overrode my body beginning to soften into his, my mouth beginning to open.

I eased away and this time he let me. I didn't have to feign shock and flustered confusion. I seized on the physical attraction and yanked it to the surface so he could see that in my eyes as well.

"I...this is unexpected."

I wasn't a woman who stammered. Ever. But I stammered now. Because I was also a woman who'd learned how to use every nonviolent tool in her arsenal to escape a threat.

"I think I need to take another walk. I need to think."

His brows drew together. "You know I'm concerned about your safety when you leave the apartment after dark. You're not weapon's trained."

Another quirk of his—his subtle fixation on the risk of assault. I'd wondered if he'd been a victim, or knew one, but it wasn't a topic I would broach before he was ready to confide.

"I can handle myself. I have before."

I often ended work late, but once I was home he didn't like me to leave at night unless he was with me. If he couldn't be with me, he exerted both gentle charm and persuasion to talk me into remaining at inside. Because none of my proposed after dark outings had ever been important, and I enjoyed the novelty of being under someone's theoretical protection, I'd acquiesced.

"Before is not now. You don't usually argue with me over this, Valencia."

Not giving in now would break pattern, and Gary was conscious of behavioral patterns.

There was something about how he said the words now, a smooth edge in them, his gaze a touch too watchful.

I gave him a tremulous smile, suppressing my growing anger.

"Just a quick walk around the block, then we'll sit down and have a proper discussion. You know what—I don't think this is going to be a cooking night. How about instead of a walk I stop at the café and grab soup and sandwiches?"

He nodded after a moment. "Alright. I suppose this once will be fine. I'll put together a salad while you're gone. Grab a small fruit tart as well, I think we'll both need the sugar. But don't linger."

I nodded and walked around him, the weight of his gaze on the back of my neck as I scooped up my keys on the way to the door.

"Valencia, you forgot your wallet."

Valencia again, not Val.

I halted, my heart in my mouth and turned slowly, smiling—not too brightly. Grabbing my wallet hadn't been instinctive; I had go bags stashed throughout the city. Mostly for clients I'd had to help over the years.

"Let me go get that. Thank you. I'm a little flustered right now." Getting away from the threat was my sole focus.

"Understandable," he murmured.

He'd be suspicious if I didn't take my wallet so I went to the bedroom, pausing to glance at the puzzle he'd been working on. He hadn't made any progress. What had he been doing alone for the last two hours then?

I grabbed my wallet, nodded to him where he stood in the living room, hands in pockets as he watched me. "Be careful, mi cielo."

Pausing, I glanced back at him, "I usually am," then slipped out of the door.

No time to wonder what must have gone wrong.

How, under my nose, a poisonous spider had woven an invisible web.

Chapter Three

VALENCIA

We lived on the top floor of a three flat, the living room window facing the street. I strolled toward the café at the end of the block, assuming he watched.

Feeling his eyes on me.

There was no time for anger, for wondering what happened, what changed, if somehow my extra ability had in this one instance failed. I'd never reacted well to betrayal, to threat.

An understatement, considering the instinct toward violence creeping up my throat. Had it been a decade since I'd last had to battle the urge to destroy something over my disappointment? Now I wondered if that was my Fae side after all. Everyone knew they were murderous bastards.

Did he plan on kidnapping me? Did he want to live out some fantasy in the Fae world and didn't intend for us to return? Was it murder he planned?

How many scenarios had I'd witnessed over the last eighty years? So many it was a miracle I'd let a man into my apartment in the first place. My home was sacred to me, the place I'd crafted over decades to be an oasis of peace and sanity and safety. And somehow he'd invaded it. I was twelve decades old. Gary was four. How had a man-boy fooled me?

Because I'd weakened. Where had I gone wrong? How had I begun to trust him?

Entering the café, I headed around the counter and through the kitchen, ignoring the startled cries around me as I used the back exit.

It came out into an alley, and Gary would have no line of sight from there.

I'd make my way to a precinct where several officers owed me favors. I'd developed relationships with all of them over the years. Relationship building was important in my line of work.

I'd ask for officers to be sent to my apartment to evict my ex. They'd ask a few questions, but my spidey sense had been right enough over the years that they wouldn't ask too many if my answers were a little vague. I'd decide later if I needed to move. It was safer to do so, because since Gary hadn't hurt me, charges would evaporate into thin air. They'd hold him as long as they could, but they'd have to let him go.

Anger burned low in my gut. Gary was very, very lucky I'd sworn an oath of nonviolence.

Very lucky.

I'd never wanted to kill someone as much as I wanted to kill him now. Somehow, he'd betrayed me.

I didn't like the feeling.

I was so rattled I almost ordered from our shared rideshare account, canceling it at the last second. If I did, the app would alert Gary to the booking and my location. As a safety feature. I chuckled.

Instead, as I walked down the block I downloaded a competing app, created an account and ordered a ride. Then waited.

Waited until a surge of adrenaline shot up my throat and I wanted to vomit, almost falling to my knees.

I whipped my head around, searching. It was a busy enough block, but not so crowded I could be easily followed. I didn't see him.

But he was there.

The spidey sense was never wrong.

I turned on my heel and began walking. Damn it. The rideshare would follow my location, of course, and it was better to keep moving than to stay still.

If Gary had followed me, it meant he was suspicious, and it was always one step from suspicious to violent.

To deadly violent.

I needed to break his line of sight.

There was a small city park I could cross, and wouldn't that be a horrible cliché. But clichés were clichés for a reason. The dumb broad fleeing a predator who ran right into a park full of trees and shade because it seemed on the surface like a good hiding place. All prey wanted to find dark holes and crawl into them.

But I needed to break his line of sight.

My cell rang; Gary's ringtone. I'd given him his own ringtone. The call went to voicemail.

It was so much easier to criticize other women's decisions when you were sitting on your couch eating popcorn, or reading a book. In real time, the decision-making process was harder, and more complicated.

I sighed, crossed the street and entered the park.

It...somewhat seemed like a good idea.

Gary's ringtone again, but this time it cut off after two seconds. A warning he knew I'd gone off course.

The third time it rang, I answered. "Hola, what's up?"

"You are not in the café, Val." He spoke gently. "Come home, please, and we'll talk. I'm sorry if I discomfited you."

"Why don't you think I'm in the café?"

He didn't respond, not even the whisper of a breath, and after a moment the call disconnected.

Mierda.

Forcibly calm, I checked my app to make sure the rideshare was updating my current location. I'd emerge on the other side of the park, meet the driver on a corner and hop in.

Funny.

I'd never considered myself to be a woman with a sense of humor, but evidently, I had one.

I gagged, stumbling, fighting the instinctive urge to vomit, a vice pressing against my skull. What was this motherfucker planning on *doing* to me? Skinning me and chopping me into pieces to stuff into a fridge? This level of spidey sense went far beyond a mere kidnapping, or even a garden variety stabbing.

"Valencia."

Of course. Of course. This was why we always paid attention to the movies. *You aren't supposed to run into the shadowy park with trees. You should have stayed on the busy block even if he was able to keep you in line of sight.* What could he have done with other people around?

Unfortunately, I knew the answer to that was quite a bit. How many times had a woman come to me after being beaten in broad daylight on the street by her man while others stood by, not wanting to get involved? Sometimes they'd call the police. Sometimes.

I made the decision to turn and confront him rather than run.

For a reason, or instinct rather, I didn't have time to examine, running felt like the worst option. Gary had once said, "*Fae are predators, even the females. If you're being hunted, hide if you can but never run once they have you locked in sight. It will only activate the instinct to bring you to ground. You can't negotiate with a beast.*"

He stood a few feet away, silvery blond hair tousled and a little too long—I'd never told him he needed a cut since I liked longer hair on men, but he kept it long enough to cover the nape of his neck. Enough for a lover to grab a handful and yank his head back.

I was annoyed with that thought, the incongruity of it in the current situation.

Gary walked forward another step, his hands in his trouser pockets as if it made him less dangerous. I had no idea of the exact nature of the danger he presented, only that it was serial killer comparable.

"Where are you going?" he asked, voice calm. Reasonable. "I thought we were going to have dinner and discuss Casakraine. Our relationship."

He offered me a smile, slow and warm, his normal smile, but this time every instinct in me continued going off like fireworks, my spine tingling.

I didn't step back. "I'd like you to return to the flat."

My voice was as calm, as reasonable. I couldn't fake a smile, but I had enough self-control not to panic further though he continued those slow, inexorable steps towards me.

"Don't come any closer," I snapped.

He stopped immediately. "I don't mean you any harm. What happened?" His eyes searched my face. "You're afraid. I can scent it."

"If you were trying to pretend you're safe, that was the wrong thing to say."

Gary paused, as if considering my words, and nodded.

"You're right. I apologize. It's not my intent to frighten you, but this situation is fraught with difficulties. Can we talk?"

"No."

"Why not? Why are you afraid of me suddenly?"

"Because you're a danger now."

He narrowed his eyes, expression still thoughtful. "Your spidey sense. Interesting. That Skill is going to be useful to us, Valencia."

Yes, like idiots all over, I'd told my boyfriend about my ability. He'd called it a Skill—wild magic, but couldn't tell me much more. Or wouldn't.

He'd shrugged when we'd first discussed it. *"Wild magic is exactly that. It pops up and is discovered mostly by accident. The only training is through trial and error."* Not many people knew, and in a moment of weakness I'd wanted mental and emotional connection.

"Who is us?" I asked.

He held out a hand. "Come with me and I'll tell you."

I'd thought he'd understand, be someone in my personal life who I didn't have to conceal the entirety of my nature from. Humans still were wary of Fae, and rightfully so. And though I was only half, that half was strong enough to have given me a quasi-immortal lifespan along with a touch of their power.

I smiled bitterly. "I don't even know who you are."

"You know. Enough, anyway, of what is important. I've said I intend you no harm. I cannot lie to you."

I'd almost been to the point of telling Gary my real age—and it occurred to me now. . .the times I'd slipped up and spoken in first person about historical events a thirty-year-old woman wouldn't have experienced, he had never blinked, or questioned me. I'd assumed he wasn't paying attention, or was simply a little slow. Which was fine. I didn't mind stupid men, especially if they were pretty and harmless and quiet.

Of course, I was now rethinking harmless, and redefining quiet.

"Talk now, and maybe I'll listen."

"A stalling tactic." Gary sighed and tilted his head back to look up at the canopy of trees, lowering his hand. "I thought if we came to know each other this would be easier. I didn't want to coerce you."

Though he was talking to me, the cadence of his voice was almost as if he was speaking to himself.

"Your life is going to be difficult enough with the House feud, and I want a quiet, happy marriage. A restful wife. Well-adjusted children. You're half-human," he added, looking at me again. "Our children will be a quarter and that will make things more complicated for them. But it'll make Mag happy—I think you'll like my cousin."

I mostly ignored his babbling as I calculated escape paths, and chanced a step back.

He tensed, stilling in a way that reaffirmed my suspicion he wasn't entirely human. I'd seen human predators, men stalking their ex-girlfriends, their wives, their daughters. The prostitute or girl next door, or classmate they were obsessed with.

Human men did not go so still. Preternaturally still. The stillness of a vacuum. The eye of a hurricane before its devastation was unleashed.

Human men couldn't unleash such focus. Focus meant placing something outside of yourself above your own internalizations.

He focused on me as if I was the only thing that mattered.

"I'm sorry, Valencia. What I do is because we both have no choice." His smile was slow, poignant with sorrow. "Humans think choice is a right of merely being alive, of having power. They know nothing."

I whirled but didn't get more than a step before strong arms enfolded me, his deep voice speaking a word in no human language I knew.

And then darkness.

I didn't wake disoriented. I understood what had happened to me. I'd been the victim of a long con, and now I'd been taken.

I was a prisoner, though there were no shackles on my ankles or chains on my wrists. Though the bed I woke in was clothed in soft white sheets, a gentle bath of sunlight streamed through an open window. It was a pleasant room. Pale blue walls, warm wooden floors. Outside the window, a breeze ruffled and birds chirped. If I didn't know better, I would think I'd woken in some kind of vacation holo.

Remain calm for now, lose my shit later.

I slid out of the bed, noting I was still clothed. There was no pain. No sense I had been touched.

My feet were bare though, and I padded towards the door, found it unlocked and exited the room into a hallway. More pale blue walls and warm golden wood floors. I walked until I saw a kitchen, butcher block counters and weathered cabinets to match the floors, the debris of a meal on the center island.

Crunchy bread, cheese. There was a plate next to it, as if it had been set out for a guest. I glanced at it, then looked away, proceeding through the open doors and onto the expanse of a grassy lawn.

There was a larger house in the distance.

I turned, looked up. A guesthouse, then. Someone had put me where I could have some privacy. All of the doors and windows were open.

What was going on?

I wasn't asleep, I wasn't dreaming. I wasn't entranced. But I didn't recognize this land, its scents, the trees not quite like the trees I was used to, the lack of busy noise; people, vehicles, pets. Nothing in the air, nothing in the distance on the streets.

I didn't panic. Instead, I walked around the guesthouse assessing my surroundings.

"Good morning."

I stopped and turned. The Fae male who approached me was dressed in long, butter yellow robes and loose pants, his silvery hair falling down his shoulders to his waist, pointed ears dressed with tiny sparkling jewels. Chocolate brown eyes watched me as he approached.

He hesitated, stopping just out of arm reach and bowed. "We have not been properly introduced. I am Garen, High Lord of House Anteyan."

I knew that voice. It was different. Deeper, more assured, sonorous. I knew those eyes, though the face was off. He was taller, his shoulders broader, the way he watched me both grave and weary, as if he understood nothing about the next few hours would be easy, or pleasant.

"Valencia," he said again, his voice softer, a whisper of almost pained sound. "Forgive me."

Staring at him, "Gary?"

I saw it then. The hint of Cary Elwes in the Fae face. The echoes of that human visage which must have been a glamour, in this male who stood before me.

He inclined his head, and there was no triumph in his expression. No darkness. Nothing but sadness, resignation a thin veneer over steel.

"You'll hate me for some time, I expect," he said. "And that is fine. I understand. But I hope you remember I never lied to you."

"You've never lied to me?" I could barely speak the words, they were so ridiculous. "This is Casakraine."

"It is."

It took me a moment to formulate a thought, and all that came out was. . . "Why?"

"The short answer? I was commanded. Our Houses are at war, yours and mine." He stepped towards me. "But I swear to you, I will never lift a hand against you. I will try to make you happy." He stepped forward again.

"You want to marry me. That wasn't a lie."

"No. It wasn't a lie." He held out his hand. Pale golden skin, long fingers. "Will you come inside with me? I'll explain everything. And I promise I won't touch you unless you give me leave."

I'd been talking myself into some semblance of calm until his last sentence.

No man, in my experience, ever had to say out loud he wouldn't touch you without permission unless he intended the exact opposite.

I turned and ran. If I could get to the big house—

Chapter Four

VALENCIA

The functioning part of my brain understood the futility of running as soon as my feet took off. The hypercritical part of my brain—the part hidden from clients—felt chastened.

Survival instinct was strong, and I was still half-human. Half-human survival instinct often focused on flight as the sole method to preserve one's life.

The few feet of distance I gained were likely a courtesy. Gary—no, Lord Garen, but I'd call him my Lord over my dead body—had always been courteous, faultlessly thoughtful.

Or maybe the Fae male was toying with me, allowing me a few seconds of triumph.

He was in front of me in moments. I ran into his chest and would have bounced off if he hadn't grabbed my upper arms, holding my weight to keep me from tumbling to the ground.

That I looked like an idiot only added to the strikes against him. I needed to get ahold of myself, fast. The slippery ribbons of my anger and fear were sliding through my fingers.

Garen sighed. "Valencia. Please, this isn't necessary. I won't hurt you unless you force me, and only as a matter of safety."

"Whose safety? *Whose* safety, *you lying piece of shit?*" My fingers twitched, curled into a claw, but I had that much self-control left. I didn't attempt to strike him.

"Surely you can come up with more creative insults. And, Val—I had no idea you had this kind of temper. I didn't account for it when I ran scenarios. You kept it concealed."

Because when I let my temper loose, property destruction always followed.

The last time I'd gotten off with probation because of my networking, the work I did with the shelter, and the fact that no one really blamed me for destroying the property of a proven wife beater and child rapist. But I'd been quietly referred to anger management counseling, which I'd accepted, and actually enjoyed. It had been nice to be the client for once.

He swung me up into his arms and I responded not with my normal rational, considered calm, but like a shrieking wild thing. Kicking, twisting, bawling up my fists and aiming them at his face. The indignity of this situation hurt as much as his betrayal. I was too old for this shit.

I'd thought he was forty.

He wasn't fucking forty.

"Ack, none of that, densafa."

Lord Garen dropped me to my feet, grabbed my wrists and warmth shackled them together. The same thing happened to my ankles, and he lifted me back into his arms, having the nerve to cradle me to his chest as if he cared.

I'd been fooled by the pretty, quiet, harmless one. "No puedo creerlo. Hijo de puta!" Never trust the pretty, quiet, harmless ones.

"The restraints are a basic use of power," he explained, ignoring the cursing. "I couldn't teach you before because that would have revealed I wasn't human, but I'll teach you how to make them in the future, if you've an interest in learning."

"Let! Me! Go!" A spurt of angry Spanish followed.

"Val, mi cielo. That isn't going to happen. I understand you have to process this turn of events the way you will, but I promise you resistance is futile."

"La madre que me parió. Cómo me he podido meter en este lío?"

"You're well aware that I don't speak much Spanish, Val. You'll have to curse at me in English for full effect."

"You motherfucker," I repeated, *as* requested, each word distinct. "I don't know how the fuck I got myself in this situation, but I'm going to make sure you regret it as much as I do."

"I see." He turned and strode back toward the guest house. "I've never seen you enraged. It's interesting. I'm glad you're. . .normally an even-tempered female, but I was beginning to wonder if all your fire was drained by your shelter. No—don't do that, Val. You'll hurt yourself."

I screamed, more in fury than in fear.

The High Lord—and something about that designation was important; Gary had lectured for hours about it once while I watched him build his then puzzle of choice, or had it been the model castle—sighed.

"There's no one on the grounds or in the main house. I ordered them all away because as you are to be my wife, I didn't relish witnesses to these early conversations in case I'd miscalculated your probable response—and, clearly, I have."

Reading between the lines; he'd thought I would be easy to manage. I was about to head butt him in the chin to show him exactly how easy I would be, but I managed to dredge the last remnant of self-restraint, mostly because I had some pride.

Ten years. It took only a man to ruin ten years of good behavior. Typical. *Typical.* I had only myself to blame.

I closed my eyes, resting my head on his shoulder and letting my body go limp. I had to stop the chemical cocktail flooding my body.

"Very good," he murmured. "Deep breaths. Calm down, assess your situation, give nothing away. What is the opposing party's goal? What is yours? What tools or advantages do you possess and what are your disadvantages?"

Mine was the position of vulnerability here. So far he hadn't retaliated with violent physical force, he'd only acted to restrain me. I was on his territory, he had the greatest strength and power. I'd do everything I could to escape, but I had to be strategic. I couldn't escalate the conflict to the point he felt justified—if he needed justification—in hurting me. I needed to find out what his title entitled him to, but if I alienated him I doubted I'd get any information.

Garen carried me into the kitchen as if I were no more trouble than a squirming toddler throwing a mildly annoying fit.

"Now, I'm not going to let you near anything sharp, but are you hungry?" he asked. "There's fresh bread, fruit and cheese, and I'm certain we have chocolate in the pantry somewhere. Maggie always keeps some on hand. I can also make horchata."

Calm shriveled. "*I don't want horchata, Gary.*"

He lowered me into a chair, his expression brightening with hope as his long hair fell into my face. "Something stronger? I have cava or vermouth."

I'd wanted him to grow his hair out but had said nothing because I had no right to criticize his body—but it had been long and silky and perfect all along. The silvery blond strands mixed with my wild honey gold waves that were a mess around my shoulders. Damn him, my brunette roots would start growing out soon, and I was stuck here.

I stared at him, curling my lip up. "What did you do, *Gary*? Google 'The Top Ten Drinks in Spain?'" I'd never had either of those beverages in our flat.

"Spiked horchata, then. I'm looking forward to introducing you to Mag. I think you two will get along quite well. As soon as you're in a better mood, of course. I understand we need to take this slowly." His expression darkened as he straightened to his full height and looked down at me. "But not too slowly, Valencia. We're running out of time."

"No, *you're* running out of time," I spat. "*You're* running out of time! Whatever this is, it has nothing to do with me. Do you hear me? Nothing!"

Whatever magical bonds he had wrapped around my ankles and wrists also tied me to the chair. Thoroughly, so I could move only my head and neck. And my mouth. My gums ached.

He rubbed his long fingers, the nails short and shiny, over his clean-shaven jaw as he eyed me. It was a little narrower, his skin satiny and gleaming with that poreless immortal shimmer makeup companies kept trying to replicate with creams and foundations.

"If I offer you food, will you take it? You haven't eaten much in the last day or two. You don't eat when you're stressed, and that's a poor decision. But I don't want you to bite me, Val. I'm a little on edge myself, and also not entirely controlled." An almost amber light flashed in his dark eyes.

"Please let me go," I said, slumping my shoulders and letting my eyes well with tears, which spilled down my cheeks. I blinked once so I could see his expression.

"Val, I recognize a negotiating tactic when I see one. Tears won't work, at least not in this circumstance. Later, it might be intriguing."

"You bloated excuse for a dickless incel brained *troglodyte*."

Garen chuckled, warmth and approval lightening his expression. "See? Much better. I knew you could devise a better insult if you put your mind to it. The traditional human expletives are rather dull. You're a bright girl, Valencia."

He stepped around me and busied himself at the kitchen island, silent for several minutes. "I expect our children will be highly intelligent. Nature as well as nurture. Though. . .I'm slightly worried considering your father, but Valyah shows great potential. So there is that. I probably needn't be concerned. We'll lean on nurture. I think we'll make excellent parents."

He came back around, pulled up a chair and sat, holding a plate, giving me a quizzical smile. "Do you think he went with the letter 'V' to name his daughters as a show of unity, or because he's particularly unimaginative?"

I stared at him.

"No, of course you wouldn't know. You haven't had the misfortune of meeting your sire. I'll try to spare you from that fate as long as I can, but. . ." he shrugged. "He'll know at the wedding. I'm quite looking forward to his expression. He has no self-control and quite a temper, so all of his anguish and impotent fury will be plain for everyone to see." This time his smile was all teeth, and I shuddered.

Garen misinterpreted my expression. "Oh, don't worry. None of the shame will fall on you—you'll be mine by then, of course. And he didn't raise you, so you're free from his taint. . .except for this temper. Hmm. Will you eat?"

I wanted him to put his fingers near my mouth. I *needed* him to put his fingers near my mouth.

I nodded, projecting chagrin at my shameful display of pointless, irrational emotion.

"Lady Valencia, if you bite me, I will bite you back, and I bite much, much harder."

I needed to work on my acting while under duress. I used to be pleased at how well he was coming to know me. Stupid. But no. . .how many times had a woman cried on my shoulder, berating herself because shoulda woulda coulda? No. This wasn't my fault. I wasn't stupid. I'd trusted someone who'd gone out of their way to be trusted.

That didn't make me stupid, and it didn't mean I should start second guessing my judgment. It just meant I'd been outmaneuvered.

That wasn't going to happen again. Ever.

"I'll eat," I said. "Thank you for your patience. This is a difficult time and I reacted poorly."

"You just overplayed your hand," he said, choosing a slice of fruit and bringing it to my lips. "Only say what the opposing party is likely to believe. Otherwise you run the risk of losing credibility, and when you do craft a genuine lie, it will fail. Also, people tend to assume your first reaction is the genuine one—so you lost ground with that show of temper."

He watched my lips, then selected another piece of fruit.

"It will take convincing to make me believe a reasonable act now. Though I admit I'm intrigued to see your strategy going forward."

I finished swallowing. "From my understanding, the Fae are magically prohibited from lying."

He smiled faintly. "Yes. But we can subvert the truth. To humans, there's no appreciable difference. Their minds aren't sophisticated enough for the difference to matter. Especially the men." He looked baffled, then shrugged and selected a piece of cheese.

Despite enough years honing my own acting abilities—it came in useful when trying to defuse a potentially violent situation—I wasn't able to feign enough calm to convince him now was a good time to continue our conversation.

The magic released me from the chair when I was done eating, and he escorted me back to my bedroom, as solicitous as any host, pointing out amenities in the bathroom and the stocked closet—this serial killer mother*fucker* had a stocked closet with clothing and everything, to my taste and sizes—with an anxious air, again as if he cared.

After inspecting the room, I turned back to him. He stood in the threshold, watching me, hands clasped behind his back. Had the yellow robes been a deliberate choice? It was a disarming color; cheerful and non-threatening, almost childlike if you discounted the elegant silver embroidery edging the hems and cuffs.

If you discounted that there was nothing nonthreatening and childlike about his dark eyes.

The threat wasn't overt, but he didn't have to be overt, did he?

"There are no locks on the doors, Val," he said as the silence stretched. "You're free to explore the grounds as you please. But do not leave the boundaries of the estate. It isn't safe if your father discovers your presence, and our defenses are stretched thin."

I almost blinked, a little nonplussed that he revealed that weakness to me.

"I'm telling you this because I trust you to do the intelligent thing," he said, a clear warning in his voice. "You're alone in a strange country in a different realm. You don't know the rules, you have no money. My own people may not all appreciate your presence at this time, either. There are dangers out there I haven't had time to apprise you of—and your father will welcome you with a knife, not open arms. Do not test this. Please. No matter how dangerous you might think staying here with me is, I promise you that it is not. My intention isn't to hurt you."

"No, but you've stated that your intention is to marry me against my will. You've discussed our children, which I haven't consented to conceiving, nor will I."

"By the time we're ready to bind ourselves, it's my hope and intention that it won't be against your will." He paused, as if mulling over his next words, then spoke slowly. "I could have used other methods to ensure your cooperation. The marriage oath is not a binding Vow. You wouldn't have to be in your right mind to take it, and you'd be legally considered my wife. Because you have no rank and no acknowledged House, you would also be considered my property. I'm a High Lord, Val," he continued, and his voice softened even further, nearly diffident. "Through whatever trick of fate and circumstances, I am a High Lord." He looked lost for a moment, then shook the mood off. "No one will gainsay anything I choose to do with you."

After he left on that lovely note, it took three minutes for my self-enforced calm to break, and another minute to realize there was nothing breakable in the room.

I exited the room and found the living area.

Chapter Five

GAREN

I surveyed the deliberate destruction of the living room, then focused on the female sitting on the remnants of a once pristine couch, her legs crossed and her arms draped across the back as if she had just had a good, hard fuck and now needed a drink.

I congratulated myself for not taking her to the main house right away. Clearly, the instinct that she'd need a transition period was proved correct.

Stepping over. . .something. . .I strolled into the room, somewhat tempted to give her that good, hard fuck. But she was in no mood.

Pity. Well, the time for such celibacy nonsense was soon coming to a close.

"Did you enjoy yourself, densafa?"

My venomous little rabbit turned her head from me so all I saw was her profile; nose with a slight bump in the middle, lush lips turned down. Her hair was more of a mess than it had been earlier, the thick dark gold waves tumbling down her shoulders as if she'd been running her hands through the strands in a literal attempt to not pull them out.

Yes, I'd somewhat miscalculated her reaction, but even I had to be wrong once. I'd expected a strong response of sorts, as Valencia was not a female who enjoyed either having her choices taken away, or being made to look a fool.

But this explosive temper...I'd had no idea. Unlike my halfling, I enjoyed surprises—a surprise oft meant there was something interesting to learn.

Not that she couldn't be fierce, but at home she'd been so thoughtful, almost reserved, mild tempered to the point I had begun to grow bored despite decades of insisting to myself I wanted a quiet, diffident, scholarly wife.

She'd put that assertion to the test, though my love for her had grown.

"You're not speaking to me?" I asked; a rhetorical question.

Val occasionally retreated into dense silence where nothing could break her introspection short of the threat of death to one of the females in her shelter. I'd learned to leave her alone during those times, understanding the need for internal silence and space. I often required the same, and our ability to navigate each other's currents was one of the reasons we suited.

"Well, we're going to have to pull some furniture out of storage," I said, clasping my hands behind my back and circling the room—remaining well out of reach. "It's all right, Val. I understand. I'll forgive you the destruction this once, though I'll ask you not to do it again. Next time, the cost will be deducted from your allowance."

The tension in her elegant body made clear she was aware of me, though she pretended indifference.

I gathered shards of a vase and set them on the fireplace mantle, glancing at her bare feet. She hadn't thought this out very well. "You consider me a threat, though I have no intention of harming you unless forced to do so for your own protection." If I said this enough times, she would come to believe it. "If you behave reasonably, that threat will never manifest."

Silence.

I sighed. Until her Skill told her I wasn't going to harm her, she would be difficult to reason with. The conundrum was I hadn't yet figured out what her Skill considered harm, so I couldn't effectively circumvent it.

Obviously, taking her from her home against her will was harmful. I might also conclude that marrying her without her enthusiastic approval was also considered harm.

"Your spidey sense is a Skill, the wild magic, but I have no idea if you've inherited other power from your father."

I continued to circle as I spoke, pausing now and again to gather debris and set it aside.

"Untrained power is dangerous and can manifest unexpectedly with disastrous results. Normally it doesn't come to that because children are trained from birth—it's rare we let our halflings run amok either."

One wondered exactly what that half-brained troll's excrement had been thinking. Clearly, he'd known of her existence since he'd gone to some trouble to conceal it.

"Why he allowed your mother to remain on Earth realm with you is the mystery of ages. I would never allow a child of mine to remain outside of my protection and guidance. Which would, of course, extend to the mother even if she proved unworthy of my seed." I shrugged. "But that's what happens when you chose bed partners indiscriminately, sometimes they fall pregnant which is, of course, the biological purpose of intercourse. I cannot fathom it. Your mother was better off, though. . .I wouldn't inflict him long-term on even a female of low intellect—whatever capacity she possessed would shrivel to nothing."

Had Narazah so little respect for the come he'd shot between the human girl's thighs that it hadn't occurred to him it would one day form an adult who'd inherit his traits and might be an asset to his House? It was almost wasteful, and lacked anything resembling foresight.

I halted in front of Val a moment later. Still, she refused to respond. "I do care for you, you know. I've been falling in love with you, and loving one's wife is more conducive to a successful marriage. Or at least, I hope it is."

I paused for a moment, thoughtful. Perhaps friendly indifference would be better. Unfortunately, since I only planned to take the one wife—they were expensive, I'd discovered, when outfitting Val's closet and drawing up estimates of her health and entertainment expenses—it wasn't something I could experiment with.

Valencia turned her head and pinned me with sharp blue eyes simmering with contempt.

"I'm not in the mood for your babble, *Gary*."

I pursed my lips. The trace of Spanish accent in her voice had thickened, her cheeks still tinged with pink.

"In fact," she continued, "I much prefer when you shut up and look pretty and play with your puzzles like a good little quiet boy."

Ah. She was completely misinformed as to our relative ages, experiences, and intellects—but I'd had to maintain the pretense of being only a slightly above average human male well below her in age.

I would correct her, gently, over time. She would learn to respect me; I'd endure these growing pains with patience, grace, and humility.

And our life together had been restive though handling her oft required a deft touch. I'd never known a female so willing to dive head first into—but, no matter. The shelter, and its dangers, were behind us now. Now that we were in my territory, I could handle her with a firmer hand.

"Well," I said, considering the matter of puzzles, "if that was one of our mutual interests you enjoyed, I can arrange for—"

"I never would have let you live with me if I'd thought you'd be talkative. You enjoy the sound your voice, don't you? I'm tempted to ask what you do in this realm for a living, but I don't want to encourage further talking."

"I'm a diplomat, though the word in English is somewhat inexact—oh, yes, I've arranged for a language tutor so you can learn Cassanian. They will be here in the morning. Now, House Anteyan is sought after and renown for—"

She held up a hand. "Please with the lectures. I'm equally disinterested in any discussion unrelated to releasing me from your illegal custody."

"My custody is not illegal, densafa. I'd apologize, but I cannot lie. I am sorry this is distressing you, though."

The simmer of anger in her eyes sparked, hardened. "Maybe not illegal, but it will be fatal. For one of us."

By the Dark she was beautiful when she was issuing ineffective, but charming, threats. Objectively, only averagely pretty with a heart-shaped face and a well-formed mouth. She had House Gisleyan's bone structure—which one must grudgingly admit was not substandard as far as Fae beauty went—and her mortal mother's well nourished feminine form. A bonus, since no one could ever accuse me of not feeding my wife properly.

But intelligence informed her expressive face and eyes, and every time she spoke, even if she was only asking me what we should have for dinner, my cock stiffened at the sound of her husky, modulated voice.

It had become a game I played with myself, how well I could disguise the hunger, dance around the mysterious trigger of her Skill by not slipping into a state her wild magic would consider threatening.

For there was nothing non-threatening about what I wanted to do to her body, or her mind.

Thus, the puzzles that served as adequate foci.

So many puzzles. I dreamed of the pieces sometimes, and they formed a single picture; Valencia. Spread out naked on my bed, her hair wild around her shoulders. Thighs open and glistening, arms sometimes tied above her head. The sheets Gislayen aqua-and-purple, stained with her blood and my come.

Sometimes, I forced that bark-skulled blight to watch as I fucked the eldest daughter he'd thought to hide and she screamed my name, her submission absolute, Narazah's silly plans to outsmart *me* dust.

More than anything, I wanted to hear her elegant, disdainful, compassionate voice hoarse with pleasure. I wanted to hear her scream my name and demand I claim her, breed her—

"Earth to motherfucker."

I blinked. We were going to have to work on her language before we released her to the public.

Valencia lifted a brow, studying me. Had my expression shifted? "What are you thinking, Gary—never mind. I don't care. Why don't you go somewhere not here? Unless you plan on letting me go?"

I stared at her, and smiled. It was time to begin correcting some of the misinformation she retained regarding my personality and character—and her ability to control me.

"You think saying my human use name in such a tone is an insult, but I only want to fuck you more."

She choked.

I stepped forward as she sat up, pulling her legs off the floor and tucking them beneath her as if there was a monster under the couch. Her eyes widened, the pulse in the hollow of her throat fluttering as she looked up at me, hands clutching the back of the couch.

"Call me a motherfucker when you're screaming and bouncing on my cock, Valencia, your breasts filling my hands. Once you've had our first child, I'll squeeze your nipples and catch the spray of your milk as your wet pussy clenches around me and—"

"That is *not* going to happen."

"*Densafaaa*. . .now you know how I love a challenging puzzle."

VALENCIA

I pushed up, sitting on the back of the couch in instinctive retreat.

This wasn't Gary, not the Gary I knew. On the heels of that inane thought I mentally slapped myself.

Of course it wasn't, because that had been the entire point. I was letting my oft buried temper get the better of me, but he didn't seem to expect any different.

"I understand what you want," I said after a long silence.

I refused to respond to the blatant sexual come-on, or the look in *Lord Garen's* predatory eyes—the look of a man one wrong move away from defiling something he'd coveted. The look of a man telling himself there was no more need for self-control.

The look of every civilized layer peeling back to reveal the true, bleeding black heart within.

How had he managed to work around my spidey sense? The raw, awful hunger staring at me through an unblinking brown gaze was the exact opposite of safe and non-threatening.

All I could do was ignore the High Fae and speak to the personality I knew. "You want me to marry you for political reasons—no, I don't care why. Just listen, damnit." I waited until he closed his mouth and nodded for me to continue. "You want me to marry you but you've also indicated you want a real marriage. A peaceful one, with children."

He'd given away his hand with that revelation; he considered my position here to be so inferior to his it didn't matter if he came to the negotiating table with all of his cards laid out. That, as much as anything, infuriated me. I would teach Lord Garen not to underestimate me.

After I figured out how to stay far away from his dark side.

Gary nodded, expression now relaxed though heat lingered in his eyes. How I'd thought him asexual, I didn't know. He made no further move towards me, hands clasped behind his back as he banked the sexual heat. Yes, Garen had been playing a long game.

But I could play, and play better. There was one factor about my personality Garen hadn't considered. I was willing to cut off a limb in order to save the body.

"I'll give you a child," I said. It was a false concession—I didn't have access to birth control here, and I was under no delusion he would allow his wife to refuse his advances. I'd grown up in a time where there was no concept of marital rape. But the concession would at least allow me to appear cooperative. "I'll co-parent with you. And after, I want us to live our separate lives."

He studied me; classic Gary, always consider one's words before speaking. After a moment he moved away, pacing. I watched as he stopped, his attention caught by something on the floor. He bent, and picked up a photograph.

He stared at it a moment then turned to me. "This is Maggie."

"I don't care who she is. She could be your mistress and—"

"She's my cousin, and like you, she's half human."

A note in his voice shut me up. I set aside the worst of my anger and focused. "Go on."

He approached and set the photograph on the couch next to me. I glanced at it once; saw a smiling young face similar to his but more rounded.

"Forty years ago she was attacked and raped by House Anteyan warriors." He closed his eyes. "They trashed her flower shop and terrorized her employees—but she was the only one they touched."

It took me a moment to talk past the surge of anger and revulsion. Was there any realm where this kind of evil didn't happen? "What reason did they give?"

"She rejected the advances of one of their warriors. She prefers females, not that it matters. No insult was intended and I know my cousin, she gave none. Maggie would have let him down kindly. To this day to remember what they'd done to her —" His hand trembled and he drew in a breath, then offered me a crooked smile as he tucked it behind his back. "My cousin is sunshine on a cloudy day."

I let myself soften enough to return the strained smile, silent comfort to ease the pain. The first time I'd sung that song to him, he'd listened as if entranced, as if he'd never heard it before. Maybe he hadn't.

"I'm sorry she and your family had to go through that." Oh, wait. Gisleyan. "My biological father's House."

"Yes."

"I see."

Dios. I sighed, glancing at the photograph again. I couldn't help but soften. She looked like so many others who'd come to me for shelter over the decades. Young, undefiled, brimming with hope for the future. "How can you not hate me?"

"That would be an illogical emotional response. It had nothing to do with you."

"You know that wouldn't matter to most men."

He shrugged. "I'm not most men. I was never meant to be a warrior, Val. You know me well enough, or at least another side of me. But this feud. . .demanded things of all of us. I couldn't let the insult go unanswered."

"Was the rapist punished?"

"The rapist," he said in an exact tone, his eyes going cold in a way I hoped was never aimed at me, "was torn apart while alive, the pieces hung in District Anteyan's square. We have a healer in our House—it took the offender some time to die. Fae are strong."

"And the ones who watched but didn't touch?"

"Were allowed to die a somewhat swifter death. Not less painful, but faster."

"Good."

Our gazes clashed, his eyes brightening to a brilliant amber. Then he looked away, suppressing the glimpse of his real nature again. I gave it about three months before he stopped.

"I'd like you to meet her. I've arranged for a family dinner. . ." he eyed me. "If you think you're feeling up to meeting a few of my cousins and Housesworn."

"You think we'd have something in common. You think I'll feel empathy for her and that will make me more cooperative."

He glanced down at the picture. "Yes. My motives in this aren't complex, and there's more to tell but I don't want to overburden you right now. I am sorry, Val. I understand what I'm doing to you is wrong. But I've been commanded by my Lord, and it's either sacrifice you to marriage, or my House to annihilation."

And I wasn't family. I was nothing, and no one would ever think my fate was worse than the deaths of Cassanians. A halfling forced to marry and live in comfortable wealth? Oh, the horrors. No one would feel sorry for me. Objectively, I recognized it as the lesser of two evils.

But fuck objectivity. I was no willing sacrifice. Let other women allow themselves to be used in that fashion, succumbing to generations of social conditions telling us we should give up everything, even our souls and especially our bodies, if only it would benefit someone else. . .a man usually, or that man's spawn.

I wasn't going sacrifice myself even for my own children. . .but I was steeling myself to the necessity of waiting. Until I was strong enough. Until I could make him, and *only* him, pay the price of my violation.

Garen met my gaze again. "I want to make you happy. I want to. . .make up for our poor beginning. I understand and expect it will take time, but for now all I ask is you try to keep an open mind."

"You know this is wrong, no matter what the circumstances are. You kidnapped me, Gary."

"I know."

"Why me? Is there no other Gisleyan woman?"

"There is, but the stipulations of the Vow Narazah and I took to secure the ceasefire states I must wed his eldest daughter. You are the eldest." He cupped my chin. "I'll do whatever it takes, within reason, to gain your willingness, Valencia. This feud isn't your fault or your problem, but you are tasked with resolving it. And for that, you will have my lifelong gratitude."

Chapter Six

VALENCIA

After I agreed to attend family dinner—and by attend, he meant not embarrass him—Garen left me to rest and prepare. I conducted a quick search of the guest house and found what I'd expected; nothing weaponizable. Not even butter knives or ceramic dishes.

"I can still stab you with a spoon, *Gary*."

There was a lived in office and from that I deduced this guest house was a work from home area.

Retreating to my bedroom, I opened my window to let in a breeze and perused the closet's contents, listening as someone entered the patio door.

I ran a bath, taking my time to sniff test the various oils and salts stocked in a corner cabinet.

The quiet time helped me wrangle my temper; I doubted he'd be so sanguine about property destruction a second time.

He'd played it off, but Lord Garen hadn't been happy. If he ever brought it up I'd frame it as an acceptable loss in order to gain his goal; my cooperation. The marriage oath must require at least verbal consent unless this society was so feudal it allowed brides to be dragged to an altar and wed under obvious duress.

A light tap sounded at the bathroom door as I slid into the water.

"Densafa? Do you have everything you need?" He paused. "I can join you if you'd like a neck rub, though I cannot promise that's all—"

"Read the room, Gary." I leaned back on the lip of the tub, closing my eyes. "Go make pretty pictures with bits of tiny colored cardboard."

"I'm beginning to wonder if you harbor some resentment for the time I spent on my hobby, Val. If you'd asked, you would have had my undivided attention." His voice thickened into rich molasses. "I certainly resented the time you spent with your little buzzing toys. Listening to you stifle your moans, imagining that it was my cock slick from your pussy. Do you know how many nights I stood outside your door, telling myself to wait, to not break it down and teach you the far superior use of my—"

I sat up, sloshing water as I glared at the door, my clit pulsing. "Go. *Away.*"

A muffled chuckle. "Soon, Val. Enjoy your. . .bath." Then the feeling of absence again; I didn't hear footsteps.

I shivered, running my fingers along my oil slicked legs. He wanted to do far more than rub my neck or drag me to an altar; if he hadn't fantasized about fucking me on it to an audience, I'd be surprised.

My fingers skimmed my clit, circling it, but I stopped. The last thing I needed to add to this situation was sexual frustration, and nothing I could do for myself would help right now. Or maybe the smart thing to do was pop the balloon so I could think.

But I sighed. Time to get the strategic submission started. The sooner I demolished his guard, the sooner I could begin to work against him from within.

I acknowledged the strong pang of regret at the thought that he'd been a mirage. Gary didn't exist. But I was allowed to grieve the loss of my relationship; it had been real to me. Loss made this situation even worse; I grieved a man I'd loved while staring his doppelgänger, my kidnapper, in the face.

He wasn't in the kitchen or living room or the other bedroom. Which left one room.

"You said you would do whatever it took to gain my willing participation," I said, and stopped short as I entered the office.

I'd noted in my prior impromptu tour that the pale blue walls and warm floors extended here. The back wall had been removed and replaced with another set of sliding glass doors, and one entire wall was devoted to floor to shelf bookcases. The overall aura of the room with something lived in, and cozy. The owner of this room valued peace and knowledge, and disavowed pretension. At least in private.

Two men turned towards me, one of them Garen, standing behind a large wood desk cluttered with papers, books, and gold ink pens. The other was just as tall, though storm gray eyes glittered at me rather than deep brown. I eyed their subtle resemblance. Fair white skin with neutral undertones, lean muscular builds, and long silvery hair. Like twin LOTR elves.

"I interrupted you," I said. "My apologies."

Garen gestured me forward. The other man stalked towards me, giving me the kind of thorough once over that begged for a backhanded slap. There was something about Casakraine that brought out my less than civilized side. Maybe that something was being kidnapped.

"So this is the Gisleyan halfling," the man said, circling me. He wore molded leather armor in green edged with gold, though no visible weapons. "Fetching. She's shades of gold, almost like she's Anteyan. Your children should suit the bloodline well enough."

I didn't look that much like them. My hair and skin were more sunkissed gold rather than Nordic pale and besides...the blonde wasn't natural. I'd darkened to an ashy brunette when I was a child.

He stopped circling me and lifted a hand as if to brush his fingers across my cheek.

I gave him a stony look. "If you touch me, I will bite your fingers off."

"Believe her," Garen murmured.

His eyes sharpened then he smiled, slow and slightly malicious. "Oh, cousin, if my bed wasn't full, I would enjoy assisting you in acclimating this one to the delights of the Cassanian Courts."

Garen cleared his throat. "Lady Valencia, may I introduce my cousin, Lord Constin, Housesworn to Andreien Sahakian-Casakraine. Constin, this is the Lady Valencia of House Anteyan, eldest daughter of Lord Narazah."

"I'm not of House anything," was my curt reply. "I'm Valencia Rubio." I paused, returning his thorough look with one as blatant and objectifying. "Does everyone in your family have the same build and coloring? Like fantasy porn elves?"

Lord Constin narrowed his eyes at me. "If you address me as Legolas, I will bite *your* fingers off. As for the porn. . .if my Lady Hasannah gives leave, we can make arrangements."

I injected all of my disdain into my silent response.

He sighed, turning to Garen. "When she's settled in, bring her to see Hasannah. Anah loathes visitors, so I'll enjoy springing one on her."

"I'm not going to facilitate violating another woman's boundaries," I said.

Constin scoffed. "Realms, she's one of those." He laughed. "You have fun rubbing the shiny off that, cousin."

"What is it you need, mi cielo?" Garen asked.

I moved closer to the desk, shifting to keep the cousin in my line of sight. "I require a pool, Gary, since you require me as a wife. This city is landlocked and it's going to drive me crazy. You know the beach is one of the few things—"

He waved a hand. "Yes, yes, you needn't state your position. It will take a few weeks, but there's room on the grounds to have a pool dug. You'll want a sand surround rather than stone, I assume?"

I stared at him, mildly disgusted. I'd hoped to pinpoint how expensive having a so-called wife would be, but both men looked as if my request was reasonable. Gary had always acted as if he came from a working middle class background. Not impoverished, but not taking a yearly trip to Disneyworld either.

"It's a reasonable request," Constin said, as if echoing my thoughts. "Lord Andreien finished Anah's home studio and we're all much happier now that she has her own interior space with a locking door." He smiled again, still sharp. "Where we can monitor the only entrance."

Maybe I would go visit this Hasannah, and explain to her the psychology behind self-imposed cages. But of course that's what I was doing by requesting a pool. Whatever time I spent on the grounds sunning myself, falsely congratulatory for swindling him out of a chunk of money, was time he didn't have to monitor my movements off the grounds.

The men were looking at me. "Do you still want a pool?" Garen asked, a thread of amusement in his tone.

My jaw tightened, but I gave him a smooth smile. "Of course."

Just because I understood how he was going to use it against me didn't mean I didn't want it. I needed water. If I was going to be forced to marry him,

I'd be the most expensive wife in the history of this city—until I was the most expensive widow.

"I'll leave you to your negotiations," Lord Constin said, giving me a half-amused, half-something else nod as he left the office.

The something else wasn't quite warning, wasn't quite chilling foresight, but seemed to be the nod a man gave a cute trapped thing he knew would be brought to heel—but there would be blood if it protested too much.

I would never be brought to heel. Marriage, children, a long life lived together—never. If I had to wait Lord Garen out, one day I would pay him back for taking away my free will, no matter how he tried to make it noble.

"Let us discuss this private beach," Garen said.

I faced him again, recognizing *that* tone of voice. "You agreed."

"I did. But you agree it's a significant expense? The lowest estimate is $120,000 USD. Labor costs in Casakraine are more expensive since we are required to pay our people a living wage." He gave me a smooth smile.

"You had estimates drawn up?"

The smile turned quizzical. "Of course. I understood what you would require. And the lowest estimate—"

I waved a hand. "I heard you. It's expensive. I thought the House Lords were all wealthy." I recalled *some* of his babble. Of course now I knew he wasn't a Faeophile, but had been trying to teach me about the city I'd be living in, unbeknownst to me.

He hummed. "Anteyan is by no means insolvent, but neither are we the wealthiest House in Casakraine. My finances are now your own as well. You may have what you desire, but have a care for our purse. Our financial recovery after the marriage will take some time."

I began to feel hunted. This was a married person discussion, and we weren't even married yet. "I could get a job."

He drew his brows down in a delicate scowl. "You'll wish to find something meaningful to occupy your time until our children come, yes. But I insist the occupation you choose be worthy of a Lord of House Anteyan. I'm afraid I'll have to forbid any menial labor as a matter of course. Perhaps you should speak to Mag and see what she suggests. She'll have ideas for suitable businesses or charitable pursuits, or perhaps you could work together in arts or genteel entertainment. Lady Hasannah is prima ballerina of Sahakian Arts, and that does not diminish her Lord's dignity."

I ignored the babbling, the classist elitism, and the remark about children—it was a classic technique. He was attempting to distract me. But from what?

I placed a small wager with myself. In the next thirty seconds he would tell me the price, the real price, of this pool. He wanted me to agree without much thought—thus, the conversational distraction.

"So considering the significant expense—which I am delighted to incur for my wife's pleasure—I would like to ask for something small in return. A token, really."

Garen, my Gary, I know you almost as well as you think you know me. You reveal far too much when you babble, because you think I'm not a threat.

"The token?" I asked.

He gave me his earnest, somber, not at all threatening and not up to anything at all look. The one that I used to take at face value before patting him on the shoulder and asking about his latest model castle so he could talk while I thought about work.

Now that I reflected, many of those seemingly one-sided conversations had ended with me somehow agreeing to think about leaving the shelter and moving away with him. I'd never taken it seriously, except for the days leading up to when my spidey sense went off. I'd realized he was right, and I needed a long break from my job.

He'd urged me outside on my walk, and now I was in Casakraine.

Hijo de puta.

"A kiss," he said. "Nothing more."

Chapter Seven

VALENCIA

My expression mirrored his former frown. "A kiss."

That was so straightforward, it had to be a trap. But what kind of trap?

"A kiss for a small private beach. Consider this my suspicious face."

He spread his hands. "Not small. Of a size to entertain my Lady's chosen guests. You may eventually entertain the Heir and consort, considering our House's connection to the Sahakians. It must not be shabby."

"Of course not, that would be a disaster."

He gave me a knowing look, then said in his Gary voice, "Yeah, Val, first world problems. But among the upper caste, the sane prefer to avoid said problems because they lead to sword fights—and brides dragged to altars. I'd like a few quiet centuries."

I examined the forfeit, and could find no loopholes. A kiss was a kiss was a kiss. It wasn't like he was going to kiss me with poisoned lips.

"Very well. A kiss. I agree. On one additional minor condition."

"Interesting. The condition?"

"Drop the boyish act. It may, I concede, may be a small facet of your true personality. . .but you're an urban warlord. You aren't harmless, or kind, or goofy."

A beat of silence, two, three, as he considered me. Then he nodded.

"If you insist, Valencia," he said, his voice rich and dark and smooth with a lifetime of manipulating silly women into the exact corner he preferred to ravish them.

The corner of his mouth curved up in a smile, his brown eyes paling a half shade, and I wondered how I'd made a mistake.

"But you may find you prefer my boyish facet, when all is said and all is done. If you want it back, simply say the name."

His posture altered to match his voice. Garen walked around the desk and as I turned to keep him in front of me, he halted, looking down.

Not for the first time, I forced myself to shove away the unease of physical intimidation. I wasn't short, after all, 5'11 was a respectable height for a woman, especially in Spain twelve decades ago when I'd been born. I'd towered over most women and several men in my small town.

But these Fae were all tall, not a single one below six feet. Was it natural, or did they breed for height?

"A kiss," he murmured, sliding his hands around my waist.

Before I could say anything, he lifted me up onto the desk. The hands he habitually kept clasped behind him or shoved in pockets as if they were untrustworthy appendages with minds of their own, slid down to my knees and gently pushed my legs apart. My robe parted on either side, and I wasn't wearing undergarments.

I flattened my hands on his chest. "You said a kiss."

"I did, Val. But you did not specify the definition of kiss. What have I told you? Definitions are the bedrock of any discussion. If you haven't agreed on definitions, you've agreed to nothing that comes after. I'll forgive poor negotiating this once, since the day has been trying."

He lowered his head, his lips hovering just over mine, but not touching. "But if you do this again, it will be my duty to correct you. I can't let you loose in our society without having mastered foundational skills. Our House has a reputation to maintain, and I won't have my rabbit taken advantage of. I'm tired of killing."

Everything in me clenched on the word correct. "I don't play those games.

I won't call you Daddy. I won't let you span—" The word choked in my throat. I tried to say it again, "I won't let you spank me," but I couldn't.

Eyes widening, I wrapped a hand around my throat, and stopped trying to speak.

Garen lowered himself to his knees in front of me, tilting his head back to maintain eye contact. "Fae cannot lie, densafa. You are Fae enough for that to apply—I've watched you closely for almost a year now."

I inhaled, horrified. I'd lied before. I lied all the time. I was adept at—I halted my frantic internal denial, and thought. Really thought back.

Did I tell outright lies, or did I skim the truth so well nothing could be used against me? I'd never deliberately lied to police or clients, and there was no reason to lie to close friends or associates. Even when I'd extricated a woman out of a potentially explosive situation, had I outright lied?

No. . .no, I didn't think I had. And wasn't that one of the reasons why Gary had appealed to me so much? His so-called negotiation training? All he'd been doing was helping me hone an already well-developed skill.

"I see," I said. "That's unfortunate."

This magical truth serum, or whatever it was, would be inconvenient.

Especially since I'd inadvertently revealed something about myself. I better understood why it always took Gary so long to speak, even in a casual conversation. I'd assumed him to be a little slow at first, until as weeks passed it became clear he was simply thoughtful. Of course once he started talking, it took a mild shock to his system to get him to shut up. The other side of that coin being he could go for days in peaceful silence.

"Oh, you'll learn to work around it," he was saying. "I'll have you trained in little time. Your mind is shockingly agile considering your sperm donor. I'm surprised he didn't shoot gremlins out of his loins but, no, you are a sane and intelligent being. Your sister has qualities to recommend her as well. It must be the mothers' genetics as the mitigating factor. Curious."

I ignored his babbling again—his antipathy towards my father couldn't be helped—and filed away the reminder I had a sister.

"I don't care if some part of me would enjoy spanking," I said when he paused for breath, keeping my voice firm. "I don't want anything done without my permission."

"Certainly not, densafa. It isn't enjoyable unless both parties want it. Have I ever attempted to coerce you into any action outside of your will?"

"You kidnapped me."

"That was not an attempt. That was a success."

His breath ghosted along the inside of my thigh, but his lips didn't touch my skin. Of course not, because any touch of his mouth against my skin could be considered a kiss, since we were using deviousness rather than intent.

Words unsteady as his breath slowly reached the juncture of my thighs, I said, "You know what I meant by kiss. You're going against the spirit of the bargain."

"We've discussed that before," he murmured. "There is no such thing as the spirit of a bargain. There is only the bargain. Separate your emotion from fact. Fact is a scalpel, and emotion is a scythe. Scalpels for peace, scythes for war."

An invisible force pushed me onto my back. He pulled my hips forward, pushing my legs farther apart.

"Enough talking," he had the nerve to say. I wasn't the one talking. "And since you didn't select your words with care, I'm free to interpret the manner of kiss in any way I choose."

Gentle fingers spread my folds, and his mouth latched delicately around my clit.

I gasped as his tongue circled the nub of flesh which rarely saw any attention either than my toy—a toy that we now knew irritated dear Gary. I'd have to retrieve it, and make sure I used it every night as loudly as possible now that I knew he'd been outside my door listening. We'd maintained separate rooms for privacy, and he hadn't protested.

He'd been so considerate. Giving me that space, never pressing for more than I wanted to give.

It all had been subterfuge.

Garen pressed now, tongue and lips on my body, pulling me closer as he devoured me.

If I'd harbored delusions that once I took him to bed I'd have to direct him, those delusions were shattered now.

"This is by no stretch of the imagination a kiss," I said on a shaky exhale.

Fingers pinched the inside of my thigh as if to say shut up. My hips ground against his mouth, and vaguely I reassured myself that this was a perfectly natural reaction and I couldn't be blamed at all. Or blamed when the only thing that left my mouth was a moan as he slid a finger inside me.

One, as if testing the waters, my muscles clenching around him.

And then a second, and a third, sliding deep inside my channel to seek my G-spot, the underside of that external bundle of nerves.

He stimulated me from above, and beneath, and I said nothing.

Not no, not stop.

I said nothing but god, and I wasn't certain that when I said god I didn't mean Garen.

Crying out, I came on his tongue and fingers, my body seizing and clamping around him, his wet thrusts continuing through the aftershocks as if he was forcing my body to chase a second release.

Chase it, hunt it down, capture it and force it into compliance, and to the distant sound of some helpless woman's moans, I came a second time.

Shattered.

Almost sobbed his name as if giving me mind numbing pleasure also meant giving him the chains to voluntarily shackle me to him.

"Think," he said in a smooth drawl, running his tongue up my slit because now he wasn't pretending to abide by the terms of the so-called bargain, "how good it will feel when it's my cock fucking you in place of my tongue. Making you come over and over again, your screams shredding your throat because I don't release you from my bed until you're too spent to lift your head. But I'm happy to have you ride my tongue until you're ready for more."

Dios. Dios.

Another long, slow lick, another thrust. "It's tradition for a Cassanian warrior to give up something in the weeks leading to their wedding. A small token of the willing deprivation they'll undergo on behalf of their spouse."

I shuddered, gasping, meeting his thrusts, my fingers now tangled in his silky hair. "You could give up your lengthy speeches. I'd get some peace."

He smiled against the inside of my thigh. "I'm giving up wine." Another lick, another thrust. "But with you on my tongue, I won't need it."

Fuck me with a double Dark Fae cock, this man could put a proverbial Latin lover to death from shame. How had I ever thought he was asexual with a strong dose of nerd thrown in?

"There are benefits to being my wife, Val." His replaced his tongue with his fingers as he whispered against my skin. "I studied pleasure. Fae, human, the other species across the realms, it didn't matter. I knew I couldn't offer a spouse great power, great prestige, great wealth. My House is modest."

He withdrew, and one wet finger trailed down the inside of my thigh and he wrapped his hand around my knee again. A light, but searingly possessive touch.

"But I can offer this. My mind is at your disposable, and the exclusive use of my body, if exclusiveness is what you desire. You can use me however you want, Val."

His clothing whispered as he rose, disentangling himself from my fingers. I turned my face away, blinking back tears. I'd never felt this helpless, this mastered as if my body wasn't my own.

I pushed up on my elbows, and then my hands, my legs still shaking. Eyes that were no longer brown but a molten gold stared at me, a harshness to the dark expression on his face, the tense slant of his shoulders as if he held himself back.

"There's nothing I won't let you do to me. There's nothing you could ask me to do to you that I would deny."

But to prove how thoroughly he owned me, Garen slid a hand around the back of my neck, tugged my head back and covered my lips with his. His soft, slick lips, the taste of my release on his tongue as it dived deep, conquering me yet again.

His arm slid around my back and he held me as I shuddered, my thighs still open and cradling him. I could do nothing but sit there and scramble for the last vestiges of my dignity, my distance.

It was just two. . .three?. . .orgasms. It shouldn't matter. It shouldn't matter at all. How many times had a woman come to me so hormone bonded to her abuser because sex was one of the tools he used, that she had to be reprogrammed and detoxed before she could let him go?

His thumb brushed my cheek. "I know there are things you want that you've told yourself you should be shamed for desiring. You've spent your adult life helping women who were abused, and though you can intellectualize your needs, it still bothers you that you want to submit. That you want a master, that you want to be forced to take pleasure."

I stared into his piercing gaze, transfixed, my horror growing as he cradled me against him.

Garen shook his head, eyes still flickering with shards of gold, his voice rougher and rougher as he spoke. "You shouldn't be ashamed, Valencia. Especially not with me. You are a Fae female, after all. It's your nature to be fucked into submission just as it's your nature to rise from the bed defiant, demanding more."

And here I was, being reprogrammed into wanting more.

I shoved him away, my breathing harsh, and scrambled off the desk. Ran.

A snarl behind me, a sound in no way human and in no way merciful. "Valencia."

I got halfway down the hall before the heavy weight of a predator slammed me to the ground. Hands slapped on either side of my head where I lay sprawled on my front.

"I've told you many times not to run from a High Lord, Valencia," he said in my ear, the words guttural. "And yet you ran. I'll take this as an invitation."

"No," I gasped as he lifted my bottom into the air, shoved my thighs apart, positioning me like I was a doll. "No. I don't want—"

This.

I tried to say that I don't want "this." And it was a lie.

And I was Fae. I couldn't lie.

"Tell me you don't want this, Valencia. Tell me you don't want me to take you up on the floor while you're sobbing and cursing my name, and I'll stop. I'll stop because if you can say it, it will be the truth."

I tried to say I didn't want him to master me, to be the key to unlocking the sexuality I'd kept suppressed even during the months we'd lived together. I didn't want to fall so deeply into him I forgot all common sense.

I tried to say it and by my failure revealed more than what I'd intended. I would have to master Garen's trick of saying nothing if I wasn't certain I could speak a truth that was to my advantage.

"I hate you," I moaned.

"But you're still going to come on my cock. I'll watch the cream drip down your thighs and that is all the truth I need, densafa."

The head of his cock pressed against my opening.

I didn't want it, but I needed it. I craved it.

"Last chance. This is your last moment to plead for mercy—but we both know you won't."

"No," I said again, my voice a hoarse whisper, and he shoved inside me to the hilt.

I screamed, though my body was open, slick, welcoming.

I screamed when he withdrew and slammed back in, pushing my cheek against the floor, his thrusts savage, relentless, his hands on my hips holding me to him when I tried to wriggle and crawl away.

"Don't make me do this, please," I begged. "Garen, please."

"You're not a child, Valencia," he said on the end of snarl. "You can face what you desire. You can claim it."

"Release," I begged.

His only response was his fingers twisting my nipples, his hand in my hair, yanking my head back as my hips met his savagery.

I sobbed as he fucked me.

Fucked wasn't the right word.

I sobbed as he rutted me, stretched me wide to the point of pain and over and over and over...

Was this what it felt like?

Was this what it sounded like, this heavy slap of flesh against flesh, his breath just as harsh, nothing left of the urbane, sometimes diffident man I'd thought I'd known.

"Ten months I waited, and that's nothing in the life of a Fae. It felt like an eternity. An abyss of denial because I could not yet take what belonged to me without risking everything. You are my enemy's daughter, but you will be my wife. And by the end of this evening, the mother of my child."

He fucked me like he wanted me to break and beg him for more, like the discussion of who owned my body was quaint.

His cock swelled inside me and when I clenched around him, climaxing, he seeded me in a flood of heat, his hips grinding with the blatant intent to impregnate me then and there.

I wasn't on birth control. I hadn't needed it, and nothing seemed worth the side effects.

"Garen," I cried out, trying to get away in truth this time.

When I said I'd give him a child, I hadn't meant *now*. Not even in five years, but eventually. I cursed myself, because of course the timeline was the first thing I should have hammered down. I'd let myself get distracted.

"Stop, I'm not on the pill."

"I know." Another snarl, and his seed pumping into me. "And you won't be. You have to have a child, Val, or the peace will break. You must birth an

Heir to combine the Houses. Until you're pregnant, everything is at risk. I gave you as much time as I could."

My shriek of fury pierced my eardrums, but I wasn't strong enough to stop him, to break away from the bruising cage of his hands on my hips.

Wasn't strong enough for my body to care about my outrage because as he continued to fuck me, another climax rose as if my cervix wanted to open, to suck up all his come and make a child.

Finally, he stilled, his hands caressing and squeezing my ass. "I want you with child when we approach the altar, Valencia. The timing in your cycle is right. I took you from Earth realm soon enough for a viable attempt. If you conceive for me, I will be very pleased with you."

I didn't move, exhausted, listening to him tell me how he'd planned my kidnapping to coincide with my fertility cycle so he could impregnate me before dragging me to the altar, an unwilling sacrifice to resolve decades of Fae savagery.

"Do you want a bath?" he asked when I didn't respond. "Before dinner. I can run you a hot bath if you're sore." He cupped my pussy as if he were feeling my temperature.

"Val?"

I didn't have the energy to tell him there was no thermometer between my thighs, and my silence wasn't because I was physically sick.

He sighed, picked me up and carried me down the hall into my bedroom, a literal pep in his step as if he felt energized—while my muscles held the strength of a dead goldfish.

"I didn't hurt you, did I, Val?" Gary asked, setting me on the bed. "I was a little rough, but you really caught me by surprise when you ran. I think we gave it a solid first try, though. You took me as if you were born to it. Well, you were, but you know what I mean." He entered the closet, murmuring about dinner and bath salts and disposable versus cloth diapers. . .and something about dressing attendants.

He emerged with clothing, stopped in front of me and studied my face. His voice altered. "Are you well, Valencia? I do not intend this to be a brutal process."

"I hate you."

Garen sighed. "I know. It will pass."

"If you touch me again, I'll fight you."

His eyes turned gold. He set the clothing aside and climbed onto the bed, straddling my waist. "Perhaps once more before dinner then? It will help you to relax. Scream no again, densafa."

He covered my mouth with his hand, pushing my thighs open. "Scream no as loud as you like."

Chapter Eight

VALENCIA

"It's a game, Valencia," he said as we strolled across the slightly overgrown lawn.

If it was a lawn, rather than grounds that were lightly manicured and maintained but otherwise allowed to grow freely. It wasn't lawn like we'd come to think of on Earth.

Whoever established the estate had cleared enough ground of forest to fit the main house, the guest house, and the vegetable and flower gardens as well as a circular stone walking path that contained a wild copse of trees and flowers.

Fingers brushed my shoulder, slid down to grasp my hand. A custom of ours, walking hand-in-hand. I didn't know if taking my hand now was an attempt at manipulation, or habit.

"Enjoying our games is not an indictment of your character, and it does not mean you've given over autonomy to me outside of the bedroom."

I stared at the main house, not seeing it other than to note it appeared to be made of glossy dark wood like the forest surrounding the property, and was only two levels. The upper level was dark though there was light and movement on the bottom; people revealed through wall sized windows, a drift of voices in the air.

"You don't think it says something about my mental health that I enjoy being raped by the fake boyfriend who kidnapped me?" I snapped.

Because I glanced at him, I caught his slight grimace at the word rape. "I am your betrothed, the male you've dated for ten months and lived with for four. Not a fake boyfriend, and a rape fantasy is normal. You are twelve decades old. You know this. Also, I understand your meaning, but I'd prefer we be specific when discussing our bed." He halted, turned to me. "Unless you feel I raped you. You ran, Val. You know—"

"Yes, I know. Running is an invitation. I'm not accusing you of rape."

"I'm glad. That's why we use specifics, to prevent unfortunate misunderstandings."

"Don't talk to me like I'm twelve, Gary."

Garen's eyes flashed with flecks of gold. "That wasn't my intent. As it wasn't your intent to accuse me of one of the viler acts known to any civilized species, after months of restraining myself."

"Would you like a cookie?"

He glared, then smoothed his expression.

I recalled a conversation several months ago. "You once told me that if I ever travel to Casakraine, not to catch the eye of a Fae Lord." Which was a spectacular piece of compartmentalization considering he was one. The male species never ceased to amaze me.

"Yes. It isn't wise. We aren't accountable to the judicial system like people in power would be in your world. In theory."

"Is rape a crime here?"

"No."

I stared at him, nauseated. He *knew* how I felt about sexual crimes. "How can you consider yourself a civilized species?"

"We don't, not the way you understand the word civilized. Understand that our words translated into English are broad at best, wildly inaccurate at worst. Rape isn't a crime, per se, because no one is going to force a Lord into a court of law to be prosecuted. Such an insult is left up to the family and allies of the victim to punish. There are less deaths if it remains a private matter rather than a criminal one."

"You said your House and my biological father's House have been embroiled in a decades long war because of this not crime."

"Yes. Until recently, due to the stupidity of your biological sire, there were no deaths outside of our two Houses. This is considered a success, Valencia. It's why this is one of the particular crimes that is not prosecuted in court. Both because no person of power would stand for it, and because it can be more satisfactorily resolved between the two parties."

"How many perpetrators get away with it?"

He lifted his brows, lowered them. "Few. We're a clan based society. It's rare an individual has no allies or family to turn to, and the Low Fae know how to avoid our gaze."

"The Lords."

"Yes. It usually doesn't take so long to resolve the matter, either," he added. "But Narazah's House is powerful, and my House is. . .strategic. Thus we were evenly matched. Their warriors thought us weak, though, or they would not have *touched* my cousin." His voice flattened. "No House will make that mistake again, unless they are certain they are the more powerful." He cupped my face. "But regarding your discomfort. What is that mortal song. . .yes. The heart desires what it will."

"The heart desires—do you mean wants what it wants?"

"Yes yes, that. I will not have you twisting yourself into a pretzel. Half of your nature is pure savagery. Accept it. Enjoy it. I intend to."

"Which half?"

Garen laughed and kissed my nose. "Perhaps both halves. The only problem is that you've spent too much time mired in human culture." Amusement crossed his face. "If you believe what we shared is dark, it behooves me to introduce you to certain aspects of our society very, very slowly."

"I still don't want to marry you. I still don't want to have a child right away."

His voice smoothed, the smile in his eyes going neutral. "I know."

"You're forcing me to do those things and that is not a fantasy."

"I know."

"How is that any different from what happened to Maggie?" It was and it wasn't, but I wanted to see if he would attempt to justify it.

His expression hardened. He didn't break. He didn't justify it. Good. At least we were on the same page.

We stared at each other. I shook my head and turned to start walking again. He caught up a second later, resting his hand on the small of my back. "I haven't tried to pretty up what is being done to you, Valencia."

"Perhaps not, but you aren't going to stop either. You'll sacrifice me for your cousin's honor."

He didn't speak for several moments, until we were at the back patio of the house. He stopped and looked down at me. "If it were a matter of choosing your honor over Maggie's, I would choose yours, Valencia, if forced to make a decision. But I am Vowed, and without this marriage—"

I pulled away and strode towards the patio doors. "Don't beat a dead horse, Gary."

It wasn't a grand entrance, but it was an entrance. I opened the patio doors as if I owned the house, and in any society with property laws related to marriage, as soon as dear Gary put a ring on it, I would own this damn house so I intended to make myself comfortable.

Stepping inside, I waited as the hum of conversation died down and people turned towards me. Fae, all Fae, not a human among them.

No. . .I recognized the softened bone structure and round ears of another halfling. Some halflings had pointed ears, but not many from what I'd been told. Illogical biology, that. Give us immortality but not pointed ears. It seemed a bit arbitrary.

The halfling walked forward, a woman slightly taller than medium height with curly light brown hair cut around her shoulders and sun-tanned skin that was probably once as pale as Gary's. Blue eyes with brown around the iris stared at me, widening.

She smiled. "Our new cousin," Maggie said.

It wasn't in me to resent her. She wasn't the root cause of my victimization, the other folks were. She'd been a victim herself, like so many of the women who'd come through my shelter seeking temporary safety for themselves and their children.

I smiled at her and held out my hand. "It's nice to meet you. I'm Valencia Rubio. You're Maggie, Gary's cousin."

"Yes, I'm Maggie, short for Magaia, not Margaret." She ignored my hand and enveloped me in a hug which I was happy to return, then she laughed. "You call him Gary? That's rich. Gary. Like one of those pet. . .ah, they look like rats but humans think they're cute? They put them in small cages."

"Hamster?"

"Yes, that." Her lips twitched.

"She's the only one with permission to do so," Lord Garen said behind me, his voice cool. But I heard the humor beneath it, the coolness a façade. "I missed you, Mag."

She pulled away from me, her hands on my shoulders as she studied my face. "I missed you too, Garen. It took you long enough to bring our bride home. We were getting worried."

No one was talking, and though I was focused on Maggie, I'd scanned the room and pinpointed a half dozen other people, all of them staring.

My smile faded. "Yes, it took him almost a year to trick me into coming to Casakraine. Though a trick implies some level of consent."

A shadow crossed her face as she looked down, letting her hands fall away from my shoulders. "I'm sorry."

"It's not your fault. I'm not angry with you, I'm angry with Garen and. . .I suppose, my biological father. Though from what I understand," I framed my words delicately, "the original fault doesn't lie with him either."

Someone snorted. "What have you been telling your halfling Gislayen bride, Garen?" A masculine voice, deep and derisive. "Or is she as intelligent as her father?"

I understood that was an insult, since Gary had done nothing but bemoan Narazah's challenged intellect. Not everyone would be as welcoming as Maggie.

"There hasn't been much time to fully outline the situation," Garen said, coming to stand at my side. His voice was a kind of pleasant I wouldn't want to meet in an alley on a dark night. "Please attribute any faulty conclusions to my inadequate explanations, rather than her lack of comprehension, and mind your manners, Leone."

I glanced at him. "It's fine. I have a fair grasp of how this situation is going to play out."

I looked past Maggie's shoulders, letting my expression settle into the reserved but friendly to you as long as you're friendly to me expression.

"The enemy daughter, half human, and the human half from a different culture," I continued, keeping my voice light. "I'm an unwilling participant here, so my loyalty is worse than unguaranteed. Your Lord is forced to wed me, bed me, introducing the loathed genetics of the man who harmed your House into your bloodline. I understand." I smiled faintly. "This story has played out in human history over and over again in multiple dynasties. Countless dramas. The Fae don't have a corner on the market for enemies to spouses marriages. It's a cliche at this point."

My gaze settled on the man who'd spoken, Leone. He drew close as our eyes locked, the same long, straight silvery hair down his back though his brown eyes were a lighter shade than Garen's and flecked with blue.

The look on his face was as friendly as mine, but he held himself with the control of a man who wouldn't translate general dislike into action.

I didn't relax, but I wasn't afraid he'd attack me in a corner some night either. I could work with that. I would have to work with that.

"You understand something of the situation," Leone said. "As for your loyalty. . .your father abandoned you with your human mother. You owe him none either."

I chuckled. "Oh, I'm not happy with him, never fear. I've no interest in some kind of daddy daughter reunion. If he runs the kind of House where his warriors didn't expect his censure for the behavior that started this feud. . ." I glanced at Maggie once, but her expression remained serene, ". . .then I don't want anything to do with him."

"You will be our Lord's wife, and mother of his Heir."

"And you're campaigning for me to throw my lot in with you?" I shrugged. "Trust takes time to build and I'm not interested in proving myself to any of you. I'm the victim here, not the perpetrator."

"You have nothing to prove, Val," Garen said, his hand once more coming to rest on the small of my back. "I've told you what is required of you. You need not court any favor other than mine."

"I know." I sighed, thrumming my fingers on the side of my leg. "This is what you can expect from me. I won't betray the interests of your House, and

I won't interfere in House business. If I can't escape, I intend to keep to myself. I'm here under duress, and it's going to take me a long time to come to terms with that. My relationship with Gary is my business, not yours."

"And will you Vow you will not go running to your father or his allies at the first possible moment? You will not expose our weaknesses to the dogs?" Leone asked.

Garen inhaled. "She will Vow nothing. Why would you ask so asinine a question?"

I smacked the back of my hand against his mouth to shut him up. He bit me, but let it be. "A Vow is magically enforced, correct? With consequences if it's broken? No, I won't make any Vow. But I'll make a personal promise. Whether you choose to believe it is up to you. I don't care."

"Your terms are fair," Maggie said. "I know what the ceasefire requires from you and you're right—" she glanced at her cousin "—it's no better than what happened to me, and Lord Issahelle cares about as much."

"Issahelle cares," Garen said when I lowered my hand. "But she won't interfere in House business, you know that. Constin's aid was invaluable, and he wouldn't have come if Andreien hadn't allowed it. That was as much debt as we could afford to accrue."

"What's happening to me is not the same thing," I said, wondering who all these people were. "I'm here under duress, but...my relationship with Gary is not the same as what happened to you."

I wouldn't demean her rape by saying that a consensual relationship with Garen, even if it was under circumstances which defined the opposite of consensual, was rape.

I was an adult. An adult of 120 years with a wealth of life experience, and I understood the facets of my situation. I wasn't tricking myself into accepting something that was coercive so I could mentally cope. I'd wanted the sex, even if some of my reasons were rooted in survival and strategy rather than desire or love.

But I'd made a choice. More importantly, I didn't want this woman standing in front of me to take on the burden of my perceived rape as well as her own.

"You don't have to worry about me putting a dagger in his back some night either," I added, glancing at Leone again. He stared back, expression flat. "I'm not particularly violent—"

"How do you get away with such lies," Garen muttered.

"Property damage is not the same as physical violence."

"I would almost rather you stabbed me. It is less expensive."

"Think of it as an investment in my long-term happiness. If I don't get it out of my system now, the cost will rise over time."

"Did he tell you?" Maggie asked. "Did he tell you that if it wasn't you, it would be your younger sister? That she's *my* lover?"

I blinked, startled, but not from the note of savage possessiveness in her voice. "No, that's a little detail dear Gary left out."

And of course Maggie would rather sacrifice a stranger than her own lover. I wasn't mad about that either. This was the kind of situation where there was too much gray, and the morally corrupt guy was easy enough to sympathize with too. Well, I hadn't met my sperm donor yet. So far I had zero sympathy for him. A team took its tenor from its leader.

"I wish you would have come to me and asked, damnit. All of you." I shook my head, sighing. "If you had asked—"

"You would have sacrificed yourself?" Leone said, the curl of his lip scornful. "Your life, your womb, your will, to our House?"

I frowned. "Have none of you heard of bribes?" Classic avoidance.

"I did consider that before I introduced myself to you," Garen said. "But after some observation I concluded that strategy was likely to fail rather miserably."

"When in doubt, a little kidnapping and coercive impregnating will do just as well."

"Ah, I believe it is time for dinner. We may continue this discussion over food and wine, with perhaps a little judicious editing of our words, densafa. Shall we?"

"Lots of it," Maggie said, shoulders slumping. "That's why I opened the cheap stuff. We're going to be drinking it like fish tonight. None of us like any of this. None. Any."

Chapter Nine

VALENCIA

Garen didn't drink the wine, making some lighthearted excuse when Maggie asked why. I wasn't young enough to blush at the quietly amused, heavy-lidded glance reminding me of his betrothal sacrifice, or maybe the day's events had inured me to that kind of embarrassment.

We were all adults here. It would take more than heated looks to put me off my guard, but nice try, Gary.

"Is this estate outside of the city?" I asked. "I can't see anything beyond the forest boundary."

We'd moved from the dining room to an open family room facing the back wall of windows. The ceilings here were high, with exposed beams in the same warm wood as the floors. I'd settled onto a brown leather couch, comfortably worn but well cared for. The entire house was the same, and I'd need more time to determine whether or not this was a statement of emotional attachment to their surroundings, or if they were hovering on the edge of genteel poverty.

Considering my betrothed could afford a six-figure swimming pool, their definition of poverty and mine definitely didn't match up.

I spared a bit of worry that bribing me with a pool was an expense they grimly accepted, rather than one they could afford. But I wasn't certain yet that they deserved my concern, so I kept my worries to myself for now.

Maggie lifted her arms above her head, stretching. "Eh. It's easier to let enemies in and kill them conveniently on the front lawn."

Garen gave his cousin a brief, neutral look I decided was code for "shut up."

"We're located in the city proper," he said. "Once you go beyond the forest boundary, you'll hit city streets. Homes are more concentrated the closer you go to the central downtown—that would be Sahakian District's square but colloquially if you say downtown, everyone will know what you mean."

I stood, setting aside my drink. "Do you mind if I go for a walk? Alone. I need some quiet time and fresh air."

He brushed his fingertips along my arm, the gaze he leveled at me contemplative. "You may go, but don't leave the grounds."

"Oh? Don't leave the grounds. I understand."

"Valencia, if you leave the grounds, I will be forced to pursue you."

I turned towards the back patio doors. "I said I understood."

"Does she really understand?" Leone asked as I exited.

"She does, but she intends on being difficult."

Oh, not too difficult. Just difficult enough to remind him not to take my willing participation for granted.

"Why?" Maggie asked. "On general principle?"

"No. It is likely she wishes to see how I will respond."

"Sounds like an evening's entertainment then."

"I'm uncertain she will continue to think so once I am done with her."

He meant me to hear those words, of course, as a warning.

Game on, Gary.

I continued my ambling pace across the lawn, pausing to circle the center wild garden, standing still for a few moments to look up at the night sky and the almost lavender tinged moon. A second moon floated farther in the distance. These were definitely not Earth skies.

So. If I went beyond the forest boundary, dear Gary would pursue. If I left, how far could I travel and how long would it take him to come after me or send minions? When they caught me, would I be restrained, or courteously escorted back to the house?

It was good data to have even though he understood my intent. Whether he knew my purpose or not, at what point he pursued me would reveal the length of my leash, though I doubted a serious escape attempt would be successful at this time; it would take time for them to let their guard down.

The moment I plunged into the forest boundary, I began to jog.

Dense ancient fir trees loomed overhead, reaching for a star speckled sky that was barely visible through the canopy. A hint of something like jasmine drifted in the breeze, and the freshly turned up earth scent of forests everywhere. Though my eyes had already adjusted to the dark, I was still half human, my night vision not as acute as a Fae's. I couldn't go on a full out run without risking tripping, so I maintained a steady pace, using my ears as a compass.

The city outside the estate was quiet except for the occasional clop of hooves, hiss of steam or clatter of wheels against cobblestone.

As the forest thinned, and I was about to step across an invisible line of demarcation between tree and cobblestone sidewalk, a force hit me in the chest.

I gasped through the dull thud of pain. It lasted only seconds as my body continued moving forward as if through thick, electrified gel, then it dissipated. I stumbled forward, bending over and resting my hands on my knees.

"*Merde.*"

This must be the all-purpose magical protective barrier Gary called a ward. I'd listened to his explanation of Fae magical systems with half an ear the week he spent lecturing me on it.

"Protective barrier." I straightened and continued forward. "Meant to repel unwanted visitors. Stationary power that can be lowered or raised with the trigger phrase and is anchored to a physical boundary."

The cobblestones were slightly rough under my slippered feet. I walked until I saw narrow buildings a quarter mile in the distance, three stories high and made of brick or dark wood or a combination of both, lights on at the bottom floors.

This was farther than I had expected to get, and I was mindful Lord Garen hadn't given me a full primer on the inherent dangers in the city, including my biological father.

A sudden force almost sent me sprawling to my knees. I stumbled, caught myself and halted. Turning, I saw Garen several feet away, tall and straight backed, his hair and skin shimmering in the moonlight, his hands clasped behind his back.

Eyes black, impenetrable.

"I warned you not to leave the grounds, Valencia."

"You did. I heard you clearly."

"Are you certain you want to play this game again tonight? You cried the last time, if I recall."

There had been a few tears in my eyes because of the heightened emotions of the situation, but I hadn't cried. "You're exaggerating."

"Am I." He lifted his shoulders in a shrug. "Very well. Then run, Val. I'll give you a head start to make it fair."

Garen shimmered, then disappeared from sight. I swore, stared for a split second then turned on my heels and ran.

Yes, yes, I knew running was an invitation.

What I didn't know was if the invisibility was some kind of glamor or a mind trick. A faint breeze brushed the back of my shoulders, like fingers, or breath on my neck.

The next block the grounds of the estate ended, merging into what looked like a mixed residential and commercial square. Townhomes with shops at the bottom, a center walking park, the sort of small, sophisticated European village type planning I'd expected from Gary's descriptions of Casakraine.

I entered a café, wanting to park myself somewhere with witnesses—he couldn't be far behind and I wasn't certain of his mood.

As soon as I entered, I realized I'd made a mistake. I'd assumed my presence would go unnoticed—halflings weren't uncommon in Casakraine and my coloring was close enough to Anteyan's.

I gained first and second glances, those second glances turning into long stares.

They stared at me like I was an unwelcome stranger, and one wrong move someone would show me the door. Very well, no one had to tell me the hard way to get out. I turned, intending to exit, and found my way blocked by a female.

I stared at her, clasping my hands behind my back. A slight shimmer in the air surrounded her, a sharpness to her eyes and a certain tilt of her head that warned me to tread with care.

She reminded me a little of Gary; the stillness, the displacement of air when he passed, the utter self-assurance. High Fae? The others I met today were considered Low Fae, and they didn't have the aura of this female.

"You're new here," she said. "I don't know your face."

I fell back on good manners and gave a little half bow. "Yes, I'm new here."

Her eyes brightened. "Who are you running from, halfling?" She stepped forward, raising her hand, and ran the tips of her fingers along my hair. "To whom do you belong?"

One hundred and twenty years of stubborn pride warred with practicality. I could end this right now and say I belonged to Lord Garen.

I might as well slap the ball and chain around my ankle myself. Or a collar around my neck with a little jingling bell on it. That would be as effective.

"I belong to myself," I said. "I'd like to exit, if you would excuse me?"

She smiled, a slow spread of her lips. "House Anteyan has been at war for forty years. No one wanders into our District that we don't already know. And I don't know you."

This was a good lesson in not allowing Fae to get too close. Fingers that had skimmed my hair now flashed into motion, wrapping around my neck.

Stamping down on my instinctive violent response, I remained still. She was the aggressor, but would anyone care.

She lowered her head, inhaling. "I recognize the stench." Her grip tightened. "Gisleyan."

Could the Fae sniff out DNA? That would have been nice to know.

Inhaled again. "But also. . ."

The hand tightened some more, and I decided to abandon dignity. "I belong to Lord Garen."

"Kithara," someone in the café murmured. "It must be the Gisleyan Heir. He won't be happy if you bruise it."

It? *It?*

"You ran from your betrothed?" this Kithara said. "I think I'll enjoy dragging you back. Maybe a little bruised, but I doubt he'll mind."

"You know he will." The same voice, firmer this time. "Don't start a fight."

She looked over my shoulder. "He shouldn't have let his prisoner escape the leash."

Internally, I debated the merits of using physical force to defend myself or letting her drag me out of the café as the safer, though still unpleasant, option.

The café door opened again.

"Kithara." Garen's calm voice.

Chapter Ten

VALENCIA

She turned, dragging me with her then released my neck as if it was an afterthought. Garen didn't glance at me. He lifted a hand, casually, and backhanded the female.

She staggered back but didn't go down, blotting a dot of blood blooming on her lip.

"You may go," Garen said. My shoulders tensed.

Kithara bowed. "Lord."

Garen held out an arm. Placid brown eyes met mine, but I wasn't fooled.

I always believed a man when he showed his true colors. His casual blow proved he was capable of meting out mild violence.

That didn't surprise me. Few people weren't capable of violence. But there was a difference between self-defense and bullying.

"Valencia?" A mild inquiry.

I took his arm and let him lead me out of the café.

"What did you learn?" he asked.

"Your people are traumatized by new faces."

An hour ago there might have been a bite of sarcasm in my response but I'd seen Kithara's eyes. Heard her voice. Considered everything I knew about the last several decades of civil warfare between these two Houses. They were all traumatized, and I couldn't make light of it.

Garen nodded. "They're somewhat hypervigilant, and it's true that we allow very little through traffic in our District. We must have safe territory in the city. It was easier to seal the District than to monitor traffic."

"You told your people I was coming."

"They knew. None of them was expecting to see you, however." The bite I'd suppressed in my tone was present in his. "Kithara was admirably restrained."

"I believe her intention was to drag me back to you by my hair, missing the top layer of my skin."

"If that was all she intended, then you would have been fortunate. Don't forget whose daughter you are."

I tried to tug my arm away from his, which he didn't allow. "That's not my fault. You can't visit the sins of a father on a child."

"Can't? Demonstrably, one can. Is it right? No. But you are not a child, Valencia. You understand how muddy are the waters of right and wrong. This is why I warned you, in part, not to leave the grounds. You made a decision, and if there wasn't anything besides your disobedience at stake, I would've allowed you to experience the consequences of defying me. I wouldn't have had to even lift my own finger."

Garen stopped walking and drew me into a break between two buildings. "I hope you also learned that attempting to escape me is futile, mi cielo. You'll get only so far as I allow."

I was watching his face, his eyes, listening to the cadence of his voice and understood a harsh truth. He might truly believe he loved me but a part of him loathed me as well. A part of him wanted to see me pay the price of Gisleyan's crimes.

"You would destroy every last Gisleyan if you could, wouldn't you?"

He met my gaze. "Every last one, save two—which is ironic, considering the two are the daughters of the House." His voice was very, very quiet. "But you are Anteyan, and your sister will be adopted into our House as well. It's only because of this that you can walk freely in my District and live. I cannot promise my people will otherwise be welcoming."

"Gary—"

He shoved me against the wall, rough brick at my back. Not a hard shove, but when he stepped close he caged me with a hand on either side of my head. I wasn't escaping until he let me go.

"You chose not to heed my warning. When you choose to disobey me, you are choosing to accept the consequences."

"You talk as if I agreed to come to Casakraine in the first place. We don't have a bargain, so I'm not required to obey any of your rules."

Garen shook his head. "The bargain we have is that made by power. I have power, you have none."

There was no point in getting angry, so I didn't. Besides, he was right. Only equals sat down at a negotiating table, and we were so far from equal here in Casakraine that I couldn't even laugh about it. Laugh, or cry.

I felt nothing.

"But," he continued, "because I love you, and because I want my wife to be happy, I'm willing to lend you some of my power. Some of my authority. I'm willing to allow you to negotiate with me in good faith as if you have something I want."

Now *that* was a miscalculation. "I do have something you want. Willingness."

His eyes narrowed, and then he smiled, slow and approving. "Yes. Yes, you're correct, of course. I want your willing cooperation, and it's within your power to withhold that. Very good, Valencia. But there's one small wrinkle in this equation."

I shifted slightly, testing him, and he moved immediately to block my knee before I got my foot off the ground.

"What's the wrinkle, Gary?"

He slid one of his hands into my hair and fisted it, pulling me forward against his body as he tugged my head back sharply. My eyes prickled because it hurt. It was meant to hurt.

But he relaxed his fingers, and massaged my scalp where a second before heat had abused it.

"The wrinkle, my dear," he whispered, lowering his head to ghost his lips across my cheek, "is that you don't want to offer me willing cooperation. You want me to take it."

I didn't move, forced myself not to portray any emotion, even discomfort, in my expression. I'd known having sex with him was a risk. I'd known revealing that much about my inclinations would give him another bargaining chip against me.

If he knew what I wanted, he knew what he could withhold.

"I liked you better when you were pretending to be a human nerd," I said.

He chuckled. "The only reason you can get away with that lie-that-is-truth is because we both know liking me has nothing to do with wanting me. And nothing at all to do with being my wife." Then the warmth from his expression vanished. "Choose your consequence, Val."

"What?" I placed a hand on his chest, trying to push him away to give myself some space.

Garen didn't move, staring down at me, and the fingers in my hair re-tightened.

"Choose. Your consequence. I gave you an instruction, and you flouted it. Worse, you placed yourself in danger. There's no telling what the extent of your injuries might have been, and then I would have had to punish one of my most loyal warriors. That would have made me very unhappy, Valencia. Kithara does not deserve to be sacrificed to your stubbornness."

"My stubbornness? Are we forgetting that you kidnapped me? You have no right to expect anything but stubbornness. This is not a scenario where I am required to be a good, cooperative little girl for the sake of the greater good. You can go fuck yourself, Lord Garen."

"I can, but I won't, because you will be doing the fucking, densafa. Not choosing a punishment is, by default, a choice. A choice to accept the consequence I deem appropriate."

"I can't wait until you bring me back home. I am going to break things. So many things. Some of them over your head, if you're stupid enough to come close to me."

His lips curved against my cheek. He released me only to wrap his hands around my upper arms. "I have no right to do to you what I'm doing. It's wrong. And it doesn't matter, because what I have is—"

"I'm a little tired of hearing it."

Power. But I was half Fae, and I had power of my own, though it was untrained. One day I would be stronger, and that day would be followed by many, many days of burrowing under Lord Garen's guard, learning his weaknesses.

And on that one day, I would use every weakness I'd learned and break him. Then we would discover who truly had power and who didn't.

"Don't think I don't see the vengeance in your eyes," he whispered. "Don't think I don't understand that one night I may wake to a blade at my throat. Or not wake at all."

"Then why let me live after you marry me, if you know I'll be a threat?"

"Because I love you. Because you're half Fae, and I'd expect nothing less. Because, in time, you'll discover that you don't want to live without me any more than I want to live without you."

The hands wrapped around my upper arms pushed me to my knees, the expression in his eyes brightening, turning them into amber flames.

"Even if you hate me. Especially if you hate me."

The warm brown now a hot, molten gold. The pretty silver hair framing ghostly pale skin.

"Say it out loud," I said, my voice slightly uneven, as uneven as my racing heart. "Tell me what my punishment is. Say it, so you can't pretend this is a game."

I couldn't pretend this was a nighttime role play between lovers.

No, this was meant to be pleasure for him, and punishment for me. A demonstration of our unequal power, and a taunt.

Because he knew that my racing heart wasn't fear, that my revulsion wasn't hatred.

It was eagerness, desire, need never met.

Lord Garen brushed the back of my head with his fingers. "Take me in your mouth, Valencia. Demonstrate the value of your penitence."

He wore the same clothes from this evening, a long loose tunic-robe that wrapped at the front, with slits up the side, loose pants beneath. I loosened the robe, my fingers trembling as I felt the prickle of magic in the air.

"No one will see or hear," he said, and I understood it was his only mercy to me in this moment. Privacy. But then, it was probably as much for his sake as mine; Gary wasn't an exhibitionist. Neither was Lord Garen.

I undid the waistband of his pants enough to draw his hard length out.

A cock I was now well acquainted with, smooth satiny skin, precum already wetting the tip. He'd tasted like burnt sugar, salt over blackened sweet, and as his hand tightened in my hair to the point of pain, he bumped against my lips, and I opened.

Opened wide, taking in the heavy girth until he damn near pressed his groin against my face.

I gagged, relaxing my throat against the reflex and he pulled out then shoved back in. It wasn't as if I had to do much but kneel there and allow him to use me as he wished.

Because that's what he wanted. To take, not to be seduced. To subjugate, to watch my face with his hot eyes as tears slid down my cheeks and saliva pooled at the corner of my mouth and I had to work to draw in breath through my nose because he was relentless.

"You'll learn," he whispered, voice hoarse with his lust, with the pulsing darkness that flooded us both as he did this to me. "You'll learn that obeying me equals your own pleasure. And you'll learn that disobeying me will force me to remind you that you are my wife, beholden to me, under my protection and in my power. I will not have a divided House, Lady Valencia."

He came with a low groan, and I gagged again. "Swallow it all down," he rasped. "All of it, or we'll begin again."

I obeyed, I had no choice. My knees were sore, my eyes blurred, and I swallowed down every last drop of his come, shuddering.

When he was done he exhaled, then pulled me to my feet and tilted my head back, his mouth diving down to capture mine.

He kissed me; a frenzied kiss, lacking skill, lacking seduction, lacking everything but wild hunger. He ran his tongue along my lips, on the inside of my mouth, tasting himself, tasting my tears.

"You did very well, Valencia," he said, finally pulling away. "And when we return home, I'll reward you for your submission."

Chapter Eleven

VALENCIA

"Do you remember what to do if you're captured?" Garen asked.

We stood in front of the coach, my hands clasped in his, the remnants of his Housesworn gathered to travel with us to the city palace where the wedding would be held.

The wedding dress was two pieces, a sleeveless beaded top and a skirt fitted around my waist and hips then flowing to the floor in sheer layers of black and silver cloth, the main colors of Anteyan.

"I remember," I said.

"Tell me."

He listened as I recited, in bullet point, a list of scenarios and responses.

He'd spent hours drilling me in what disaster might befall us, when, and how I was to respond in order to survive, unveiling a canny, strategic mind.

Garen squeezed my hands and released them when I'd finished, approval in his warm brown gaze, then pressed his palm against my stomach.

"It hasn't been two weeks," I said, not bothering to hide my irritation. "We won't know for at least another three days. Not even Fae can determine pregnancy before the body produces hormones."

He sighed. "I tried to delay the wedding, but Lord Issahelle refused. She's eager to begin her not-retirement and wants this matter resolved before she gives the city over to her son for a few years."

Since he changed the pitch and cadence of his voice, I assumed he was repeating near verbatim what Lord Issahelle had told him.

"I'm half Fae, Gary," I said. "It's going to take a while." Please, Darkness, or whatever these people called their vague deity, let it take forever.

I should be frothing with rage, and I seriously considered the possibility that I was under some type of enchantment to make me cooperative. Nothing else made sense.

Garen gave me an oblique look. "You are also half human. It should take you no time at all."

He'd certainly been doing everything in his power to achieve his goal. His cousins watched me like a hawk. No one was coarse enough to broach the subject, but the question lingered in their eyes.

The day after the first family dinner, we discussed Garen's reasoning behind his urgency.

"I don't see how a pregnancy will secure the ceasefire where a wedding doesn't," I said. *"Do you think he's going to play nice if he knows he has a grandchild on the way? He doesn't care about me."*

Garen shook his head. *"It's a matter of succession, not sentiment. You are his eldest child, his Heir. Your child will stabilize your claim to his House."* Garen paused. *"A fourth of Gisleyan is ready to defect already; he won't risk it. Your sister will throw her loyalty to you."*

"You want me to take the House."

He held my gaze. *"Yes. I want you to take the House. I want you to crush Lord Narazah under your heel. But not yet. Once our children are older—"*

"More than one now?"

"Once our children are older they will combine their strength with ours. The threat of their existence should be enough for now to buy us time to strengthen Anteyan."

So here I was, my betrothed assisting me with courtly grace into a horse drawn coach, accepting with resignation that slowly these people were winning me over to their side.

"I'd advise you to relax," Garen said as he settled opposite me. "But it would be a waste of my breath. So instead, I will advise you to remain alert. What can go wrong, will. If you expect it, you will not fear it."

"I'm not so sure about that, but it's an interesting way to view things."

I watched the city pass as we traveled. Blackwood buildings and cobblestone streets. Tall, graceful lamps lit by balls of softly glowing magic, and trees everywhere, as if the city was built around them. Why wasn't I fighting this more? I couldn't. My best chance would be to bide my time and in immortal terms, time could mean decades or possibly centuries.

I'd been told Dark Fae were adepts at a long grudge.

But. . .Garen Anteyan hadn't started this feud. The reason the conflict began was the core of my life's work—a violent act senselessly committed against an innocent woman. The part of me that was outraged by what happened to Maggie wanted to throw myself into the fight wholeheartedly.

The situation wasn't simple, not when the solution involved dragging me to an altar and taking away my reproductive choice.

"Will you forgive me one day, Val?" he asked, sounding almost like my old Gary.

I glanced at him. The top half of his hair had been brushed back into a braid and then left to fall loose down his back, so nothing obstructed his clear, somber gaze.

"No," I said. "But I think in time I can set it aside. It's not that I don't understand. It's a matter of principle, Garen. I would be betraying everything I've stood for if I gave in. But I won't do anything to jeopardize Maggie. I. . .won't defect to Gisleyan."

Garen reached out and took my hand, pressing it between his. "You're stubborn." He spoke with affection, not exasperation. "You'll need to be stubborn in this city. In this Court. Did I tell you I only rose to the High caste two decades ago?"

"You did." In one of his long monologues this week.

The monologues and lectures weren't a part of his normal routine like I'd assumed, but were an attempt to squeeze a lifetime of information into weeks, to bridge the gap of culture and ignorance between us. Left to his own devices, he was an introspective man. Odd for a diplomat to be an introvert.

Such tangled webs. Webs of truth and lies, webs of right and wrong, virtue and evil.

And my High Lord standing at my side, whispering in my ear, weaving his spell around me so I would do as he asked without fighting him, without introducing further strife into his home.

Garen tensed, dropping my hand. "Now is the time to be alert, Valencia. This is the section of the city where, if there's an attack planned, it's most likely to happen."

I set aside my thoughts and focused as we waited.

He'd sent decoy coaches ahead, the one carrying us plain and unmarked, no decor or House insignia to betray its passengers.

"Almost," he said, meeting my gaze.

Almost out of the hot zone, the section of the city that was a District allied to Gisleyan, where warriors might be posted.

In this scenario, we'd be attacked.

Warriors would separate me from Garen through overwhelming force.

They'd take me, and either I'd be killed outright or allowed to live for some political use. Maybe as a hostage against my betrothed if they thought Garen cared for me. But if he didn't, he had Vowed to wed the Gisleyan eldest daughter. Without fulfilling that Vow, he would suffer the consequences. Whether he cared for me or not, he would be required to retrieve me.

If I were Narazah, I would order my death and be done with it.

"Two blocks," he murmured, "then we're clear."

We were going to make it. Once we were on Sahakian grounds, Narazah would be limited in what mischief he could stir.

I gasped, pressing fingers to my temple. "We're not going to make it."

Garen's attention sharpened. "How much time do we have, and how great is the threat?"

I bent over, wanting to vomit, my vision going black for a second with the pain.

He cursed. "No time, and great. Is this worse than when I kidnapped you?"

"Yes," I managed to breathe out.

"Valencia, prepare." A tingle of heat in the coach I'd come to associate with defensive magic, and the electric zings of offensive magic. The standard spells anyone with basic power could master. "He may have decided to eliminate you."

He didn't have to tell me.

A sharp crack, and a thin stinging pain across my cheek woke me.

I blinked, gasping at icy water thrown in my face—as if the blow to my cheek hadn't been enough.

The windowless room was dim, empty of furniture, the walls a soft gray.

My gaze locked on a male standing several feet away, staring at me with no expression. He'd crossed his arms over his broad chest, and it occurred to me that the lack of expression was boredom.

It also occurred to me that Garen hadn't told me I had my father's eyes.

Blue eyes, dark around the rims but paling into softer color towards the iris with striations of that darker blue throughout, like tiny bolts of lightning. The kind of eyes that looked average unless you gave them a second glance. My mother had been brown-eyed.

"Lord Narazah, I presume," I said. "I'm Valencia Rubio. I'd hoped we would meet under better circumstances."

I should have waited for him to speak first, but I wanted to set the atmosphere now. Brisk, impersonal but cautiously friendly, as if I had no idea how much danger I was in.

Also, I was motivated to determine which scenario we were dealing with. The one where I died right away, or the one where I sold my continued existence as a benefit to House Gisleyan.

After a day of stories about Narazah's proclivities, I'd abandoned any energy spent on crafting an escape in favor of learning whatever Garen and his cousins could teach me to survive in the immediate future. After the wedding I'd go back to making Garen's life miserable for kidnapping me.

Narazah's gaze flickered over my shoulder; a second later another blow against the back of my head. Hard enough to hurt, but not hard enough to injure. But then, I was more difficult to injure than I'd previously known. That blow should have knocked me out.

"Well, at least you're not weak," my father said. "You didn't scream. That's good. I would have had to cut your tongue out. I cannot abide screaming. My first rule is this, girl; do not speak unless invited to do so."

I managed to control my expression as the hair on the back of my neck rose.

What in the holy psychopath was this and why had my mother slept with it?

He was handsome enough, all Fae were, but that was no excuse. My spidey senses writhed, the pain in my head not only from the blow.

Had she a choice? She'd never said my conception wasn't consensual. My skin crawled.

"Remember, she needs to be able to speak, my Lord," a ragged female voice said behind me. "Or she will not be able to execute her part in the plan. She will not be able to prove that she is a worthy Heir and keep her life. You desire to live, don't you, elder sister?"

As soon as she began to speak, I'd guessed who it was behind me. Garen had hoped Valyah would be present. He'd been willing to pin quite a bit on the assumption that even if she appeared to be loyal to her father, she wasn't.

"I know she loves Maggie," Garen said. *"She could have betrayed us a dozen times. She told us where to find you, that you existed at all, thereby saving my life from a danger I hadn't known. If she's present when Narazah takes you, don't give her away. He may not know she's a traitor."*

"I'd like to leave Casakraine if at all possible," I said. "But if that doesn't please my Lord, then I will earn my place. I have no other family left."

All truth. I'd been drilled what to say, in what tone, with what expression. Drilled in how to make myself as harmless but potentially useful as possible to give Anteyan time to rescue me.

If Narazah intended I miss the wedding in the first place.

Which lead to the scenario I'd been dreading, but Garen had hoped for.

"Live, Valencia. Do anything you must, but live."

Chapter Twelve

VALENCIA

I must kill Garen. There was no choice; his death was what I wanted. His death would free me.

Narazah's fingers bit into my upper arm as he escorted me out of the coach. His escort was a hair short of a drag, and I almost tripped on my gown, catching my balance. I didn't have to pretend to shake, there was enough pain and adrenaline running through my veins to take care of that for me.

I finally understood the slow torture of a Vow. Garen had been living with this for almost a year. Almost—*almost*, I forgave him, and certainly I better understood some of his motivations. But understanding his motivations had never been our problem.

I'd do anything to get rid of this Vow. Even kill my betrothed.

"Remember the price of failure is your sister's life," Narazah said without moving his lips, a smile on his face. "And remember the rewards of success."

"Of course, Father."

He'd invited me to call him father once he'd felt I'd earned the honor through a show of proper respect.

During our scenario discussion, Garen warned, *"Don't appear too eager if he makes overtures. Whatever he wants, he'll expect to have to convince you.*

Agree readily, and he'll suspect a trick." He hesitated, lowering his voice as if he had to force the next words out. *"He may resort to torture, though if I were him, I would extract a Vow. It is the only sure way to control you."*

This was the scenario my betrothed hoped for, that if kidnapped, Narazah would use me as an assassin at the wedding. Anteyan wouldn't have to search since Narazah would deliver me to them.

I only had to execute my part of the plan, which was easy; kill Garen.

"Are we late?" I asked, my voice trembling as my father escorted me across the grounds and into the palace.

Another time I would have stopped to marvel at the clusters of wild gardens, the forest pressing on the palace boundaries.

"Don't speak."

"I don't want to disobey you, but if Lord Garen is suspicious, what do you want me to tell him?"

"What will he believe?"

I didn't grimace. "I can tell him that you took me because you thought the wedding was against my will and when I reassured you I was willing to sacrifice myself for the peace, you agreed."

His fingers tightened. "Stupid halfling. He'll never believe that. He knows I don't want this wedding."

"He'll think you fooled me. What would I know? I don't know anything about Court politics."

"Fine, you may tell him that. Whatever you need to do to put him off his guard. You must succeed."

"Of course. I Vowed to do so."

A murmur of conversation began as we entered a hall made of the same polished, gleaming blackwood as everything in this city, the floors a reflective onyx pool, the ceilings high and arched, inlaid with green and gold.

A crowd of Fae in rich and varied dress milled, people turning to face us as Narazah and I halted, his retinue at our backs.

On one side of the hall stood House Anteyan, family and Housesworn in formal black-and-silver with accents of yellow; warriors in molded leather armor, non combatants in whatever took their fancy. On the other side stood those of House Gisleyan already present, clad in purple-and-aqua.

They formed a loose circle which opened to reveal my betrothed, who turned.

Garen strode forward, glaring at Narazah, one hand clenched at his side as if he were angry, humiliated and worried but attempting to control himself.

"Lady Valencia. Are you well?"

Narazah released me and I stumbled towards Garen, collapsing in his arms. He clasped me against his chest, one hand smoothing the back of my head, pressing my face into his shoulder because I couldn't quite work up the acting skills to make tears.

"She's here now," Narazah said. "Let's get this over with."

"We'll begin when I've ascertained my bride is well," Garen said in his cold, smooth voice. "Val?"

I nodded against his shoulder. "Lord Narazah didn't mean to keep me away from you. You know how I feel about this wedding."

"If you'd wanted to ensure she was not under duress, Lord Narazah, I would have granted an audience."

"Enough," Narazah said brusquely, placing a hand on my shoulder and squeezing. The sound of pain I made was real. "The High Lord waits. Remember your duty, daughter."

As if I could forget a Vow strangling my throat. I straightened. Garen gave me a brief glance, the press of his hand on the small of my back reassuring. He must see the sweat beading my temples, feel the trembling in my body. I felt faint and dizzy, as if my airways were slowly being constricted. I'd been warned that if my will deviated from fulfilling the Vow, the magic of the Fae would retaliate.

Once we took our places, the officiant began to speak. No oaths of obedience, and I supposed the till death do you part was a matter of course—divorces among the High caste were rare.

I focused on breathing, on maintaining the will to kill Garen. It was difficult. I had to believe that killing him *was* my intent, and that I would succeed.

". . .let this binding represent a promise of blood and seed, a peace between two Houses in accordance with the will of our Lord. Let none seek to sunder those who willingly come forward to be united. . ."

Garen held out his hand, palm up, and I slid mine over it until I was grasping the bend of his elbow and he mine. Someone drew out a long, fine chain of silver and gold links and began wrapping them around our clasped arms.

The Vow was cutting off my breath.

"Valencia?" Garen's voice, pitched softly under the drone of the officiant.

"It's almost over now," I said, the only other warning I could offer. "I'm ready."

He smiled, eyes sparkling with flecks of amber. "As am I."

I slid my free hand into the slit cut along the side of my dress.

"If a Vow senses your will weaken, Val, it will retaliate, possibly kill you. You must convince yourself the will of the Vow and yours are the same. Even if the Vow is to kill me. You must believe with all of your heart and mind that my death is what you intend."

The moment before I instinctively felt the Vow seek to remove my head from my shoulders—literally, it felt like—I swiped the dagger out of my dress, then angled it up, aiming for the space between the second and third rib.

A strike to the heart.

Panic choked my throat for a second because I'd thrown everything I had into the strike, and believed it would find its mark.

Garen moved, proving diplomats were warriors. He allowed me to carry through to the point where I was fully committed and if he didn't disarm me, he would die.

The blade pierced skin. Blood.

It clattered from my numbed fingers to the floor. Garen wasn't gentle in disarming me; there was no time. He shoved me at Leone and waded into the sudden chaos.

"You did well," Leone said, whisking me away.

I'd tried to kill his Lord at our wedding. The cousin who didn't like me said I'd done well.

Fae.

Leone stood guard over me until my husband came to retrieve me. I listened to the sounds of battle with no desire to wade in above my pay grade.

"Are we married?" I asked, looking up at Garen as he stepped into the ante chamber where I'd been stashed.

He grinned. "We have to finish the last bit. Your timing was impeccable, Val, though I worried that slime-bait would catch on."

"Her warnings were a little obvious, weren't they?" Leone agreed. "It almost took the fun out of it."

"Fun," I echoed.

"Live for a few more centuries," my husband said, bending to scoop me up in his arms. "But I agree. I would like a few quiet years, with gentler pursuits."

"The wedding is ruined."

"Nonsense. No Cassanian wedding is complete without a death or two. Especially when the spouses are bound at knife point."

"The High Lord gifted the wine," Leone said, already striding out of the room. "I'm in a hurry to abandon sobriety, so can we finish the rite and get to the party?"

"You mean the kegger?" I asked.

He waved his hand, disappearing from view.

Garen had not been lying.

We completed the ceremony, signed a stack of documents, and stood at the beginning of the receiving line to accept the bows and congratulations of Lords and High Lords and assembled guests. No one looked at all perturbed, in fact there was a disturbing amount of color in cheeks and glittering eyes.

I met Lady Hasannah, the human bonded consort of the Heir. A brown skinned beauty with enigmatic dark eyes and a drape of glossy black hair over her shoulder. The effortless grace with which she moved, and the cool reserve of her manner, fascinated me. I reminded myself not to stare.

"I'm Han," she said once formal introductions were over. She glanced at Garen. "I'm told your entry into Cassanian society was similar to my own."

"You were kidnapped?"

Her brow flicked up, then lowered, and she smiled. "They always dance around that word."

"It's public relations. They can't go around admitting how morally depraved they are."

Our Fae males let us converse, neither of them looking ruffled.

Andreien. . .a prince, in human terms, glanced at his consort, his teal eyes gleaming. "You know you like my depravity, cignet."

She gave him her back then said over her shoulder, "Come see me, Valencia, when you've settled in. I could use a sane feminine presence."

"I resent that," an obsidian skinned female in gold-and-green armor muttered, following Lady Hasannah as she retreated, leaving Andreien behind without another glance. "I'm sane. Mia laments about that all the time."

"I would like to say her manners aren't usually so abrupt," Andreien said, "but it would be a lie." He bowed, and excused himself after assuring me I was welcome to call upon his consort at her pleasure.

"That sounded like a command," I said when the Heir was gone.

"It was," Garen said. "I'm pleased, Valencia. That will be a beneficial relationship to cultivate and Lady Hasannah isn't known to make alliances among the Court."

"I'm not part of the Court."

"You are my wife, and Lady of Anteyan."

I didn't bother with a sigh. The tidal wave sweeping under continued to grow larger.

"It was a Vow like you thought," I told him later that evening.

Garen, lounging in nothing but his drape of silver hair, glanced at me, sipping wine. "Oh? How was it?"

"Difficult, like you said. I used to think I had excellent focus."

"Hmm. There is nothing quite like a Vow to challenge your mind. It was a good learning experience."

"Oh, a definitely a learning experience, *Gary*. I wished I could say I'm yearning to repeat it."

He set aside his wine, eyes brightening to pure amber. "Come here, wife. Our evening is not yet done and since you're of a mind to use your mouth, I'm of a mind to put it to excellent use."

Chapter Thirteen

VALENCIA

"I came to see you once when I was a girl," a female voice said behind me. "I was only about sixty. You were an adult by then, of course, being a halfling—I was envious. You were forced to ask no one's permission to live your life as you wished. I wanted to ruin it, to drag you home and make you take my place."

I turned and looked at the woman who'd entered the greenhouse where I'd retreated for some time alone, struggling to deal with news that was neither a surprise, or welcome.

If she'd passed me on the street, I wouldn't have known she was my sister, but I should have. We had the same eyes, our sperm donor's eyes, the same cheekbones and pointed chin—though she didn't have my Spanish mother's nose bump. Her hair was lighter than my natural color, but still more ash brown than blonde, long and slightly wild as if she'd given up trying to keep it neat and sleek a long time ago.

I sympathized.

"How is Maggie?" I asked.

Valyah smiled, and the expression ballooned across her entire face taking her from merely lovely to beautiful. I understood what Garen's cousin saw in my sister.

But the smile didn't quite reach her eyes. There was a level of reserve present, which didn't bother me.

"She's fine." A pause. "We both owe you a great debt."

I flicked my fingers, then turned back around and wandered deeper into the greenhouse, choosing a stone bench and sitting. I patted the seat next to me.

"Sit."

She stared at me for a minute, a little startled, eyes widening, but she wasn't the first slightly wary, slightly reserved woman whose confidence I'd had to talk my way into.

And Garen was right. I needed Valyah firmly on my side if we were going to win this internal war against our own House.

After I'd recovered from the mind-numbing rage of having my first, and last, escape attempt thoroughly crushed days after the wedding, I'd turned my mind to the only avenue open to me.

Integrating myself into Anteyan, taking control of Gisleyan. Giving Garen on the surface everything he said he wanted from me—and then, in time...

In time.

And surprisingly, I felt a level of responsibility towards Valyah. I'd learned I was two decades her elder. In mortal terms, that was quite a bit of time though to the Fae it made us nearly twins. Evidently even a hundred-year age difference would have made us practically playground buddies.

But she sat, giving me a side-eyed glance.

"You don't owe me a debt," I said. "This whole mess started because of your father—"

"Our father."

I paused, then nodded. I didn't like to think of him as my father, but what I liked had nothing to do with reality, and I didn't want to alienate my little sister.

"Our father," I amended. "This started because of him. So I suppose in a way it was fitting that I finish it." As I always did when someone brought a fight to my porch.

"You didn't even know we existed."

"Funny, I keep trying to tell my husband that, and he keeps telling me that my lack of knowledge means nothing to the High Court."

Not in those blunt terms, and certainly not without the requisite husbandly empathy, but I understood the subtext. No one cared if I was an innocent bystander.

Bloodlines condemned everyone in Casakraine, especially lofty bloodlines such as mine. Being born into the highest caste in the city came with rights, but also with crushing responsibility, and whether I wanted either was irrelevant.

Children gnashed and wailed against what they couldn't change. I hadn't been a child for a very, very long time.

"And how are you?" I asked more gently. "Lord Garen told me you were injured."

This time the silence was longer, weighted with both pain and anger, which she swallowed.

She hadn't been a child for a very, very long time either.

"I'm healing. Nothing that was inflicted on either of us comes even close to what happened to Maggie."

I understood her purpose now. She felt they owed me a debt, and in the Fae fashion I was entitled to extract it as painfully or inconveniently as possible. She was attempting to protect Maggie from me.

"Did anyone tell you what I did for a living?" I asked.

"You. . ." she paused, as if gathering her thoughts. "You Housed homeless women and children."

I nodded. "All of those women and children were displaced because of violence, mostly at the hands of husbands or boyfriends or fathers. I've spent my life sheltering and protecting those women to the best of my ability. Killing for them when I had to."

Dios, how freeing it felt to say that out loud and know that I would face absolutely no consequences for the admission. Here, no one cared. Here, the murder of someone I deemed worthy of death was considered about as consequential as swatting a bee.

The bee shouldn't have stung its superior. For its crime, it died.

Of course, it had been some *time*. I'd taken my personal oath of nonviolence for a very good reason.

Maybe part of my anger over this situation was also disquiet that I fit in so well with these people, these Fae who called themselves descendants of the Darkness. Seamlessly well.

"I meant it when I said you and Maggie owe me no debt," I continued. "I don't blame her, or you, for my current circumstances."

Next to me I felt tension slowly seep out of her as she probably did what I often did—sift the words of the person speaking to me for any possible way they could have been twisted. But what I'd said was straightforward, there was little way to creatively interpret.

"Then if you won't accept a debt, accept my gratitude," my sister said. "And if you choose to take our House, my backing."

"I appreciate it. It's a little premature. There's a lot I have to learn, and I'm told we're both still very young." I sniffed.

"There's time," she said. "And I'll help you. Narazah—" she stopped.

Narazah was going to be a problem. To my husband's seething fury and disappointment, the Lord of Gisleyan had not died during the festivities at the wedding. Instead, he'd retreated so quickly I wondered if his lack of intelligence was a front.

He'd retreated so quickly, it was almost as if he expected the double cross and had worked out beforehand that retreat was the best method of survival.

But I would deal with him later.

"I came to ask you something else as well," Valyah said.

I glanced at her.

"Your permission."

Well, I hadn't been expecting that. "My permission?"

"You're the head of our House by default, while our father is missing and presumed dead."

I braced. None of those words sounded like they came with anything less than a massive headache.

"Valyah, my permission for what? We'll quibble over head of Household details later."

"To wed."

I turned and stared at her. "You want to marry Magaia? Now?"

"Yes. You are Heir. Her rank is unequal to mine. Your permission is required. Not legally, but in reality if the head of House objects, bloodshed usually ensues. It's easier to ask permission."

"Would this be considered a political alliance?"

She was silent so long I could only conclude she was attempting to choose her words carefully. "Yes."

"And can I assume that Lord Garen wants the happiness of his cousin above all things?"

Valyah blinked at me. "Not above your happiness."

"Even better. My dear sister. . .we're about to enter marriage negotiations. And I am going to bleed my husband dry."

I was already standing, and at that she rose to her feet, eyes widening with alarm. "Anteyan can't afford a marriage price."

"Oh, I don't want anything as common as money."

Valyah stepped toward me. "Please don't start another feud."

I laughed. "Of course not. Don't worry, I probably won't nail him to the wall for anything more taxing than a handful of undisclosed future favors. After all, I can't give my sister away without the respect due my interim Heir, now can I?"

"Interim?"

I said nothing.

"I see. Then you have much to discuss with your husband, and leverage." Valyah sighed. "This is why no one likes the High Fae."

That evening, I sipped an iced chai latte, staring at my husband across the small table in our private suite. At least once a week we dined alone together rather than with the family, and I'd requested one of those dinners for this evening.

He'd agreed readily enough, with the kind of placid happiness that let me know he half suspected the reason for the summons.

We'd only been married for three weeks, consign him to the Darkness.

I'd told Valyah that I was probably going to extract undisclosed future favors, and probably I was. And probably I was not. A future favor could be construed as just about anything, couldn't it? My sister had been too anxious to pay attention to details though, and I was learning more and more how to tell the truth creatively.

"You've been quiet tonight," Garen remarked. He toyed with the stem of his wineglass, giving me an oblique look. "Is something troubling you?"

I set my chai down and settled back in my chair, holding his gaze. "Something is. Though it won't trouble you at all."

He smiled, the expression both warm and smug before he cleared his throat and attempted to look sympathetic. "You haven't bled. Are you with child?"

This motherfucker was tracking my periods. I wouldn't be surprised if he'd been tracking my periods while we were living together, in anticipation of my ovulation cycles. Hadn't he admitted as much the first time we fucked?

"I'm pregnant," I said, not bothering to soften my flat tone. "As you intended. You spider."

Garen rose immediately and came around the table, cupping my cheek with his palm. "I know this is difficult for you. You will be well rewarded, Valencia. We will say nothing, and when your condition is too obvious to conceal, you will retreat to the grounds until the child is born. Anything I can provide to ensure your comfort, I will."

I'd already concluded this would be the plan. If Narazah was in hiding, the news of an Anteyan-Gisleyan Heir would draw him out, and there would be nowhere in the city I could go without looking over my shoulder. But once the child was born, the baby at least would be safe. Cassanians had few absolute laws, but harm to a child was one of them. Lord Issahelle personally saw to the punishment of offenders. Unsurprising, since she was a mother of two herself.

"That's not my only news."

"Oh? What could be more important?"

"Lord Valyah has requested the hand of Housesworn Magaia in marriage."

"Already?" He lifted his brows. "The timing is a little unstrategic, but I won't stand in the way."

"Excellent. Because we both agree Maggie deserves this happiness, doesn't she?"

"Of course." He paused, some of his happy glow diminishing. "What are you up to?"

"I am Heir of House Gisleyan, and as such my sister requested my permission. Which I'm happy to give, if the demands of my House are met." I lifted my chai to take a long sip.

Garen lowered his hand. "I repeat, what are you up to? Why would you negotiate on behalf of Gisleyan?"

"Am I not Heir? Is Gisleyan not the House that is mine by right of blood, and right of force when the time comes to take it?" My voice was as slippery as a marble floor coated with fresh blood. I found I was enjoying myself. "Is this not what you wanted, Lord Garen?"

"Valencia."

"No, don't worry. I don't intend to extract too high a price from Anteyan. But my interim Heir will not be dishonored by being given in marriage with no regard for her rank and status, and the great risk she took on behalf of a House not yet her own. Which is why Anteyan will ask Gisleyan for nothing."

A long, long moment of silence. "And that is your price? That we give our Housesworn to wife like a Low Fae?"

"Oh, my dear Gary, not at all. That's simply a courtesy extended from your House to mine."

I stood.

"My price is this; when the time comes, when I successfully take my House and I'm acknowledged as Lord of Gisleyan, you will release me from our marriage. Not death, but divorce."

He froze, all expression draining from him until he was as lovely and lifeless as a statue. "What game are you playing, wife?"

"No game. But I will not be a High Lord of the Court and subservient to a husband."

"Have I demanded subservience?"

"Did you allow me the right to refuse conception?"

He watched me, saying nothing.

"You will grant me that, or I will deny my permission for Valyah to wed—and I will forbid her from having anything further to do with Maggie. And then Gisleyan and Anteyan *will* be at war again."

I felt him gather himself to speak and held up my hand. "There is one more thing. This child."

Ice crept into his eyes, making them hard, cold chips of agate.

It was the first time I'd seen him look at me like death.

I didn't flinch. He wouldn't lift a finger against me. He wouldn't dare.

"This child," I repeated. "I will carry it, I will bear it, and I will help raise it to be loyal to Anteyan—and in time, my House as well. I'll even love it, because it's mine and I would never deny a baby it's mother's love. But."

He waited me out. I wanted him to speak first, but mentally shrugged. "But for your use of my womb, I require you to legally sign over full custody of the child to me."

"No."

"If you don't, I will not carry it to term."

He lifted his hand; it hovered at shoulder level, near my face, but still I didn't flinch though I understood his visceral desire to wrap that hand around my throat and squeeze.

"And how," he said, biting off each word, "do you think you will achieve a termination? I can lock you in this bedroom, Valencia Gisleyan. I can tie your wrists and your ankles to the posts and feed you through a tube and have you pissing from a catheter. How, exactly, do you think you can carry out that threat against my House?"

Interesting. My spidey sense wasn't going off, at all. Which meant his threat wasn't real.

He would never hurt me.

I suspected he'd spent the last ruthless bone in his body dragging me from my home and imprisoning me in Casakraine.

"I will make a Vow, Lord Garen."

The hand hovering close to my face dropped to his side, like a rock. "What?"

"I will make an unbreakable Vow, one with simple, clear, and immediate terms that if I don't fulfill, will cause the Vow to extract its price." I smiled at him. "Probably death. And if it doesn't work the first time, well, I'll just make another Vow, and another, until one does the trick. You could threaten to sew my mouth shut, I suppose, but no one said a Vow must be spoken out loud."

All the color drained from his face as he stared at me.

I confirmed that interesting suspicion about my husband, standing there confronting him.

He *wasn't* ruthless. He hadn't lied when he'd said he started out as a peaceful man, a diplomat, one who preferred learning and knowledge and puttering with his hobbies. He didn't have a warrior's instinctive predilection for killing.

I did.

Because in his shoes, I would have balled up my fist and slammed it into my jaw, rendering me unconscious. I would have kept me unconscious, tied to that bed until the child was delivered. Because no, a Vow didn't have to be spoken out loud, but a person did have to be conscious.

But a woman didn't have to be awake in order to successfully carry a child to term and give birth.

It had happened to humans before, women in comas.

This didn't occur to Gary, not once. Or if it did, he was unwilling to carry through with that action.

Which further told me that if we were going to win a war against Gisleyan, we would need me. His strategy, my...killer instinct.

I almost laughed. That was what I was calling my spidey sense these days.

It really would have been a match made in heaven except for the fact that I loathed, more than anything, having my rights taken away.

That kind of behavior just doesn't agree with me outside of a romance novel, Gary.

"Valencia," he said. And stopped. Because he couldn't say "you wouldn't." I'd said it, so demonstrably I would.

"What will you do with full custody? Take my child from me when you take your House?"

"The child will be an adult by then," I pointed out, "or near enough to adulthood that they can decide whom they wish to live with. I'm not interested in denying you the parenting of our child."

"Then why do you want full custody?"

"Because of the look on your face, Lord Garen. The look on your face is only the slightest fraction of what I've been feeling since you took me from my home, dragged me kicking and screaming to the altar, and then forcibly impregnated me."

"You were not kicking and screaming. You—"

"Please. Let's not quibble over semantics. I was screaming on the inside."

I let out a breath. Not taking pity on him but allowing some of the tension to deflate. I had no intention of having an unhappy marriage, while we were married. I was simply building boundaries, adjusting expectations.

Giving him the tiniest glimpse of just who the fuck he was messing with.

"Every action," I said gently, "has a consequence."

"I agree to your terms."

Garen turned away from me.

I stepped towards him, holding out a hand. "Gary."

He paused, didn't move when I laid my hand on his shoulder, then followed it with my cheek, sliding my arms around him until I was hugging him from behind.

"I didn't know you could be so treacherous," he said. "So cold. I thought you loved me."

"I do. Isn't this how High Fae love?"

I felt movement under my arms after a moment, and then he laughed. And laughed.

Then turned in my arms, sliding his hand into my hair at the nape of my neck and tugging my head back, his fingers tightening, his eyes warm and hard.

"Well played, densafa. I am pleased—my wife cannot be weak, or stupid. But I won't forget." He lowered his head, planted a sweet kiss on my ear, and whispered, "I know what you're doing, Valencia. You are a mere child in this game and I have lived for centuries. So play, and I will play, and we will see who wins in the end. Neither of us will be bored, mi cielo. And I am always learning."

I smiled at him, rolling in my temporary triumph. Let him lift me into his arms and stride to the bed, lowering me down, gently, because after all now I carried precious cargo.

Then my smile was gone, replaced by begging. By his cruel fingers and taunting laughter. By my screaming hatred for him, for this, for us.

By his gentle kisses and anxious, dangerous fussing that reminded me why *hating* a Dark Fae Lord was a wild, slippery slope.

Holding my shuddering body, my tears dampening his chest, he murmured, "This is how the Darkness loves."

About the Author

Alisyn Fae, the pen name of PNR & SFR author Emma Alisyn, writes high heat adult fantasy romance with heroines over 30, for readers who like their romance slightly dark, grown as *uck, with slap in the face tension and adventure.

Dear Mortal Reader, this is not the end. Our Lords will resolve their war. Even Dark Fae know happiness.

Lord Andreien and Lady Hasannah are proof. Read their story, *Lord of Dance & Desire*, here: https://emmaalisyn.com/courtcasakraine/

Coming Soon From Our Authors

Of Thistles and Talons by Elayna R. Gallea

Bound to the Prince by Priscilla Rose

The Gilded Survivor by Daniela A. Mera

Quest for Love by Danielle Hill

Fae Court of Caskraine #4 by Alisyn Fae

The Laurentian Mountain Clan Series by Mimi B. Rose

And follow Ruthie Bowles and E. Milee to watch their publishing journeys!

Printed in Great Britain
by Amazon